A girl on a bike p
went by.
'Watcher, Bubbles,'
'I'm Patsy,' she said,
'Boston, Lincs?' said L
'My Boston is in Massachusetts,' she said.
'Got you,' said Daniel, 'you're an American girl.'

They walked along together, Patsy recounting at length all the details of how she and her dad crossed the Atlantic, how they toured bomb-damaged London, and the frightening ordeal of their first air-raid. They reached Red Post Hill, and Daniel said, 'Would you like to come home with me and have a cup of tea?'

'OK, I give in,' said Patsy, and she sat sideways on the carrier as Daniel rode the bike. He whizzed her down the hill as if Hitler's demons were on their tails. What a fun guy, she thought, even if he is a bit skinny.

and published by Corgi Books

THE WAY AHEAD

Mary Jane Staples

CORGI BOOKS

THE WAY AHEAD
A CORGI BOOK : 0 552 14785 0

First publication in Great Britain

PRINTING HISTORY
Corgi edition published 2000

1 3 5 7 9 10 8 6 4 2

Set in 11/12pt New Baskerville by
Phoenix Typesetting, Ilkley, West Yorkshire.

Corgi Books are published by Transworld Publishers,
61–63 Uxbridge Road, London W5 5SA,
a division of The Random House Group Ltd,
in Australia by Random House Australia (Pty) Ltd,
20 Alfred Street, Milsons Point, Sydney, NSW 2061, Australia,
in New Zealand by Random House New Zealand Ltd,
18 Poland Road, Glenfield, Auckland 10, New Zealand
and in South Africa by Random House (Pty) Ltd,
Endulini, 5a Jubilee Road, Parktown 2193, South Africa.

The Random House Group Limited supports The Forest Stewardship
Council (FSC®), the leading international forest certification organisation.
Our books carrying the FSC label are printed on FSC® certified paper.
FSC is the only forest certification scheme endorsed by the leading
environmental organisations, including Greenpeace. Our
paper procurement policy can be found at
www.randomhouse.co.uk/environment

MIX
Paper from
responsible sources
FSC® C018072

Printed and bound in Great Britain by Clays Ltd, St Ives PLC

*To Sheila, Liz, Janet, Lyn, Fay, Joan, Ron and all
other friends who gave so much
happiness to Florence.*

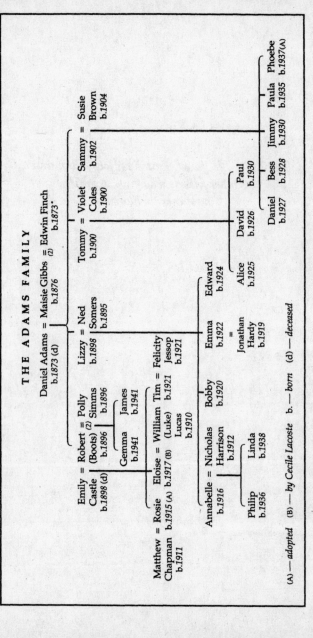

THE ADAMS FAMILY

Daniel Adams = Maisie Gibbs (2) = Edwin Finch
b.1873 (d)   b.1876*   b.1873*

Emily = Robert (Boots) (2) = Polly Simms
b.1898 (d)   b.1896   b.1896

Gemma   James
b.1941   b.1941

Matthew = Rosie   Eloise = William   Tim = Felicity
Chapman   b.1915 (A) b.1917 (B) (Luke)   b.1921 Jessop
b.1911   Lucas   b.1921
                    b.1910

Annabelle = Nicholas Harrison
b.1916   b.1912

Philip   Linda
b.1936   b.1938

Bobby
b.1920

Lizzy = Ned Somers
b.1898   b.1895

Emma
b.1922
=
Jonathan Hardy
b.1919

Edward
b.1924

Alice
b.1925

Tommy = Violet Coles
b.1900   b.1900

Daniel   David   Paul
b.1927   b.1926   b.1930

Sammy = Susie Brown
b.1902   b.1904

Bess   Jimmy   Paula   Phoebe
b.1928 b.1930   b.1935   b.1937(A)

(A) — adopted   (B) — by Cecile Lacoste   b. — born   (d) — deceased

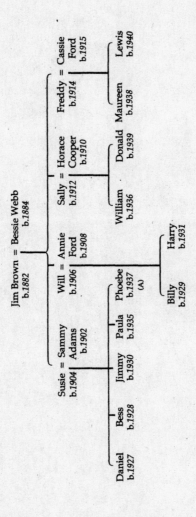

THE BROWN FAMILY

Jim Brown = Bessie Webb
b.1882   b.1884

Susie = Sammy   Will = Annie   Sally = Horace   Freddy = Cassie
b.1904   Adams   b.1906 Ford   b.1912 Cooper   b.1914   Ford
         b.1902   b.1908   b.1910   b.1915

Daniel   Bess   Jimmy   Paula   Phoebe   William   Donald   Maureen   Lewis
b.1927   b.1928 b.1930 b.1935 b.1937   b.1936   b.1939   b.1938   b.1940
                                 (A)

                                 Billy   Harry
                                 b.1929 b.1931

Chapter One

March, 1944

Moonlight over France. An RAF Lysander was flying low over the department of Marne, famous for its champagne vineyards.

Lysanders, high-wing planes that could land almost at a walking pace on a short strip of level or rough ground, had proved superb in the carrying of SOE agents to and from German-occupied France. Tonight was no exception for this particular machine. It flew ahead of desultory flak thrown up by an anti-aircraft battery manned by a French crew under the supervision of German officers. The gunners seemed incapable of hitting a flying elephant, much to the disgust of the Germans. But perhaps there was more to it than inefficiency. Perhaps the image of General de Gaulle and his Free French Army was looming larger day by day, for there were few people in France who did not suspect the Allies would open a Second Front sometime in the near future, and that de Gaulle would arrive with them to settle his account with Marshal

Pétain, Pierre Laval and other men who had sold France to the Germans in 1940.

The Lysander flew on in the moonlight. All flights undertaken in aid of the French Resistance took place during the full moon periods. Navigation demanded visibility to enable pilots to accurately pinpoint landing strips.

On this mission, the pilot, descending at decreasing speed, searched for the prearranged tiny lights marking the selected strip. Three lights, hand torches fixed to sticks in the form of an inverted 'L', were the established way of guiding a Lysander in, always providing a fourth torch, hand-held, flashed the coded all-clear signal.

There it was, the inverted 'L', clearly visible, and there too was the flashing code giving the pilot the signal to land, and he brought the plane safely down on the rough grassy ground with the lightest of bumps. The moment it stopped, out jumped a man and a woman, and from a point just beyond the nearest light several men and women of the Resistance came running. Stoutly bound packs containing arms, explosives and detonators were quickly hauled from the plane, and within minutes the Lysander was moving again, turning to taxi. It took off with a wave of good luck from the pilot.

The landing lights were switched off and collected, and the men and women melted away in company with the two SOE agents from London, Captain Bobby Somers, RA, and Lieutenant Helene Aarlberg, FANY, both of whom had survived other missions of underground activity in France.

'Bobby, how far this time are we from my home?' It was a quick whisper from Helene.

'Only a few hundred miles,' whispered Bobby. 'Were you thinking of dropping in for Sunday tea?'

'Idiot.'

She had called him that countless times, but not without a note of endearment. There was no-one quite like Bobby to Helene Aarlberg, daughter of a Belgian father and French mother. They were lovers, she and Bobby, and from him she had a firm promise of marriage when this disgusting war was finally over.

They ran on with the partisans, and the little group disappeared into a wooded valley, packs of arms and explosives strapped to backs.

There was work to do of a dangerous, hair-raising kind, and Bobby and Helene were as much committed as the men and women of the Resistance.

April, 1944

By this time, the extensive family of Mrs Maisie Adams, known as Chinese Lady because of her almond eyes and her addiction years ago to the quality work of Walworth's Chinese Laundry, had experienced all the shifting patterns of a war that seemed to have no end.

Britain, along with its Empire, was well into the fifth year of the conflict with Germany, and its people were bruised and battered. But so were the people of Germany who, suffering continuous assaults from the air by the bombers of the RAF and the USAAF, were at last coming to realize exactly what kind of hell their demonic *Fuehrer* had fashioned for them. That hell was about to become an inferno, for not only were the Russian hordes scorching German armies in the east, but the South Coast of England was soon to receive the men and machines of a colossal seaborne invasion force designed to set fire to Germany's defences in the west. An armada of ships and landing craft was to assemble in ports, and the South Coast to become a guarded encampment of men and machines. The Press printed nothing and the radio breathed not a word about these forthcoming preparations for the opening of the long-awaited Second Front.

'Well,' said Mrs Lizzy Somers to her husband Ned over breakfast, 'the news is getting more cheerful every day.'

Their kitchen wireless was in full flow, the BBC announcer as measured of tone as he had been all through the war, come storm or sunshine. The Allied armies in Italy were hammering away at the Germans, the Americans and British beginning to crack the Japanese in the Far East, and to get the better of the U-boats in the Battle of the Atlantic.

'Yes, everything's more encouraging, Eliza, no doubt about it,' said Ned. He was now forty-nine, with greying hair, and as manager of a wine merchant's in Great Tower Street, he was forever striving to survive a shortage of imports. That, of course, didn't help to slow the greying process. However, having lost a leg in the Great War, he made do very well with an artificial limb, and carried out his ARP duties in the kind of valiant way that aroused emotional pride in Lizzy. Nearly forty-six herself, she still owned her admirable Edwardian figure, despite food rationing. Improved corsetry, lighter and better designed than formerly, was a delightful friend to her. She looked an extremely well-preserved woman, her wealth of chestnut hair and the deep brown of her eyes matchless. Ever a supportive wife and a caring mother, Lizzy represented to Ned a very rewarding investment in marriage. 'I suppose we still can't look forward to seeing much of our sons and daughters,' he said, tackling his breakfast toast with strong, crunching teeth.

Their sons, Bobby and Edward, were twenty-four and nineteen respectively, Bobby an artillery officer, Edward an aircraftman in the RAF. Their daughters, twenty-seven-year-old Annabelle and twenty-one-year-old Emma, lived in the country. Annabelle and her two children had been in Wiltshire since the bombing began in 1940. Her husband, Nick Harrison, was a fighter pilot in the RAF. Emma and her husband, Jonathan Hardy, were in Somerset, Emma working for a farmer, Jonathan a gunnery instructor at an artillery training camp.

'Oh, we'll be seeing Emma and Jonathan soon,' said Lizzy. 'I did tell you Jonathan's getting seven days' leave, and that Emma will be with him.'

'So you did,' said Ned. 'Well, that's something. They're two of my favourite people.'

'Ned, you shouldn't have favourites,' said Lizzy, 'it causes little ructions.'

'Well, if big ructions arrive,' said Ned, 'don't open the door to them.'

'You're just like Boots,' said Lizzy, 'you've always got an answer that's a bit comical.'

'My other favourite people', said Ned, 'are Annabelle and Nick, Bobby and Helene, and our one and only Edward.'

'You said that just in time,' smiled Lizzy. 'Listen, love, about Bobby and Helene. Don't you wonder sometimes what they get up to?'

'Well, they're young and healthy, of course, and Helene's French, and there's a war on,' said Ned, 'so I daresay they—'

'Ned Somers, I don't want to hear what you're going to say,' said Lizzy, refilling his teacup, 'and I wasn't meaning that, anyway, which you knew I didn't. What I do mean is that we get hardly any letters from them, and when we do they never give us a hint of where they might be or what they're doing. It's worrying sometimes. I mean, what sort of a regiment are they in, for goodness sake?'

Ned had long had his ideas about what kind of a war Bobby and Helene were engaged in. Helene was French, her home in the agricultural region east of Dunkirk. Bobby was familiar with France, and spoke the language fluently. Everyone knew the British were giving all kinds of help to French Resistance groups, and it was reasonable to suppose Bobby and Helene had been recruited to work with them. Ned, however, was not going to let Lizzy know he suspected exactly that. It would give her sleepless nights. She'd think about them being caught, tortured and shot as spies. If I'm right, thought Ned, that's actually a frightening possibility.

'Whatever unit they're in, and whatever they're doing, I'll wager they're giving a good account of themselves,' he said, and washed down toast with hot tea. 'Rely on it, Eliza.' He had always called Lizzy by her baptismal name.

'I hope you don't mean Helene is firing guns,' said Lizzy. 'Mum's been saying ever since the start of the war that it's not natural turning women into soldiers. I admit she goes over the top a bit sometimes, but she's right generally speaking.'

'Women in khaki are supportive, not combative,' said Ned. 'They don't take part in battles, and I think you know that, Eliza.'

'It's what my commonsense tells me,' said Lizzy, 'but Helene's very independent, and the sort of woman who'd think she could fire a gun as good as Bobby. When we've had them staying here, we've heard her tell him she's as good as he is.'

'Which she is, of course,' said Ned, 'but she's not the same. No woman is the same as a man, and *vice versa*. Look up the biology of the sexes—'

'Do what?' said Lizzy.

'Yes, we're biologically different,' said Ned.

'Are you showing off?' asked Lizzy.

'Only a bit,' said Ned. 'Helene won't be firing big guns, Eliza, or be charging at the enemy. She'll be doing a good job in regimental administration work, or something like that.'

'Wait a minute,' said Lizzy, as Ned rose from his chair, 'isn't she something to do with that special women's thing?'

'I could ask what special thing women have got,' said Ned, 'but I won't, in case you mean *that* women's special thing, and even at my age I can still get embarrassed.'

'A thick ear is what you'll get in a minute, my lad,' said Lizzy. 'I was talking about that special unit called FANY, and you know I was. What do FANY officers actually do?'

'Oh, all kinds of work, including driving generals, driving ambulances, or making express deliveries of the choicest cigars to our Prime Minister,' said Ned. 'Very special, that, and good luck to the girls and the old boy. Must go now, love. See you on time this evening, if the railways don't get bombed during the day.'

'But Hitler hasn't done any daylight raids for ages, or at night,' said Lizzy.

'For which we're all truly thankful,' said Ned, 'but I don't trust the bleeder.'

'Now, Ned.' Lizzy got up.

'All right, blighter,' said Ned. 'And in addition to that, he's the world's number one gangster. Now I'm off. So long, Eliza.' He kissed her. Lizzy detained him for a moment.

'Ned, I just want to tell you how glad I am we're seeing this war through together,' she said. 'There, now you can go.'

'You're still my girl,' said Ned.

'I'm glad about that too,' said Lizzy with soft affection.

While she was washing-up the breakfast things, she thought about her day ahead. She was going to Kennington to have Camp coffee with Jemima Hardy, Emma's very likeable mother-in-law, then on to Walworth to enjoy a light lunch with Rebecca Cooper, adoptive mother of Horace, who was married to Sally, Susie's sister. And in the afternoon she was going to share a pot of tea with her mum and Susie. Susie and Sammy, whose house had been flattened by a bomb ages ago, were still living in the large family house in Red Post Hill.

For all that she had a full day ahead, Lizzy still couldn't help wondering and worrying about Bobby and Helene.

The phone rang. Answering it, Lizzy heard her stepfather's voice.

'Hello, Dad,' said Lizzy, 'what can I do for you?'

'I'm at the office,' said Mr Edwin Finch, second husband of Lizzy's mother and an important cog in the high-powered wheels of British Intelligence. 'I promised your mother to ring you. She doesn't trust our own phone at the moment, since she's convinced it's in one of its contrary moods. You know, of course, that she still regards it as a new-fangled contraption capable of electrocuting her.'

'Yes, I do know, Dad,' said Lizzy, 'but we can't do much about her funny little ways. When Boots first bought his car, she didn't trust that, either. He told her it would get from A to B safe and easy because it had four new-fangled round things. When she asked what they were, he said "Wheels, old girl." He's always been his own kind of comedian.'

'Which we all relish, Lizzy,' said Mr Finch. 'Now, I promised to ring you as soon as I reached the office, rather than interrupting your breakfast by ringing from home. Your mother wants to know if you've heard from Bobby or Helene.'

'Not a word for ages, Dad,' said Lizzy. 'No letter and no phone call. It's a bit worrying, really.'

'You'd have heard, Lizzy, if anything had happened to them,' said Mr Finch reassuringly. He was always in tune with the sentiments, emotions and worries of his wife's large family. 'It's possible that because Helene is French and Bobby speaks the language so well, they're working on liaison duties with the Free French divisions somewhere.' Like Ned, Mr Finch suspected the work was with the French Resistance. 'So don't worry.'

'Oh, worries have been everyday things for all of us since the war started,' said Lizzy, 'and we have to live with them, don't we?'

'It helps to some extent, living with them,' said Mr Finch. 'My love to you, Lizzy, and my regards to Ned. Goodbye now.'

'Goodbye, Dad, and bless you,' said Lizzy, and put the phone down. Going back to her kitchen, she again wondered about Bobby and Helene, where they were and what they were doing.

Chapter Two

When the Allies invaded Italy in September, Hitler ordered the whole of France to be occupied, and the Vichy Government, tolerated on the basis that it would co-operate with Berlin, found itself a puppet stripped even of its clothes.

At this moment, the SS and Gestapo establishment in the department of Marne was in a state of fury. With the war now going badly for Hitler on the Russian front, and American and British bombers wreaking havoc on German industry, the French Resistance was becoming bolder, and a group had succeeded in effecting the hold-up and capture of *Standartenfuehrer* (Colonel) Furstein and his deputy, *Sturmbannfuehrer* (Major) Grasse. Their car, driven by an NCO, came round a bend on its way into Epernay to find a bicycle lying in the road, a woman sprawled beside it, her face apparently a mask of blood, and a man kneeling beside her, trying to help her. Naturally, the compassion of Herr *Standartenfuehrer* induced him to tell the driver to stop. As soon as the car came to a standstill, a body of men and women materialized to surround it. It was a plant, a hold-up by obvious partisans, who threatened the occupants with British Sten guns. The driver was knocked unconscious, pulled out of the car and dumped on the verge, while *Standartenfuehrer* Furstein and *Sturmbannfuehrer* Grasse were speedily hand-tied and gagged. Three of the scoundrels crowded into the car and it was driven away. The driver subsequently reported the hold-up and what had happened to himself. Being unconscious he did not know what had happened to the officers.

A telephone call from one of the insolent partisans to the German headquarters in Epernay established the fact that both officers were being held as hostages against the release of six Resistance men and women who were under interrogation. The release was granted on orders from Paris.

Immediately, as the fleeing Resistance group anticipated, the area became thick with SS men, Gestapo officers and pro-German French police, who flung out a wide cordon in their determination to lay violent hands on the swines, and to retake the released prisoners.

The Resistance group was led by a man called Roget, and included two very useful and experienced SOE agents from London, code names Maurice and Lynette respectively. Bobby and Helene, in fact. This was their fourth mission to France, and each had been prolonged and dangerous. However, because Roget knew the area as well as he knew the shape of an apple, it did not prove difficult for his group to break through the enemy ring at night, and by morning they were on a barge carrying potatoes up the Marne river to the German garrison in Epernay.

The bargee had an escort, two German soldiers, as was usual on river craft carrying supplies earmarked for Hitler's occupying forces. Swinish French partisans had a stinking habit of boarding a barge, removing the cargo and sinking the vessel. Several of the German hunters, SS men, arriving at the river, hailed the escort from the bank, shouting questions about escaping partisans. One soldier shouted back that nothing had been seen of them.

'You are sure?'

'Yes! Totally!'

'Well, damn you for your blindness!'

'We aren't blind, we can't afford to be!'

'Then keep your eyes open!'

'Of course!'

'Shoot on sight! Not to kill, but to bring them down! We want the swines alive! You hear, you hear?'

'Yes! Loud and clear!'

The barge went on, under sail, its engine out of action due to a serious lack of fuel. Germany was producing only half of what it needed to maximize its war effort. The Allied bombing raids were causing disastrous damage to sources of supply.

The hunting SS patrol raced along the bank to hail a following barge that was a dot in the distance. The two soldiers on the first vessel winked at each other, and the bargee showed a smile. All three were Roget's men, one a 1940 refugee from Alsace, a Frenchman who spoke perfect German. The genuine bargee and his undressed German escort lay trussed and blindfolded below, Roget, Helene, Bobby and the rest of the group keeping them close company.

The barge went on until dusk arrived, when the bow was grounded at a place gloomy with marsh and devoid of inhabitants. But it was also devoid of Germans. The partisans and the SOE agents disembarked, booted feet disappearing into the marsh. The stern of the barge swung in clear water, and all together, they pushed the bow sideways until the vessel floated off and caught the tide, taking the trussed bargee and German soldiers with it, as well as the potatoes.

Roget, using a torch, led the way, the marsh sucking at them for two hundred yards before their feet began to tread firmer ground.

'I am soaked,' breathed Helene.

'So are my feet,' said Bobby.

'I meant my feet,' said Helene.

'A small price to pay, my infant.'

'Ah, yes, the luck was ours, but who is an infant?'

'Slip of the tongue, considering your qualifications,' murmured Bobby. Helene was tall, strong-bodied and robust.

'Never mind, you are always very English, and I like you for that. How glad I am you were not born a German, a Nazi Boche.'

'We can both thank my parents for that.'

Whispers mutually encouraging ran up and down the line of trekking men and women, boots squelching but spirits high. Roget took them on sure-footedly, and they melted into the darkness, heading for their primitive hideout in the hills to prepare for an operation even more audacious than the one just accomplished.

Helene's hand touched Bobby's. He took it, she squeezed his fingers. She was far from her parents, he far from his family, but they had each other, and they had Roget and their other French comrades.

Chapter Three

Mid-April

A tram travelling along the Walworth Road from the Elephant and Castle came to a stop at East Street. An Army sergeant alighted in company with a young lady, he limping a bit from a gammy knee, she lithe of limbs and colourful of dress, and accordingly a fetching picture of approaching summer on this warm spring day.

'Old home ground, Emma,' observed Sergeant Jonathan Hardy, gunnery instructor to recruits at a Royal Artillery training camp.

'For my family as well as yours,' said his wife Emma, younger daughter of Lizzy and Ned Somers, and much like her mother in her attractive looks, especially in respect of her chestnut hair and brown eyes. Her face was tanned. So was Jonathan's. She worked on a farm not far from his training camp in Somerset, and the open air of that rural county had made its healthy mark on them. 'Mum and her brothers were all born and brought up in Walworth,' she said.

'But well gone by the time my family arrived from Sussex,' said Jonathan, a tough sergeant and playful husband. He was twenty-five, and owned the kind of physique much admired by Emma. It has to be said that he was even more admiring of her feminine line and form. Ergo, what she liked about him and what he liked about her led to very agreeable marital togetherness. They were always able to meet once a week, on either Saturday or Sunday, and to make use of Emma's room at the farmhouse.

They were an engaging couple, Jonathan's habit of lapsing into rural Sussex dialect often sending Emma potty, provoking her into having her own back by taking him off or belabouring him with rolled-up magazines. Sometimes, during their moments of agreeable togetherness, a teasing urge to take him off would rise above her palpitations, and she'd say, albeit throatily, 'Be that your tin leg rattling, Jonathan?'

Jonathan, wounded in action in 1941, had been fixed up with a metal knee joint. It left him with his limp, but he appealed successfully against the possibility of being discharged, and won himself a posting as a sergeant gunnery instructor down in the county he called Zummerzet.

He was on seven days' leave, and Emma's employers, a farmer and his wife, had given her the week off to be with her soldier husband. They were presently staying with his parents, having spent their first three days at her parental home.

The light of the Saturday afternoon was kind to old Walworth, softening the smoky grey of its Victorian buildings and brightening shop windows.

The main road, bustling with traffic, did not seem to have suffered too badly from air raids, but Emma and Jonathan had come across heavy damage elsewhere. Many streets of solid terraced houses were rent with jagged gaps.

'Come on, Jonathan,' said Emma, 'let's see what the market's like these days.' The East Street market, known as the Lane, was still functioning, despite severe shortages of fruit and vegetables. It had been a favourite pre-war shopping place for Jemima Hardy, Jonathan's mother, and for Emma's much revered grandmother, known as Chinese Lady, in long-gone years.

They entered the market. Stalls lined each side of the street, which was crowded with people looking for bargains in the way of domestic items and un-rationed foodstuff. Not that pre-war poverty still existed. No, jobs were plentiful, wages good, but the housewives of Walworth had an acquired addiction for bargains, as well as a great fondness for the market and its familiar stallholders, who had been fighting the trade setbacks of war for four and a half years. Among the crowds were a few American GIs and their Walworth girlfriends, the latter introducing the former to the atmosphere of a cockney market, and the former saying things like, 'Well, I'll go to Coney Island on a mule, I got to believe there's no hamburger stalls?'

Shoppers had their eyes open for fruit, for home-grown produce in the main, since imported varieties were scarce. Bananas, grapes and pine-apples were only distant memories, but oranges sometimes miraculously turned up, and whenever they did there was a rush of feet, bodies and wide-open purses, the latter a temptation to pickpockets who had become lamentably operative in the knowledge that wartime purses were more richly laden than in former years. Much to Emma's delight, she spotted a stall heavy with crates of dates from the Middle East. Two crates were broken open, the dark gleaming fruit standing in square blocks, the stall-holder carving out large sticky chunks with a knife.

'Dates, Jonathan, dates,' said Emma, 'let's buy some.'

'Right,' said Jonathan, with the authority of a sergeant, 'you get a pound, I'll get a pound.'

People had formed a queue, and Emma darted and joined it. Jonathan followed on.

'Here, mind me eye,' said a young woman, arriving at the same time. Turning, she found herself looking at a brown-faced and personable Army sergeant. Jonathan found himself close to saucy eyes and a bright orange sweater on which was a gaudy brooch bearing the name of Lola. 'Oh, howdyerdo, sarge, excuse me hot temper,' she said. 'I don't have no quarrel with the Army. You can queue next to me, if yer like.' Somehow, she was elbow to elbow with Jonathan, and between him and Emma.

'You be keen on dates, I reckon,' said Jonathan.

'Eh?' said Lola, nicely made-up, her full-lipped mouth moistly pink.

'Well, dates be a tidy bit nourishing,' said Jonathan, with Emma more amused than put out. She knew her country bloke and his tendency to make himself sound like a village yokel. Village idiot, she sometimes said.

'Here, excuse me for asking,' said Lola, the queue moving slowly forward and other shoppers joining it, 'but where you from?'

'Durned old Army,' said Jonathan.

'No, I mean where'd you come from?' said Lola.

'Just lately, mostly from down Zummerzet way,' said Jonathan.

'I dunno I ever met anyone from there,' said Lola.

'Born in Sussex I were,' said Jonathan, 'according to my Ma and Pa, and they should know, I reckon.'

'Crikey,' said Lola. Emma was splitting her sides, while the stallholder was bawling compliments about his dates as he served customers a pound each. 'I never heard no sergeant talk like you,' went on Lola, a young lady given to offering immediate friendship to people in a queue, as long as they were wearing trousers and didn't have tea-stained whiskers. 'I've met American sergeants, y'know, and me latest is Gus, but blowed if I know where he's got to this morning.'

'Gone off, maybe, to find out where the war is?' said Jonathan.

'No, course not, he's in the market somewhere,' said Lola.

'Then speaking friendly, like,' said Jonathan, 'I join you in hoping he'll turn up sometime.'

Lola let go a giggly laugh.

'You're a card, you are, sarge,' she said. Yes, he's that all right, thought Emma, and wait till I get him home. 'Have you got any medals?' asked Lola of Jonathan.

'Only a handful,' he said, 'but my three stripes pay better than medals. Did you say if you liked dates?'

'Well, I wouldn't be queuing if I didn't, would I?' said Lola. 'Nor waiting twenty minutes to get served. It's worse than lining up for lunch at our fact'ry canteen.' The long queue moved forward a little. 'Here, would you like to come to a party tonight?'

'Durned if that don't be real nice of you,' said Jonathan, noting Emma was struggling to keep her face straight. 'Might I ask if I could bring a close friend?'

'Not 'alf,' said Lola, who hadn't taken any notice of Emma. Well, she didn't know the young lady on her right was very well-known to the sergeant on her left. 'All Army blokes are welcome, and sailors too.'

'My close friend is a female farmhand,' said Jonathan, as more people attached themselves to the queue. I'll give him female farmhand, said Emma to herself.

'She from Somerset too?' said Lola.

'Regular Zummerzet dairymaid,' said Jonathan, at which point a large body pushed in, a large finger tapped him on the shoulder, and an aggressive voice landed in his ear.

'What's your game, buddy?'

Jonathan turned, Lola turned and Emma turned. Emma quivered. A huge American sergeant was eyeing Jonathan with glowering suspicion. Jonathan was hardly insignificant at five feet eleven, and was considered fearsome by conscripted gunners when bawling them out for being on close terms with uselessness, but the American sergeant was six inches taller, broad all over, and decked out with the mountainous shoulders of an American football player.

'Did you say something?' asked Jonathan.

'Sure. What's your game?'

'I'm lining up for dates,' said Jonathan, one half of the queue in front shuffling forward, the other half now held up.

'The way I see it, buddy, it ain't dates you're sold on, it's Lola.'

'This lady's Lola?' said Jonathan.

'That's her, and she ain't first prize in a Fourth of July raffle.'

'We met by accident,' said Jonathan. 'Well, you never know who you might find yourself next to in a queue.'

'Don't get smart.'

Emma quivered again. The GI sergeant's fists looked as if they could knock large holes in an iron lamppost, and she hoped Jonathan was ready to duck. Lola made herself heard amid the noises of the market.

'Now then, Gus, leave off,' she said.

'See here, Lola—'

'And don't start hollering, either,' said Lola. 'There's people lookin', and you're 'olding the queue up. Go and buy some spuds for me mum, and some onions as well, if there's any.'

'I ain't leaving, Lola,' said Gus, 'not while—'

'I don't want no arguments,' said Lola, a mere midget by comparison with Gus.

'I ain't arguing,' said Gus, 'I'm letting this Limey sergeant know he'll have trouble finding his teeth if he keeps getting fresh with you.'

Restive people in the held-up section of the queue began to complain.

'Here, what's goin' on?' demanded a plump woman.

'That's it, what's goin' on?' echoed a thin one.

'It's a Yank, a sergeant,' said a fretful bloke. 'A big one.'

'Well, get 'im out of it,' said the thin woman.

'Me at my time of life and my size?' said Fretful. 'Ain't I got enough troubles?'

'Anyway, leave him be,' said the plump woman, 'I like them Yanks, and me daughter's goin' steady with one.'

'Well, that's her lookout, and someone's got to shift that sergeant,' said the thin woman. 'I ain't got time to stand 'ere all day. What's he doing of?'

'Having a barney with an English sergeant, it looks like,' said a long lanky bloke, who could see over the tops of ladies' hats.

'Can't they have it somewhere else?' bawled a fed-up woman.

'That's it, somewhere else,' hooted Fretful, 'I've had enough aggravation round here from bleedin' Hitler.'

'There, listen to all that,' said Lola to Gus. 'See what you're doing? Upsettin' people, that's what. 'Oppit. Go and get them spuds and onions, or I won't put me party costume on for you tonight. Go on now.'

What a character, thought Jonathan, talk about the female of the species at five feet four being deadlier than a GI at six feet six.

A shadow flitted alongside the queue, a nifty hand reached, grabbed and snatched. Emma's precious handbag, hanging from her wrist, went the way of the shadow, which materialized into a fast-running skinny bloke. Emma yelled.

'Jonathan, he's pinched my handbag!'

'And right in front of my fat eyes,' said Gus, and away he went, Jonathan on his heels. Gus tore holes in the crowds in his bruising chase, holes that Jonathan promptly filled for a split second. He could move fast, despite his tin knee. The slippery bag-snatcher eeled his way towards bomb-damaged King and Queen Street, but something like a tank caught him up and fell on him as he turned the corner. Down he went.

'Oh, bleedin' Amy,' he gasped, 'someone get it orf me.'

Jonathan arrived.

'You hurting?' he enquired, stooping and tugging the handbag free.

'Course I bleedin' am,' panted Slippery Sam, or whoever he was, 'I got a bleedin' bus on top of me, ain't I?'

Gus came to his feet, used one hand to pluck the geezer up and to bounce him up and down on the pavement, feet first.

'How's he doing, buddy?' he asked.

'You're giving him flat feet,' said Jonathan, 'and I don't think he likes it.'

Gus dropped him.

'Oh, yer bugger, now you've broke me back,' groaned Slippery Sam. Gus yanked him up again, planted a boot in his backside and sent him careering. He did a double somersault before he came to a stop, when he then complained bitterly about gorblimey Nosy Parkers interfering with a war-crippled bloke's way of earning an honest living.

'Now what's eating him?' asked Gus.

'Lost his teddy bear,' said Jonathan.

Gus roared with laughter and clapped Jonathan on his shoulder. Jonathan, fortunately, was made of sterner muscle than the bag-snatcher, and he stayed on his feet.

'Let's get back to the ladies,' said Gus.

The date queue was in minor uproar, Emma the centre of it.

'Did he hurt yer, love?'

'It's what the war's done, you can't trust nobody these days.'

'Oh, yer poor gal, have a good cry, if yer want.'

'Where'd yer come from, love, round here?'

'Yes, where'd you get yer sunshine looks?' asked Lola.

'Somerset,' said Emma.

'Crikey, you're the one?' said Lola. 'Well, don't you worry, our blokes'll get your bag back.'

'It'll come back one way or another,' said Emma, implying complete confidence in Jonathan and the Yankee man-mountain, although she had an uneasy feeling the skinny thief was slick enough to vanish. The loss of one's handbag could be the loss of something very personal and private.

Despite the happening and its aggravation, no-one had vacated the queue to go looking for a copper. The acquisition of ripe and luscious dates kept everyone standing their ground.

A woman said suddenly, 'They're coming back.'

'Yes, that's them,' said the plump woman, 'and look, they've got the handbag.'

Gus and Jonathan arrived, and the return of the handbag delighted Emma and struck a happy note throughout the queue.

'Any damage?' asked Lola.

'Not to the handbag,' said Jonathan, and Lola eyed Gus suspiciously.

'Gus, you ain't done for the bloke, have you?' she said. 'You ain't put him in hospital, have you?'

'Treated him gentle,' said Gus.

'I bet,' said Lola. 'You bent me mum's best iron saucepan just by takin' hold of it. Still, I suppose the bloke deserved a broken leg. Well, here we are at last.'

The four of them had reached the stall. The crates of dates had diminished, but the stallholder sold each of them a pound of the imported fruit. They moved aside, grouping on the pavement, and Gus large-heartedly referred to Jonathan as his Limey buddy.

'And I'm forgetting about you going after Lola,' he said.

'Big of you,' said Jonathan, 'except I'm an innocent party.'

'You got three stripes as an innocent party?' said Gus, and roared with laughter again.

'Well, he don't wear them upside-down like you do, so stop making loud noises,' said Lola. 'Excuse me,' she said to Emma, 'you really a dairymaid like your friend mentioned?'

'No, I'm his wife,' said Emma, 'and when I get him home I'll give him a reminder of that.'

'Crikey, and there was me starting to fancy him,'

said Lola. Gus emitted a growl. 'Oh, me Yank's off again,' she said, 'I'd best take him home to me mum. She'll quieten him down. He's a bit noisy sometimes, and I dunno why he calls me Lola when me name's Ada. I kept telling him, but he still went and bought me this Lola brooch, the daft haddock. Still, a girl can't help liking him.'

With that, she and Gus parted from Emma and Jonathan on friendly terms.

'Well, my word,' said Emma, 'weren't they an entertaining couple?'

'I think Lola wears the trousers,' said Jonathan, as they resumed their stroll through the market. 'Or could it be her mum?'

'Whatever, you and Gus did a lovely job rescuing my handbag,' said Emma, 'but I owe you a wallop for getting too close to Lola's sweater.'

'Came up and bumped into me when I wasn't looking,' said Jonathan.

'Giggle, giggle,' said Emma, and laughed. There was an atmosphere of cheerfulness throughout the market, much to do with the people feeling the worst days of the war were over, and that the Allies were now powerful enough to get the better of Hitler and his formidable armies.

Emma and Jonathan ate a date each, then found a stall where they bought a lettuce, a bunch of spring onions, a cucumber and some radishes. They took them home, along with the dates, to Jonathan's mother in Lorrimore Square on the border of Kennington.

'My, my,' said Mrs Jemima Hardy, rosy-cheeked

and contentedly buxom, 'the dates be a treat, Emma, and it were thoughtful of you to get the salad items too.'

'Only too pleased, Mum,' said Emma, 'but I nearly lost my handbag.' She recounted details of the snatching of her handbag and how Jonathan and a big American sergeant took only ten minutes to get it back.

'Well, Emma, there be some of our own people who pester us even in a war like this,' said Jemima. 'But then there's other people, like the American sergeant, who make up for the kind we can't abide. And then there's the war itself, it's better news these days, and making you and Jonathan think about going out one day to look at houses to give yourselves an idea of the kind you'd like to have come the end of the war. That be a happy thing for a young couple, thinking about their future home. It's turned in our favour, the war, so your dad says, Jonathan.'

Jonathan reckoned the most significant turning-point had come when the Eighth Army finally and decisively defeated General Rommel and his Afrika Korps at the end of 1942. Prime Minister Churchill had said that that victory was only the end of the beginning, but couldn't hide his satisfaction and optimism.

And that had been eighteen months ago. The country had made more progress since then, and it was bound to be ready now with the Americans to open up the Second Front. That, thought Jonathan, might be the final step towards the end of this durned old war.

Chapter Four

'Say that again,' said Mrs Rosie Chapman to her husband that same afternoon.

'Saying it six times over, Rosie, won't put a difference on it,' said Captain Matthew Chapman, officer in charge of a specialized workshop at Bovington. He had just arrived home at his cottage in Dorset. 'This is my first day of embarkation leave, after which, along with a team of our best mechanics, I'm going on a boat trip to China.'

'China?' said Rosie. 'China?'

'Just a code name for the real destination,' said Matt, 'and I daresay it won't sabotage the war effort to tell you I think it'll be Italy. Damned old shame, Rosie, but when Dorset husbands a ship do find, Dorset wives get left behind.'

'That old piece of Dorset doggerel needs a burial service,' said Rosie. 'Are you telling me you're being sent overseas despite your crippled ankle?'

'Well, that's it, Rosie, seems I'll have to take it with me,' said Matt. He'd broken an ankle when a boy, and a faulty repair job had resulted in lameness. But it had never been a serious impediment as

37

far as he was concerned, and eventually the Army agreed with him, enlisting him as a first class auto engineer with the rank of second lieutenant. He'd been twice promoted since then, much to Rosie's pleasure. Her faith in his expertise had always been total.

'I'm not in favour of your going,' she said, making a face. 'You do know, don't you, that you're a husband and father, that you've a wife and two children?' The children were Giles, born in May 1942, and Emily, born in August last year. Emily had been named after Rosie's late adoptive mother, a gesture that touched everyone in the Adams and Somers families. Rosie, almost twenty-nine now, was the bright star of Matt's little world in the heart of Dorset, her hair the colour of golden corn, and her clear expressive eyes as magnetically blue as her Aunt Susie's. She had an extraordinarily warm and engaging personality, and a deep well of love and affection for all who were dear to her. Her natural father, Sir Charles Armitage, had been killed in action at Tobruk, and that had saddened her, although it was her adoptive father, known as Boots, who had always meant more to her. 'Matt,' she said firmly, 'a man with a wife, two children, and a gammy leg can't go off on any boat trip to China or wherever. I object. Giles and Emily object. We'll write protest letters about it. Giles and Emily might only come up with inky blobs, but they'll be blobs with a clear message of complaint.'

'Where are our blobs?' asked Matt, his uniform giving his sinewy frame the kind of man appeal Rosie thought sexy.

'Emily's asleep in her pram, and Giles is in the garden with Felicity,' said Rosie. Felicity, her blind sister-in-law, had accepted an invitation to come and stay with her for a couple of months. The immediate development of a warm friendship turned the temporary stay into one that looked like lasting until the end of the war, when Felicity and her husband Tim, a Commando, would find a home of their own. Felicity fought the disability of blindness with resolution and courage, and at the moment was so taken with little Giles that she'd been wondering if she could cope with a child of her own. You could cope as well as the best of us, said Rosie, so have a private word with Tim on his next leave. Hell, said Felicity, a private word with your brother about something like that might land me with a lot more than I bargained for. Tim's a Commando of vim, vigour and virility, she said, and all that could add up to triplets, absolute disaster for a woman who can't see for looking. Oh, chance it, said Rosie, give it a go. 'Matt,' she said now, 'I'm going to hate not having you home once a week, but as there's nothing we can do about it, I'll put my long face in the broom cupboard and keep it there. Come and see Emily, and you'll know what an angel in a pram looks like. Then come and talk to Giles and Felicity.'

'I'm damn glad to know you'll still have Felicity here while I'm away,' said Matt, whose gifted affinity with engines was responsible for his posting to Italy to set up a new repair workshop for tanks. 'She's a walking advertisement for guts and courage.'

'Yes, darling, I know,' said Rosie, 'I know it a

hundred times over, and so does Tim. He'll be here later this afternoon, he's managed to get three days leave before disappearing again on some crucifying Commando exercise.'

'He told you that in so many words?' said Matt.

'In so many words,' said Rosie, and as she and Matt bent over the pram to gaze at the soft relaxed face of the sleeping child, Matt thought that a crucifying exercise pointed to the Commandos making ready for either a special assignment in war-torn Italy or something else. What? An invasion of France? Could the long-delayed opening of the Second Front be in the air at last?

'Where are we?' asked Felicity later that day. She and her husband Tim, Boots's son, were out in the dogcart belonging to Rosie and Matt, the nag a placid ambler only inclined to break into a trot if the driver was cussed enough to insist.

'Where are we?' echoed Tim, Commando officer with a number of barbaric raids to his credit (or discredit from the point of view of those on the receiving end). 'Well, Pussy Willow—'

'Objection,' said Felicity.

'Well, Puss,' said Tim, 'we're still on a road, but I've no idea where it's taking us. There aren't any signposts, and I'm only an occasional visitor to Dorset.'

'What a case,' said Felicity. 'I'm married to a chump who doesn't know where we are.' Dark glasses, as ever, covered her scarred eyes, but her complexion was healthy, her body vibrant, her spirits buoyant. As Tim's wife, she always thought of

40

him as the man who had dived into her slough of despond, pulled her out and convinced her that her blinded eyes didn't mean a life of no hope and no fun. 'Listen, useless, you at least know the way back to the cottage, don't you?'

'Believe, Mrs Adams, I'll make as good a guess as I can,' said Tim.

'I've heard that good guesses can be bad news for a girl,' said Felicity. 'On a par with running out of petrol on a lonely road.'

'Don't worry, Dobbin will get us back,' said Tim, enjoying the slow wandering around lanes where hedgerows were bursting with growth. 'As soon as I turn him round, he'll make straight for home.'

'He's called Humpy, not Dobbin,' said Felicity. 'By the way, I want to ask you something, but first tell me what you think of Giles and Emily.'

'Love 'em both,' said Tim, 'and not just because they're Rosie's.'

'I'm besotted with Giles,' said Felicity, 'and I daresay I will be with Emily too when she's older.' On a slightly flippant note, she added, 'Even if I've never seen either of them.'

'Point taken,' said Tim, and lightly patted her knee. 'Rosie says you're a marvel with Giles.'

'Oh, we toddle up to the chickens together, and feed them together,' said Felicity. 'Giles looks, I listen, he sees them pecking and I hear them clucking.'

'That's fair,' said Tim, and glanced at her. In profile, her good looks were clearly defined, her expression containing nothing of self-pity. He wondered if any other person could have fought blindness as well as she had. Her jolly, breezy self had taken a terrible hiding, but had refused to be broken. 'What's on your mind, Puss, what was it you wanted to ask me?'

'Oh, I'd just like to know if you think I could cope with children of our own,' she said matter-of-factly.

'Come again?' said Tim, sitting up.

'I'd like to hear you say I could and then do something about it,' she said, placing her hand on his left thigh and applying a caress.

'Message received and understood,' said Tim. 'Let me think.' He reflected. As a lively young ATS subaltern, Felicity had seemed just one step up from a jolly-hockey-sticks type, the kind who ended up as a games mistress at a girls' school. Bugger that, he'd thought at the time, am I going to let her spend her life running about with a whistle on a playing field? Not if I can help it, and not while I'm sure she can do me the world of good as my legal bedmate. Well, that had come to pass, but children when she was as blind as a bat? 'Felicity, you're serious, you want children, and you want them now?' he said.

'Allowing for the fact I can't have them tomorrow,' said Felicity, 'yes, I'd like us to start a family, and to begin now, while you're here on leave.'

'I did think that if we decided to have children, we'd wait until after the war,' he said cautiously. They had always practised birth control.

'I know, but must we wait?' asked Felicity. 'Need we, if you think I could cope? I'd have Rosie's help.'

'If you're sure of your feelings, I'd bet on you

being able to manage,' said Tim. 'As long as you did have Rosie's help.'

'I will have,' said Felicity. 'And you know now Matt's going overseas, Rosie would like me to stay on indefinitely.'

'You and Rosie, well, there's a gilt-edged partnership,' said Tim. 'As for doing something to help, well, God bless you, Puss, it's—'

'I'm not relying on God,' said Felicity, 'I'm relying on you. I'm entitled to, I'm married to you.'

'Happy is the day,' said Tim. 'Let's see, begin now, that was the idea, I think. Well, it's a warm afternoon, and that's in our favour. What else is?' He surveyed shelving green slopes, farmlands and a farmhouse away to their left. Not far from it was an open barn full of light and shade, and hay. 'This is a lovely spot, and that over there is promising.'

'Could you enlarge on this and that?' asked Felicity.

'Yes, the spot's quiet, we're by ourselves, and there's a barn not more than fifty yards from here,' said Tim. 'I could walk you over the field to it.'

'You shocker,' said Felicity, 'you're talking about a roll in the hay with the well-brought-up daughter of a Streatham gent recently promoted to bank manager. Little did I think, as a growing schoolgirl with romantic ideas about chivalry and men of honour, that I'd end up marrying a first-class bounder.' She expelled a little laugh. 'Oh, well, some girls are lucky. I'm one of them, I like my own particular bounder.'

Tim smiled and gave the reins a little tug. The ambling nag stopped, its nose dipped and it began nibbling at the grass verge of the lane. Its own attitude to hay was to eat the stuff while it was still grass.

'The barn's a washout?' said Tim.

'Well, I ask you, lover,' said Felicity, 'a barn when we've got a room and a bed all to ourselves at Rosie and Matt's cottage? That makes some farmer's hay a ticklish joke.'

'So how about if we go for an early bedtime and a discussion under the bedclothes to make certain, before we get reckless, that you really are sure about this family planning idea?' suggested Tim.

'I'm already sure about one thing, even if I sound soft in the head,' said Felicity, 'and that's that I'd like us to have our own versions of Giles and Emily.'

Tim put an arm around her.

'We'll go for it, Puss,' he said, but he was painfully conscious of the fact that whatever children they had, she would never experience the joy of actually seeing them. Never. She must know she'd have to live with that, and he was certain she'd taken it into account. His pride in her and his admiration for her had never been more acute. He had to survive this uncivilized war and be around to help her in her inevitable moments of frustration and stress. He had only narrowly survived a Commando raid on Sicily last year, a raid designed to test the German coastal defences of the island before the Allies invaded it. Those defences proved vigilant and deadly. German machine-guns caught the vanguard of his group, which lost seven men killed and two taken prisoner in a matter of minutes. He himself and Colonel Lucas, his brother-in-law, both took leg wounds. They were evacuated only just in time. Having been wounded on other occasions during his time as a Commando, Tim had a feeling the Jerries were out to get him one way or another. Sod that, he thought, I need to stay alive for Felicity and the kids we're going to have. There's something special blowing the way of the Commando group, something that makes me think I've got to take extra care. I think we're going to be geared up for a real blood-and-guts operation that'll make all others seem like larky tea parties. He shook the reins. 'Walk on, Dobbin,' he said.

'It's Humpy,' said Felicity.

'Well, I love the nag and you too,' said Tim.

'Mutual all round, old soldier,' said Felicity. 'So let's look forward to the patter of tiny feet.'

That, of course, was Felicity thinking of sounds. Sounds were her substitute for images. Tim reached and took hold of her hand. Her fingers curled and squeezed, and he interpreted the gesture as one that meant his jolly-hockey-sticks bedmate really did want children.

He thought later about the two Commandos taken prisoner during the raid on Sicily. The Germans had reported to the Red Cross that they were shot while attempting to escape. Tim and Colonel Lucas, when learning of that, both expressed doubt and suspicion. Shot while attempting to escape was becoming too commonplace.

They would have known the truth if they had seen a copy of Hitler's top-secret Commando Decree issued in October 1942.

'I order that from now on all opponents engaged in so-called Commando operations in Europe or Africa, even when it is outwardly a matter of soldiers in uniform or demolitions parties with or without weapons, are to be exterminated to the last man in battle or while in flight. Should any of these individuals, on being discovered, make as if to surrender, all quarter is to be denied on principle . . .'

In other words, shoot all Commando prisoners. This from a man who was constantly declaring what an honour it was to be German.

Chapter Five

Mrs Polly Adams was still living in Dorset, but her husband, Boots, had departed over a year ago for North Africa with the corps formerly under the command of General Sir Henry Simms, Polly's father. Sir Henry had been forced to relinquish that command because of ill-health, but incorrigible in his persistence once he'd recovered, he secured an appointment in an advisory role at the War Office. It was a desk job, but he was listened to on occasions. He grumbled, of course. Lady Simms, as energetic as ever in her work for the Red Cross, patted him, soothed him, and sometimes drove him to Dorset to see Polly and her twins, his grandchildren. He missed the daily contact he'd enjoyed with Boots, his logistics expert, and he missed the man. So did Polly.

The corps under the command of Lieutenant-General Montrose had played its part in the Tunisian campaign, which ended in the complete defeat of the Axis armies, and was marked by a victory parade through the streets of the Tunisian capital. In a letter to Polly, Boots referred to a well-attended fête at which bands played rousingly but couldn't quite make up for the absence of Women's Institute stalls selling homemade jams and marmalade. Polly guessed what he meant by a well-attended fête, and that told her exactly where he was at the time.

Hitler was furious with the German surrender. It did not accord with his uncompromising demand that in any losing situation, German soldiers should fight until the last man was dead. Mussolini didn't make such demands of his Italian troops, who surrendered happily. The Allies subsequently used their battle-hardened North African armies to invade and conquer Sicily. This was followed by an invasion of Italy itself, when the Italian Government immediately made peace with the Allies and gave Mussolini the order of the boot. Incensed by this treatment of his portly Italian partner, Hitler sent hordes of German troops into Italy to occupy it and to defend it against the invaders. They were unable to prevent the Allies securing a foothold, however, and since then the fighting had been bitter.

The corps in which Boots was serving as a staff officer was now part of the British Eighth Army in Italy. His letters, arriving at very irregular intervals, never said much about what was happening. However, Polly knew from wireless broadcasts that the Americans, British, Poles, Canadians and Free French forces were presently locked in titanic battles with the Germans who, to give them their due, were always the toughest of soldiers.

She endured nail-biting moments thinking of

Boots all too close to the costly fighting around Monte Cassino, never mind that he was a staff officer. His last letter, as usual, gave no details of military events. He kept mainly to personal and family matters, most of which related to his attachment to her, the twins and home. The twins, Gemma and James, were now two and a half years old, and children of delight to Polly. Sometimes she could still not believe they were hers, that in her forty-eighth year she was actually the mother of two bundles of fun and mischief. She spoke constantly to them of their father, for she was determined they would not see him as a stranger when he eventually turned up.

Her erstwhile help and companion, Kate Trimble, was now in the WAAF. Kate's young man, Boots's nephew David, was working on a farm in Devon prior to his own call-up, and he intended to opt for the RAF. All Kate's visionary wartime heroes were RAF pilots, and David had promised he'd do his best to fill such a role. He hoped, he said in a letter to her, that German pilots would help him achieve that status by not shooting at him. Kate wrote back to say she quite liked him as he was, that he didn't have to be heroic as long as he looked the part.

Polly made light of being without her. She never allowed the twins to be an encumbrance instead of a blessing. She was more than a match for their childish tricks and tantrums. She had lived through the country's most difficult years, the years of the decimating Great War, the years of economic depression and demoralizing unemployment, the rebellious years of the wild Twenties, and the years of this war against Hitler. There were also her years of frustrated longing for a man whose marriage kept him apart from her until Goering's bombers robbed him of his wife, his Emily.

As Boots's second wife, all her frustrations vanished. The scourge of London bobbies in the wild Twenties, she became almost soppy with happiness, and such an uncritical wife that his mother told her it didn't do for any woman to put her husband on a pedestal. It was bound to make him believe he was her lord and master, which was never what God had in mind. Polly said she'd never had it in mind herself, but somehow it happened. His mother, registering shock, said she'd never brought her only oldest son up to be any woman's lord and master, and something ought to be done about it. Polly said she was doing her level best to get on equal terms, but everything bounced off him, as one might expect with lords and masters. Chinese Lady, as his mother was called, registered more shock. Well, I don't want to interfere, she said, but I'm going to have to talk to him. Which she did, with Polly eavesdropping.

'Now just look here, Boots, I won't have you treating Polly like you were the Lord of the earth, which she says happens every day.'

'Come again, old girl?' said Boots.

'Don't call me old girl, it's airy-fairy and disrespectful,' said Chinese Lady. 'Polly's a very nice woman and a good wife to you, especially considering her worries about the war. Now I know she

50

thinks highly of you, but I won't have you taking advantage of that to make her bow down to you.'

'Come again, old girl?' repeated Boots.

'Don't keep saying that,' said Chinese Lady, 'you know what I'm talking about. Of course, it's not my place to interfere, but some things have to be said. Polly says she didn't think you'd act like her lord and master, but it happened somehow, she said. She told me she's trying to change you, but that you don't take a blind bit of notice.'

'Old lady, I'm lost for words,' said Boots.

'H'm, that'll be the day,' sniffed Chinese Lady.

'I'll talk to Polly,' said Boots, and did so at a suitable moment. The only response he received came in the form of shrieks of laughter. There was no way any lord and master could get the better of hysterical glee by mere dialogue. So, in a manner of speaking, he dragged the lady up the winding stairs to the bedroom. Polly liked that.

'What happens next?' she asked when they arrived at the bedside.

'Something heavy's going to drop on you from a great height,' said Boots.

'Oh, yes please, m'lord, thank you, m'lord, carry on, m'lord,' said Polly.

Today, she was motoring back to her wartime home in the village of Corfe Castle after spending three days with her parents in Dulwich, London now being free of air raids. On no account would Polly have taken her precious twins to the Empire's battered capital if there was still a threat from the skies. Her main family visits were to Rosie and Felicity, who weren't all that far from her.

The car wasn't short of petrol. Her versatile brother-in-law, Sammy, kept her supplied with coupons without disclosing how he acquired them. Polly always expressed thanks, but asked no questions, knowing that among Sammy's useful wartime connections were a spiv or two. Polly was far too sophisticated to feel guilty.

Gemma and James were sitting together on the passenger seat, where she could keep an eye on the little darlings. While they were inseparable, they weren't identical. Gemma was fair-haired, hazel-eyed and round-faced. James had the dark brown hair, grey eyes and leaner features of his father. They were arguing about who was the first to see the squirrel that had crossed the road a little way back. Arguments alternated with agreements in their existence as twins.

A few miles from Corfe Castle, Polly approached a cross-roads and came to a stop. Passing by was a long line of trudging American Army troops. Dorset and Devon had been swarming with men of the American divisions for a year and more. Thousands of GIs had conducted regular countryside man-oeuvres, bestowing on the land a host of muddy footprints, gouged earth and large dents, and leaving chalked messages such as 'Kilroy was here, OK?' Lately, however, Polly's impression was that they were thinning out, that an exodus from the West Country was taking place for some reason or another, and she made her guesses about that.

She sat there in Boots's old Riley, its hood down on this bright day, and the foot-slogging GIs eyed her as they went by, rifles slung, packs on their backs.

'Room there for me, lady?'

Polly smiled.

'Here, kids.' One man, diving a hand into his fatigues, brought out a wrapped candy bar and tossed it into the car. Gemma and James fought for its possession. Polly thanked the GI with a smile and a little hand gesture. He slowed as if he had it in mind to ask her for a date.

'Move it, Private Brewster!' bawled a sergeant, and the GI picked up his feet and went on. It didn't prevent another man from trying his luck.

'Could I meet ya somewheres, lady?' he asked, giving Polly a wink. Polly was only a few months short of forty-eight, but with every assistance from herself, the passing years had been kind to her. She still looked very much like Colleen Moore, piquant-faced Hollywood film star of the Thirties. Her natural elegance and her Mayfair accent intrigued Americans with whom she had come into contact. They cast her as a typically fascinating upper-crust Englishwoman by no means middle-aged. Wearing a light brown hat and dark brown costume, she watched the American soldiers trudging by. It made her think of how she had watched British Tommies going up the line to the trenches of the '14–18 war. Even now, those memories were quick to come back. There was, thank God, no trench warfare in this present conflict, although death from mighty machines was no less hideous.

The rearguard passed. An officer gave her a friendly salute.

'Thanks, ma'am,' he said in appreciation of her patience. She had made no attempt to disrupt the column.

'Goodbye, mister,' called little Gemma.

'Goodbye,' echoed young James.

Polly crossed then, and the twins began to argue again over the candy bar. Gemma glanced at her mother. So did James. Polly took no notice. She rarely took any notice of arguments, yells and friction, and that seemed to shorten their duration. She always gave attention to the twins' sweeter moods, which let them know that that was how she liked them best. She sometimes wondered if her life had become the humdrum one of conventional motherhood and routine domesticity. But then she'd look at the twins, feel the sense of wonder that they were hers, and follow that by thinking of their father, the man who had helped in the creation of the miracle.

God, she really did miss him, she thought, as a battered old taxi, coming from Corfe Castle village, passed her with a rattle and a wheeze.

Reaching her wartime home on the outskirts of the village, the cottage Boots was renting for the duration, she turned in, brought the car to a stop in the short drive, switched off the engine, and alighted. She went round, opened the passenger door, and out scrambled perpetual motion in the form of Gemma and James. They were still rabbiting on about ownership of the candy, tightly clutched in Gemma's hand.

'If I confiscated it,' said Polly, 'would that settle the matter?'

'But, Mummy, it's ours,' protested James.

'Oh, you've finally settled it yourselves, have you?' said Polly. 'It's yours and Gemma's?'

'Well, it's mine really,' said Gemma, 'but I'd best share it with James.'

'Hooray,' said Polly, and opened the front door with her key. In rushed the small boy and girl. There were three letters on the hallstand. Odd, how did they get there from the mat? Had Mrs Clowes, her domestic help, been in? She must have. The top letter was a blue airmail missive. Polly, picking it up, recognized her husband's handwriting. She slit it with a quick fingernail.

James called from the living-room.

'Mummy, Daddy's here.'

'What? What did you say, James?'

Gemma answered.

'He's down the garden, Mummy.'

Polly ran into the living-room. Through the open French windows the garden showed clear and green, the borders colourful with spring bulbs. An Army officer turned at the bottom of the garden and began to stroll back to the cottage. Out through the French windows scampered the twins.

'Daddy!'

'Daddy!'

It had been a year since they had last seen him, but they hadn't forgotten him, young though they were. They pelted up to him. Boots stooped and put an arm around each of them.

'Hello, little poppets, I think you've both grown a bit,' he said.

'Daddy, we been to Mummy's home to see Granny and Grandpa,' said James.

'We just come back,' said Gemma.

'So have I,' said Boots, 'but not from your grandparents.' He sat down on the garden bench and brought the twins up on the seat with him, Gemma on his left, James on his right. He planted a kiss on James's cheek and one on Gemma's nose. Gemma giggled and chattered. James used his own tongue. Both children knew without question who their father was, even if he had been away for ages.

Polly, out on the patio, stood quite still, watching the exuberant reunion. Emotion coursed through her. Boots saw her.

'Hello, Polly.'

'Hello, darling.' Polly's response was slightly husky.

'Be with you in a tick,' said Boots.

'Don't hurry, give them a fussing,' said Polly, and waited while he talked to the twins, hugged them, and listened to piping voices delivering words that tumbled over each other. It pleased Polly immensely that during his absence she had succeeded in keeping his image alive in their young minds. She noted his demonstrations of affection, of delight in his twins. It touched her emotions. Eventually, Boots sent the boy and girl into the cottage to play the game of standing guard over his valise, which he'd left in the kitchen. Polly took her turn then for

56

a reunion. She sat down beside him. Boots put an arm around her and kissed her with warmth and feeling, which helped her to make an admission. 'Do you realize, you old darling, that I'm close to needing a hankie?' she said.

'I realize your nose is slightly pink,' said Boots. 'I liked your neutral one best, but I can live with the pink. Um, is there a good reason for needing a hankie?'

'Yes, there is,' said Polly. 'You're the one man I've been aching to see, but the last one I expected. How did you manage it, have you been given home leave? If so, for how long, and why didn't you let us know you were coming?'

'How many questions is that?' asked Boots.

'Never mind how many, you can roll them all into one,' said Polly. 'Just tell me – oh, ye gods, what are you doing?'

Boots had opened up her jacket and placed a hand on her blouse, where a firmly defined curve was a tribute to her well-preserved figure.

'I'm delighted to find you all present and correct, Mrs Adams,' he said.

'Boots, you old warhorse, if you're delighted, I'm delirious,' she said. 'You're here, you're home.' There he was, his familiar smile all for her, his years sitting so easily on him. His face was tanned, his impaired left eye a little more deeply grey than the right. Close to him, Polly experienced that which he so often aroused in her, the incredible feeling of being young again. She had fallen in love with him years ago, on the day she first met him in Sammy's grotty Army surplus shop, and had never been able to cure herself of her intense attachment to him. 'Speak to me.'

'First,' said Boots, 'I arrived in Southampton from Gibraltar this morning, where I was able to catch a train and finish up at Wareham. I phoned you from there, hoping you'd be able to come and pick me up. No answer. Well, according to our cherubs, it seems you were on your way back from Dulwich, but I simply thought you were out in the village with them. So I convinced an old bloke with an ancient taxi that he'd do the Army a favour if he'd drive me here.'

'I think the old rattler passed us a little while ago,' said Polly.

'Well, it helped me to beat you to the door by about ten minutes,' said Boots.

'So it was you who picked the letters up from the mat,' said Polly. 'Boots, I want to hear how long you're going to be with us, how much leave you've got, why you were in Gibraltar, and yes, what you think of the twins after a year away from them.'

'I'm still in wonder that those two treasures should be ours, Polly,' said Boots.

'Darling, is that how you feel about them?' said Polly. 'So do I. Sometimes I simply can't believe they belong to us. What happened to make us so privileged?'

'A little extra togetherness on a certain night,' said Boots and kissed her again. Polly, melting, asked herself if it was absurd that, when they were both nearing the frightful age of fifty, they should be as heady as young lovers. If it was absurd, if it is, then I like absurdity. 'As to answers to your other questions,' said Boots, 'it's a long story. Is there any chance first of a cup of tea?'

Polly laughed out of sheer happiness.

'Tea,' she said, 'tea. Is there anything you and your mother, and the rest of your family, like more than a teapot?'

'In my case, several things,' said Boots, 'including watching you put your stockings on.'

'At my age, that's a pleasure to you, you old ratbag?' said Polly.

'You can believe me,' said Boots. 'Which reminds me, there are six pairs of fully-fashioned stockings for you in my valise, with the compliments of an American major.'

'How can I thank him?' asked Polly.

'We'll invite him for a weekend sometime after Hitler's dead and buried,' said Boots. 'Meanwhile, I'd still like a cup of home-brewed tea.'

'Dear man, you can have anything I'm able to give you,' said Polly. 'Only ask and you shall receive.'

'Then put the kettle on while I talk to Gemma and James again,' said Boots. 'But not until this evening, when they're in bed, will I tell you what's brought me home.'

'Why not?' asked Polly, getting up.

'Just one answer to that, Polly,' said Boots. 'Not in front of the children.'

'Is it grim, then?' asked Polly, wincing.

'It won't make good listening for Gemma and James, Polly. Yes, it's grim, but it doesn't directly affect you and me, or our cherubs. Hang on until they're in bed.'

Chapter Six

Evening. Gemma and James were in bed, sound asleep after a long, exciting day. Boots and Polly were seated in armchairs in the living-room that was bright with pretty chintzes. The owner of the cottage, a sweet old lady now living with her widowed sister in Taunton, had made a pretty thing of the cottage as a whole.

Boots recounted the events that had brought him back to England. The prolonged battle for Monte Cassino, defended in depth by the Germans, who held all positions of advantage, had been savage, the Allied casualties heavy. One day, Boots and his Corps Commander, Lieutenant-General Montrose, together with a Captain Francis, also on the staff, were driving back to headquarters after a consultation with unit commanders at the front. They slowed to edge a way past a truck containing Germans taken prisoner. A British sergeant in charge of the escort jumped down from the cab and ran to hail the staff car. Lieutenant-General Montrose ordered his driver to stop, although the sky was being repeatedly invaded by German fighters and Stukas.

The sergeant, noting the pennant on the car and the presence of a general, saluted and said, 'Sergeant Rogers, Middlesex Regiment, sir. Permission to have a word, sir?'

'Make it a quick one, Sergeant Rogers, and it had better be worth my while,' said Montrose.

'Yessir, right, sir,' said Sergeant Rogers. The noise of gunfire to the north-east was a persistent low drumming on every ear. 'It's like this. We've got a corporal among these here prisoners, and he's raving, sir.'

'Raving?' said Montrose.

'Like bloody hell he is, sir, and in good English, all about what Himmler's SS are doing to Jewish people, according to his brother, who's an SS sergeant. He's shell-shocked, so it's all coming out like he's on his deathbed, poor bleeder.' The sergeant, grimy-faced and battle-worn, was blunt. 'He's been gabbing on about some concentration camp in Poland, called Auschwitz, and about what his brother has told him the SS are doing to Jews there. Bloody flaming murder, sir, they're gassing them by the thousand and burning the bodies.'

'Sergeant, are you sure you haven't been listening to the ravings of a lunatic?' asked Montrose.

'Sir, we've all heard rumours, but I'm believing I've been listening to facts. Gassing the poor bleeders and then burning them down to their bones, right, yes, that does take some believing. It's bloody horrible, and it's not all, it seems there's other

61

camps where the SS are doing the same thing, so the prisoner says. It's my opinion, sir, that my best bet is to hand him over to you. Well, what he's got coming out of his mouth is information of a kind special to my way of thinking, and he ought to be taken care of as a special case.' A case for Intelligence, thought Boots. 'He's up in the cab, he's been sitting between me and Corporal Harris, the driver. That's for his own safety. The other prisoners, fourteen of 'em, jumped him as soon as he started to open his mouth to me. Well, it was all coming out in German, and they were getting earfuls of it and not liking it. I had to order the escort to use rifle butts on the buggers. Then he started to talk to me in English, so I had him out of the truck, and a bit later, up in the cab. Corporal Harris is holding on to him right now.'

'Sergeant Rogers, are you serious?' asked Montrose.

'Too bloody true I am, sir. I've got this feeling it's no fairy story. Permission, sir, on account of the nature of the information, to place prisoner in your charge?'

Montrose, seated with Boots in the back of the car, said, 'Get him down, Sergeant Rogers, bring him here.'

The German corporal, helmetless and ashen-faced, his chin darkly stubbled, arrived at the car, Sergeant Rogers with him. Boots, out of the car, had the back door open. Sergeant Rogers pushed the man's head down and shoved him in.

'Good work, sergeant,' said Boots.

'I'm relieved to hand him over, sir,' said Sergeant Rogers.

Boots resumed his place, so that the German corporal was between him and the Corps Commander. Sergeant Rogers closed the door, Montrose gave an order to his driver and the car moved off. Sergeant Rogers saluted.

The car raced for headquarters, passing Army vehicles moving up to the front. German fighter planes caught it out in the open after five minutes. All hell erupted around the car and other Army traffic.

'Bale out!' shouted Montrose. The car stopped, and out surged the driver, the Corps Commander, Captain Francis and Boots. Boots pulled the prisoner out after him, and they all ran for cover. Self-preservation was paramount as they went to ground off the road. There was a chance now for the German corporal to escape, but he flung himself down next to Boots and stayed there while cannon shells whistled, hummed and exploded. He vibrated and trembled, spilling words.

'Auschwitz, *Mein Gott*, Auschwitz.'

Boots thought him a man shot through with the violence of war and demons of the mind.

The German fighters screamed and shrieked. Cannon shells struck the car forty yards away and it blew up and burst into flame. The heat fanned the grounded men.

It lasted only a few minutes, the strafing attack from the air, but it caused casualties among men and machines. However, although Captain Francis suffered a flesh wound in his thigh, Boots, Montrose and his driver emerged unscathed. The German corporal had taken another psychological hammering, but came out of it with his teeth clenched and a strange resolve intact.

In good English, he said to Boots as they clambered to their feet, 'I wish to speak with someone important, I have much to tell, which I must tell or live in hell.'

'British Intelligence?' said Boots, brushing himself down while an officer in charge of an armoured truck radioed for ambulances.

'Yes. Yes. I am Corporal Hans Thurber, and my brother Ernst is an SS sergeant serving in a concentration camp. Are you a good officer, a good man?'

'Can I say so?' said Boots, feeling an odd kind of pity for this haggard German. 'No, you must find that out from other officers, other men.' He scanned the sky. The *Luftwaffe* was still a force of might and power in Italy. 'But I can tell you that if you have information you think we need to know, you'll be listened to.' As a measure of reassurance, he added, 'Sympathetically'.

'I will be grateful,' said Corporal Hans Thurber.

The torched car blazed away. Lieutenant-General Montrose commandeered the use of a replacement vehicle, and on arrival at headquarters was immediately called to a conference. He gave Boots the responsibility of taking exclusive charge of the prisoner, and Boot was present the following day when Corporal Thurber was interviewed by two Intelligence officers.

What he told them had been recounted to him by his brother Ernst when they were on leave together two months ago. His brother, a tough SS specimen though he was, had begun to find his life and his duties at a concentration camp called Auschwitz unendurable. He put aside his oath of secrecy and poured out details of unimaginable horror. Thousands of Jews, thousands, arrived at the camp month by month, and all were gassed or worked to death, then shovelled into crematoria to be burned down to ashes. Men, women, and children. Ah, the children. Some no more than infants, who died in their mothers' arms.

If Sergeant Ernst Thurber of the SS eased his conscience in any way by confiding horror to his brother Hans, it did nothing for Hans except to land him with images and thoughts appalling to dwell on. Ernst asked for nothing to be said. Hans, aghast and bitter, asked if he was expected to take such a tale of enormities to his grave. Yes, you must, for the sake of Hitler and the German Reich, said Ernst. Accept, he said, that it has helped me a little in confessing to you, in sharing my sickness with you. I am not your priest, shouted Hans, I am a German soldier sworn to die for our *Fuehrer* if necessary. Our *Fuehrer!* Have I sworn such an oath for such a man? Stop shouting, for God's sake, said Ernst, our *Fuehrer* has not done these things with his own hand. Damn him, said Hans, and damn you, I would rather you had shot yourself than saddled me with the knowledge of what you have done to help in the murder of thousands of Jews. Could it ever be right to murder one single person because of his religion or race? To murder them, small children as well, is that what we are doing at Auschwitz and other concentration camps? May God forgive you and our *Fuehrer.*

All this and more was relayed by Hans Thurber to the two British Intelligence officers in the presence of Boots. Every word was difficult to believe, but belief hovered because the man was so convincing, although there was a suggestion of a suffering mind that might have been the result of a recent Allied bombardment of the Germans defending Monte Cassino, a bombardment that lasted forty-eight hours.

Was there any proof? Did the prisoner have anything in writing or by way of photographs?

No, he had only his brother's emotional and turbulent verbal confession.

A pity. All the same, London must know of this. London must decide the issue. The prisoner would be flown to England under escort. The prisoner asked for a favour, that Colonel Adams might be a member of the escort.

Colonel Adams had other duties.

The prisoner dug his heels in, and was told he was not in a position to ask for any kind of favours. The prisoner responded by saying he was a man unable to live in peace with himself, and therefore what he was asking for was a sympathetic favour.

'Colonel Adams?' said one Intelligence officer.

'I'm more than willing to go, to have charge of him,' said Boots.

'Good.'

The prisoner, dismissed, was taken away under escort.

'That's a man unable to come to terms with the infamy of Hitler,' said Boots. 'Or Himmler.'

'Or with the sickness of his own imagination.

Colonel Adams, one of our officers and a sergeant will keep you company on the flight, and it looks as if you'll have to be present at London interviews. Any objections?'

'None,' said Boots.

'We'll ask Lieutenant-General Montrose to release you, perhaps for a month, in view of the fact that the man regards you as his confidant.'

'I think that what we've heard will be enough to make London jump out of its skin,' said Boots.

'It might, yes, if we had any proof. As it is, we're dealing with hearsay, Colonel. There have been hundreds of rumours and some accusations, but never any proof. Hearsay alone won't do.'

'But prolonged interrogation in London might dredge up a few bones with meat on them,' said Boots.

'Yes, so it might. But meat on those kind of bones? God Almighty, it'll be meat that'll stink to high heaven. We'll signal London.'

For two days, Boots spent much time with Corporal Thurber, establishing a close and reassuring relationship with him. The German willingly, if in a distressed way, offered extra details of his brother's outpourings. All amounted to the same thing, however, a picture of the appalling fate suffered by Jewish people in the concentration camp called Auschwitz. On the morning of the third day, with Boots temporarily detached from Lieutenant-General Montrose's staff, a flying-boat carried prisoner and escort to Gibraltar, where they were met by informed Intelligence men from London.

There, Corporal Hans Thurber was interrogated for four consecutive days, always in the presence of Boots, who had succeeded in reducing the man's hysteria and brought him to a calmer recounting of his brother's confession. Calmer, he was more credible. And there were no variations in his story, only an unbreakable thread of bitterness and a sick disillusion with the glorified SS.

Credibility, however, was still not proof.

He was eventually flown to Southampton Water, with the Intelligence men. Boots went too. On arrival in Southampton itself, Boots was offered a break, either at home or in London. He chose home. He would be contacted there when he was needed again, say in three or four days.

'And there you are, Polly, here I am,' he said.

'I'd be very happy if I weren't so appalled,' said Polly. 'Boots, for God's sake, do you believe this man?'

'I've spent days with him, observed him, talked to him and listened to him,' said Boots, 'and yes, I do believe.'

'That thousands and thousands of Jewish people are being gassed and cremated monthly?' said Polly, incredulous.

'I reserve my judgement on numbers,' said Boots. 'I can put thousands and thousands monthly down to the exaggeration that goes with disordered and tortured minds.'

'But even a count of hundreds doesn't bear thinking about,' said Polly. 'And children, Boots? Infants?'

'Is it possible, Polly, that Hitler's Germany is

more of a hell than any of us could ever imagine?' said Boots sombrely.

'If it's responsible for the murder of little children and their mothers, yes, it's a hell built by Satan himself,' said Polly. 'But could it be, could even the most devilish nation cover up the murder of hundreds of men, women and children, and by gassing them?'

'That's what puts a chink in belief,' said Boots, 'that's why Allied governments need positive proof. You're right, Polly, how could murder on that scale be hidden if it's been going on for a year and more? I'd like to talk to Corporal Thurber again, and will do when I'm called to London. They're giving him time to recover from disorientation. They want him stone cold sober, if that's possible. He's calmer than at first, but he still has spasms of hysteria.'

'Darling, do you feel sick about all you had to listen to, and are you tired?' asked Polly.

'I feel a sympathy for Corporal Thurber,' said Boots. 'As for tiredness, it's a little early for bed, isn't it?'

'I don't think I mentioned bed, did I?' said Polly.

'It's a thought,' said Boots.

'Bed?' said Polly.

'With you, Polly,' said Boots, 'but not now, later.'

'At our ages?' said Polly, finding a smile.

'Polly old girl, I'm not done for yet,' said Boots.

'Oh, good show, mighty man of everlasting iron,' said Polly.

'There's one thing that's happily constant,' said Boots.

'And what's that, old sport?' asked Polly.

'You're a lovely woman to come home to, Polly.'

Polly's eyes turned misty.

'Don't do it to me again,' she said muffledly.

'Don't do what?' asked Boots.

'Put me in need of a hankie again,' said Polly.

Boots got up, took hold of her hands and brought her to her feet.

'It's a frightful world, Polly,' he said, 'made so by frightful men, but some of us are blessed with civilized and forgiving women. Women like you. Let me say that it was painful to lose Emily, but you've been a joy and delight to me.'

'Dear man, don't you know how much I always wanted to be?' said Polly.

The phone rang. Boots answered it. The conversation he had with the caller lasted more than a few minutes, and when he came back he looked stunned.

'My God,' he said.

'Boots?'

'Corporal Thurber hanged himself an hour ago, Polly. He was housed comfortably, with two Military Police sergeants to keep an eye on him. But he managed to hang himself in the bathroom by standing on the lavatory seat, tying his braces around the high window sash, then around his neck and simply letting himself fall. He was a man in torment, Polly, a man who considered himself monstrously betrayed by his brother and his Fuehrer. In common parlance, a decent man. I wonder, are there other Germans like him, others who can tell us what he told us, and would tell if they were free to do so?'

'If all he said is true, Boots, then there must be, there must,' said Polly. 'Did he say who runs these concentration camps?'

'Himmler's SS,' said Boots. 'That's believable, if so much else isn't. I'm still struggling with some doubt.'

'So am I,' said Polly.

'Now Intelligence not only has no proof, but no Corporal Thurber, either,' said Boots. He grimaced. 'There's a suggestion he might not have hanged himself if I'd been there, for he asked once or twice if I had deserted him, if I considered him a man who belonged to an insufferable people.'

'Boots, you're not going to blame yourself, are you?' said Polly.

'No, Polly, I'm going to have a whisky, a stiff one,' said Boots.

'And then?' said Polly, aware that he was a shaken man.

'There's always you, Polly, thank God,' said Boots.

'That's one thing you can always believe,' said Polly.

Chapter Seven

Little Phoebe Adams, adopted daughter of Susie and Sammy Adams, ran around the bedroom she shared with their natural daughter, Paula. She was shrieking with laughter, Sammy in chase of her. She scrambled over the bed, Sammy popped up on the other side, cut her off and collared her.

'Got you, little sausage,' he said.

'Daddy, you cheated,' she said, flushed and indignant. But she was happy to be up in his arms and to look into his smiling blue eyes. She was seven, a girl of giggles and responsive affection, and as much of a delight to Sammy as Paula, almost nine. Two of his other three children, Bess and Jimmy, were still in Devon as evacuees. The third, elder son Daniel, seventeen, had returned home three months ago, and was working at the factory in Belsize Park.

Phoebe, with her dark curling hair, dark eyes and elfin prettiness, had her own special place in the affections of Sammy and Susie. They cherished her as if she had been their own, and in the same way that Boots and Emily had cherished Rosie as a young girl.

'Did I cheat?' asked Sammy.

'Yes, you went so's you could get in front of me,' said Phoebe, who had a strange belief that Sammy and Susie were her natural parents. That was something Sammy and Susie were going to have to deal with eventually. 'Daddy, again.'

'I'm supposed to be getting you ready for bed,' said Sammy, as mentally and physically up to the mark at nearly forty-two as he had been when running a market stall at eighteen.

'Just once more, please,' said Phoebe, so he set her down and a new chase began, Phoebe shrieking as she scampered around. Up the stairs and into the bedroom came Paula.

'Well, I just don't know, I'm sure,' she said, taking off Chinese Lady, her never-failing grandma. Her fair hair, loose, was shining from a brushing, and she wore a dressing-gown over her nightie. 'I simply don't know what I'm going to make of you two, and Mummy says that if you bring the house down, Daddy, you'll be for it. And Daniel said he can hardly hear what the wireless is saying. And Grandma says she didn't bring you up to make a racket.'

Sammy and Susie, still living with his mother and stepfather in the Red Post Hill house, had decided to stay until the war was over, when they would rebuild on the site of their bombed home. Chinese Lady and her husband, Edwin Finch, had no objections whatever to an indefinite stay by Susie, Sammy, the two young girls, and their brother Daniel. The large house had six bedrooms.

'Mummy and Grandma said that, did they, Plum Pudding?' said Sammy.

'Yes, Daddy, they did,' said Paula.

'Oh, my eye,' said Sammy.

'Oh, crikey,' said Phoebe, and darted a glance at Sammy. He tried to look like a guilty man, but failed. A little grin came and went, and Phoebe smothered a giggle.

'And another thing,' said Paula, a young lady with a tongue, 'Mummy says to remind you that Emma and Jonathan will be here in five minutes.'

'Ah,' said Sammy. 'Emma and Jonathan, right,' he said. 'Teeth, Phoebe. Jump about.'

'Daddy, I already done my teeth,' said Phoebe.

'Have you?' said Sammy.

'Oh, dear, oh, dear,' said Paula, 'I think you're a bit wobbly from making a racket, Daddy. Never mind, you'll be better later.'

Only a little later, in fact, when the girls were in bed, Sammy was well enough to answer the door to Emma and Jonathan himself. It was the last full day of the young couple's week at home, and Sammy had asked them to drop in.

'Here we are, Uncle Sammy,' said Emma, fresh as a bird at morning's first light, despite spending the whole afternoon in and around the Denmark Hill area. She and Jonathan had been trying to decide on the kind of house in which they would like to begin their post-war life. It was a prolonged outing embracing ideas, visions, hopes and optimism.

'Glad to see you,' said Sammy, and gave his like-able niece a hug and a smacker before shaking Jonathan's hand. 'Jonathan, forgot to ask you about your tin knee when me and Susie saw you at the beginning of your leave. How's it doing?'

'Rattling a bit,' said Emma.

'I call it operative,' said Jonathan who, like all the younger relatives, thought Sammy an eternal live wire. 'So, I'm grateful to it, fond of it, and hanging on to it.'

'I'm fond of it too,' said Emma. 'We're a proud trio, Mum and Rosie and me, we all fly the flag for our husbands' brave legs.' She spoke light-heartedly, then made a little face. 'Considering everything else, Uncle Sammy, we're lucky.'

'We're all lucky, Emma, all of us who are still alive,' said Sammy, remembering the months of the sustained blitz on London, and the night when he, Susie and Paula, in their air raid shelter, had heard the shattering roar of the exploding bomb that had razed their house. 'And I'll say this much, Jonathan looks as if he could climb trees all day, and you look as if you'd never be far behind.'

'Yes, him Tarzan, me Jane,' said Emma. 'Oh, hello, Aunt Susie, love your dress.'

Susie, coming through the hall, was wearing a jersey wool dress of royal blue, a blue that always did so much for her fair looks. She was thirty-nine and the thought of being forty in August didn't exactly exhilarate her. Every year seemed to fly, even in wartime. She could hardly believe the country had been involved in an utterly vicious conflict with Hitler's Germany for well over four years, and against Japan for more than two. Susie could sense the country being drained of its best men and its strength. Soldiers, sailors, airmen and yes, merchant seamen too. Time after time the news referred to the loss of merchant shipping and the drowning of the crews. The German U-boats were the wolves of the Atlantic and the North Sea, hunting in packs, although the Royal Navy and the American Navy, with the help of long-ranging Sunderland flying-boats, were gradually getting the upper hand. And no U-boats could touch those fast-running troopships and armament carriers, the *Queen Mary* and *Queen Elizabeth*, in their voyages to and from New York.

Susie still put her faith in Prime Minister Winston Churchill, a bulldog turned lion. She was still sure he could outmatch Hitler, especially as his American allies were proving awesomely powerful. And their GIs were proving irresistibly fraternal. Shy girls shrieked and ran home to their mothers when they saw them coming. Most girls did no such thing. They liked the breezy, extrovert gum-chewing Americans.

Susie greeted Emma and Jonathan affectionately, exchanging kisses with them.

'Lovely to see you again,' she said. 'We'll talk in the parlour, shall we? Sammy has something to say to you. We won't keep you long as it's your last evening.'

On the table in the parlour were glasses, a bottle of beer and a bottle of port. They sat down around the table, and Sammy poured port for Emma and Susie, and beer for Jonathan and himself. The beer frothed to a fine white head on which bubbles sparkled and popped.

'Now,' said Sammy, 'here's to you two young people, well and truly married, which my dear old Ma is all in favour of and said so on the happy occasion when your Aunt Susie had the good sense to marry me. Or was it the other way round?'

'Well, I think the world of you, Uncle Sammy,' said Emma, 'but I also think it was the other way round.'

'Granted,' said Sammy. 'My lucky day that was, and I won't deny it.'

'Granted,' said Susie.

'I weren't there myself,' said Jonathan, 'but durned if I don't believe you, Aunt Susie. No offence, Uncle Sammy.'

'None taken,' said Sammy genially. 'You two have been looking for your kind of dream castle today, right?'

'Oh, a kind of wander into the realms of wishful thinking,' said Emma, 'to give ourselves lovely ideas of what we'd like for our post-war home, even if we know we'd have to start with something modest. Jonathan's saving as much as he can out of his sergeant's pay, and I'm saving as much as I can out of my farm pay.'

'Well, it's a fact you'll need somewhere to live,' said Sammy.

'It's the usual thing, Uncle Sammy,' said Jonathan, enjoying his light ale, which an off-licence keeper had produced from under his counter for Sammy, along with another bottle. Sammy had his way of getting various shopkeepers to forage about under their counters for consumables and other items in short supply. 'We go along with having a roof and a front door.'

'Well, Jonathan, we don't want you to be like Flanagan and Allen, living underneath the arches,' smiled Susie.

'Too draughty, Aunt Susie,' said Jonathan, returning her smile, and Emma thought what a nice face her country chap had, firm and manly, with good humour written all over it. That didn't mean he was a soft-speaking sergeant, an easy touch for recruits. She'd met some of his fellow NCOs, and they'd told her that when Jonathan was delivering reprimands to a squad of trainee gunners, the shock waves cracked teacups in the camp Naafi. 'Yes, we'd prefer a roof and a tidy old amount of bricks and mortar,' he said.

'With a garden,' said Emma.

'Emma,' said Sammy, 'd'you happen to know the firm's in the property business?'

'Oh, I know,' said Emma, sipping her port. 'Grandma keeps us all informed of everything.'

'Ought to be Minister of Information,' said Sammy, lively blue eyes conveying a hint that an interesting announcement was about to come forth. 'Now it so happens that our property company has just acquired a house in Ferndene Road off Denmark Hill.'

'For you and Aunt Susie to rent from the firm?' said Emma.

'Rent's money down the drain,' said Sammy, looking pained.

'In any case,' said Susie, 'Sammy and me are going to have a new house built on the site of our bombed one, just as soon as the war is over.'

'Incorporating some of your own ideas?' said Jonathan. 'I'd call that exciting.'

'Mentally, Susie's already built the kitchen,' said Sammy, 'a bit on the lines of Buckingham Palace. She's well known to me and our kids for being mental.'

'You'll be well known for having a large hole in your head in a minute,' said Susie.

'Noted,' said Sammy. 'Where was I? I got it, yes. In regard to this lately acquired desirable residence in Ferndene Road, we thought we'd hold it for you two, Jonathan, and to let you buy it from the firm on an instalment basis if you'd like to move in after the war. Of course, there'd be a bit of reasonable interest chargeable. When I say reasonable, I mean it won't give you and Emma heartburn or fainting fits, unlike the arm-twisting interest charged by loan companies. What we had in mind was a fair return for the firm.'

'Uncle Sammy!' Emma sat up straight and looked Sammy in the eye.

'Do I suspect you're offended?' said Sammy.

'Offended?' said Emma. 'I should say not. Well, I'm not, and neither is Jonathan, are you, Jonathan?'

'I don't feel any kind of offence coming on,' said Jonathan. 'I feel more like I'm falling off this chair.' That reaction out of the way, he eyed Sammy seriously. 'Mr Adams, are we talking about a house and home waiting for Emma and me as soon as the war's over?'

'That's the idea,' said Sammy.

'It's a lovely house,' said Susie, 'fully detached, with four bedrooms, a boxroom, large kitchen, and apple trees in the garden.'

'Oh, my sainted aunt,' said Emma.

'Is that me?' smiled Susie.

'No, I meant – well, yes, why not?' said Emma. 'I know Ferndene Road, and I know the kind of properties there. Jonathan knows it too, but only because it was one of the roads we took in this afternoon.' She looked at Jonathan, her mouth parted and excited little breaths escaping. 'Say something, Jonathan.'

'I will,' said Jonathan. 'Could I ask you to outline the terms, Uncle Sammy?'

'It was an offer, fully furnished, for a sum that hurt me ears,' said Sammy. 'But the firm acquired it for five-ten, which was only slightly painful. Terms for you and Emma? Well, you pay for it at the rate of seven pounds a month for six years, plus ten per cent simple interest, which is fourteen bob a month, and which means that at the end of six years it'll have cost you five hundred and sixty-one quid in all. That's a lot less than if you took out a loan or a mortgage. Fair?'

'Fairer than anything else I ever heard of,' said Jonathan.

'Especially as Aunt Susie says the house is lovely,' said Emma, flushed with sheer delight. 'I can always believe you, Aunt Susie.'

'Thank you, Emma,' smiled Susie.

'Uncle Sammy, we adore the prospect of having the house on those terms,' enthused Emma. 'Jonathan will tell you so too, won't you, Jonathan?'

'I think I've already made that clear,' said Jonathan. 'It's a very fair deal, Uncle Sammy.'

'All in the family,' said Sammy. 'Right now, it's let on a lease for the duration of the war to an American major and his wife. He's holding down a centenary job with the Allied Command's London headquarters.'

'Centenary?' said Jonathan.

'That's it, it's a desk job,' said Sammy.

'Sedentary?' suggested Jonathan.

'Knew it was something like that,' said Sammy blithely.

'Yes, something like that,' smiled Susie.

'The rent from this happy Yank, who wangled a passage over for his Philadelphia missus, helps us look after genuine maintenance costs as landlords,' said Sammy. 'Which means we don't pay for any furniture or windows they break if they have a ding-dong. Just any natural deterioration. It'll leave a bit over for the property firm's bank account, which is a consideration that accords with Susie's business principles.'

'Mine, Sammy?' said Susie.

'Glad you've got the right kind, Susie,' said Sammy. 'What I'm saying, Jonathan, is that when you and Emma move in after Hitler's been fried, the house'll be in good order. Mind, I won't be able to speak for the furniture, which'll depend on how Major Happy Yank and Mrs Happy Yank use it.'

'I'm not going to object to them having happy times on the sofa, and I won't be bothered if the armchairs take a beating,' said Jonathan. 'I've got a job lined up with a firm of City accountants after the war, so I'll sign up on your terms, Uncle Sammy.'

'As Jonathan's better half,' said Emma, 'I'll sign up too. Aunt Susie, I don't believe in wives being left out of important documents, do you?'

'I've had some problems with Sammy, Emma,' said Susie, 'but I've straightened them all out. And Sammy too,' she added as a thinking woman's after-thought.

Sammy grinned.

'Have you got problems yourself, Uncle Sammy?' asked Jonathan with a grin.

'Only Susie,' said Sammy. 'Well, that's it, then, glad you young people are happy about everything.'

'Uncle Sammy,' said Emma, 'why are you doing this for me and Jonathan?'

'It's a family business,' said Sammy, 'and what we're doing for you and Jonathan is good business for all concerned.'

'Well, bless you and the business,' said Emma.

'It's still light,' said Susie, 'so if you and Jonathan have got time, would you like Sammy to run you up to Ferndene Road to look at the house?'

'Oh, yes,' said Emma.

Ferndene Road wasn't far, being on the opposite side of Denmark Hill to Red Post Hill, but Sammy took the young couple in his car. He pulled up outside the house in question, and Emma and Jonathan took in its aspect. Double-fronted with a central porch and latticed windows, it was built of attractive multicoloured brick. It was typically suburban. The Denmark Hill area, close though it was to Camberwell and Walworth, did have a look more suburban than urban. Emma, well-read, knew a certain kind of knowing people would call the house pseudo-something-or-other, but as far as she was concerned it represented a dream post-war beginning for herself and Jonathan. And their post-war children. It was like other houses in the area that they'd admired, larger than they thought they'd be able to afford, but Uncle Sammy's offer brought it within reach, even though he hadn't offered it on a long-term basis. Six years was better business for the firm, and Emma could understand that.

'Just say if you think it's not what you'd like,' said Sammy.

'Love it,' said Emma.

'Family house,' said Jonathan.

Lights were on and there was a faint sound of music.

'Seems like the tenants are throwing a party,' said Sammy, 'so I can't ask 'em to let you look around. But you've got my word it's pretty handsome, and you can always decorate to suit your own tastes.'

'We're happy as things stand,' said Jonathan, thinking he'd be able to afford nearly two pounds a week out of his wages. He'd been promised a starting salary of eighteen pounds a month because of his pre-war experience with accountants at Camberwell Green. The offer of the job had come from Captain Bradshaw, a peacetime partner in the City firm, and presently an officer on the cadre of the training camp.

Sammy drove the young couple back to Red Post Hill, where they spent some time with Chinese Lady, Mr Finch and Daniel, a young man with some of Sammy's electricity. Emma was bubbling over, and Chinese Lady, approving of the arrangement, said it was going to be nice having her and Jonathan living in the family area, and that Sammy had always had his good points, even if he wasn't always as respectful as he ought to be and spent too much time thinking about money.

'Oh, well, he doesn't keep it in his old socks any more, Mum,' said Susie. 'Most of it's in the bank.'

'It should be fairly safe there,' said Mr Finch.

'I'll have a look at it, if you like, Dad,' said Daniel. 'Say at a charge of one per cent.'

'Sammy, that makes me ask if you go and count it sometimes to make sure it's all there,' said Chinese Lady.

'In a manner of speaking, once a year at audit time,' said Sammy.

'Well, I suppose once a year's enough if you trust the bank,' said Chinese Lady.

'Just as much as old socks, Ma,' said Sammy.

'I don't know what Emma and Jonathan think of you calling me Ma,' said Chinese Lady. 'I've told you a hundred times it's common. Still, you've been very family-minded about the house for them, so I won't go on at you. We all hope it'll make a nice home for you and Emma, Jonathan, which I'm sure you both deserve, and I must say it's a blessing you've got a healthy job on a farm, Emma, instead of being a woman soldier like Eloise. I can't say I'll ever believe women ought to be soldiers. Look what might have happened if Rosie and your Aunt Polly had been soldiers when their babies were due. A fine thing that would have been, having their babies with guns going off.'

Mr Finch coughed, as was his wont when Chinese Lady's observations were a bit over the top.

'Um, I think that would have been avoided, Maisie,' he said.

'I should hope so,' said Chinese Lady.

'I never fancied soldiering myself, Grandma, and I like doing my bit on the land,' said Emma, thinking how alert and sprightly her grandma was at sixty-seven. She still seemed to keep an eye on everyone, whether they were at home or away. Grandpa Finch was beginning to age a bit, but even at seventy he still had a distinguished look, and went to his Government work every day, being determined to give his services until the war ended. His department must think a lot of him, or they'd have insisted on retiring him. 'Uncle Sammy and the family firm have made Jonathan and me very happy, Grandma, but we really must go now.'

She and Jonathan said goodbye, Jonathan leaving pocket money for Paula and Phoebe. On their way by bus to Kennington, Jonathan said, 'Our own house, Emma.'

'Our own house and home, Jonathan, for us and our own family,' said Emma.

'You reckon you like that idea, Emma?'

'I reckon, Jonathan.'

In bed with Sammy later, Susie said, 'I'm really happy for Emma and Jonathan, and you can go to the top of the class for being so good to them, and for saying it cost the firm five hundred and ten pounds instead of the real price of five hundred and fifty.'

'Well, family, y'know, and Emma's sister Annabelle and her husband Nick have already got their own house,' said Sammy. 'But the firm will consider approaches from other nieces and nephews when their time comes. Further, Susie, it's good business right enough in this case, considering the happy Yank is paying rent of forty-eight quid a month.'

'How much?' asked Susie.

'Forty-eight smackers per calendar month, Susie. I've got to admit it, the blokes from over there are loaded and generous. And Mrs Happy Yank is likewise generous and also friendly.'

'Pardon?' said Susie.

'Just friendly, Susie.'

'And how generous, might I ask?'

'Just a whisky and soda on the two times I popped in, Susie. She calls it a highball. Apart from that, she's six feet tall and wears boxing gloves lined with iron filings in case a German paratrooper drops in with ideas about a bit of naughty pillaging, if you get me.'

'I get you, Sammy.'

'Susie, even if the war only lasts another year, at that kind of rent we'll bank nearly six hundred quid, and maintenance costs won't amount to much, seeing the place is in first-class condition.'

'Just a minute, didn't you tell me a rent of twelve pounds a month originally?' said Susie.

'No, twelve a week approximately, Susie.'

'Sammy Adams, at the end of a year that'll nearly cover what the firm paid for it,' said Susie.

'Um, a bit more actually,' said Sammy.

'Then what you'll get from Jonathan and Emma will be all profit. Sammy, it won't do.'

'But, Susie, if the war ended next week—'

'Some hopes,' said Susie.

'The proposition is fair business, Susie, and still doing Emma and Jonathan a good turn.'

'Sammy Adams, I don't want the firm making that kind of profit at their expense. Jonathan's serving in the Army and been wounded, and Emma's working on a farm. They deserve some discount.'

'Eh?'

'How much discount is it if you lower the firm's price to four hundred and twenty-five pounds?'

'Susie, that's enough discount to turn me hair white.'

'I like white hair on men, it makes them look distinguished. So write to Emma and Jonathan and tell them four hundred and twenty-five, not five-ten.'

'Oh, me gawd. Susie, I'll—'

'Or I'll divorce you.'

'Susie, d'you want me to have an anxiety collapse?'

'I want you to tell them you're able to make the reduction after thinking things over. You hear me, Sammy?'

'You're a hard woman, Susie. Didn't I already give 'em forty quid discount?'

'Not enough,' said Susie. 'Sammy, you're crafty, you know you'll still make a handsome profit for the firm, while Emma and Jonathan will think you're their Father Christmas. You'd like them to love and bless you, wouldn't you?'

'Sometimes, Susie, I'm not sure you understand what business is all about.'

'I know what family-mindedness is all about, Sammy, and so do you.'

'Well, all right, Susie,' said Sammy. 'You still awake, are you?'

'Of course I'm still awake – here, wait a minute, what's going on?'

'Just trying my luck at a bit of pillaging, Susie.'

'Where's my boxing gloves?' asked Susie.

Chapter Eight

Boots, as expected, was called to London. He took Polly and the twins with him, first phoning his mother to tell her they'd like to stay for a couple of nights. Chinese Lady couldn't hide her pleasure at the prospect of seeing the twins, who in some confusing way were the uncle and aunt of the two children of Lizzy's elder daughter, Annabelle. Those children were actually older than Gemma and James. I just can't work it out, she said on the phone to Boots. Don't bother to, old lady, said Boots, just accept they're two more additions to your family. But it's not natural, an uncle and aunt being younger than their niece and nephew, said Chinese Lady, and is it legal? Hope so, said Boots, or I'll get locked up. Chinese Lady asked if that was supposed to be funny. It won't be, said Boots, if a policeman comes knocking.

That made Chinese Lady smile, but she didn't admit to it.

Boots drove up in the morning, and dropped Polly and the twins at Selfridges, where she was going to take them to lunch in the restaurant, and then shop for them and herself at the expense of clothing coupons. Whatever damage had been wrought in the West End by air raids, no effort had been spared by shopkeepers in keeping up appearances. Flags were flying on some buildings, and the sun, rising obligingly at dawn, was still bright. It helped Oxford Street to cheerfully receive strolling American GIs and hefty American WACS, although there was no shop that was not limited in what it could offer. With some wartime visitors, it was being there that counted.

Boots, out of the car, brought the twins onto the pavement.

'Oh, thanks, Daddy,' said Gemma.

'You're welcome,' said Boots.

'Can't you come in the shop with us?' asked James.

'Unfortunately, old chap, I'm wanted by some gentlemen who are more important than I am,' said Boots.

'Oh, blow,' said James.

'Daddy, you do look ever so nice,' said Gemma, and Polly, noting a passing WAAF officer giving Boots a glance, thought it's a little more than that, Gemma. Boots, distinctively masculine in his uniform, was always a target for feminine eyes. Even his long legs had their own kind of sex appeal. Very much.

'Daddy, can't you just come and have lunch with us?' asked Gemma, and she and James gazed up at their tall father. Boots thought both of them irresistible. He looked at his watch. Twelve-twenty. His appointment was for two o'clock, and he'd been told he'd be free at four, when he would pick Polly and the twins up from Selfridges.

'Well, if we had lunch immediately,' he said, 'I could have it with you.'

'Oh, come on, then, Daddy,' said James.

'Yes, do join us, old sport,' said Polly.

So they had lunch together in Selfridges. The menu was limited, but no-one complained. The twins put aside their natural fidgets, sat up straight and exercised fairly faultless behaviour. Boots took note of women's dresses, coats, hairstyles and hats. The dresses and coats were square-shouldered, hairstyles composed of lacquered curled rolls, and hats had sharp angles. The overall effect wasn't feminine enough for Boots. He looked at Polly. Her light spring coat had soft shoulders, her hair was softly waved, and her hat of soft light brown velour was round and brimmed. A country woman's hat. Damned if she isn't the most feminine woman in the place, he thought, my ageless, vivacious Polly who made a name for herself as an ambulance driver in that mud-drowning war of '14–18. He thought of Emily. There was always a little pain present whenever Emily came into his mind. Gone with only half her life lived, and she had lived every day in spirited fashion from the time she was old enough to realize that in Walworth you had to fight elements and circumstances. And so she became a holy terror long before she became a wife and a godsend.

'Daddy, I'm talking to you,' said Gemma.

'Sorry, little poppet, what were you saying, then?'

'You're not eating your pudding,' said Gemma.

'He's studying the talent,' said Polly.

'What's that mean?' asked James, digging into red jelly.

'Oh, a man's observation of what's around him,' said Polly.

'What's that mean?' asked Gemma.

'I asked that,' said James.

'Well, I can ask it too, can't I?' said Gemma, eating a wartime version of college pudding.

'You don't have to,' said James.

'Yes, I do, if I want,' said Gemma.

Boots and Polly exchanged glances across the table. Each read the other's thoughts. By a miracle, they were parents of twins articulate, bossy, argumentative and forward at two and a half. In the middle of a fiendishly destructive war they had in their mid-forties given the world two little angels.

Boots thought then of little Jewish children being gassed and cremated by the hundred. Could that possibly be true?

In a house in Bloomsbury, very much like other houses in that area of pre-war literary giants, Boots was received by two Intelligence officers he already knew, and introduced to an Army major and an American colonel. As the man who had spent so much time gaining the confidence of Corporal Hans Thurber, he was required to give his considered opinion of the German and to relate everything that Thurber had said.

'It'll be everything I can remember,' said Boots, 'and most of it already known.'

'Go ahead, Colonel Adams. You can include repetition.'

Boots said that first of all he believed what Thurber himself believed. At no time did he hint that he felt his brother was suffering delusions. Far from it. He was truly convinced his brother had reached such a traumatic state that he sought some kind of relief in confessing to participating in the elimination of the Jews of Auschwitz concentration camp, while at the same time asking Hans to keep it all to himself.

Boots's recitation of hearsay and of Thurber's confidence was detailed. It was a fact that the man never contradicted himself or gave a different version of any part of his brother's confession. The Intelligence officers could probably confirm he never varied in anything they had listened to themselves.

Boots's lengthy exposition turned into a question-and-answer phase, and that turned into a discussion on whether or not there was a precedent, that of taking hearsay seriously.

Colonel Lawrence, the American, said, 'Gentlemen, far-fetched though most of it is, I'm taking all of it damned seriously.'

'On the face of it, and if we can believe it,' said Major Dipworth of Security, 'it's not merely serious, it's infamous to the final degree.'

'God damn it that there's no proof, nothing to show my Secretary of State,' said Colonel Lawrence.

'Colonel Adams,' said an Intelligence officer, 'have you thought about one particular thing? If it's true that thousands of Jews have entered this concentration camp every month to be murdered or worked to death, and that similar death camps exist, isn't it odd that apparently not one man or woman has escaped to give the facts to the world? Allied prisoners of war, held in every kind of restricted circumstances, produce regular escapees, and these are men who at least know they aren't going to be murdered.'

'Perhaps some Jews have escaped,' said Boots, 'but failed to cross a border.'

'But it's reasonable, isn't it, to expect one to have shown up in the free world?'

'Very reasonable,' said Boots.

'So?'

'It's a question I can't answer,' said Boots. 'All I'd say is that despite obvious doubts, I'd recommend some investigation. We all regard thousands murdered every month as appallingly unbelievable. So did Corporal Thurber. But he believed the unbelievable, and his belief crucified him.'

The discussion went on, and Boots knew that both Colonel Lawrence and Major Dipworth were in favour of an investigation, and that the Intelligence officers were under pressure to accept hearsay as evidence. Nothing altered the fact that they were dealing with hearsay. The meeting had been another going-over of everything that had come to light in the first place, and no actual facts had emerged, only a repeat of words spoken by a man now dead.

The meeting ended promptly at four. Colonel Lawrence, saying goodbye to Boots, added, 'Glad to have met you, Colonel Adams. It's my guess from listening to you that your guys and ours are going to run up against a pack of howling SS hyenas one day, the bastards.'

'And what will your guys do?' asked Boots.

'Hang 'em on the spot, using a slow rope.'

'I think ours might lend yours a hand,' said Boots.

He picked Polly and the twins up at Selfridges. Polly was minus a certain amount of money and a quantity of clothing coupons. On the plus side, she was in possession of parcels. The twins reunited excitedly again with their father before scrambling into the car, where they enjoyed a bit of a free-for-all in working out who was to sit where. Boots relieved Polly of the parcels, and then drove through the West End and over Waterloo Bridge on his way to Red Post Hill.

He reached the bomb-devastated Elephant and Castle.

'The Hun passed this way,' said Polly.

'With his rampaging elephants,' said Boots.

'Did the Hun ride elephants?' murmured Polly.

From the back, James asked, 'What's that you said, Daddy?'

'Daddy said elephants,' shouted Gemma.

'Is James deaf?' asked Polly, as Boots drove along Walworth Road, still as familiar to him as Chinese Lady's chiding voice.

'Crumbs, Mummy, he must be deaf if he didn't hear Daddy say elephants,' said Gemma.

'Daddy didn't just say elephants,' protested James.

'Rampaging was the word,' said Polly, 'which

means running wild, like two little harum-scarums I know.'

'Who's them, Mummy?' asked Gemma.

'Guess,' said Polly.

'Gemma, I bet you're one of them,' said James.

'I bet I'm not,' said Gemma.

Boots passed Browning Street, and a swift glance told him of severe damage some way down on the right of the street. Polly lightly touched his knee.

'Old places make sad old ruins,' she said.

'Well, Germany's bomb-laden chickens are coming home to roost now, Polly, with a vengeance,' said Boots. American and RAF raids were devastating German towns and cities with increasing regularity. Dr Goebbels, Hitler's Propaganda Minister, made broadcasts to the effect that all enemy bombing raids that killed innocent Germans were foul and disgusting. Oh, dear, what a bleedin' shame, Dr Gobbler, said the London cockneys who'd been on the receiving end of German bombs.

Approaching East Street, Polly saw a plump woman turning into the main road from the market.

'Boots, stop,' she said, 'there's Susie's mother.'

Boots saw the woman too, and pulled up. Mrs Lily Bessie Brown, always called Bessie, spotted the open car and its occupants. Motherly, equable and eternally comforting, she came out of her usual placidity to give a little shout and to hasten over, carrying her shopping bag.

'Oh, bless me,' she beamed, her round face showing pleasure, 'it's you two. Goodness, I haven't

seen you for I don't know how long. I heard you got
married, and me and Jim was that pleased for you.'
Jim was her husband.

'How are you both, Bessie?' asked Boots, and Mrs
Brown looked at him, at his uniform, and his smile,
and thought what a friendly man he always was.

'Oh, we're handsome, Mr Adams, as you might
say, we moved back to Walworth from Peckham
when the air raids stopped, being fond of that old
house you grew up in before we took it over. My, Mrs
Adams, don't you look nice? Jim always said he
didn't know a nicer or more fashionable lady.'

'Bessie,' smiled Polly, 'I have my other moments.'
There was no side with Polly, she took everyone as
she found them. All upper class prejudices, if she
had ever had them to any obvious degree, had
vanished during her time among the Tommies
of the Great War. She liked her sister-in-law and
Susie's brother and sister, and she liked their
parents, two cockneys of the old resilient kind, born
in the time of Queen Victoria. 'You haven't met our
children, have you? The imp is Gemma, the scamp
is James. They're twins.'

'Hello, lady,' said Gemma.

'Hello, lady,' said James.

'My word, hello,' smiled Mrs Brown, who knew
about the twins. She was part of the grapevine
nurtured by the Adams family. 'Pleased to meet
you, I'm sure.'

'Daddy, can I say "same to you"?' asked Gemma.

'Go ahead,' said Boots.

'Same to you, please,' said Gemma to Mrs Brown.

'How many birthdays you had?' asked James.

97

'No, you can't ask that,' said Polly.

'Mummy, he's already done it,' said Gemma.

'I've had a lot more than I can count,' smiled Mrs Brown, sixty. 'Little pickles you've got, Mrs Adams, bless 'em.'

'How's Cassie?' asked Boots. He had fond memories of Mrs Brown's chirpy daughter-in-law.

'Oh, she's coming home soon, after all them years in the country with her dad and the children,' said Mrs Brown. 'She wrote saying she was having a chronic spell of being homesick, and was going to chance air raids starting up again. I'll be that glad to have her back, I must say. Well, it really is nice seeing you two after all this time, and meeting your twins.'

'What about Freddy?' asked Boots.

'Oh, lor', he's in that awful Burma,' said Mrs Brown, 'and goodness knows when he'll get home, but Cassie's bearing up remarkable. Jim and me hope you and all the Army can get the war finished quick, Mr Adams, or it'll wear everyone out and make them white cliffs of Dover fall in the sea.'

People passed by, traffic buzzed, trams clanged, and all that together with the beaming air of this cheerful cockney woman brought back to Boots the atmosphere of the Walworth of his former years. It was part of him, Walworth, its cockneys and its bustling heart, and war hadn't changed the place, although it had knocked it about a bit.

'Give our regards to Jim and Cassie,' he said.

'Yes, I will, Mr Adams,' said Mrs Brown. 'Might I ask if you're on leave?'

'For a week,' said Boots, who'd been asked to

stand by and await orders from the War Office.

'Well, I'm sure all our soldiers are deserving,' said Mrs Brown.

'Goodbye now,' smiled Polly.

'Goodbye, lady,' said James.

'Goodbye,' said Gemma.

'I said it first this time,' crowed James.

'Goodbye, Bessie,' said Boots, and drove off. Mrs Brown waved to them, then went plumply and happily on her way. My, she thought, those two with twins and all. Such a nice couple, and like Mrs Maisie Finch had said to her, after Boots lost poor Emily, he wasn't going to remain a widower for the rest of his life. He wasn't cut out for that. But fancy him marrying Polly Simms, that upper class lady whose father was a lord or something. Mind, Freddy had always liked her, saying she was a genuine sport who'd won medals as an ambulance driver in that other war. And imagine her and Boots having twins, that must have been a lovely surprise for people their ages.

Mrs Bessie Brown hummed a song as she went on her way to the house that had known Chinese Lady and her family for many years. What a happy thing it was not to have to worry about them Germans dropping their bombs at night.

'My, you angels,' said Chinese Lady.

'You pets,' said Susie.

'Daddy's with us,' said Gemma.

'He come home the other day,' said James.

'He kissed Mummy,' said Gemma.

'We saw him,' said James.

'Who's got big eyes, then?' asked Boots.

'Gemma,' said James, and Gemma giggled.

'Come on, you sweeties, Daniel's not home yet, but you can come and meet Paula and Phoebe,' said Susie.

'Susie, should we put all four together?' smiled Polly.

'Oh, I think their grandpa's got everything insured against breakages,' said Susie.

Chinese Lady smiled. This was her world, family members and children. Four children. Sometimes, the war made a woman despair. Then children appeared, children who were going to know peace, she hoped, although she didn't trust what Stalin and his Bolsheviks might get up to after Hitler had been beaten. Something ought to be done to make sure peace was peaceful, especially as her grandchildren looked like they weren't going to know the kind of poverty their parents had. Well, except Polly, of course.

When Sammy and Daniel arrived from their work within minutes of each other, they joined forces to go into immediate chase of Gemma, James, Paula and Phoebe. The house resounded to shrieks, yells, squeals and laughter upstairs and down.

'That Sammy,' said Chinese Lady.

'Can't help laughing, though,' said Susie.

'That's the fun of it,' said Polly.

'Kids?' said Susie.

'Including Sammy and Daniel,' said Polly.

When Mr Finch arrived, Boots and Polly had a private word with him in his study. Boots gave him, in confidence, the story of Corporal Hans Thurber.

'Yes, I've heard, Boots old chap,' said Mr Finch, 'it's circulating in my department.' His department was Intelligence. Not that Chinese Lady knew. 'But only this afternoon did I hear your name mentioned.'

'What's your opinion, Edwin?' asked Boots.

'It's no secret that Hitler has been looking for a solution to what he calls his Jewish problem since he became Germany's leader,' said Mr Finch. 'Has he found one in the form of physical elimination?' He sighed. 'What gets into the German people that they make a fetish of obedience to a figurehead? This time their obedience seems to be an act of sheer criminality. Thousands and thousands of Jews, Polly, including women and children, what does their ghastly elimination do to you?'

'Horrifies me,' said Polly, 'but Boots and I are still asking ourselves if thousands and thousands count as believable.'

'There'll be an investigation if Allied Security Services can put together a team capable of entering Poland and coming out alive,' said Mr Finch.

'I think an investigation would help Hans Thurber to rest in peace,' said Boots.

'I'm sure it would, Boots old love,' said Polly, 'even if I never met him.'

From the hall, a bump and a yell were heard. Someone knocked on the study door and opened it. Elfin-faced Phoebe put her head in.

'Please, Daddy's fell down the stairs,' she said.

'Phoebe little poppet, is he hurt?' asked Boots.

'Oh, no, but he's saying awful swear words and Gemma and James is listening. And Paula.'

'What awful words?' asked Mr Finch, the philosophical one.

'Oh, crikey, Grandpa, I fink he's saying—'

'Stop!' said Polly, and Phoebe gulped. Polly went out into the hall. Sammy was lying at the bottom of the stairs. Paula, Gemma and James were looking at him. Daniel, also present, wore a grin. 'Sammy Adams, are you swearing in front of the children?'

'Me, Polly? Me?' Sammy looked innocent and hurt. 'Yours truly, when all I've been doing is having a game with the kids?'

'Crikey, Daddy,' said Paula, 'you did say—'

'Stop!' said Polly again. Elegance combined with experience as a teacher combined with a touch of aristocratic verve made her quite awesome to the children, even her own. Her own gaped. Boots and Mr Finch joined her. 'Sammy Adams?' she said.

'Never said a word,' declared Sammy.

Paula chanced her arm in favour of her playful dad.

'Oh, it wasn't much, Aunt Polly,' she said, 'just "Oh, bleedin' hell". Well, he did fall with an awful bump.'

Silence. Polly put a hand to her mouth. Boots looked at the ceiling. Mr Finch coughed. Daniel's grin spread. Phoebe hid behind Boots.

Susie, appearing, said, 'What's happened? Sammy, what're you lying on the floor for?'

'Bruised *derrière*, and that's no lie,' said Sammy. 'Oh, dear goodness, me pain, what a blessed nuisance,' he said.

Polly let go and shrieked with laughter.

A small hand stole into Boots's hand. He looked

down and saw Phoebe gazing up at him like a child not sure if laughter was right. He smiled, winked and lightly squeezed her fingers. Phoebe's return smile preceded a little giggle.

Great God, he thought, how many young girls of her age and her sweetness, but of the Jewish faith, might have perished in the death camps?

And what of the family's ever-faithful Jewish friend, Rachel Goodman, and her girls, what if they had been citizens of Poland or Germany?

Chapter Nine

Saturday, 1 May

During the morning, the merry month had forgotten it was the herald of summer by delivering some overlooked April showers on London. It repented at midday, however, and bestowed sunshine and warm breezes. In Hyde Park, a quite beautiful girl with raven hair and velvety brown eyes, was watching people enter by Speakers Corner. They had come, many of them, including Americans and home-grown ladies, for a lunchtime stroll or a prearranged 'howjerdo'. A 'howjerdo' was the term some cockneys used in this context for a shady meeting between an American serviceman who might have a wife back home, and an English lady who might have a husband serving abroad. The proliferation of uniformed men and women, particularly the ubiquitous and freedom-loving American GIs, was a sign that London was the Allied headquarters of European endeavours. The capital showed in its flags, its barrage balloons and its sandbag-bolstered buildings, the trappings of a nation still applying aching muscle to the necessity of defeating Nazi Germany's monstrous regime. The girl, intent on her watching brief, did not have her mind on the war at the moment, and was startled when the circumstances of war introduced a voice that crept up behind her.

'Looking for me, honey?'

She turned. A fine figure of American military manhood smiled at her. She recovered her cool and said, 'Well, no, I'm not.'

'Not my lucky day?' he said.

'I'm sure you're very nice,' she said, 'but I've a date.'

'With one of us?'

'No, one of ours,' she said.

'How about if I stick around in case he doesn't show up?' suggested the GI hopefully.

'Oh, he'll be here,' she said, glancing over her shoulder. She saw him then, a young man in RAF uniform. Her eyes grew warm and bright. Impulsively, she ran. The young aircraftman opened his arms to her, and people smiled as he embraced her and kissed her.

'Got you,' he said.

'Edward, oh, my life, I'm so happy to see you,' said Leah Goodman, younger daughter of Mrs Rachel Goodman, a widow.

'Mutual,' said Edward Somers, younger son of Lizzy and Ned Somers. 'But let's see, who are you?'

'Me,' said Leah, and looked up at him, searching for a sign that he was as thrilled to see her as she was to see him. Edward, soon to be twenty, was tall, thin, earnest and matriculated. He was saved from being called a bookworm by his sense of humour. Like some of his relatives, he had the fine grey eyes inherited from his maternal grandfather, Corporal Daniel Adams, who had lost his life when soldiering against the Pathans on the North-West Frontier a few years before the outbreak of the '14–18 war. In three weeks' time Edward was due to begin a pilot's training course, which he hoped would enable him to emulate his sister Annabelle's husband, Nick Harrison, promoted some time ago from sergeant-pilot to pilot officer. Nick had incurred serious injuries following a dogfight over Malta, when he was forced to crash-land his crippled plane. Fully recovered, however, he was back on active service. Edward wondered how long it would take to join him.

'What's up?' he asked, aware of Leah's searching look. People ebbed and flowed around them, and the hopeful GI, disappointed, went on his way. 'Have I come out in a rash?'

'No, I'm just making sure it's really you,' said Leah, close to eighteen. She was home after spending years as an evacuee at a boarding school in Wiltshire. It was in Wiltshire that she and Edward had come to know each other, to like each other, and to gradually acquire deeper feelings than mere liking. Leah had to ask herself if she was in love and if she ought to be, since she was Jewish and he was Church of England. He had phoned her at her Brixton home last night to say that today he could stop off in London for the afternoon by breaking his journey from Tangmere in Kent to Cranwell in Lincs, where he was to attend lectures. Could Leah meet him in Hyde Park, say? Leah said yes, not half. So here they were, with the green of the park in front of them. 'Well, I haven't seen you for months,' said Leah, 'not since your week's leave in February.'

'That's a coincidence, I haven't seen you since then, either,' said Edward.

'That's not a coincidence, that's a joke,' said Leah.

'No joke considering what I've been missing, you angel,' said Edward.

'Me, I'm an angel?' said Leah, laughing. 'Becky doesn't think so.' Becky was Rebecca, her sister, now studying law at university. 'Never mind, if you do, I won't argue. One can overdo modesty, can't one?'

Eyes met and held. Each felt oblivious of others. Edward frankly thought this Jewish girl stunning. Leah thought her pulse was jumping about.

'Let's walk and talk,' said Edward, and she slipped her arm around his. They began to stroll amid the bright colours of the park, where shop girls, free for the lunch hour, were sitting with their GIs, or sauntering with them, or standing close to them. 'What's your daily grind, Leah?'

'I'm working for your Uncle Sammy until I'm old enough to volunteer for the WAAF, I told you so,' said Leah. 'And didn't he let me finish early this morning so's I could meet you?'

'Good old Uncle Sammy,' said Edward, whose time so far in the RAF had been mainly concerned with wireless telegraphy. Useful enough, but not very exciting for a bloke who had finally decided he wanted to climb high into the clouds. 'Remind me what kind of work you're doing for him.'

'Oh, typing, taking turns to answer the switch-board, making tea, stamping letters, posting them and filing the copies,' said Leah. Sammy Adams liked girls of all work in the general office. 'Your Uncle Sammy has lots of labour problems. Girls keep going off to volunteer for more exciting war work, and even his senior bookkeeper has gone off to live in the country and take a job with a firm of accountants in Leamington. Mama, who's general manager, found someone to take his place. He's a bit of an old buffer who's come out of retirement, but your Uncle Sammy is now saying out of a museum, more like. Well, you know how he prefers people who fizz a bit.'

'Uncle Sammy's the number one family fizzer,' said Edward. 'Uncle Boots is the family fixer during a crisis, and Uncle Tommy is the honest family stalwart. Anyway, I'm tickled that you're working for the firm along with your mother. It keeps you away from all these American GIs.' Perhaps he shouldn't have said that, for almost at once a couple of husky specimens materialized. One addressed Edward breezily, while casting an admiring eye at the ravish-ing young beauty beside him.

'Say, old buddy, we'd sure like to meet your sister.'

'That wouldn't do you much good,' said Edward, 'I've got two sisters and they're both happily married.'

'This heah young lady ain't yo' sister?' enquired the second GI.

'Hand on my heart, I can say she's not,' said

Edward. 'She's the young lady I'm proposing to marry.'

Leah gulped.

'Well, old buddy,' said the first GI, 'you're a lucky old buddy.'

'Granted,' said Edward, after his Uncle Sammy. 'So long, guys.' And he went on with Leah.

'Excuse me, Edward,' she said, 'but did you actually say what I think I heard you say?'

'I can't say I didn't,' said Edward, 'because I heard it myself, and it reminded me that I've been thinking of writing a letter to your mother and grandfather. With your permission, of course.'

'What kind of a letter?' asked Leah, as they passed the bandstand, the rendezvous at this moment of several young ladies of the United Kingdom and their young gentlemen of the United States Army. 'Is it relevant to what you just said to that American soldier?'

Edward cleared his throat and addressed her with the formality of a young Victorian gent.

'My dear Miss Goodman, I want to let your mother and grandfather know that in a year's time when I'm twenty-one, I hope to be so bold as to ask you to do me the honour of becoming my wife.'

'Crikey,' said Leah, a born Londoner, 'what a lovely mouthful. Edward, could I ask you to say it again?'

'Certainly,' said Edward, taking in a lungful of the park air. 'In short, if I still feel the same about you next year as I do now, Miss Goodman, I'll definitely be asking you to do me the aforesaid honour, and I'll have to let your mother and grandfather know of my prospective intentions in advance in the hope of receiving their approval.'

'Crikey,' said Leah again, 'that's in short? It was more than before. I never heard such a lovely mouthful. Could I ask you to—'

'No, you couldn't,' said Edward, 'I'm out of breath.'

'So am I!' said Leah, giddy.

'D'you think you could tell me what you think will be your own feelings in a year's time?' asked Edward.

'Well, they're all giddy at the moment, and so am I,' said Leah. 'Edward, excuse me for asking, but do you mean you love me?'

'Does it embarrass you?' asked Edward.

'I should be embarrassed?' said Leah. 'How could I be?'

'You don't feel you're too young to be told?' said Edward.

'Pardon me, I'm sure,' said Leah, brown eyes brilliant and pulse rate galloping, 'but I'm not in pigtails and socks. I'm a working girl with prospects of being a WAAF. Edward, are we serious about all this?'

'I am, believe me,' said Edward, 'but I'm not sure if your mother and grandfather are going to be in favour.'

'Because of religion?' said Leah. The atmosphere of the park, a green oasis, was not a place for contentious issues. It encouraged agreement, compromise and tolerance. 'Edward, we'll have to talk to them. I'm sure they'll listen.'

'Yes, but I'd like to write to them first to give

them a chance to think about it,' said Edward.

'My own thinking's very positive,' said Leah. 'I mean, if you do ask me to marry you, I'm certain I'd say yes. Will you have to give your own family time to think about it?'

'Mum and Dad already know how I think about you,' said Edward, feeling extraordinarily chuffed that this stunningly lovely girl favoured him.

Leah, who had met his parents and liked them a lot, said, 'You've actually told them that when you're twenty-one you'll ask me to marry you?'

'I spoke to them on the phone a couple of evenings ago,' said Edward. 'Dad thought I'd be lucky if a girl like you said yes, and Mum asked if I'd take on your religion or you'd take on mine. I said I wasn't bothered about that, and she said well, she didn't think there was anyone in Grandma's family who'd ever been anything except Church of England. I said that could change, and Mum said well, she'd always liked your mother and that you struck her as being a nice respectable girl, which Grandma would approve. Grandma's great on respectability, although Mum said the old lady might get a bit confused about having different religions in the family. That meant Mum was thinking she'd probably get confused herself, and she's like Grandma in believing families should avoid confusion and not let it sneak in through a letter-box.'

'Edward, if you say much more like that,' said Leah, 'I'll get confused myself, especially as I'm still a bit giddy.'

'Religious differences are something our elders

will think about a lot more than you and I will,' said Edward soberly.

'Oh, bother differences, it's feelings that count much more,' said Leah, 'but isn't it a happy thought, Edward, that in our country a mixed marriage won't cause a blood-letting riot?'

'I've heard that people of mixed marriages in Germany are executed,' said Edward soberly.

'Mama is sure terrible things are happening there,' said Leah. 'Thank goodness that here we've still got our Parliament and Mr Churchill. Isn't he splendid? You can actually hear him growling when he's on the wireless and talking about what he thinks of the Nazis.'

'He's working up to a roar,' said Edward. 'Something's going to happen that Hitler won't like. Well, that's what slipped out of my section sergeant's mouth the other day. He's a friend of mine.'

'Your section sergeant's your friend?' said Leah.

'Yes, he says do this or do that, and I do it,' said Edward. 'But about you marrying me, Leah, you might find some people getting spiteful.'

'Yes, some,' said Leah, 'but most people won't fuss. They don't in our country. Edward, do you realize we're talking as if we've already agreed to get married?'

'Yes, I'm noticing that, but I think we'd be sensible to wait a year before we become engaged, don't you?' said Edward.

Something told Leah he was right. Well, he wasn't yet twenty and she was still only seventeen. But she couldn't quite come to terms with being sensible, not in this sunny park, and not when she was high on adrenalin.

'Oh, I suppose so,' she said, 'but I think I'll be counting the days.'

'Is that a fact?' said Edward, an arm around her waist.

'Edward, I just know I'd love to be married to you,' she said.

'Blimey,' said Edward, 'then I think I'll be counting the days myself. You're a lovely girl, Leah.'

'Oh, my life,' she said happily. It didn't matter to her that Edward wasn't husky or broad-shouldered or a Clark Gable. She knew, she just knew, he was kind and sincere, and comforting to be with. He was manly and protective, and he belonged to the family that her mother always said was the finest in the land, made so by their remarkable matriarch, Mrs Maisie Adams. Show me, her mother said once, any woman who has given the country three sons more splendid than Boots, Tommy and Sammy Adams.

Loitering GIs whistled at her. She simply walked on with Edward, pushing the problems of their different religions to the back of her mind, where they settled down without twitching.

Chapter Ten

Sunday

Mr Harold Ford, weatherbeaten in his middle age, and known as the Gaffer, was at the gate of a house in Wansey Street, Walworth, when an expected taxi from Waterloo Station pulled up. The cabbie got out, opened the passenger door and helped Mrs Cassie Brown and her children to alight. Six-year-old Maureen, called Muffin, and four-year-old Lewis, scampered up to the open gate and into the arms of the Gaffer, their granddad. Although the house was strange to them, Muffin being only two and Lewis an infant when their mother took them to live in Wiltshire, she had spoken of the place so often that they knew they were home.

'Granddad!' cried Lewis happily.

'We're here, Grandpa!' exclaimed Muffin.

'As expected and on time, which is a compliment to me old railways, eh?' smiled the Gaffer, a ganger foreman, who had just transferred from Swindon back to his old working habitat with South-Eastern Railways. 'Here I am, Cassie,' he said, moving from the gate to help with the luggage the cabbie was depositing on the pavement.

'Hello, Dad,' said Cassie. She was in her twenty-ninth year, and still looked at life out of eyes that always seemed to be in search of unexpected gifts. A clear crisp sunny morning in December or a new balancing act by Lewis counted among the delightfully unexpected. She and her good old dad, together with the children, had been living in Wiltshire out of the way of bombs for well over three years. Finally, and because air raids on London were now rare, she had decided she could no longer wait to get back home. Home was here, in Walworth, and Walworth was the place of a hundred happy memories for her, most of them relating to her times with Freddy. Her decision had been helped by the moving out of wartime tenants from the house a month ago, and she had chosen to make the journey on a Sunday, when travel was just that much easier for a woman with two children and lots of luggage. 'Dad, what d'you think now of us coming back?' she asked.

'I'm happy because I know you are,' said the Gaffer.

'Home's home,' said Cassie. Her dad, a great handyman who could plug leaks in tin kettles, create a built-in wardrobe, and successfully fight the animosity of a burst pipe, had left Wiltshire a few days in advance to get the house in complete order for her and the children. Hubby Freddy, overseas with a battalion of the East Surreys, had written by Forces airmail five weeks ago in response to her letter telling him she was thinking of returning to

Walworth. He said that as long as she was sure they weren't going to run into any air raids, the move was fine by him. Being head of the family, he said, I'm appreciative of you asking for my approval, which I'm giving. Keep the kettle warming on the hob, he said, in case I turn up myself. Freddy love, I wish you would, she'd said in her reply. As for him being head of the family, she reminded him that Queen Victoria was old bones now, and that there were two equal heads to the family, except hers was more equal than his, which they'd agreed on ages ago. She was now waiting for his next letter, although letters from him were beastly irregular. He always apologized for keeping her waiting, but she knew why irregularity persisted. Freddy was in Burma.

She paid the cabbie, and gave him a generous tip.

'Well, bless yer, lady,' he said, 'and good luck. You're the kind the lads are fighting for. Wish I had two kids like yours. Instead, I've got four racketin' gals, all in the Wrens and all a danger to the King's Navy. Lucky they ain't Queenie's kitchen maids or they'd of blown up Buckingham Palace by now. They're what yer might call accident-prone, like. Still, I've got a soft spot for all of 'em, specially as they ain't blown me up yet, nor me dear old Dutch. Well, so long, lady, been a pleasure.'

'Ta-ta,' said Cassie, and took a look up and down Wansey Street as the taxi moved off. The street was just the same, just a little bit superior to most others in Walworth, and it had escaped bombs, the bombs Germany had unleashed in fiery storms on all its opponents, thus creating reigns of terror from the skies, for which its people, so triumphant at first, were now paying dearly.

However, there were no hideous gaps in Wansey Street, no brick-torn desolation, just the quiet street in which she and Freddy had started their married life. Across the way, a little farther down, was the bright front door in which lived Mr and Mrs Cooper, adoptive parents of Horace, husband of Freddy's younger sister, Sally. I'll call on them tomorrow, thought Cassie, following her dad into the house, he carrying the last of the luggage. She heard the children romping around in the parlour, discovering everything that was new to them. Her dad left all the luggage in the little hall for the time being, and went through with Cassie to the kitchen. The range fire was alight, a kettle on the hob, and the room was warm, homely and comforting.

'I'll make a pot of tea,' said the Gaffer, and transferred the kettle to a gas ring in the scullery. Back he came, tireless.

Cassie looked at him, weatherbeaten and iron-grey, and just about the best dad in the world. He'd been a tower of strength all through their time in Wiltshire.

'Dad?'

'Well, Cassie?'

'Wiltshire was lovely, I know, but it really is nice to be home, don't you think?'

'Bless yer, Cassie, that I do. I'm thinking of having a pint of old-fashioned wallop down at the pub tonight.'

'You do that, Dad.'

'I'm hoping to run into an old acquaintance, Henry Williams.'

'Him?' said Cassie. 'But you never liked him.'

'Sanctimonious geezer, always was, always will be,' said the Gaffer. 'Met 'im down the market yesterday. Know what he said? That it was criminal of Churchill to approve all this bombing of Germany.'

'Well, I like that, I don't think,' said Cassie. 'If any people's asked for it more than the Germans, I don't know who.'

'If I see him in the pub tonight, I've got a few things to say to him,' said the Gaffer. 'Things I've thought about.'

'Yes, go get him, Dad,' said Cassie. 'You've got everything in order in the house?'

'Everything, Cassie, including the beds all aired. You can put yer feet up soon as you've had a cup of tea, eh?'

'I'm fine, and the children were no bother,' said Cassie, taking off her hat and pushing at her thick black hair. Boots would have liked her hairstyle. There were no curled rolls, only long shining hair down up in a crown. Cassie looked after her own hair to save what money she could out of her allowance from the Army. 'Dad, all we've got to do now is wait for Freddy to come home.'

'He'll walk in one day, Cassie, you bet he will,' said the Gaffer. He knew just how much Cassie missed her bloke. They'd been inseparable from the moment they first met, when Cassie was only ten. By the time she was fourteen, she was pulling out the hair of any girl who threatened to be a rival. But the perishing war had done what nothing else could have. It had taken Freddy into the Army and away from Cassie, and there were times when she was pretty down in the mouth. 'Soon as we've laid ruddy old Hitler low and chopped 'is block off, Freddy'll walk right in, you'll see,' he said.

'Dad, I love you,' said Cassie.

'Well, bless yer, Cassie,' said the Gaffer, and coughed.

Lewis yelled from the parlour.

'Mum! Granddad! Muffin's jumping on me! Mum!'

'No, I'm not,' called Muffin, 'I'm just sitting on him, that's all.'

But perhaps Lewis did have something to complain about. Muffin was plump and he was a lightweight. Cassie smiled. Wiltshire or Walworth, one was the same as the other to lively, runabout kids. For herself, the atmosphere of home was what counted most. Old Walworth was grey and sooty. Wiltshire was green and clean. But Walworth was where she and her family belonged, where she and Freddy had enjoyed endless years of togetherness, first as boy and girl, then as husband and wife, and then as parents.

Don't be long coming home, Freddy.

The Gaffer enjoyed his stand-up face to face confrontation with Henry Williams in the pub that evening. Henry tried to stick to his guns about the heavy bombing of Germany, saying Churchill had a lot to answer for. Churchill, actually, had his reservations about the efficacy of the raids, but allowed the chiefs of the Allied Air Forces to have their way.

The Gaffer flayed Henry with a barrage of words and got him so steamed up that he invited the Gaffer to step outside, where he swung punches. The Gaffer took a few, then responded in kind.

'Hold that, Henry. That's from me. And hold this one. That's for me daughter Cassie. And here's one on behalf of me son-in-law Freddy.'

Henry gave up, and well before any copper arrived.

Freddy at this stage of his commitment to the war was with a group of the late General Wingate's Chindit guerrillas of the 14th Army behind the Japanese lines in Burma. They were fighting for survival in the steamy heat of the terrain, while repeatedly hitting Japanese lines of communication during the mighty battle for Kohima. The lurking presence of the enemy made every sortie a threat to life and limb. Dysentery, malaria and other kinds of malignant diseases also took their toll, and while Freddy had earned the three stripes of a sergeant, it was the high incidence of death that placed them on his sleeve well before he might have expected. As lean as a whippet, he was teak-brown and teak-hard, his cheerful nature submerged beneath the grim necessity to kill or be killed. Survival was the keynote.

Not that any of the Chindits fell easily by the wayside. They were hard and lethal fighters, many resistant to diseases by now, and they had learned from the Japs how to apply cunning and trickery to the art of disposing brutally of the enemy. They were also bitter men, for they'd been away from home for over two years, and felt they belonged to the Forgotten Army. But it did not make them less dangerous, as the Japanese were finding out. Their epitaph was already in the making, an epitaph addressed to their descendants.

'For your tomorrow we gave our today.'

In Britain, the country from which the 14th Army was so remote, men and machines were on the move. At night huge motorized convoys of regiments, battalions and squadrons, together with guns, tanks and other armour, were heading for the South of England, and from every direction north, east and west.

The armada was beginning to gather, and Churchill's promise to one day get at the throat of the Nazi beast was taking shape. His teeth had become formidable fangs the moment the Americans and their massive weight of armour entered the war as his allies.

Chapter Eleven

Emma's sister Annabelle was still in Wiltshire with her children, Philip who was eight now and six-year-old Linda. Cut off from her parents and her Adams relatives, she was nevertheless determined not to put the children at risk by returning to her home off Denmark Hill. Air raids looked to have stopped, yes, but she simply didn't trust that gang of Berlin rotters. What had happened to the commonsense of the German people in placing their trust in such a clique of odious men was a mystery to her. Hitler had hardly been able to wait to lead them into another terrible war.

Her husband Nick, a fighter pilot, had almost become a fatal casualty of the conflict when he had to crash-land his plane. His injuries kept him hospitalized overseas for three months, and it was another three before he was able to return to duty. But that, he told her when he was finally home on leave, had probably saved him from becoming one of the RAF's many dead in the battle for Malta, where the skies were another form of hell. His squadron, what was left of it, had been posted home for rest and recharging, and the move had coincided with his convalescent leave.

His squadron was eventually sent to Italy when the Allies invaded Mussolini's Fascist state. Today, however, she was going to see him again, because he and other fighter pilots were once more back in England, this time training to handle new and faster planes. In his letters, Nick hadn't said what planes they were. Well, he wasn't allowed to tell her everything. But in his last letter he'd said he'd be with her for three days, after which he and the other pilots would depart overseas for what to Annabelle was the umpteenth time. She hoped it wouldn't be Burma, a world away, and a nightmare world at that. By all accounts the war against the Japanese in Burma was of a kind that belonged to one's worst dreams. Annabelle could have killed Hitler herself for starting a war that had encouraged Japan to join in.

It was just two in the afternoon, and she was shopping in the high street of the Wiltshire village, Philip and Linda being at school. Nick was due to arrive about three, and had told her he was getting a lift in Bloggsy's car from his present station in Somerset.

'Bloggsy?' said Annabelle, who by pre-arrangement with Nick was receiving a call from him in the village phone booth at the time.

'Roger Blewitt-Broughton actually,' said Nick, 'so we call him Bloggsy, of course. First-class pilot, but mad as a dog.'

Annabelle was now experiencing a sense of happy anticipation. She was a demonstrative woman, and more temperamental than Emma. Twenty-seven now, she had her highs and lows, and she had

had her disagreements with Nick, but she was equipped, by virtue of family traditions, to work at her marriage, because sustaining the bond was far more worthwhile than breaking it. Sometimes dissatisfaction reared its unwelcome head on account of Nick's prolonged absences from her life and the lives of their children. Such moods were partly due to worry that his time as a fighter pilot would come to an end from enemy action, for she was well aware that losses among his kind were heavy. However, all dissatisfaction melted away immediately leave brought him back to her, and there was always the knowledge that the RAF would ground him for executive duties when he had completed his maximum tours of active service.

An open sports car was racing along the winding country roads not far from the village. Five RAF flying men, including the driver, were crammed into the car, nominally a two-seater. The owner-driver, Pilot Officer Blewitt-Broughton, was taking bends in hair-raising style.

'Keep this pram on the bloody road, Bloggsy!' yelled one passenger.

'Don't wet your pants, Kipper,' shouted Bloggsy.

'I already have, you lunatic.'

They came out of a bend on the wrong side of the road, the car skewing and squealing as Bloggsy wrenched at the wheel. A police constable, riding a bicycle, stopped, dismounted, moved to the middle of the road and held up an authoritative hand. The car came to a giddy, scarifying halt on tyres almost bald.

'Afternoon, officer,' said Bloggsy, 'what can we do for you?'

'You in charge of this vehicle, sir?'

'Right first time,' said Bloggsy, sporting a flowing moustache, 'it's my own baby.'

'Well, it's overloaded, sir, and by the evidence of my own eyes, being driven in a manner dangerous to behold, which is an offence. It 'ud be safer for your passengers to catch the afternoon bus that'll be coming along shortly.'

'Have a heart, officer,' said Bloggsy, 'most of us have got another ten miles to chew up.'

'Well, I don't wish to spoil the day for you gentlemen, but I have to caution you to drive with due care and attention, as is required by the law. Understood, sir?'

'Hearing you loud and clear, officer,' said Bloggsy.

It was a little later when Annabelle, emerging from the grocer's old-fashioned but spicy-smelling establishment, saw the sports car entering the village at racing speed. She stared in horror as it rushed towards a woman crossing the street. Brakes went on, wheels spun, tyres shrieked, and the car, skidding, slewed past the paralysed woman at an ungovernable rate. It struck the kerb sideways on and turned over with a sickening crash. Men in RAF uniforms hurtled from it. The engine died, but the upper wheels were still spinning, the car on its side, the driver a crumpled heap, half in, half out, the passengers limply sprawled over the pavement.

For a moment, Annabelle and other shoppers

were paralysed themselves. Annabelle, appalled by the fact that the casualties were RAF officers, that Nick might be among them, came to and rushed across the street. She saw the driver, doubled up and unconscious. The other men were all on the pavement, inert, their caps off and blood oozing from one man's cracked forehead.

Annabelle's horrified eyes searched frantically for Nick, since she was sure the car was the one he'd spoken about, even if it had appeared well before three o'clock. The grocer himself was on the scene, but only for a few seconds, when he then ran back to his shop to phone for ambulances.

'Oh, Lordy, Lordy, what can we do?' gasped a woman.

'They're hospital jobs, that they are,' said an elderly man, 'and I don't think we should try to move 'em. There's broken bones, that's certain sure. Can anyone bring blankets to keep 'em warm? That's the most we can do for the poor chaps till ambulances come.'

Two shoppers hurried off to get blankets. Annabelle was suffering for the casualties, but shaking with relief at realizing Nick wasn't among them. She also felt grief and helplessness that so little could be done for the injured until ambulances arrived with a medical team. People stood around, numbed and shocked, staring at limp bodies that eventually began to stir and twitch. At least the officers were alive, thought Annabelle, but how tragic and yes, how foolish, if a car crash had crippled these men of the skies.

The blankets arrived, and willing hands helped to cover the casualties.

The afternoon bus pulled up at the stop outside the Post Office opposite the crash. Three people alighted, one of them an RAF officer. Annabelle, turning, drew a loud noisy breath and made another wild run. Pilot Officer Nick Harrison, her husband, saw her coming. He dropped his valise and Annabelle rushed into his arms.

'Nick!'

'Annabelle—' Nick checked as the overturned car came to his eyes. 'Oh, my God,' he breathed.

'Nick, it crashed,' gasped Annabelle. 'They're all badly hurt, they were thrown out – is it the car you spoke about?'

'Christ, yes, it is, but I got out and caught the bus about a mile from here.' Nick raced across to the car, and the knot of people made way for him. He went down on one knee beside groaning men. 'Oh, Christ,' he said. There had been just that mile to go when the police constable stopped the car. Just a mile that was all, for himself. But Bloggsy, a wild and reckless character, really had been driving like a madman. So even a mere mile offered too many risks to a man whose wife and children were expecting him. Further, the police constable's advice touched an instinct. So Nick left the car and waited for the bus, Bloggsy derisive of his caution.

He felt distraught as he regarded the faces of the blanket-covered men, his fellow pilots. He used his handkerchief to wipe away blood that was oozing from Johnny Gardner's forehead, Bloggsy, unconscious, was breathing stertorously, the others issuing small painful groans. One man, Ian Kipling, opened his eyes and regarded his immediate world in a vague and puzzled way.

'What happened?' he asked faintly.

'Crash landing, Kipper,' said Nick. 'Bloggsy did it in, the careless bugger.'

Bloggsy was beginning to groan.

Annabelle was there, down on one knee beside Nick, her hand pressing his arm in a gesture of compassion.

'Perhaps it's only broken bones, darling,' she whispered. It was spoken fervently, but it was, of course, a wish and a prayer, and they both knew it.

More time went by before two ambulances arrived, a doctor aboard. A police car turned up soon after.

When Philip and Linda came out of the village school, their mum and dad were waiting for them. Seeing their father, they yelled in glee and ran to him. Nick put aside feelings of lingering shock to give his kids the kind of welcome they wanted, boisterous and affectionate. Philip had the lively, beguiling nature of Nick's father, once a con man who'd come unstuck and served a prison sentence. Linda was a bundle of cuddlesome fun who liked attention, especially from her father. She had the large brown eyes of her maternal grandmother, Lizzy Somers. She clung possessively to her dad's hand as they all walked through the village to the small cottage being rented for the duration. The battered car had been towed away, and the four casualties were in hospital. Philip and Linda were ignorant of the crash.

As always, when their dad arrived on leave, they received presents from him, and so did their mum. They clamoured for Nick's attention, which made Annabelle wonder what happened to the affections of children who rarely saw their absent fathers. Would such men eventually become total strangers to their sons and daughters, and even close to being forgotten by their wives? It was common knowledge that in this village alone, the wives of three absent servicemen were having affairs with American soldiers.

While Nick enjoyed a romping reunion with Philip and Linda, Annabelle wondered if her interests were being looked after by God or Nick's lucky rabbit's foot. Well, something had made him leave that car and catch the bus.

Not until after supper and Linda and Philip were in bed that evening did she and Nick enjoy their own kind of reunion, much as Polly and Boots had a short while before. Hugs and warm kisses prevailed, and Nick said it was wizard to be in close touch with her person again.

'My person?' said Annabelle.

'That's you, yourself,' said Nick, aiming for her lips and kissing them.

'Bull's-eye,' said Annabelle when she came up for air.

'Smack on operational target, I'd say,' said Nick, and let go to look at her. She was definitely her mother's daughter with her rich chestnut hair and her fulsome figure. Emma was slimmer. 'My kind of target,' said Nick.

'Stop making me sound like a dartboard,' said Annabelle, but she gave him another hug. He had once had a vigorously muscular look, but his time with the RAF had fined him down, giving him lean lines. He still liked soccer and during off-duty days he played for RAF elevens in friendly matches against Army or Navy teams. That is, they were billed as friendlies, he said, but it was often necessary to stretcher off victims of mayhem. 'Nick, I think you'd like to ring the hospital, wouldn't you?'

'Frankly, I would,' said Nick.

'Go and use the public phone by the Post Office, then,' said Annabelle, 'because I'd like it myself if you'd find out how your friends are.'

Nick went. He was back in a while and able to tell her that injuries were extensive, but all patients were stable and not in danger. Bloggsy was the worst, with a damaged chest and a fractured pelvis. Broken bones and fractured ribs had laid a painful curse on the others, while Johnny Gardner also had a hairline skull fracture. But he was notoriously thick-headed, said Nick, and just some sticking-plaster would be enough to mend him. Annabelle accepted that comment as an attempt at light relief.

'They're all in no real danger, Nick?' she said.

'They'll live,' he said, 'but God knows how long it'll be before they can fly again.'

'Don't let's worry about that,' she said, 'let's begin to enjoy your leave now.'

'Every minute of it,' said Nick.

'I miss you very much when you're away, you know,' said Annabelle. 'I value the companionship of marriage.'

'Can you hang on until we've settled with Hitler and his jackboots?' asked Nick soberly.

'Yes, if I can trust you not to take unnecessary risks,' said Annabelle, and Nick thought of the instinct that had induced him to get out of the car and catch the bus.

'I'll never take the chance of throwing away what means most to me,' he said, 'you and the kids.'

'The point is, love, we'd like our post-war future to include you,' said Annabelle.

Three days later, Nick was on his way back to the war in Italy, travelling by air in company with other pilots of his squadron.

Annabelle found consolation in her children, as she always did, as she always had to, when Nick was away. Was this war never going to end?

President Roosevelt and Prime Minister Churchill were presently set on bringing it to a conclusion inside the next twelve months. They not only had millions of war-weary people to consider, they also had Joe Stalin on their backs. The dictator of the Soviet Union had a fixed belief that only the Red Army was fighting the war.

Chapter Twelve

Saturday, 8 May

The phone rang down in Dorset.

'Phone, Mummy!' called little Gemma.

'It's ringing,' said little James.

'Yes, I've called Mummy,' said Gemma.

Polly, appearing from the kitchen, picked up the hall phone.

'Hello?'

'Hello?' The masculine voice was deep, warm and vibrant.

'You old darling, it's you, isn't it?' said Polly.

'Your lord and master, so I believe,' said Boots.

'Don't crack the whip, O Mighty Sultan,' said Polly, 'or I'll speak to your mother.'

'As you did a while ago,' said Boots.

'Noticing my cowed look, she dragged it out of me. However, I've assured her I'm still fighting.'

'You're still fighting what?' asked Boots.

'My weakness for bowing down to you,' said Polly.

'Let me know when your next attack is coming on,' said Boots, 'I'd like to be there.'

'Unless you are here, it won't happen,' said Polly.

'And if I am, and if it does,' said Boots, 'watch out for fireworks.'

'Oh, m'lord, could you get here in ten minutes?' begged Polly. Boots laughed. 'I hope you don't think that's funny,' said Polly.

'What's she saying?' asked Gemma of James.

'Dunno,' said James.

'Well, who's she talking to?' demanded Gemma.

'Daddy,' said James.

'Crumbs,' said Gemma.

Polly was now listening, Boots letting her know he wasn't returning to Italy, that he'd been transferred to 30 Corps. She stopped listening to interrupt.

'Where is this corps?'

'Here at home, Polly.'

'Oh, really, old sport? In your stepfather's back garden?'

'Hardly,' said Boots, keeping to himself the fact that he was now in Essex, and that the corps was constituted of units strongly equipped and ready for the greatest adventure of the war. No specific details had been given to him by a General Richards of the War Office, only that he'd be obliged if Colonel Adams would accept the transfer, since the corps, in view of what lay ahead of it, was in urgent need of one more staff officer of proven experience. When Boots asked exactly what did lie ahead, General Richards replied that was a question the Corps Commander would answer at the right time. Boots felt he did not need an answer, that what lay ahead was the opening of the Second Front. 'Not to worry, Polly.'

'Not to?' said Polly. 'But I do. Listen, old war-horse, you're mine, not the Army's. Their claim on you is secondary, so don't let them muck you about. I'm against you coming back to me and the twins with a hole in your head. Saints and sinners, do you realize the women of your family are living on their nerves instead of relaxing happily with their knitting or whatever? Rosie, Eloise, Annabelle, Lizzy, Vi, your mother and myself? That's a whole tribe of worrying women.'

'Bake a cake,' said Boots.

What a man, thought Polly. She'd given him a hundred words to think about, and what had he said in response? Bake a cake? Dear God, she thought, is this a man who could listen to Hitler delivering a thousands words all at the top of his voice, and then tell him to take an aspirin? Yes.

'I'm a frightful cook, you know that,' she said.

'Never mind, Polly, give it a go,' said Boots. 'I'll keep you posted. Kiss the cherubs for me. Must hang up now.'

'Wait, isn't there something else?' asked Polly.

'Yes. Love you.'

That night, roads leading to the South of England rumbled again to the passing of troop-carriers, tank-carriers, mounted guns and a host of other armaments. From the West of England, where concentrations of American troops had been conducting manoeuvres for many months, travelled the formidable units of the Stars and Stripes.

'Pretty at night, ain't it, this old island?'

'You seeing in the dark, Felix?'

'I ain't Felix. Who the hell's Felix?'

'A cat that can see in the dark.'

'Listen, it ain't a question of seeing, Ratty, you can smell it's pretty.'

'Murphy, you dope, that ain't this island, that's Sergeant Tucker.'

'Who said that? Answer up, that man.' No answer. 'Gimme his name, Murphy.'

'Honest to God, sarge, all I know is that one of us guys has just jumped out of the truck, and it ain't me. Hell, sarge, did you hear that?'

'Did I hear what, Murphy?'

'A squelch. I guess he's just been squashed by a gun carriage. Who's gonna tell his Ma and Pa?'

'Private Ratcliffe?'

'Here, sarge.'

'Private Ratcliffe, shoot Private Murphy.'

A letter for Felicity.

'Read it to me, Rosie?' she said, and Giles came up to listen. Emily toddled up behind him. 'Is that Giles and Emily?'

'Afraid so,' said Rosie.

'Well, if I know my bounder of a husband,' said Felicity, 'there's sure to be something your innocents shouldn't hear.'

'Let's risk it,' said Rosie.

'Up to you, you're their mother,' said Felicity.

'Here goes,' said Rosie. '"*Dear Puss—*"'

'Typical,' said Felicity.

'I am at present in the throes of being given the run-around by other ranks who've got aggravating ideas

that I was commissioned by Girl Guides, not by courtesy of His Majesty Georgie. As you know, or should know, I was brought up in a family believing in respect, and I'm getting none right now. Just some shocking language. I'll set down here a list of words you've probably never heard of and some of which are even new to me. Rosie will read them out, I suppose.'

Rosie paused.

'You pass, I pass,' said Felicity. She heard Emily close by and reached for her. The child turned and Felicity brought her up onto her lap. Emily wriggled until she was comfortable, then settled. 'What's up, Rosie, has the letter caught fire?' asked Felicity.

'Tim's cheated,' said Rosie. 'All he's put down are rows of dots.'

'That's not cheating,' said Felicity, 'that's Tim remembering for once that he's an officer and gentleman. Oddly, I think I like him best as a bounder.' She applied a little hug to Emily's warm body. Her world of darkness was still a bitter world at times, but Rosie's children and Rosie herself were always able to brighten the darkness. 'Carry on, Rosie.'

Rosie carried on.

'Of course, suffering does lead to a bit of blasphemy, but I keep telling these cowboys it's all necessary if they want to grow hair on their chests. You should hear what they say to that – correction, no, it's not fit for your hearing. While I'm prepared to reason with them, my brother-in-law Luke – Colonel Lucas – prefers to break a leg or two, which lets them know

they're in a war, not a netball match. It's a special kind of war in this outfit, meaning as ever, and as you'll remember from Troon, that anyone with a broken leg is still expected to complete a forced march in full kit. What our next objective is I don't know, but I think it's something like wiping out Berlin and bringing Hitler back with us. I understand it's a fact that Churchill wants a word with him. I think I'll go sick and stay where I am. It'll be safer.'

'Rosie,' said Felicity, 'if they're training for something unusual, what's your guess?'

'I'd like to guess it's going to be a month's leave,' said Rosie, 'which is about as unusual as you could get, but they don't train for leave, do they?'

'You can do better than that,' said Felicity.

'There's only one thing that's obvious to me,' said Rosie, 'an objective that's overdue.'

'Second Front?' said Felicity.

'Don't you think so?' said Rosie.

'It's going to be—' Felicity wanted to say 'bloody desperate and dangerous'. No, not in front of Giles, who'd be quick to pick the word up. 'For something like that, Rosie, they've all got to be hairy-chested men. Finish the letter, there's a sweetie.'

Rosie concluded.

'I enjoyed my time with you, Puss, very much I did, and with all of you, so if you're reading this, Rosie, consider yourself a sister who's always been the best ever to me, and tell Giles and Emily I love 'em. I can't wait to see all of you again, but I don't think it'll be tomorrow. If it's summery when I do arrive, let's go

on seaside picnics, and bring your swimsuit, Felicity.
Love you all over, as you well know.
Yours ever, Tim.'

'Rosie, has he put that down in black and white?' asked Felicity.

'Put what down?' asked Rosie with a smile that made her children beam at her.

'The "all over" bit,' said Felicity.

'Yes, what's wrong with it?'

'Some things are private, and the swine knows it,' said Felicity.

'But it's lovely, isn't it, for the swine to say so?' said Rosie.

Felicity laughed.

'Rosie, he's my kind of swine,' she said.

Rosie thought of the first letter she'd received from Matt since his arrival in Italy. He'd said several things like that in his long missive, and she'd loved them all, except that she wondered if an Army censor had seen them.

She was waiting now for another letter.

Wives waited. Husbands served. Children asked after them. War did its best – its worst – to keep families divided. That was something Grandma Finch considered more upsetting than many other consequences of war.

'Let's harness Humpy to the dogcart and all have a ride to Tolpuddle, shall we?' she said.

'Oh, could we, Mummy?' begged Giles.

'Count us all in,' said Felicity.

'Up, everyone, up, up, on your feet,' said Rosie, 'and let's enjoy the great outdoors.'

*　　*　　*

Leah entered Sammy's office to place a cup of tea on his desk.

'Well, ta muchly,' said Sammy, who'd been wading through the more artful clauses of a new set of regulations from the Ministry of Supply. They might have been framed by Civil Servants in stiff collars, but they were still the work of blokes who knew the advantages were all theirs in the matter of giving out contracts. 'That'll cure my headache.'

'Oh, d'you have a headache, Mister Sammy?' said Leah.

'Sometimes, Leah,' said Sammy, 'I'd be better off leaving my head at home, where Susie could look after it with a piece of old-fashioned affection, which is one of the things married wives are good at. When you're a married wife—'

'But all wives are naturally married, Mister Sammy,' said Leah. She called him that in the office, as the other girls did. Outside of that, she called him Uncle Sammy, for he'd been like an uncle to her and Rebecca for as long as she could remember. 'You can't be a wife unless you are married.'

'I can't?' said Sammy, taking a welcome mouthful of hot tea.

'No, not you, you're a man,' said Leah.

'I'm glad you said that,' murmured Sammy. 'By the time I get home some days, I feel like a fairy penguin with no flappers.'

'Mister Sammy, stop making me giggle,' said Leah.

Sammy took a kind look at the lovely young lady, so like her mother at her age.

'How's your love life, Leah?' he asked.

'Mister Sammy?' said Leah, slightly pink.

'Well, you and Edward are still going strong, are you?' said Sammy.

'You don't mind about us, do you?' said Leah.

'Mind?' said Sammy.

'Well, there's our differences,' said Leah.

'What's that got to do with young love?' asked Sammy. 'Listen, if Susie had been a Buddhist nun, would that difference have made me back off? Not on your Nelly. I'd have broken into her Chinese nunnery, carried her off and married her at the first church we reached in Hong Kong, even if she'd yelled it was against her vows to wear wedding garters and a frilly nightie.'

'Oh, my life, Mister Sammy, stop making me giggle more,' begged Leah.

'I can't hear you giggling,' said Sammy.

'Well, you will in a minute,' said Leah. 'Suppose Edward asked me to marry him—' She let that hang in the air.

'I happen to have heard that's a possibility,' said Sammy. 'Edward's mum and dad mentioned it to me and Susie. Leah, I seriously recommend you don't let differences muck your life up. You and Edward can both do your own kind of praying. What's the biggest difference between people in this country? Conservatism and Socialism. Sometimes they could beat each other to death with spiked copper sticks. But some Conservatives do marry Socialists, male and female respective, of course, and they get happy beating each other with rolled-up pamphlets. Rolled-up pamphlets are more loving than spiked copper sticks. You got that, Leah?'

'Yes, Uncle Sammy, and you're a dear,' said Leah, who had heard from Edward to the effect that after considering how to frame the letter to her mother, he'd decided to put everything down in plain English. Any moment now, she expected her mother to receive the letter. 'Well, I'd better get back to my work, I suppose.'

'Well, we should all do a bit during business hours,' said Sammy. 'It helps us to remember we're working to help the Army and the RAF look well-dressed, which I presume is noticed by the enemy and accordingly puts the wind up 'em.'

'Mister Sammy, you're making me giggle again,' said Leah, and went back to her work.

Chapter Thirteen

Italy, mid-May

The Allies had taken Monte Cassino at last, and had begun their advance on Rome. American, Canadian, British, Free French and Polish forces were all involved. The Germans were retreating to a new defensive position, a prepared one, the Adolf Hitler line, but fighting all the way. South-east of the town of Frosinone, their artillery was giving 13 Corps of the British 8th Army a brutal pounding, checking its momentum and inflicting heavy casualties.

At dawn, a flight of Bristol Beaufighters took off from the rear of 13 Corps to attack the German guns. They flew straight for their target, several batteries of camouflaged heavy artillery within an extensive ring of protective anti-aircraft batteries. On their way they passed high above regrouping German units, which issued radio warnings to a squadron of Messerschmitt fighters based north-west of Frosinone. The Beaufighters, however, arrived before the Messerschmitts, and their leader, coming in low, spotted the camouflaged guns. He gave orders through the intercom, and his flight manoeuvred at once into the attack formation. Down came the Beaufighters, one after the other, screaming through the bursting flak, to deliver their explosive rockets. The German gun crews scattered for shelter. The rockets struck home, and from the explosions huge balls of fire leapt.

The Messerschmitts arrived as the last of the Beaufighters completed the mission. The RAF leader, high in the sky, was turning for home, his flight following. The Messerschmitts, higher, swooped.

'Leader! Bandits! Twelve o'clock!' The warning came from the pilot of the RAF tail-ender.

'Break!'

The Beaufighters broke formation, peeling off in an avoiding action. A frenzied dogfight took place. The Beaufighters, lightning-fast and superbly manoeuvrable, were an elusive target for the Messerschmitts and quickly turned their avoiding action into attack. The sky crackled with fire, and tracer bullets flashed streams of light. The Messerschmitts pressed home their own attacks. Two of them cut out a Beaufighter and downed the plane, its tail splintering and disintegrating. A revengeful Beaufighter screamed in pursuit of the victorious Messerschmitts which, warned by their leader, soared upwards. Too late. Cannon shells from the Beaufighter caught one amidships as it became a rising silhouette against the sky, and it blew up.

'No apologies,' grated the RAF pilot, and then shuddered as cannon shells from a pursuing

Messerschmitt smashed into the tail of his own plane. Sparks flashed and blazed, plumes of black smoke streamed. The Beaufighter tottered in the sky, fell away and began a crazy spiral to doom a few miles south-east of Frosinone.

It was late afternoon when Caterina Angeli came out of the school in the village of Asconi. She mounted her old jangling bicycle, and a lingering residue of young pupils called '*Ciao!*' to her as she rode away. She smiled, heading for the quiet out-skirts of the village. Into her vision as she reached her house five minutes later came a limping figure from the fields beyond. Her house was the last in this street. Dismounting at her door, she watched him, a man in a dusty flying kit, helmet under his arm. Seeing her, he hesitated, then made up his mind and limped quickly towards her. From the south-west came the sound of guns. It was said that the Allies were advancing from the south and the Germans retreating north. Perhaps, in their retreat, some German units would pass through Asconi. If so, everyone would be wise to stay out of their way.

Here was a flying man, yes, that was obvious, but German or British or American? He approached in a positive way, despite his limp and she noted that the right leg of his combat trousers was raggedly torn. When he was close enough, his partly un-zipped flying jacket disclosed a glimpse of what she was sure was the blue of an RAF uniform. She thought him a fine-looking man, despite a bruise on his right jaw. He spoke from a dry throat.

'*Signorina?*'

'*Signora*.'

'Speak English?'

Caterina Angeli did not answer that. She turned, opened her front door and said, 'Go in – quick.' He stepped in. She followed, with her bike. One did not leave any bicycle unattended these days. The RAF man closed the door for her. 'Yes, I speak English,' she said with a lilting Italian accent. 'I taught English at the high school in Frosinone before coming here to live with my husband, and to teach at our village school. You are RAF, yes?'

'Shot down this morning behind the German lines and landed about four kilometres from here,' he said. 'I've been keeping clear of the foe ever since.'

'If they know you are alive they will search everywhere,' said Caterina. She took off her black headscarf, and fluffed at her glossy black hair. Her dark lashes framed the melting brown eyes of Italy. She was twenty-eight, her colour healthy, her looks pleasing, her mouth full-lipped, and she was clad in a simple white blouse and black skirt. 'You were limping, yes. Are you hurt?'

'I'm not,' he said, 'my leg is.'

'That is a joke?' she said.

'My leg's no joke, *signora*, it's gashed.'

'Go in,' she said, pointing, and he limped through from the little hall into a kitchen that exuded an aroma of lemons and spices. It was a neat, well-kept kitchen, its window looking onto the fields. 'Sit, please,' she said, 'and show me your leg that is hurting.'

'Have I found a friend?' he asked with a smile. He

was in good shape, apart from his injured leg. He put his helmet on the table, and took off his flying kit and his boots. Caterina saw at once that the right leg of his blue trousers was also torn and ragged. And badly stained. He sat down on a chair beside the table, and gingerly uncovered a leg that would have been a good-looking limb if it had not been foul with dried blood in some places and wetly red in others. The side of his calf showed a gash six inches long and still wetly raw. 'A can-opener did that,' he said.

'A can-opener?' she said, bending to examine the wound.

'Jagged edge of a rock,' he said. 'I landed close to it, my chute pulled me over it and dragged my leg over the sharp edge. It felt just like a can-opener at work. Made a swine of a mess. Look at it. You could feed a sandwich into it.'

'Ah, not good,' said Caterina. 'Or pretty, eh? But no artery is cut, so it is not as bad as it might be. I will clean it for you and disinfect it. Also bind it, and fetch a doctor to you when it's dark. He will stitch it, I will ask him to. I will be careful, so will he. Even here, there are German secret police and some *fascisti*, some who still love Mussolini and Hitler.'

Italy had come out of the war against the invading Allies last year, much to the relief and delight of a people who, unlike Hitler's Germans, preferred a happy-go-lucky existence to conflict. It was to the grief and sorrow of most of them that, after Mussolini had been ousted and peace made with the Allies, a furious Hitler sent in hordes of jack-booted Nazis to occupy the country and to fight the

Allied armies. Some Italian fascists became collaborators and informers, and some men and women became partisans.

'I hope I don't land you in trouble, *signora*,' said the RAF pilot.

'We will avoid that if we both take care,' said Caterina. 'First, this, I think, yes.' She fetched a bottle of red wine from the rack on the stone floor of her larder, produced a glass and filled it. He moistened his dry lips with his tongue, took the glass and drank the wine in deep draughts.

'Many thanks,' he said. 'I've been moving about for most of the day, carrying my ruddy leg with me. What luck to finish up in the house of a Florence Nightingale.'

'Yes?' Caterina smiled and her teeth showed moistly white. 'I have heard of her. Who has not, eh, *Inglese*?'

'Am I to know your name, *signora*?'

'No, not wise, I think. Better no names, then you do not know me and I do not know you. Excuse, please.' Caterina disappeared, but did not take long to return. She was carrying a white enamel bowl with a blue rim. It contained cotton wool, lint, bandage, ointment, and a small bottle of medical disinfectant. She placed the contents on the table, and half-filled the bowl from the tap. She added some disinfectant, then went down on one knee to examine more closely the RAF man's gashed leg. 'Please to bite your teeth, *Inglese*.'

He shut his mouth tightly, and she doused the gash with pure disinfectant from the bottle. His wound went redhot with fiery pain, and he let out a sharp breath and an involuntary imprecation.

'Bloody hell.'

'Ah, it helps to swear, yes?' she said. 'But it's best for me to do this myself and not ask the doctor to come here in daylight, or to take you to him. You understand?'

'Right,' he said, and bore the pain as she cleansed his wound and his leg with a pad of cotton wool dipped in the disinfected water. The pad quickly turned a soiled, dirty red. She made another from the supply, and continued the cleansing. 'Where's your husband, *signora*?' he asked.

'Ah, my husband.' She sighed. 'Because of my teaching, I did not marry until a year ago. Later, after the Germans invaded Italy, my husband joined the partisans who were fighting them.' Bitterness edged into her voice. 'He was betrayed and taken. They tortured him, then hanged him. Slowly, you see, because he was against Hitler, and that is a terrible crime in the eyes of Germans. What an unfortunate people they are, and how unforgivable for what they did to my Pietro. This is his house, and I stay living here because that is the only way I can feel close to him.'

'Hitler's men have fiendish ways of making people suffer,' said the RAF pilot. The wound was clean now, if still slowly seeping, and he watched as this caring Italian woman applied ointment-covered lint. Around it, she wound the bandage firmly, and fixed it with a safety-pin she had lodged in her hair. 'I'm sorry about your husband,' he said, 'but thanks a thousand times for this.'

'It's a small thing to do for someone who is fighting Hitler and his Gestapo,' she said, straightening up. 'Now you may have more wine.' She refilled the glass and gave it to him. 'I will take you to a room where you can sit behind the curtain and watch the street for Germans, yes? Good. I will make a meal for both of us. It will not be much. Italy is being robbed of everything by the Germans. Come, *Inglese.*'

She led the way to a charming room, and to an armchair by the unshuttered window over which lace curtains hung. He sat down with his glass of wine, and his smile conveyed admiration for her lack of dramatics and gratitude for her help. She asked him if he was going to attempt to get back to the British lines. He said yes. She asked if the Allies were definitely pushing the Germans back. Yes, he said. Then perhaps the British soldiers would be here in a few days, she said, and if so she would hide him until they arrived. That would save him from wandering about in hope.

'You're priceless,' he said.

'No, no, I am only doing what my husband would have done,' she said.

'You're still priceless,' said Pilot Officer Nick Harrison, husband of Annabelle and father of Philip and Linda.

He was thirty-one, had returned to the war in Italy only a few days ago, and was now trapped behind enemy lines as his brother-in-law Bobby Somers had been during the retreat to Dunkirk, but his situation was different in that he had found a Samaritan, whereas in Helene Aarlberg, Bobby found a Tartar who took a long time to turn into a saviour.

149

*   *   *

General Eisenhower, in command of Overlord, the planned invasion of Normandy, was in daily conference with his field commanders, among whom was the extrovert Montgomery, famed destroyer of Rommel's Afrika Korps, arguing constantly for the privilege of using his British and Empire troops to make Caen the anvil on which to break the major strength of German resistance. He was accordingly looked on by his American counterparts as a bigmouth.

'Doesn't that guy ever shut up?'

'Not even in a dentist's chair.'

When these kind of asides got back to him, Monty grinned. He liked being noticed, and being talked about.

From the moonlit sky above the flat area north-east of Ipswich in Suffolk, a troop-carrying plane, one of many that had left Scotland hours earlier, discharged its complement of airborne Commandos. The men came floating earthwards as part of a final practice exercise before they were called on to help form the spearhead of the invasion force. One after the other, they touched down, supple limbs and bodies freely rolling. Collapsing parachutes tugged and strained in the night breeze. Harnesses were released, parachutes gathered and folded, and the men moved to rendezvous at speed with their commander, Colonel Lucas, the first man down. He waited in silence until the roll call had been completed.

'No weaklings, Sergeant-Major?' Which meant no fractures, no sprains?

'None reported, sir,' said Sergeant-Major Dawson.

'Weaklings know they'll get sent home to mother?'

'They know, sir. Broken legs will march with the detachment. Sir.'

'Time check,' said Colonel Lucas to Captain Tim Adams, his deputy.

'02.21,' said Tim.

'Right. We've a fifteen-mile trek to our rendezvous. Get going.'

The detachment of Commandos moved off at a brisk pace, in single file behind Colonel Lucas and Captain Adams. Elsewhere in the area, other detachments on this final exercise were beginning their trek to the collective assembly point. Tomorrow they were scheduled to join the main division of airborne troops.

That was the extent of their orders. If they guessed something big was in the offing, that guess pointed them at what was obvious at this stage of the war, an attempt to establish a front that would attack Germany from the west. Wondering about this did not prevent Colonel Lucas thinking of his wife Eloise, an ATS subaltern and Tim's French-born half-sister. After another spell of duty at Troon following her return from the Middle East, she had been transferred back to liaison duties at the London headquarters of the Free French. Tim had suggested she'd have a fight on her hands. Luke, as

Colonel Lucas was known to his intimates, said it wasn't a fight that any oversexed French officer would win. He'd leave the ring awkwardly injured. Eloise had always been a handful, a woman whose French temperament surfaced all too easily, but she was nevertheless a lovely, beguiling witch and a challenge. Not that Luke had any real wish to tame her. As herself, she was endearing, exasperating and exciting all at once. Let her be. He had last made love to her on a leave three and a half months ago. During the early overtures she had suddenly begun to laugh.

'What's funny?' he asked.

'You are,' she said, 'your trousers have fallen down, and you look so comical in your shirt, with your trousers collapsing.' And she laughed again. Then she shrieked. 'Luke! What are you doing?'

'Trying to get hold of your pants,' said Luke.

'No, no! I'm in uniform! It's not permitted! Luke!'

'Now who's laughing?'

'Let go! Luke! Oh, you terrible man, you're uncivilized!'

'Stop kicking, I've let go,' said Luke.

'Oh. Have you? But look at my skirt.'

'Shouldn't be there,' said Luke. 'Get it off.'

She sat up on the bed. He was stepping out of his trousers. A little smile showed itself on her flushed face.

'A man in his shirt and socks, oh, that is really comical,' she said, and laughed again.

'Well, let's see how comical this is,' he said, and leaned over.

'Luke! Oh, I'll divorce you! Luke, let go!'

Eloise did not know why she loved this rugged, purposeful soldier so much, or why his infamous conduct became exciting instead of abominable.

Still, she put up a fight for the sake of appearances and for experiencing exhilaration.

However, since masculine muscle always took unfair advantage over a female, Eloise allowed herself a muffled yell of defeat, then became a happy loser.

Colonel Lucas permitted himself a reminiscent smile as he marched in the van of his contingent, Tim beside him, a long-established comrade by now, a tough and efficient Commando, a survivor of ferocious raids on the enemy and, to his great credit, the victor in an escape attempt from the Germans in Benghazi. It was damned good to have him as a brother-in-law and as his deputy in what lay ahead of them.

Tim was thinking of his own wife, Felicity, once an ATS officer attached to 4 Commando at Troon. For her, the war struck its bitterest blow on the night a bomb destroyed her eyesight. But what a woman in the way she'd fought the handicap of blindness, and what a relief it was to know she was living with Rosie. Rosie's life with her children and Felicity, according to her last letter, was as much fun as she could expect in the absence of Matthew. It was like Rosie, thought Tim, to be able to extract fun from a life in which she not only had a small boy and an infant girl to look after, but a blind sister-in-law as well. In that letter, however, she assured him Felicity was far from helpless.

*Believe me, Tim love, Felicity's courage and her sense
of humour have made her a lovely companion and a
boon. She's overcome the worst of her disadvantages.
As you know, we've a new lot of chickens, and you
should see her take Giles by the hand, lead him out
of the kitchen and up to the chicken run. She knows
exactly where the run is, she tells me it's easy, by the
number of steps she takes and by judging how close
she is to the clucking. She makes distance and
hearing her guide. I'm proud of her, and I know it
goes without saying that you are too. She's always at
her chirpiest when we're talking about you. She loves
you, you lucky man, so take care always.*

Tim wondered how his wife was after their
purposeful get-together last month. She'd written,
through Rosie, to tell him she'd enjoyed his letter,
but had said nothing about her condition. Well, it
was too soon, he supposed. When would she know
if she was pregnant or not? And if it turned out she
was, a bloke had to ask himself again, exactly how
would a blind mother cope with an infant, including changing nappies? She had said she could
and would.

Good luck, Puss. You're one of life's great girls.

He knew what Grandma Finch would say about
her.

'Your Felicity, Tim, I never admired anyone
more, but she's an Adams now, of course.'

Chapter Fourteen

Pilot Officer Nick Harrison awoke to a knock on the bedroom door. His night had been a fractured one, violent dreams of falling and plunging aircraft repeatedly bringing him out of sleep until with dawn approaching he lapsed into deep and welcome slumber.

Awake now, he stirred himself into awareness of his surroundings, whitewashed walls adorned with religious paintings, mostly of Madonna and Child. A Catholic house. Was it only a little over two weeks ago that he had been with Annabelle? Damn it that on only his second combat mission following his return to Italy, he'd let a Messerschmitt down him. In his time as a fighter pilot, he'd chalked up ten victories, but had been downed three times. One sea landing, one crash-landing and now this.

Knuckles rapped on his door again, and it opened. His Good Samaritan showed herself, fully dressed in her black headscarf, white blouse and black skirt.

'Ah, I disturbed you?' she said, her Italian good

looks fresh with morning, while he felt bleary and unshaven.

'It's late?' he said.

'I knocked an hour ago,' she said, 'and saw you were very much asleep. So I left you. You were very tired, yes? Of course. But I have to tell you I must go in a few minutes and begin my day's work at the school. There is coffee keeping hot for you in the kitchen, and some bread with dried figs. It is not much, and the coffee should be drunk with not too much complaint. You understand, *Inglese*?'

'I understand that what little you've got in the way of food, you're sharing with me,' said Nick, and sat up, bare-chested.

From the doorway, Caterina Angeli observed him, a man of lean muscular physique who belonged to the famed RAF. Even the most arrogant Germans had a respect for the RAF.

'Your leg is not hurting too much this morning?' she said.

'It's a lot happier,' said Nick. She had fetched a doctor to him last night, and the doctor had made an excellent job of stitching the wound, the while prattling cheerfully away in Italian. But he asked no questions, either in Italian or English, and bestowed an encouraging pat on the patient's shoulder when he left. 'My leg, in fact, feels as good as new.'

'But not to jump about on it, eh?' said Caterina. 'To rest it, I think, would be best. See, you must not go out, anyway, or show yourself, and I will look at the dressing this evening.'

'You can take it from me, I'm happy to wait here until some of our advance units show up,' said Nick.

He was hoping the Allied forces were knocking holes in the stubborn Germans, who were, he knew, contesting the issue grimly in a slow, fighting retreat to the Adolf Hitler line. There was no rout, nothing in the nature of a headlong retreat. The German Army was not like that, and the Waffen-SS divisions were made up of fanatics who never gave an inch.

'I will try to bring you some news,' said Caterina. 'We have been robbed of our radios, as well as many other things, but there are still some hidden radios on which friends can listen to Allied broadcasts. Ah, a moment, *Inglese.*' She disappeared. She returned with a man's dressing-gown and placed it over Nick's bed. 'There, you can be lazy in that and dress later. Be careful now and do not answer the door if anyone comes.'

'Understood,' said Nick.

'Once, doors were open, not closed,' said Caterina.

'I understand that too,' said Nick. 'The war's changing habits and people.' He thought of the pre-war years in Walworth, where 'Open Sesame' in the form of a latchcord was a feature of many homes, and his mother's only worry was what her erring husband might do next. 'Have a peaceful day with your pupils, *signora.*'

'Yes?' Caterina smiled. 'I hope so. *Ciao, Inglese.*'

'*Ciao, signora,*' said Nick.

She left. He heard her ride off on her creaking bicycle, after which there was silence, a silence that was all very well in its way, but told him nothing about what was happening south of the village. There were no sounds of gunfire or air activity, at least none close enough to be heard. He estimated, from the position of the German artillery the Beaufighters had attacked yesterday, that the Allied forces in this region were locked in battle with the retreating enemy some twenty miles south of Asconi. That retreat was governed by the Germans' determination not to be overrun before they reached their Adolf Hitler line, the line intended to prevent the Allies beginning an advance on Rome.

Nick sank back, lay inert for a while, then slipped from the bed to face a day of waiting inactivity. He went down to fix the catch on the lock of the front door, checked that the back door was bolted, then washed in the bathroom, the water only lukewarm. His chin was bristly. A man's shaving kit in an old leather case lay on the shelf below the mirror. That, of course, belonged to her late husband. Was there any price to pay for using a dead man's brush and razor?

Well, thought Nick, unless I shave I'll feel rough all day. He picked the brush from the case. The bristles were dry, very dry, a sign that they hadn't been used for some time. He saw a shaving mug which contained a residue of soft soap that had become discoloured. He wet the brush under the tap, dipped it into the mug, applied it to the soap, created lather and covered his chin. He gave himself a welcome shave. Cleaning his chin, he heard a faint noise. The bathroom overlooked the street. He moved to the little shuttered window and took a cautious look through the slats. A hatless man with black curly hair, and wearing a dark suit, was approaching the house, disappearing from Nick's sight as he came close. Nick stayed still and listened, waiting for a knock on the front door. Nothing happened. He strained his ears and caught the sounds of the man moving about. The sounds arrived at the back door, and Nick was sure there was a careful turning of the handle and an attempt to enter. The door, however, was bolted. Feet faintly trod hard surface, and after a minute or so Nick, still at the little window, saw the visitor reappear and make his way back down the street.

If the bloke was a friend or neighbour, thought Nick, he would have known the lady of the house was at the school, and that it was useless to knock. So what had he come for? To do a brief scouting job around the house on behalf of the German authorities?

What am I, thought Nick, a suspect presence?

However, the rest of the day was uninterrupted, and he was able to put his feet up and rest his gashed leg.

The sound of the rusty bicycle heralded the return of Caterina Angeli from the village school. Nick had let the catch down on the front door lock, but he made no attempt to let her in. It would have meant showing himself, even if only for a second or so. The front door was visible to the last house on the other side of the street, although it was some way down. His Good Samaritan's abode stood very much on its own.

She came into the house, standing her bike in the little hall, and entered the kitchen, taking her head-scarf off as she did so, and fluffing her wealth of hair.

'*Come va, Inglese?*' she said with a smile. How's it going? Nick managed to interpret.

'All quiet,' he said, 'except there was a morning visitor.' He told her about the man, and described him. Caterina's warm brown eyes sparked.

'A snake,' she said, 'a secret fascist. Enrico Bonetti. One of those who still support Mussolini and Hitler. Everyone else is much happier to support the Allies. Someone, perhaps, saw you coming over the fields. Whispers here reach many ears, but because we are now against Germany no-one would betray you, except a man like Enrico Bonetti, and then he would have to be sure and also careful. Other men would strangle him if it was known he betrayed an RAF man to the Germans here. We must do nothing that will give him a chance to know you are in this house.'

'*Signora*, I think I should go,' said Nick.

'No, no.' Caterina was vigorously against that. 'I will tell some of my friends to watch the snake. My Pietro would never forgive me if I sent you away. I will go now and speak to some of my friends.'

'You'll tell them I'm here?' said Nick.

'I will tell them anything but that,' said Caterina. '*Inglese*, to help you rejoin your comrades will be an honour for me.'

'If it turns unpleasant,' said Nick, 'it'll be a running job for both of us. We'll take your honour and my safety first instincts with us. After all, we both value your honour and I respect my cowardice.'

Caterina laughed.

'Ah, you are an amusing man, *Inglese*,' she said. 'Now I will go.'

Out she went, and her bike jangled and creaked as she rode away.

When she returned, she informed Nick that certain of her friends would keep a watch on Enrico Bonetti. It would not go on for long, she said, because the news was that the Germans were being pushed back and that the Allies would liberate this region in a day or so.

'That's the kind of news I like,' said Nick.

'I shall take you to your comrades when they arrive, and watch them embrace you,' said Caterina.

'They're all hairy,' said Nick, 'so tell them to leave out any kisses.'

Caterina laughed again.

'*Inglese*, I like you,' she said, 'so let us drink some wine together, and then I will find some food for both of us.'

'I know beggars can't be choosers,' said Nick, 'but I'll duck any more figs. I had some for lunch as well as for breakfast.'

That amused Caterina very much.

At home, Annabelle came out of her sleep halfway through the night, and found herself wide awake. She slipped from the bed and drew the curtains apart. She looked out at the darkness. The night was wild, she could hear the wind gusting, and the window transmitted a coldness that belonged more to March than May. The weather was suffering fits of temper that were making the month a disappointing one.

Was it like this in Italy, was the weather there of a kind to keep RAF squadrons grounded? How many more combat missions did Nick have to get through before RAF Command brought him down from the sky?

In the South of England, the concentrated formations of men and armour awaited the day of assault.

'Hope to Christ it's not as rough as it bloody well is now.'

'They'll no' send us if half of us are going to sink.'

'Listen, Jock, if I get seasick, I won't care if I sink or not.'

'Aye, ye're a cheerful laddie, Willy. Have a wee sup.'

'Is that your flask?'

'Aye, and a wee sup, I said, nae more.'

'God bless you, Jock, I'll buy you a French haggis for Christmas.'

'New Year, Willy, New Year.'

'Your say-so, Jock. Hang on to your kilt.'

Chapter Fifteen

Wednesday, 19 May

'Maisie?'

'Yes, my dear?' said Mrs Maisie Finch.

'What happened?' asked her husband, Edwin Finch.

'You've been working too hard,' she said gently. He was seventy, the silver in his hair advancing rapidly. But he was still a man of distinguished looks. A gentleman. He should have retired from his Government job years ago, but once the war began in 1939 he had said, quite firmly, that he would not give up his work until Hitler and his Nazi thugs were destroyed. Chinese Lady often thought the Government ought to enforce his retirement, but she had no idea his actual work was for British Intelligence, and that as a cypher specialist he was second to none. He had spent the whole winter of '43–44 at Bletchley Park, the nerve centre of cypher intelligence, returning to his department in London at the beginning of April. He was a tired man by then.

Today, a Government staff car had brought him home in the early afternoon. A doctor was with him. He had collapsed on his way to lunch, from mental and physical exhaustion, the medical man said. He was to rest for a week, in his bed, and was not to get up except for ablutions. Here are some tablets. He is to take three each day at intervals of four hours. His local doctor has been advised, and will call, if necessary. Rest, Mrs Finch, is his primary need. There's no real ailment apart from exhaustion.

Chinese Lady was shocked. Edwin was so pale, so weak. The doctor helped to get him to bed. It was now gone four, and she had been sitting with him for nearly two hours, watching him doze, watching him come awake every so often, when he said something, something irrelevant and she spoke reassuringly in return. She had loved her first husband, Daniel Adams, a corporal in the West Kent Regiment and long since gone from her life. For Edwin, the kindest of men and the most understanding of husbands, she had a deep abiding affection, and it pained her to think he might be failing. She was holding his hand which lay on the bedcover, watching him as his eyes closed again.

But he said from faraway, 'The wheels are running down, Maisie.'

'They need a rest, Edwin, that's all.' She hoped that really was all. 'It's the war, my dear, it's made your work tiring and nerve-racking for you.'

A murmur from him, again as if his mind was faraway.

'There's a hopeful dawn coming, Maisie.'

'Edwin? What hopeful dawn?'

'Did I say something, Maisie?' His voice was suddenly stronger.

'You said there's a hopeful dawn coming.'

'Did I?' He sounded like a man who had committed an indiscretion. He knew what was happening in areas of the South Coast. 'Let us hope for the hopeful,' he said, and with that innocuous comment he lapsed back into a doze.

Chinese Lady, still holding his hand, sat there and reflected on her life with him in peace and war. There was no time when he had not been a quiet strength and an unfailing support to herself and the family, more especially during these years of war. The country and its people had endured a cruel war, the people constantly in mourning for the casualties of sea, land and air battles, and air raids. Edwin, however, had never wavered in his belief that, given time and allies, the Empire would win the last battles of all. And lately he had been a happy and confident man in that respect. He must have been listening a lot to the wireless. Well, their own wireless, which had been a source of aggravation to her for years with its gloom and its unending talk about Hitler, had at last been consistently cheerful about the tide of war turning in favour of the Allies. The Russians, in winning back huge tracts of lost territory, had smashed great holes in German armies, the Americans were winning the war in the Pacific, the British 14th Army in Burma was inflicting on Japanese armies their worst casualties of the war, and the Royal Navy was hunting and destroying German U-boats week after week. Hitler was in his lair, foaming at the mouth. Well, the wireless didn't actually say that, but some newspapers did, which gave Chinese Lady the satisfaction of a woman who had long thought Hitler the kind of man who ought never to have been born.

The war. Still going on. It was a wonder the family had survived. But they had, all except poor Emily, killed by a bomb almost four years ago. Boots had married Polly Simms later, and now they were the parents of twins, Gemma and James, lovely infants of two and a half years. Polly was still living in Dorset, and Boots had a new job somewhere or other, with orders that meant going overseas again. Chinese Lady thought it downright unresponsible of him to accept such orders, especially as he hadn't long been back from Italy. During his leave, when he and Polly, with the twins, had spent time here at home, she had asked him what he thought he was up to at his age, going off to Italy as he had.

'Ah,' said Boots.

'What d'you mean, ah? That's not an answer.'

'Well, the fact is, old lady,' he said, 'your question has foxed me.'

'Now you know what I mean,' she said.

'Perhaps I do,' he said, 'but I'm sound in wind and limb.'

'Boots, it won't be long before you're fifty,' she said, 'and you still can't see properly out of your left eye. It's disgraceful if the Army sends you somewhere else, and they ought to be ashamed.' Her querulousness hid her affection and concern for her eldest son, as distinguished in his looks as Edwin had always been. 'After Dunkirk, I thought you were going to spend the rest of the war safe behind a desk.'

'That was the idea,' said Boots. 'Unfortunately, old girl, the idea got torpedoed.'

'It'll upset Polly and the twins, Boots, if you do go overseas again.'

Polly, in fact, had been a mixture of optimism and gloom.

'Boots is a born survivor, Maisie. Any man who survived the hell of the trenches in the last war can survive this one. I'm relying on that. Or is that wishful thinking? God, I can't lose him, Maisie, I need him for my old age.'

'Now, Polly, you won't lose him,' said Chinese Lady. There was a surprising rapport between Boots's cockney-born mother and her upper crust daughter-in-law. 'Don't say such a thing. Boots was never a careless man or a careless soldier. And besides, think of the twins.'

'I know about children, Maisie, I know about them growing up and going their own way,' said Polly. 'I want to grow old gracefully, and I need Boots there for that, or I'd turn into a complaining and sour old biddy. I only hope he'll land a job that'll keep him stuck to a desk. Heaven help me, why am I talking like a wet blanket when you know and I know he'll always duck at the right moment?'

'Well, at least we're doing a bit more winning than losing now, Polly.'

That was true, as the wireless had been saying lately. Included among the happier items of news this morning was the announcement that the British Eighth Army, famed for its defeat of

Rommel's Afrika Corps in the Western Desert, was part of the Allied force advancing in Italy. Alongside the British was an American army, its boisterous GIs demonstrating to the Italian ladies of liberated towns and villages Uncle Sam's way of celebrating glad days. In return, the flushed Italian ladies asked only for candy bars, cigarettes and fully-fashioned stockings. This, however, the wireless didn't mention. The BBC was conservative to the point of discreet silence concerning happy-go-lucky American soldiers with a pronounced sex drive. If it had decided to be forthcoming, its roving reporters could have gathered a mine of information without going to Italy. They could have gathered it at home, from many girls and women of the United Kingdom, including housewives whose husbands had been away for years.

Chinese Lady was not the sort of woman who would have thanked her wireless for broadcasting what she didn't want to hear. It would have upset her and her kind if it issued details of unfaithfulness at home. The fact was, however, that the influx of red-blooded GIs into Britain had resulted in many women losing their heads and hearts, and a sad number of men with the 14th Army had received what had come to be known as '*Dear John*' letters. These were letters from wives saying they were awfully sorry, but they would like a divorce so that they could marry their favourite GI. Or from sweethearts saying, '*I hope you won't mind too much, but I'm going to marry Elmer, an American soldier who lives near Hollywood, would you believe. He's ever so sweet.*'

It was true, however, that certain rumours did

float about to land in Chinese Lady's ears. She chose to dismiss them. She liked an ordered world, in which the right and proper kind of behaviour prevailed, according to the Ten Commandments.

She glanced at Edwin. He was sleeping now, not dozing. That pleased her. Sound sleep was what he needed.

Boots wouldn't like it that his stepfather was an exhausted man. Boots and Edwin were close friends, and always had been.

Air raids on the United Kingdom were no longer a positive menace, and some younger members of the family had come home. Daniel, for instance, and Vi and Tommy's daughter Alice. Alice, just nineteen, would be going to university in September unless she decided to volunteer for one of the Services. Vi and Tommy's sons, David and Paul, were still in Devon, Paul at fourteen to finish his schooling there, and David, eighteen, working on a farm while waiting to join the RAF. Paul had given up dissecting dead rabbits in favour of a more socially acceptable occupation: that of having his first girlfriend. Jenny Lymes, the daughter of neighbours, was a live-wire madcap who, he advised his mum and dad, would go off bang one day. He felt, he said, that as she wasn't a bad bit of Devon plum duff for a girl, he had to stay near enough to her to pick up the pieces and take them home to her mum and dad. Meanwhile, he'd be grateful to receive a two-bob postal order, as Jenny was getting a bit hard on his pocket lately.

Lizzy, retailing this to Chinese Lady, but leaving out the plum duff bit, received the comment that while a girl shouldn't be after what a boy had in his trousers, it was always right for a boy to treat a girl.

Lizzy, coughing, said, 'You mean what a boy has in his trousers' pocket, Mum.'

'What did I say, then?' asked Chinese Lady.

'Never mind,' said Lizzy.

Seventeen-year-old Daniel, Sammy and Susie's eldest, was a lively one, like his dad. And like his Uncle Tommy, he was a natural mechanic and was working at the firm's garments factory in Belsize Park as assistant on the maintenance of the sewing and cutting machines. The machines were over-worked in fashioning Army and RAF uniforms day in, day out, and Tommy, factory manager, was often stretched to the limit to make sure breakdowns did not exceed the number of spare machines available. New machines were difficult to come by. Daniel was proving invaluable, the son of his dad in his energy and application. Good old Gertie Roper, charge-hand of the machinists and seamstresses, mothered him, and the younger girls teased him. So Tommy said. Chinese Lady, suspecting the machinists were a bit common because they were mainly from the East End, hoped the teasing wasn't vulgar or down-right suggestive. She told Sammy she also hoped it wasn't catching, as she didn't want Daniel, now growing into a nice young man, to turn common. Don't worry, Ma, he's fighting it, said Sammy. Don't call me Ma, said Chinese Lady, if anything's common, that is.

She thought about Polly. With her twins, Polly was now on another visit to her parents in their grand house in Dulwich. Her father, General Sir

Henry Simms, had been forced by ill-health to retire from active service and take a desk job. Polly and her children were making up for the frustrations he felt at losing his command. It was nice for him, thought Chinese Lady, to have his happy little grandchildren close at hand, especially as he doted on them. He was a natural gentleman, like Edwin, with an admiration for Boots, his son-in-law, for the part he had played in making Polly a mother when she was well over forty. Damned fine man, your eldest son, Mrs Adams, he'd said, and healthier than many men only half his age. Chinese Lady hadn't wanted to talk intimately about Sir Henry's admiration for Boots's virility, so she said well, I must say he's always had his good points, although he still says things I can't make sense of sometimes. That changed the subject.

As for dear Rosie, still living down in Dorset, she said in her letters or phone calls how much she was missing her husband Matthew. But her children, Giles and Emily, filled her time, and Tim's wife Felicity, she said, was always an invaluable help and companion. Chinese Lady thought what a blessing that was, a blind companion actually being an invaluable help. Well, of course, Felicity was an Adams now, and any Adams seemed to take on something that Chinese Lady felt was to do with the sterling qualities of her long-dead first husband, Corporal Daniel Adams. But it didn't seem right, so many of the family being away in places as good as foreign. Chinese Lady liked things to be more natural. More natural to her was having her children, grandchildren and, yes, great-grandchildren, within walking distance. There was always something right and proper about being able to put one's hat and coat on, and slip out for a family visit down the road, up the road or somewhere else not far away. This war was as bad as it could be in interfering with family life. Even if the last battles were won, as Edwin was sure they would be, the country and its people would end up tired out from all they'd had to put up with and a bit bitter from the results of long separations.

Someone tapped lightly on the bedroom door.

'Come in,' said Chinese Lady.

The door opened and in came Phoebe, bringing her beguiling prettiness with her. She wore a blue dress common to the girl pupils of the local nursery school.

'Grandma?' She whispered the word. 'Mummy told me and Paula about Grandpa when she fetched us from school. We've just come in. Is he all right?'

Chinese Lady was touched. There she was, Phoebe, the little girl who, orphaned and sad, had been cared for by Sammy and Susie, and adopted by them two years ago to become Phoebe Adams, a child happy at last. She had not suffered a single accident in bed since the night Susie and Sammy told her they were her mum and dad.

'He's sleeping, pet,' said Chinese Lady, and Phoebe ventured to the bedside to look down at the sleeping man.

'I like Grandpa, don't I?' she whispered. 'He's nice. Grandma, I'm awful sorry he's not very well. Still, he'll be better soon. Mummy and Paula's coming up in a minute to see him, and Auntie Lizzy too.'

'Oh, your Aunt Lizzy's arrived, has she?' said Chinese Lady. She had phoned daughter Lizzy earlier.

'Yes, she's come to see Grandpa,' said Phoebe, still whispering. 'And Daddy, well, I fink he's sure to come and see him when he gets home. Will Uncle Boots come and see him too?'

Bless the child, thought Chinese Lady. She hadn't seen a lot of Boots, but he'd quickly become a likeable uncle to her.

'You remember your Uncle Boots, Phoebe?'

'Yes, I liked him lots, didn't I?'

Boots, of course, had made a great fuss of her, and she had laughed and giggled her way into his affections.

'He can't come to see Grandpa just yet, Phoebe, he's a soldier and he's having to go overseas.'

'Oh, dear,' said Phoebe. 'Still, when he does come, Grandpa will be better.'

'We hope so,' said Chinese Lady, and Susie and Lizzy came in then, with nine-year-old Paula – Paula tiptoeing so as not to disturb Grandpa Finch.

'Grandma, is Grandpa ill?' she asked.

'He's tired,' said Chinese Lady.

'How is he, Mum?' asked Susie.

'Yes, how is he?' asked Lizzy, very attached to her stepfather. Years and years ago, in her early teens, she'd thought she'd like him to take the place of her dead father.

'He's been a bit restless, but he's sleeping nice and quiet now,' said Chinese Lady.

'Mum, it can't be serious, or the doctor would have had him taken to a hospital,' said Susie. She owned an undiminished fairness and was slender compared to her sister-in-law Lizzy, who still retained a fulsome Edwardian figure. Happily so. Lizzy, in her forty-sixth year, believed women should be well-endowed. Her husband Ned concurred. Well, he'd been close to Lizzy's generous endowment for years, and always found it very comforting.

'He does look pale, Mum,' she said, regarding the sleeping man with concern.

'I hope he'll be sitting up and looking fairly perky by the time Sammy gets home,' said Susie with forced cheerfulness. She and Sammy now had their eldest son, Daniel, living here with them, much to the pleasure of Paula and Phoebe, who played rousing, racketing games with him. That pleased Chinese Lady. She liked the noisy sounds of family life.

'Yes, Daddy won't like seeing him not very well,' said Paula.

'Oh, he'll be better soon,' said Phoebe.

'Well, we all hope so, don't we, lovey?' said Lizzy, wishing she had small ones like Phoebe and Paula to mother. Little moments of that kind went out of a woman's life when her children became adults. 'We hope that very much.'

'Oh, yes, Grandpa's the bestest,' said Phoebe.

'Darling, we'll tell him that,' said Susie. She loved her adopted daughter, and found her endearingly quaint sometimes.

'Phoebe, you sure he'll be better soon?' said Paula.

'Yes, I fink so,' said Phoebe a little shyly.

'It's instinct, I expect,' said Lizzy.

'Well, I'm sure it's a nice sound instinct,' said Chinese Lady, who believed, anyway, that the Lord bestowed exceptionally sound instincts on women, much more so than on men. Which was why women were more sensible than men. If the Government had taken notice of her own instincts, they'd have arranged to do something about Hitler long before he went to war.

Humane though she was, Chinese Lady meant something nasty.

Edwin Finch slept on, soundly. Perhaps his own instincts told him that the people around him loved him.

Chapter Sixteen

Saturday morning

Mrs Rachel Goodman picked up a letter from her mat on her way out of her Brixton house in company with her younger daughter, Leah. They both worked for Sammy Adams. Rachel read the letter on the bus taking them to his offices at Camberwell Green. It was from Leah's Gentile boyfriend, Aircraftman Edward Somers, whose parents were old and close friends of Rachel herself. In the letter, Edward put down in clear terms his feelings for Leah and went on to say that when he was twenty-one he intended to ask her to marry him. By then, he hoped the war would be over, and that Leah would accept his proposal. If so, he also hoped that Mrs Goodman and Leah's grandfather would give the marriage their approval. He was writing in advance, he said, in order to allow them plenty of time to think about this. You can be sure, he said, that your combined blessings would be very welcome. He finished by mentioning he had spoken to Leah about his intentions, and that she had been helpful and encouraging.

Rachel sighed.

Leah, glancing at her, murmured, 'Mama?'

Rachel came to and said, 'It's from Edward, but we can't discuss it now. We'll wait until this evening.'

'Yes, all right,' said Leah, but experienced little quivers.

Rachel, placing the letter back in its envelope, said, 'Did you know Edward was going to write to me?'

'Yes, Mama.'

'I see,' said Rachel, and thought about the implications, the uniting of Jewish and Christian families. And of all of the latter, Leah was choosing the Somers family, a branch of the Adams', of whom so many members had been Rachel's warm and steadfast friends for many years. Her reservations about the marriage concerned the possibility that Leah would gradually absorb all the tenets of the Adams' religion and finally adopt them herself. Rachel felt, however, that such reservations would probably not cause her to withhold her consent and approval. She was far too attached to Lizzy and Ned, and all the others, to feel any real dismay. But her father, while not strictly orthodox, was devoted to his faith and she knew he would prefer both his granddaughters to marry their own kind. He would almost certainly mention her late husband Benjamin, and suggest Benjamin would not have been happy.

Later, Rachel spoke to Sammy in his office about Leah and Edward.

'Eh?' said Sammy.

'Weren't you listening?' asked Rachel, currently eschewing her meat ration and all potatoes in favour of apples and salads. In her forty-second year, the fulsome nature of her figure was threatening to become expansive. I should want to look like a barrel wearing a hat, she asked herself, not likely.

'Did you say my well-educated nephew Edward is going to ask Leah to marry him?' enquired Sammy, still holding on to his blue-eyed electricity.

'Yes, Sammy.'

'Well, upon me soul, Rachel,' said Sammy, 'if that's what his good education has done for him, I extend me congratulations to his educators.'

'Sammy, be serious,' said Rachel.

'I am serious,' said Sammy.

'You're in favour of having Jewish relatives?' said Rachel.

'I'm in favour of having your family as relatives,' said Sammy. 'In fact, I'd be tickled. If I'm not mistaken, Rachel me old friend, we've talked about Edward and Leah before, and I believe I told you, you can't stop a clock from ticking unless you jump on it with both plates of meat. If Edward and Leah want to get married, let it happen.'

'Will Lizzy and Ned think like that?' asked Rachel.

'Lizzy's a bit old-fashioned,' said Sammy, 'but if she likes Leah enough, she won't throw a fit. Ned won't worry either way. Ned's an old soldier, and old soldiers like peace and quiet. Besides, they've already told me they won't mind. But what about Isaac?'

Isaac was Rachel's father. Isaac Moses.

'He'll put up a fight,' said Rachel.

'Well, I know he's of the faith, and has been all his life,' said Sammy, 'but he won't fight with the gloves off, will he?'

'No, he won't make loud noises or bang a drum, Sammy,' said Rachel, 'but I know he'd prefer Leah to marry into the faith. I think he'll say so.'

'How exactly do you feel?' asked Sammy.

'I feel, Sammy, that I want Leah to be happy,' said Rachel.

'She's a sweet girl, and deserves some happy-ever-after,' said Sammy. 'Wartime's not much fun for girls her age. They're stuck in no man's land, if I might coin that as suitable wordage. They're not old enough to fit themselves into a uniform, and nor are they ready to slip into something silky and come-on.'

'Sammy, could you fascinate me by explaining something silky and come-on?' asked Rachel.

'Yes, the kind of frock Mattie Harry wore as a spy for Kaiser Bill,' said Sammy, 'and which sent French generals cross-eyed on account of there not being much of it.'

'God help me if you give me hysterics at my age,' said Rachel. 'You're talking about girls like Leah wanting to be old enough to be a Mata Hari.'

'Well, we've all had dreams,' said Sammy. 'I just suppose girls like Leah don't like having to wait while old-enough females are swanking around in uniforms. Listen, me remarkable friend, I'll consider myself a fortunate bloke if Leah ends up as a niece of mine, and that's my last word on this particular subject.'

Rachel smiled.

'You're a good man, Sammy,' she said.

'Pardon?' said Sammy.

'I should say you aren't?' said Rachel.

'Rachel, you ought to know by now I've been a hard-hearted and armour-plated businessman for years,' said Sammy. 'I've had to be, and it's – Rachel, is that you laughing?'

'I should be crying, Sammy?'

'No, but laughing?' said Sammy.

'Yes, I think you said you were hard-hearted and armour-plated, didn't you?'

'I don't mind people knowing it,' said Sammy.

'Sammy, you're priceless,' said Rachel.

'Granted,' said Sammy. 'Shall we do some work?'

'Yes, Sammy, and thank you,' said Rachel softly.

'Don't mention it,' said Sammy, whose attitude to many things was entirely easy-going unless they constituted a threat to his business. It was then that he put on his armour-plating.

Saturday afternoon

Mr Finch was much better, and Sammy and Susie's eldest son, Daniel, had helped to buck him up.

Seventeen-year-old Daniel, named after his late grandfather, Chinese Lady's first husband, was perky, self-confident and voluble. He had his mum's blue eyes, his dad's dark brown hair, and the lanky legs of the family's males. Like his cousin Edward, he was on the thin side.

Working at the Adams garment factory in the Belsize Park area, he had been asked by his Uncle Tommy to pop down to the local ironmonger by Camberwell Green this afternoon for a supply of sewing-machine needles. The factory was running short, and an expected delivery from the suppliers hadn't yet arrived. Would Daniel get some and bring them in on Monday? Certainly, said Daniel.

After he'd arrived home from work and eaten lunch, he went down to the shop in Camberwell New Road. He was now looking at a selection of nails.

'Look, Mister Broom, I said sewing-machine needles, not nails,' he expostulated to the iron-monger, whose shop he admired. What a place. It was a cavern of treasures with its multitude of shelves, cupboards, drawers and boxes full of this, that and the other. As a young man with a leaning towards the fundamentals of turning wheels, he was in tune with ironmongery that related to the mechanical. Things like cogs, springs, ball-bearings, spanners and so on.

'Now now, hold yer horses,' said Mr Broom, aged but not simple. He had grey sideboards, thinning grey hair, tea-stained whiskers and gaps in his teeth. 'I pride meself I can hear as good as the next man, but I ain't able to hear all that good when me customers mumble and gargle. Nails, that's what I thought you said. Are you sucking a gobstopper?'

'Give over,' said Daniel, looking pained. 'I grew out of gobstoppers when I was ten, didn't I? Besides,

181

the war's taken them out of sweetshop jars. Come on, Mister Broom, sewing-machine needles, if you please. I've been requested by the management to get a handful from you and take them in on Monday. The factory's still waiting for its ordered supply. That's the war again. I tell you, Mister Broom, I've never been in a war like this before, you can't even get stick-on rubber soles for footwear. That's boots and shoes, y'know.'

'I'm obliged for the information,' said Mr Broom, a pencil stuck behind his right ear, and an old brown shop coat draping his stringy but enduring body. 'And regarding orders for needles, might Hi be so bold as to say I notice you don't place orders with me? It's a pleasure for me, is it, to have you bounce into me shop once a year just for a handful of minor odds and ends?'

'If you'll excuse me saying so, Mister Broom, I don't happen to have been working at the factory for a year, just a few months,' said Daniel. 'But I'd like to point out that in those few months, I've come to give you some personal custom at least six times.'

'And ain't I bowed to you each time, Yer Worship?' said Mr Broom. It was always a lively and enjoyable set-to whenever Daniel Adams appeared in his shop. 'Now, sewing-machine needles, is it? Could you speak up in the affirmative, like?'

'Certainly,' said Daniel. 'Sewing-machine needles!' he shouted, but with a grin on his face.

'That's it, you young rip, wake the dead,' said Mr Broom, and his lined brow darkened. 'There's been a lot of that about these last four years, dead and dying. Still, it's not my doing, it's them German hooligans. Time they was all put under the ground. They'll complain, of course, like they did after the last war. Can't stand being beat. Now let's see.' He turned, pulled open a drawer, produced three tobacco tins, placed them on the counter and released the lids. Each tin was full of gleaming steel needles. 'What's your pick, young man?'

'That's 'em,' said Daniel, pointing to one tin. He already knew a lot about the factory's sewing-machines and the right kind of needles. 'I'll take a hundred.'

Mr Broom spilled a quantity from the tin into one dish of small brass scales. He weighed them, added a few more and said, 'That's a hundred, or d'you want to argue?'

'I don't think so,' said Daniel, 'and in any case I wouldn't argue with an expert. Would you put 'em in a bag, Mr Broom, as I don't think it would be clever to slip 'em as they are into my trouser pocket. They might vaccinate my leg. Listen,' he went on, as Mr Broom transferred the little gleaming heap into a brown paper bag, 'if in a few years you thought about selling your shop, I might consider buying it.' Daniel was very much the son of Sammy. He was in regular touch with his cousin David, Uncle Tommy's son. David had ambitious ideas, and Daniel reckoned that together they could make a profitable go of something like a hardware shop. 'Would an offer interest you, Mr Broom, at the right time?'

'Seeing I've decided I'm going to die in here on me feet,' said Mr Broom, 'perhaps you'd like to wait for that to happen, when Hi might leave the shop to you in me will.'

'That's a really kind thought of yours, Mr Broom, and it won't hurt me to exercise patience,' said Daniel. He took the bag of needles, paid for them, said a perky goodbye to the proprietor and left. He began his long walk back home, whistling as he went. It was another breezy day and walking was an invigorating exercise. He turned right by Camberwell Green and made for Denmark Hill. Buses rumbled by and trams clanged in a way reminiscent of pre-war days. Camberwell had known German bombs, but the Green was intact. He began his ascent of Denmark Hill. He crossed to the left-hand side after leaving Ruskin Park behind. A girl on a bike passed him.

'Hi,' she said as she went by.

'Watcher, Bubbles,' said Daniel.

She stopped and waited for him to catch up.

'How did you know my name was Bubbles?' she asked.

'Just a guess,' said Daniel, and she looked at him. He didn't seem to have much flesh on his bones; he was close to being skinny, but he had a clean, fresh look and the kind of blue eyes that could make some girls blink. 'Good guess, was it?' he said.

'No, you boobed,' she said, and cycled away.

'Gladys, then?' called Daniel, loose-limbed and quick-moving.

Again she stopped and waited for him to catch up. She was wearing a white woollen pull-on hat over dark hair, a summer dress of ivy green, and fully-fashioned nylons. Pert hazel eyes and a small retroussé nose gave her a saucy look.

'Gladys?' she said. She had an American accent. 'You sure that's a name?'

'I'm positive,' said Daniel.

'Nuts to positive and to Gladys,' she said, and rode away again.

'Betsy, then?' called Daniel, and again she stopped. Again he caught her up.

'Patsy,' she said.

'Patty?'

'Patsy. You deaf or something?'

'Patsy, not Betsy?' said Daniel. 'You look more like a Betsy.'

'That's it, get cute,' she said.

'Not my style,' said Daniel, 'and in any case, I'm on my way home for a cup of tea and a slice of cake, if there is any. The war's ruined the regular availability of homemade cake. Still, nice to have met you, Betsy—'

'I don't know what all that means,' she said, 'but I'm Patsy. Don't I keep telling you?'

'Patsy, right, I'll remember,' said Daniel, and went on his way. She kept up with him, wheeling her bike close to the kerb. She had slim, vigorous legs that made easy work of climbing the hill.

'I guess you want to know where I come from,' she said after a while.

'Brighton?' said Daniel.

'Brighton? Brighton?' She obviously thought that a daft guess. 'Brighton, you said?'

'Down in Sussex,' said Daniel, thinking she ought

to be spoken to by her dad for talking to strangers. Mind, he knew that a lot more people did talk to strangers these days, especially after an air raid. It was a kind of coming-together due to everyone being in the same rocky boat. 'I'm only guessing.'

'Try Boston,' said the girl.

'Boston, Lincs?' said Daniel, not stopping in his walk.

Still keeping up with him, the girl said, 'Boston where?'

'Lincolnshire,' said Daniel.

'My Boston is in Massachussetts,' she said.

'Got you,' said Daniel, 'you're an American girl.'

'Patsy Kirk.'

'Kirk?' said Daniel.

'You've got something against that?' said Patsy.

'No, should I have?' asked Daniel.

'It's OK with you, then?' said Patsy.

'Fine,' said Daniel.

'Are you in the Army?' asked Patsy.

'I'm not eighteen yet,' said Daniel.

'You look as if you could be, and you could say you were,' said Patsy.

'Well, I've got a grandmother who'd knock my head off if I did,' said Daniel.

'Couldn't you sneak off without telling her?' asked Patsy.

'Some hopes,' said Daniel. 'Can I confide in you?'

'Oh, please do,' said Patsy, 'I'd be thrilled, wouldn't I?'

'Well, Grandma gets to know everything,' said Daniel. 'She's the kind of second-sight character you come across in books about Ancient

Rome. You've heard of Ancient Rome, have you?'

'Sure I have,' said Patsy, 'and I've heard of Nero too, but I've never heard anything about Ancient Rome grandmothers with second sight.'

'Well, I'm glad to be able to inform you that Ancient Romans revered their grandmothers, whose second sight was useful when Caesar's army was going to war, which it often did,' said Daniel. 'Even Nero revered grandmothers. After he poisoned his own, he made a special offering to the gods, sacrificing a dozen Ancient Briton slaves. Generally, Ancient Roman grandmothers gave all the orders and all the people obeyed, and if they didn't their grandmothers flung them to the lions. Horrible sight it was, believe me.'

'I'm not believing any of that, you dope, not a single word,' said Patsy.

'It's your own funeral if you want to stay ignorant,' said Daniel.

'If you think I'm going to believe old Roman grannies threw people to the lions, you're crazy,' said Patsy. A bus passed, going up the hill, while she and Daniel walked on in chummy fashion. 'Of course, I know Nero was a homicide, but he didn't really poison his grandmothers, did he?'

'Alas,' said Daniel.

'What did you say?'

'Alas, he did,' said Daniel.

'Oh, you kook,' said Patsy, 'alas is archaic.'

'How'd you spell it?' said Daniel. 'Listen, Patsy, Nero put arsenic in his grandmothers' lunchtime helping of jellied eels. The poor old dears fell dead off their couch after only three mouthfuls. Then—'

'Hey, slow down,' said Patsy, 'I'm not believing jellied eels. What are they?'

'Cylindrical lumps of eel cooked in jelly,' said Daniel. 'My cockney forebears loved 'em.'

'You're disgusting, d'you know that?' said Patsy. 'And so are your forebears. Still, I kind of like the way you talk. You've got a musical tone.'

'Eh?' said Daniel.

'Sure,' said Patsy. 'Have you ever thought about being a singer? You could develop into a great baritone. They're favourite with me, baritones. How much farther is your home?'

They were halfway up the hill, a residential thoroughfare of handsome properties.

'It's still a bit far,' said Daniel. He stopped then, stepped off the kerb and relieved her of her bike. 'How far do you have to go to your own home, Topsy?'

'Patsy,' she said. 'How many more times? And it's Danecroft Road.'

'That's only a little way on from me,' said Daniel, and gave her a more interested look. He still wasn't sure she ought to talk to strangers, but then he hadn't yet discovered Americans were a gregarious people given to offering friendship at the drop of a hat. He'd lived as an evacuee in a quiet Devonshire village, away from American Army training areas, for most of the war. Deciding this particular female American was likeable, he said, 'I'll push your bike for you.'

'I'd like to know your name first,' said Patsy, as they stopped. 'You might be anybody.'

'Yes, so I might,' said Daniel. 'As anybody, I could give you a false name, then set about you and pinch your bike.'

'You wouldn't do that, I read you as a good guy, even if you're unbelievable about Nero's grannies,' said Patsy. 'So what's your name?'

'Daniel Adams.'

'Adams?' said Patsy. 'That's a proud name in Boston. If you remember, when we licked you in the War of Independence—'

'No, I don't remember,' said Daniel, 'I wasn't there. But I daresay it hurt a bit.'

'While we were fighting you,' said Patsy, 'John Adams, a lawyer who practised in Boston, did such a great job for the cause of our independence that he became the second President after Washington.'

'Was John Adams English?' asked Daniel. 'His name sounds as if he was.'

'Well, I guess he might have had English parentage,' said Patsy, 'but being born in America, he was American.'

'D'you mean that if you'd been born in China, you'd be Chinese?' enquired Daniel.

'I'm going to find out if I can sue you for saying a thing like that,' said Patsy. 'In Boston, folks still talk about heroes of the Revolution like John Adams and another Adams, Sam Adams.'

'I don't think we ever talk about them over here,' said Daniel. 'Bad losers, I suppose,' he said with a grin. 'Well, good old Boston. See you there one day. Say when I'm a travelling baritone.'

Patsy took a new look at him. She thought even

when he was standing still, like now, he had a supple energy that issued vibrations and made him kind of doubly alive.

Patsy Kirk was nearly seventeen, the daughter of a radio newsman. Her mother had been a lawyer, but tragically, in March 1941, lost her life in a car accident when driving herself to her office. Her father, grieving, decided a change of background would help, and received accreditation from his radio station to go and cover the war in Europe from London. He took Patsy with him, but because of the air raids had sent her to a boarding-school in Somerset. Other American girls, mostly daughters of resident diplomats and military attachés, were there, forming a sisterhood to rival the cliques of snooty English girls. Patsy quickly took the lead, which frequently meant being carpeted by the principal.

'You're a troublemaker, Miss Kirk.'

'Me, ma'am?'

'You. You have a problem. What is it?'

'I just wish this was a co-ed school.'

'A school for girls and boys?'

'Yes, I like boys better than girls. Boys are fun guys. Girls – well, they're just girls.'

'But better behaved than boys, allowing for exceptions. You're an exception, Miss Kirk. You, in fact, are a holy terror.'

However, it was said with the hint of a smile. Further, Patsy gradually adapted and made many friends among the English boarders, who invited her to their homes during vacations, where she sometimes had the thrill of meeting elder brothers on leave from the Army, Navy or Air Force, and wished herself old enough to swan around in pink satin while blowing smoke rings after every puff on a cigarette in a long holder. That, she imagined, would wow the British Army, the Royal Navy and the RAF. She was probably right. The flappers, the Bright Young Things of London in the wild Twenties, had wowed a nation in such a way.

Patsy had finished her schooling last autumn, and because German air raids had become less worrying, her father allowed her to come and live with him in his rented apartment, which the English called a flat, in a large house off Denmark Hill, in South-East London. He commuted from there to town at all times of the day and night in an old English Ford banger, since his work was governed by the events of the war and by the broadcasting facilities available to the American Press Corps in the sandbaggy heart of London. But when he could relax, he did so in the apartment, and was delighted now to have Patsy there. Patsy, a versatile and affectionate daughter, did whatever housework and cooking were necessary. Her Pa said he liked living among the people of the host nation, and residing out of town helped him to avoid the prolonged drinking sessions so favoured by overseas newsmen. Liquor was ill-received by his sensitive stomach.

Patsy made up her mind about her new acquaintance.

'OK, Daniel,' she said, 'I think I like you, or that I could get to like you, so you can push my bike for me.'

'Ta for the privilege,' said Daniel, and his mouth

spread in a good-natured smile, a smile that she liked.

They resumed their walk, Patsy recounting at length all the details of how she and her dad crossed the Atlantic in the *Queen Mary* to England after her mother's death, how they toured bombed London, and experienced the frightening ordeal one night of their first air raid. This made her Pa send her off to some gruesomely stuffy boarding-school just for girls, where she had to organize other American boarders so that they could form a united front against the English and sock them silly on dormitory raids.

'We licked 'em,' she said.

'Any blood?' asked Daniel.

'You bet,' said Patsy, 'and it earned us their respect. I've got lots of English girl friends now.'

'We all need friends,' said Daniel. The occasional bus hove into view, and the occasional car. Other than that, Denmark Hill seemed peaceful, even if a few ruined houses were a stark reminder of a murderous war. 'Would you mind telling me how old you are?'

'Eighteen,' said Patsy. 'Well, seventeen, I guess. Well, nearly seventeen.'

'Would your father like you talking to strangers?' asked Daniel.

'Strangers?' said Patsy. 'Oh, you mean talking to you. But there's the war, you have to talk to all kinds of people, and you don't seem like a stranger to me.'

'Do I strike you as being honest, upright and trustworthy?' asked Daniel.

'Sure, and cute as well,' said Patsy.

'Cute?' said Daniel, and laughed.

'Oh, some guys can be really cute,' said Patsy. 'By the way, Pa says this war's going on for ever.'

'Tell your Pa to keep that sort of opinion to himself,' said Daniel. 'Mr Churchill discourages that, y'know. It's—'

'Now there's a great guy,' said Patsy. 'Pa and me have a lot of admiration for Mr Churchill, your country's sheepdog.'

'Bulldog,' said Daniel.

'Oh, all right, bulldog,' said Patsy.

'Anyway,' said Daniel, 'warn your Pa not to talk about the war going on for ever. It's what's called enemy talk. He could get pelted with bricks picked up from bombed buildings if he said it out loud in public. The public want the war over well before they get all worn out.'

'I'll thank you not to criticize my Pa,' said Patsy.

'I'm sure he's a good old Pa, like mine,' said Daniel.

'Lucky us, then,' said Patsy. 'I like being out of school and looking after mine. He's up in town today, broadcasting news to the folks back home.'

'Good old Pa, I'm getting to like the sound of him,' said Daniel, the bike between him and Patsy. It was friendly of her to keep him company. She could have ridden the machine up the hill, although it would have been a plodding ride.

'I hope we win the war, you and us,' she said.

'Same here,' said Daniel, and stopped at the entrance to Red Post Hill. 'This is where I live, Patsy, and you're a bit farther on. Nice to have met you, good luck, and give my regards to your Pa—'

'Oh, that's it, is it?' said Patsy who, besides having no hang-ups or inhibitions, was typically American in her willingness to make friends, except with furtive characters who had shifty eyes and BO. 'You're showing me the door?'

'Unless you'd like to come home with me and have a cup of tea,' said Daniel.

'Daniel, you mean that?' said Patsy, looking distinctly pleased. 'I've gotten used to English tea.'

'Got,' said Daniel.

'Got what?' asked Patsy.

'You've got used to English tea.'

'Yes, I said so.'

'OK, fair enough,' said Daniel. 'Let's ride there. You sit on the carrier.'

'Nothing doing,' said Patsy, 'it's my machine.'

'I've got more leg muscle,' said Daniel.

'I could dispute that,' said Patsy.

'Don't muck about, Patsy. Sit.'

'Shan't. I'm as good as you are, and it's my machine, I tell you.'

'Sit, Patsy.'

'Daniel, stop making me mad.'

'You're not mad, you're laughing.'

'OK, I give in this time,' said Patsy, so she sat sideways on the carrier and Daniel rode. He whizzed her down the hill as if Hitler's demons were on their tails.

What a fun guy, she thought, even if he is a bit skinny.

Chapter Seventeen

As Daniel let himself and Patsy into the house, Susie appeared in the hall.

'I'm back, Mum,' said Daniel.

'So I see,' said Susie, eyeing his companion with curiosity.

'Oh, this is Patsy, Patsy Kirk,' said Daniel. 'She's American, and I found her on my way home from the ironmonger.'

'Found her?' said Susie.

'In a way,' said Daniel.

'No way,' said Patsy. 'Finding me is as good as saying I was lost.'

'Well, we met and got talking,' said Daniel. 'Patsy, now meet my one and only mother.'

'Hi, Mrs Adams,' said Patsy.

'Hello, Patsy,' smiled Susie, and Patsy noted another pair of blue eyes, a Pacific blue.

'I invited her for a cup of tea,' said Daniel.

Their voices brought Chinese Lady from her kitchen. Seeing an unknown young lady, she said, 'My, have we got a visitor, Susie?' She liked having visitors, providing they weren't hawkers who wanted to sell something, or tramps who wanted to pass on their fleas. She was in a pleasant frame of mind at the moment, because although Edwin was still keeping to their bed, he was perceptibly better.

'Grandma,' said Daniel, 'this is Patsy Kirk from America. Patsy, meet my grandmother.'

'Hi, Granny,' said Patsy.

Chinese Lady blinked, and not at the diminutive alone, for the front door, not yet closed, swung wide open to the breeze and let in a shaft of sunlight. With her back to it, Patsy's light summer dress became gauzy, revealing the outline of her legs.

'Oh, my goodness,' said Chinese Lady, feeling as if she should blush for the young lady. 'Daniel, close the door.'

Daniel closed it, and Sammy appeared, with Paula and Phoebe in tow.

'Are we missing something?' he asked.

'Patsy,' said Daniel, 'that's my dad, that's Paula, and that's Phoebe. They're my sisters, and there's another one, but she's still an evacuee in the West Country. Dad, this is Patsy Kirk from America, a new family friend.'

'Welcome,' said Sammy.

'Hi, everyone,' smiled Patsy, and she knew then where Daniel got his blue eyes from. From both parents.

'Crikey,' said Paula, staring at Patsy, 'is she yours, Daniel?'

'Well, young sis, I haven't made a bid for her yet,' said Daniel. 'We've only just met, and we're both hoping for a cup of tea. Any chance of putting the kettle on, Grandma?'

'I'll make a pot for all of us,' said Chinese Lady, halfway towards recovering from the shock of discovering the American girl wasn't wearing a slip. Chinese Lady automatically associated that with girls who hadn't been brought up proper. 'Bring Miss Kirk through, Daniel.'

They all went through to the large kitchen, bright with light from two windows. Patsy thought it looked old-fashioned with its out-of-date wallpaper, its big heavy dresser, solid iron range, and table covered with a check-patterned oilcloth that must have come out of the Ark or some hillbilly shack. But it also looked like a family gathering place. So she gave it plus points, even if it did need pulling down and rebuilding.

'Help yourself to a seat, Patsy,' said Sammy, wearing his Saturday afternoon sports shirt of Cambridge blue with Oxford blue trousers. Patsy thought him an engaging man, with the same kind of inner energy as Daniel.

'This one,' said Paula, touching a chair, 'and I'll sit on the next one and you can have that one, Phoebe.'

'Oh, fanks,' said Phoebe.

Patsy sat down between the two girls. Chinese Lady put the kettle on.

'How is it you're in England?' Susie asked the question of Patsy with a smile.

Patsy, having enjoyed the privilege of growing up in a country in which everyone was encouraged to speak his or her piece, willingly began a new recounting of the events that had led to the arrival of herself and her Pa in the little old island from which her forebears had emigrated. She was in luck, for she was talking to good listeners. Chinese Lady and most members of her family liked to absorb information as much as deliver it. Paula and Phoebe added wide-open eyes and mouths to wide-open ears. Daniel's new friend, all the way from America, fascinated them.

Patsy, concluding with how much she liked looking after her good old Pa, said, 'I took his best shirts to the Camberwell Green laundry this afternoon, and it was on my way back that Daniel said hello to me. Listen, Mr Adams, d'you know anything about Ancient Rome?'

'It was a bit before my time,' said Sammy, 'but I did hear they carried on some profitable business with Cleopatra and her Egyptians. Didn't they sell Cleopatra a barge?'

'Oh, I guess they might have,' said Patsy. 'And did you hear that Ancient Roman grandmothers threw people to the lions?'

'Eh?' said Sammy.

'Pardon?' said Susie.

'What's that?' said Chinese Lady.

'Lions,' said Paula, 'oh, crikey.'

'Oh, help,' breathed Phoebe.

Daniel made a surreptitious movement.

'Yes, d'you know if it's true, and that Nero's grannies liked some gruesome food called jellied eels?' asked Patsy.

'Oh, I remember friends of mine in the Old Kent Road liking jellied eels,' said Chinese Lady, 'but I brought my own family up on Sunday shrimps and winkles, which you can't get a lot of now. I just don't know that this war isn't worse than the other one.'

'Patsy, did you say Nero's grandmothers liked jellied eels?' asked Susie.

'It's what Daniel said, and that Nero did away with them by poisoning the eels,' declared Patsy. Daniel made another surreptitious movement. Susie had her eye on him, but said nothing. 'I told him he was crazy,' remarked Patsy. 'Is it OK to ask if he really is?'

'Blessed if I know,' said Paula, 'he's just one of my brothers.'

'But, I mean,' said Patsy, 'Roman grannies throwing people to the lions, that's got to be – hey, excuse me, but where's he gone?'

'I think he's just slipped out into the garden,' smiled Susie.

'What's he do that for?' asked Chinese Lady.

'I've got a feeling it's for safety first reasons on account of some Ancient Roman porkies he's been telling Patsy about Nero's grandmothers,' said Sammy.

'Well, could someone go and tell him the tea's nearly ready?' said Chinese Lady, to whom Nero's grandmothers, having been laid to rest well before her time, should be left in peace.

'I'll go get him,' said Patsy, and up she came and into the garden she went through the back door.

'Crumbs,' said Paula, looking at Phoebe. One moment the visitor had been between them, the next she had vanished.

'Was that a flash of lightning?' enquired Sammy.

'She's like quicksilver,' said Susie.

'Like Emily was,' said Sammy with sober reflection. He missed Emily, Boots's first wife.

'I fink Patsy's nice,' said little Phoebe.

'Yes, but fancy Daniel finding a girl that's come all the way from America,' said Paula.

'It's working both ways,' said Sammy. 'There's a lot of girls finding a lot of blokes that've come all the way from America.'

'We don't want to hear about unrespectable goings-on, Sammy,' said Chinese Lady.

'Daddy, could I meet a bloke?' asked Paula. 'He might be an American uncle.'

'Listen, Plum Pudding the Second,' said Sammy, 'you don't need an American uncle, you've got plenty of homegrown ones.'

'So have I, don't I?' said Phoebe.

'And grandparents and cousins,' said Sammy.

'Crikey,' said Phoebe in blissful awe.

Outside, Patsy made her acquaintance with a long lawn framed by flowerbeds. Beyond the lawn was a kitchen garden. Up there was Daniel. She ran towards him, calling.

'Daniel, your granny says tea's ready.'

'That's my granny,' grinned Daniel, 'she never fails. Sorry I slipped out while you were telling the family what you knew about old Roman grannies, but—'

'I like that,' protested Patsy, 'I was only repeating what you said.'

'You sure?' said Daniel. 'Sounded far-fetched to me. Anyway, I slipped out just to look at some seed potatoes I planted a while ago. There they are, see? New potatoes on the way.' He stooped double to touch burgeoning foliage. A little yell escaped him.

He straightened up as fast as a sprung bow, dived a hand into his trousers pocket and pulled out a folded brown paper bag. From the bottom of it a score of gleaming needle points had thrust through and pricked his thigh. 'Look at that lot,' he said. 'Vaccinated me, all of 'em. Another half-inch or so nearer and I'd have been a sad case, I tell you, Patsy.'

Patsy shrieked with laughter.

Daniel conceded it had its funny side.

Later, when he was doing the friendly thing by accompanying Patsy to her own home, Chinese Lady had a discreet word with Susie.

'I don't know, I'm sure, Susie, but it was a bit of a shock when that American girl was standing at the open door with all that sunshine behind her. It showed right through her frock. Susie, I could hardly believe my eyes at seeing she wasn't wearing a slip.'

'I noticed too, Mum,' smiled Susie.

'I don't know why it makes you smile, Susie,' said Chinese Lady. 'I mean, only vulgar girls go about with no proper underwear on.'

'I don't think Patsy's vulgar, Mum,' said Susie.

'Well, I hope not, Susie,' said Chinese Lady, 'we've never had vulgar girls come visiting, except that Lily Fuller that used to call on Tommy and wore jumpers that – well, you know what I mean.'

'I don't think I ever met Lily Fuller,' said Susie, 'but yes, I do know what you mean about the kind of jumpers vulgar girls wear.'

'Mind, I liked the girl,' said Chinese Lady.

'Lily Fuller?'

'No, not that hussy,' said Chinese Lady. 'The American girl. Perhaps Sammy could find out if she's too poor to afford proper underwear, and if she is, he could bring her some from the factory.'

'She didn't look poor,' said Susie, 'and her father's job must pay well, I should think.'

'Well, you can never tell,' said Chinese Lady. 'Some people put a brave face on poverty and such-like.'

'Like my mum and dad did,' said Susie, 'but I'm sure Mum's brave face didn't include not wearing a slip.'

'Susie, I should think not,' protested Chinese Lady. 'I don't know anyone more respectable than your dear mother. As I mentioned to Sammy once, if he'd been only half as respectable, I'd of been a happier woman. Of course, he didn't take any notice of me, he kept on consorting with people I wouldn't open the door to. Still, he's got his good points, I won't say he hasn't.'

'Yes, they show up now and again, Mum,' said Susie tongue in cheek.

'Well, that's a comfort,' said Chinese Lady. 'Now I think I'll go up and sit with Edwin for a bit. I wonder if he knows where the Government's going to send Boots? It didn't ought to be sending him anywhere, not after all he's done for his country, but . . .' Her voice was lost to Susie as she left the kitchen to go upstairs. She was still talking on her way up.

*　　*　　*

'Leah,' said Rachel, at home with her younger daughter, 'this letter from Edward. Am I to believe it's completely serious, that he definitely intends to propose marriage to you next year?'

'Yes, Mama,' said Leah.

'He's in love with you?'

'Yes, Mama, and he asked if it embarrassed me,' said Leah.

'And did it?' asked Rachel, gentle with her daughter.

'Mama, I should be embarrassed at Edward being in love with me?' said Leah. 'My life, I should say not. I'm still giddy with happiness.'

'Well, I've thought about his letter since receiving it this morning,' said Rachel, 'and I want you to know I'm not going to be against it. Your life is your own, and if—' She paused. She had been going to say that if she had been able to follow her own wants and wishes, she herself might have married outside her religion. 'And if some mixed marriages don't work out, others do, and so, I hope, will yours to Edward if it comes about.'

'Oh, Mama, thank you,' said Leah.

'However,' said Rachel, 'I'm not sure that your grandfather won't object. I can't speak to him at the moment.' Isaac Moses, her father, was staying with a lawyer and his family in Hampstead. The lawyer was acting for Isaac in regard to obtaining restitution for all he had lost in the way of bonds, share certificates, deeds and other items when his apartment in Lower Marsh had been bombed out of existence during one of the most destructive German air raids on London. 'When I do have a little talk with him, I hope to make him understand that your happiness must be our first consideration. There, will you leave it to me, darling?'

'Mama, I'm always ready to leave everything about everything to you,' said Leah. 'I'd marry Edward tomorrow, but he thinks we're not old enough yet.'

'He's a sensible young man,' said Rachel. 'Much could happen in a year at your ages. Perhaps what you both want now won't be what you want in twelve months' time.'

'Oh, I'm sure we both understand that,' said Leah. 'Edward thinks the war could be over by this time next year, and that in peacetime we could examine ourselves more calmly than in wartime.'

'Examine yourselves?' said Rachel.

'Well, perhaps he didn't say exactly that, but I'm sure it's what he meant,' said Leah.

Rachel smiled.

'Did you know that Edward's brother Bobby is waiting for an armistice before he marries his French sweetheart, Helene Aarlberg?' she asked.

'Oh, yes, Edward mentioned it to me quite a while ago,' said Leah.

'Then I suppose Bobby is being wise too,' said Rachel. 'I should mention one thing, and that's that I think our way of life is in favour of you and Edward, or we wouldn't be working for Sammy Adams on our Sabbath, would we?'

'Rabbi Symonds doesn't mind,' said Leah.

'Well, he's an English rabbi who guards our religion, but accepts the sensibleness of conforming to some English customs,' said Rachel.

'What shall we do now, praise Vera Lynn and the white cliffs of Dover?'

'Turn the radio on,' said Leah, 'and perhaps she'll be singing the song.'

She wasn't, but there was more good news about the Allied advance in Italy. Although it was slow, the Germans were being pressed remorselessly.

Chapter Eighteen

Mrs Cassie Brown, about to prepare a light midday meal for her dad and the children, answered a knock on her front door. A burly balding bloke in shirt, trousers and braces addressed her.

'Kids,' he said.

'Beg pardon?' said Cassie, looking quite nice in a floral-patterned apron.

'Kids. They yourn?'

'I do happen to have a girl and boy,' said Cassie.

'Well, young missus,' growled the burly bloke, 'do us a favour and keep 'em to yerself. Me domain ain't a penny bazaar, it's me private 'ome that I share with me old lady.'

'Might I request your name and what you're talking about?' asked Cassie, taking umbrage.

'I'm Jack Hobday, and so's me old lady—'

'Your wife's Jack Hobday, same as you?'

'Mrs Jack Hobday, and she ain't keen on kids running in and out,' said the burly man. 'I dunno, you leave yer front door open to let a bit of air in, and what happens? I asks yer, what happens?'

'Draughts?' said Cassie, always capable of standing her ground, especially in defence of her children.

'Draughts? Draughts? Now would I come and knock at yer door on account of any draughts? I tell yer, ten seconds after I open me front door in come kids, two of 'em. In and out they run, in and out, jumping on me mat, and when I holler at 'em about where they come from, it's here, they say. This house, young missus, which makes 'em yourn.'

'Oh, dear,' said Cassie. Muffin and Lewis had been used to playing with next door's children in the Wiltshire village, and that play included taking advantage of an open front door. The neighbours didn't mind. It was scampering play, with a bit of jumping, but if kids weren't lively, said the neighbours, if they didn't go racketing and scrumping, you'd have to think about taking them to see the doctor.

'Well, I'm sorry, Mr Hobday,' said Cassie, 'I'll talk to them.'

'Yus, I'd recommend that,' said Mr Hobday, giving his braces an aggravated flip. 'You're new round here, ain't yer?'

'No, my husband and me lived here until just after the war started,' said Cassie, 'but he's in the Army now and I've been living in the country with our boy and girl.'

'Well, me and me old lady – here, what's going on?' Mr Hobday stepped back to scowl up the street. 'Well, can yer believe it? They're at it again, the little perishers.'

Cassie came out and looked. There were Muffin

and Lewis, six doors up, running in and out through the open gate.

'Oh, lor',' she said.

'Kids, I dunno,' said Mr Hobday. 'Hello, hello, Maudie's on the ruddy warpath.'

Out of the house lumbered an oversized woman, yelling. In her right hand was a saucepan. She was waving it about, and it had GBH written all over it.

'I'm after yer, yer little devils!' she bawled. 'I'll tan yer both!'

Muffin and Lewis fled far up the street. The woman heaved herself rapidly through her gate, her buxom bigness loosely shaking, as if most of it had come adrift. It had rained earlier, and as soon as she put one foot on the wet pavement, the sole of her shoe skidded, and she collapsed in slow, heavy motion. Her expansive bottom softly thudded on the pavement. She didn't howl, she only heaved the sigh of a body sadly put upon.

'That's unfortunate, specially on a wet pavement,' said Mr Hobday. 'Kids. I knew it, I knew this wasn't going to be me old lady's lucky day. I can tell, yer know, I'm prophetic. I told her first thing this morning. Don't go out today, I told her, do some ironing. Then I had second thoughts. No, don't do no ironing, I told 'er, the iron'll drop on yer foot.'

'Mr Hobday, is that your wife that's sittin' on the pavement?' said Cassie.

'That's her, that's Maudie,' said Mr Hobday. 'Kids, I tell yer. We've had Hitler and his ruddy bombs, but we ain't had too many kids, seeing most've been in the country. Pity you brought yourn

208

back, young missus.' He shook his head gloomily.

'Mr Hobday, aren't you goin' to see to your wife?' asked Cassie.

'Not while she's still holding that saucepan,' said Mr Hobday.

Mrs Hobday gave up sighing. She hollered.

'Jack Hobday, come 'ere, you 'ear me?'

'Be with yer in a tick,' called Mr Hobday. 'I got me foot caught in this here lady's gate for the present.'

'Come 'ere!'

Cassie hurried up to the aggravated lady, who had managed to unfold her abundant self and clamber to her feet, saucepan still in her hand.

'Mrs Hobday, pleased to meet you,' said Cassie. 'Sorry about my children, they're sort of over-active. I hope you're not hurt, are you?'

'Hurt? Course I ain't.' Large Mrs Hobday's well-padded body did look pain-proof. 'Just me dignity. Them kids yourn?'

'Well, yes—'

'In and out, in and out,' growled the fat lady, 'jumping in over me step onto me mat, jumping out again, I ain't been more sorely tried since we was bombed out of Bermondsey and moved in here. Them kids, where are they?'

'Mrs Hobday, you're not going after my children with that saucepan, are you?' said Cassie.

'No, course not, I've had some of me own, ain't I? I sent me old man to talk to you about me inter-rupted privacy, and what did he do? Left the door open again, didn't he? And in come them kids again, jumping like circus fleas, didn't they? Where is he? I ain't brought me best saucepan out 'ere for nothink.'

Cassie turned, just in time to see Mr Hobday doing a fast runner that took him into Walworth Road. He disappeared. I don't believe this, she thought, it's like the old South London Palace that used to put on music hall turns.

'He's gone, Mrs Hobday,' she said, 'but I'm sure he didn't leave your front door open on purpose.'

'Wait till he comes back,' said Mrs Hobday, 'I'll learn 'im.'

'I'll speak to my children,' said Cassie, noting that Muffin and Lewis were keeping well out of the way.

'You do that, dearie,' said Mrs Hobday, 'I don't want no more running and jumping on me doormat.'

I'm home, thought Cassie, I'm home in Walworth.

Mrs Polly Adams, back in the delightful cottage by the village of Corfe Castle in Dorset, was gardening. If she was middle-aged (as she was, much to her disgust) she was still a woman with a flair for ex-uberant living, and a vivacious personality that had never allowed the years to blunt its fine edge. For her gardening, she wore gumboots, skirt and shirt-blouse without looking like a cabbage. While hoeing, she was thinking about the disappearance from Dorset of the larger part of the American troops. Reasons for? Plenty. But there could be a particular one. Very particular. Was Hitler going to get it in the back of his neck at last, and while he had his work cut out in dealing with successive Russian offensives?

The twins were running about.

'Mummy!' yelled Gemma. 'There's a rabbit!'

'A baby one!' yelled James.

'Curses,' said Polly.

'What, Mummy?' asked Gemma.

'Shoo it off, darlings,' called Polly, 'it'll bring its whole family to eat my lettuces.' She had taken determinedly and then enthusiastically to her vegetable plot.

'Mummy, it's there!' shouted James.

A small white-tailed bunny whisked past Polly.

Gemma and James came running. The bunny disappeared into the bushy hedge.

'Oh, it's gone,' said Gemma, and she and James gazed dolefully up at their mother. Polly smiled, loving the wonder of knowing they really were hers. Life in one's middle age would be heavenly, she thought, if only the war wasn't going to take Boots away from her for God knows how long. Whether he and the battalion had embarked or not, she didn't know. She'd had a letter from him two days ago, but he'd said nothing about date or destination.

'Darlings, we can't encourage visits from bunny rabbits,' she said, 'they'll eat up everything we grow.'

'Couldn't we share?' asked Gemma.

'Yes, couldn't we?' asked James, in whom Polly always saw Boots.

'We'll see,' she said, and off the twins went to search for the rabbit and give it news that held a promise of hospitality.

A very attractive young lady in a WAAF's uniform came out from the kitchen.

'I'm back, Aunt Polly, but I'm goin' out again this evening,' she said, and Polly regarded her silently. Kate Trimble was on leave from her station at the moment. Orphaned, she was encouraged to regard the cottage as her home. 'Something wrong, Aunt Polly?'

'Are you going out with Captain Walters again?' asked Polly.

'Well, yes,' said Kate.

'Does David know you're becoming very attached to Captain Walters?' asked Polly. Captain Elmer Walters was an American Army officer based near Wareham with a unit still in position. David was Boots's nephew, the son of Tommy Adams, waiting at the moment for a call-up that would enable him to go into the RAF.

'No, David doesn't know,' said Kate, looking a little guilty.

Polly knew David felt he had an understanding with Kate, but she also knew a uniform had a glamorous appeal for this young lady, especially an American uniform. David had been an exceptional help to Kate when her only close relative, her Aunt Hilary, had been arrested over two years ago on suspicion of being an agent for Germany. It left Kate, sixteen at the time, completely alone, and David had galloped to the rescue immediately. Polly didn't think Kate should easily forget that. On the other hand, she accepted that a good deed, however exceptional, didn't mean Kate was bound to David for life.

'Kate,' she said gently, 'I think you should tell him.'

'But I'm not actually in love with Captain Walters,' said Kate.

'Is it possible, though, that he's in love with you?' asked Polly.

'Oh, lor',' sighed Kate, a cockney from Camberwell, 'he keeps saying he is. Oh, here's a letter for you. It was on the mat, a late delivery.'

The post wasn't as punctual as in former days, nor were there twice-daily deliveries.

The letter was from Boots to tell her the corps was in position for embarkation, and that only by a stroke of luck had he been able to catch the post. He couldn't, unfortunately, tell her when she might next hear from him, but to remember that out of touch didn't mean out of mind. Well, she wasn't the kind of woman – or wife – who could slip easily from the memory, and as for the twins he'd be thinking of them every day. He dealt cheerfully with family matters, saying he was happy to know his stepfather was upright again after his horizontal spell, the kind of position he'd never favoured except for his nightly sleep, and that his recovery had made Chinese Lady count her blessings. All in all, the letter in its lighthearted nature was what his mother would have called airy-fairy, and it made Polly suddenly feel it hid a lot more than it revealed. One phrase caused her to think. 'In position for embarkation.' In position? She'd never come across that before. A unit simply travelled by train or road to the relevant port and went aboard a waiting troopship. It could take time, of course. Hours. All day sometimes. Did being in position mean the corps was camped indefinitely on a dockside?

Never. Troops under orders for overseas duty did not arrive at a dock until the day of sailing or, at a pinch, the day before.

'Aunt Polly, is there something in the letter you don't like?' asked Kate. 'It's from Uncle Boots, isn't it?' She had recognized the writing on the envelope.

'Yes, Kate. It's just that he's about to go overseas again.'

'Oh, that's hard luck, Aunt Polly, is he goin' back to Italy?'

'God knows,' said Polly, keeping to herself her suspicion that Boots was set to be involved in an invasion of France. It had to be that, it had to be the overdue Second Front. Oh, bloody hell, she thought, and wondered, as she often did, why love never went away to let simple content settle in.

Boots, in fact, was incarcerated, with his corps, and thousands of other officers and men, in a designated area that no man was permitted to move outside or to communicate by letter or phone with any person beyond it. Such letters that were written would not be posted until the day after departure.

The wait for the off was going to be nerve-racking, the date governed by conditions, the need for secrecy absolute. Nothing could be done about Germany's acceptance that an attempted invasion was inevitable, but everything possible had been done to deceive them as to time and landing area. Field-Marshal Rommel was in command of Hitler's Western defences, and represented a formidable foe indeed to catch off guard.

*   *   *

A Commando force, in which Colonel Lucas and Tim were present, waited at an airfield.

In London, at the Free French headquarters, liaison officer Subaltern Eloise Lucas, wife of Colonel Lucas, was being kept in the dark, but there were hummings and murmurs that created tingles of excitement.

That night, suspicions burning, Polly lay awake. I'm going to have a breakdown at the thought of Boots being thrown into France against a million iron-jawed Nazi fanatics. They're freaks. They like marching into hell for demon Hitler. That man's unfortunate mother must have had a carnal visitation from Satan himself. On the other hand, Polly old girl, it's got to be opened up, this Second Front, and in the years to come when the twins ask me what their father did in the war against the mad *Fuehrer*, I'll be able to tell them he landed on his doorstep and asked to have five minutes alone with him.

Oh, good thinking, Polly, now have hysterics.

Hysterics didn't arrive, however. Instead, she dropped off. She had not driven an ambulance for four years over the muddy roads of France for nothing.

Polly could look at the devil without flinching.

Chapter Nineteen

Saturday evening

They sat at the kitchen table, Caterina Angeli and Pilot Officer Nick Harrison, playing a card game by the light of a candle lamp. There was no electricity in the region. Supply was cut from eight every evening until six in the morning, and sometimes later. Under the German occupation, Italy was becoming an impoverished country, although in the south, the Allied armies had liberated the people. In the north, however, the Germans were still thick on the ground, and doing their worst in their hunt for Italian Jews. They had received help from collaborators in other occupied countries. They received none from Italians, not even from those who were still adherents of Mussolini, currently the head of a tinpot Fascist state in the extreme north of Italy.

The Allied advance was grinding on slowly, and it was Nick's fifth day in the house of his Italian Samaritan. They knew each other now. They had exchanged names, after all, as well as personal details. She had told him a great deal about her late husband, Pietro Angeli, a courageous partisan who had died a vicious death at the hands of the Gestapo. Nick had told her about his wife and children, and the bombing raids suffered by the people of Britain since 1940. Caterina said war was always terrible, but who could forgive the German people for the way they had turned this war into the most barbaric conflict ever known? They had caused the Allies to reciprocate in kind, for it was true, wasn't it, that German towns and cities were being devastated by Allied bombers?

'Very true,' said Nick.

'They cannot complain,' said Caterina, 'they worship Hitler as if he were God, and they carry out evil deeds for him. When they are defeated – and you must defeat them, Nicki – they will try to make excuses. My Pietro told me there can be no excuses, that they knew how Hitler and his SS treated the Jews well before the war began, and they stood aside. Worse, many of them informed on Jewish neighbours, and Pietro said thousands have been sent to die in terrible camps. Mussolini at least did not attempt to deliver a single Italian Jew to Hitler, and nor did he wish to fight Britain or America. France, yes, perhaps, because of Corsica. He always said it would be a mistake to fight your country, and I am happy to make up for that mistake by looking after you until your soldiers arrive.'

'I'm happy that you're happy,' said Nick.

'Ah, we are happy friends, yes?' said Caterina.

'As a friend, I'll do something about that old bike

sometime, say tomorrow, while you're at church,' said Nick.

'But what is old is old,' said Caterina.

'I'll give it a lift before old age collapses it,' said Nick.

'A lift?'

'I'll perk it up.'

'What is perk it up?'

'I'll get rid of its creaks and make it sing sweetly instead,' said Nick.

'But who would bother?' asked Caterina. 'In Italy, everything is used until it falls to pieces.'

'I'll bother,' said Nick, 'and give it a few more years of life.'

Caterina smiled and shrugged. What did a few creaks and jangles matter?

All the same, Nick gave it a go. On Sunday morning, he took the bicycle to pieces while she was at Mass. He got rid of much rust, cleaned the wheel spokes and rims, oiled everything that needed oiling, took the kinks out of the mudguards with a muffled hammer, polished all metal surfaces, and reassembled the machine. When Caterina returned from church, the bike was shining. She tried it, and it hummed very sweetly. She expressed delight. For Nick, it had been something to do, since she insisted every day that he must not go out and show himself, however much he needed exercise, nor answer the door if anyone should call. She reminded him frequently that there were German SD men in the village, as well as the man Enrico Bonetti, who called himself a patriot, but was still a Fascist in her opinion. Friends of hers were watching him all the time, for she knew something had made him sneak up on her house and prowl around it. She had persuaded her friends to believe that Bonetti suspected she was a partisan herself.

'That bike will last a few more years now,' said Nick, while she was still purring over it.

'Ah, you are a lovely man, Nicki,' she said. 'See, you have turned it into a new one. But you have not been outside with it, have you?'

'No, I haven't shown as much as a toe out of your door,' said Nick.

'Good,' she said. 'There are no whispers about you, but a toe would be enough to bring eyes to my door and then there would be many whispers. If only one reached the ears of Enrico Bonetti, it would be enough to satisfy him that you are here, and you would have to run.'

'That's the man you think is a Fascist?' said Nick.

'Yes,' said Caterina. 'He denies it, of course, and laughs at the idea, but if I ever found out he was the one who betrayed my Pietro, I would have to kill him. You would agree, Nicki?'

'Yes, as long as you had an alibi,' said Nick.

'Who needs an alibi in such a war as this, when everyone is killing everyone else?' said Caterina.

'There's no answer to that,' said Nick, and thought of his parents, his resilient mother, his care-free father, and his likeable sisters. What was the war doing to them, was it changing them, making them hard and revengeful? He hoped not, although he knew himself to be very different from the young man whose world was happily governed by his enthusiasm for football and his love for Annabelle.

'Nicki,' said Caterina, 'I heard after Mass that the fighting is very fierce, but that the British and Poles are pushing at the Germans every day. So they will be here tomorrow, perhaps. They are expected in this region, yes, because the guns are getting louder, and the German secret police in the village are getting ready to leave.'

'Louder means nearer,' said Nick.

'Then so are your comrades,' said Caterina. 'It is not too bad for you, waiting here?'

'If I'm impatient,' said Nick, 'I'm also well off. I'll wait a day or two longer.'

In the evening, they played another game of cards by the light of the lamp. Cribbage. Caterina knew the game and was quick at it.

'Seven,' said Nick, placing the card face up on the table.

'Fifteen for two!' exclaimed Caterina exultantly, showing an eight, and pegging her score.

'Twenty-one for a run of three, six, seven and eight,' smiled Nick, putting a six down. He was in fine fettle, his leg healing nicely, and he frankly found Caterina enjoyable company. 'Got you there, Catie.'

'Ah, you think so?' she said, and put down a ten. 'Thirty-one for two. Now who is winning this game?'

'You are,' said Nick, 'but I warn you, I don't like losing.' He stiffened, sure he had heard a little noise outside the back door. Caterina heard it too. She sprang to her feet, darted and locked the back door with a silent turn of the key. She looked at Nick. He nodded and disappeared fast. Someone knocked on the door. Caterina took her time to answer it.

From out of the darkness, a man smiled at her, then spoke to her. Caterina was friendly, responsive and natural. A few minutes later, she softly called from the foot of the stairs.

'Nicki?'

He reappeared and came silently down the stairs.

'No trouble?' he whispered.

'A friend to tell me he has been listening to Allied short-wave broadcasts on his concealed radio, and that the Germans are now retreating fast. The Allies have broken through. He says the Canadians are going straight for Frosinone, that the British and Polish are east of the Canadians, and in the west the Americans are on the coastal roads that will take them to Rome if they can break the Germans again. It is good, yes?'

'If it's good for you and Italy, it's good for me,' said Nick.

'My friend also told me it's not known if either the retreating Germans or the advancing British will pass through Asconi, but if some of the Germans do, no-one is to demonstrate or to provoke them.'

'Who is your friend?' asked Nick.

'Our priest,' said Caterina.

'Have you been to confession since my arrival?' asked Nick.

'Yes,' she said.

'Was that why he came to give you this news?' asked Nick.

'He did not say so, and would not,' said Caterina.

'But he knows I'm here?'

'I never speak of my confessions,' said Caterina.

221

'But you are a good man, Nicki, and if someone brings news that is happy for you, let us be grateful. I will remember you when you have gone.'

'We'll remember each other,' said Nick. 'Shall we finish the game?'

'Of course,' said Caterina, 'and with some wine, eh, my *Inglese*?'

'You talk my language in more ways than one,' said Nick.

'I am pretty good, yes?' she smiled.

'Wizard,' said Nick.

They finished the game and what was left of a bottle of wine, and then Nick said he'd go up.

'I'll get some sleep in,' he said, 'in case the Eighth Army gets here at the crack of dawn.'

Caterina, taking up the lamp, asked softly, 'Do men of the RAF make much love to women?'

'Not while I'm looking,' said Nick. 'Myself, I only make love to my wife, and that's not been often this last year or so. It's the bloody old war.'

'Do you love your wife, Nicki?'

'Yes, very much,' said Nick, 'and my children.'

'Then I wish victory to the Allies and your happy return to your wife and children,' said Caterina.

She rode her refurbished bicycle to school in the morning. Three minutes after she'd gone, Nick swore to himself. He'd made a mistake, a mistake neither of them had realized. The damned bike. Her pupils and anyone else who saw it would want to know who had improved the look of the machine and done away with its creaks and jangles. What would she say to them, that she had done it herself? She must.

A little after ten, when he was busying himself by cleaning the white-washed walls of her kitchen, the sudden noise of heavy vehicles stunned his ears. He ran up to his bedroom, the place of religious pictures, and from the window his view brought to his eyes two troop-carrying German trucks full of soldiers of the Third Reich. They were preceded by two open cars containing officers, and followed by two German Tiger tanks that looked enormous against a cluster of houses roofed with warm brown tiles. Behind them were other military vehicles. People were out of their homes, staring at what was passing through. Germans in retreat. The people melted away. Germans in retreat were never good-tempered.

The convoy stopped, and two minutes later Caterina ran into her house.

'Nicki!'

Nick was down in a flash.

'The ruddy foe,' he said.

'Yes, and the bicycle, and many questions about it, and I laughed but made no answer. Enrico Bonetti was looking on and smiling, and telling me the Germans are searching for an RAF pilot. How did he know they were unless he has been in touch with them? Now they are here.'

'If they're retreating, they won't stop to look for an airman who might or might not be here,' said Nick.

'They are talking to the men, and Enrico Bonetti

is among the men,' said Caterina. 'He will make a loud protest, they will drag him away, and then, having made himself look a good patriot in front of people, he will talk. He will tell them about an old bicycle on which someone has performed a miracle, and which belongs to the widow of a man who was hanged as a partisan. Nicki, we must both go, south over the fields, and quickly.'

Nick noted her deep concern, thought about her husband, tortured before being hanged, and said, 'Yes, quick, then.'

They were out of the house and away in a very short time, Caterina wearing a jacket over her blouse and holding her handbag, Nick fully kitted and carrying a bottle of wine. He knew the necessity for keeping thirst at bay if their flight lasted all day. The weather was cloudy and fresh, the fields of common land running adjacent to vineyards. The uneven ground made the going a little rough, but they went at a good pace, alternately running and walking, Nick's healing leg no great problem, and they left the village well behind after ten minutes.

'It is only a kilometre and a half to the road that will take us south,' said Caterina, flushed and heated.

About a mile, thought Nick.

'What are the odds, I wonder, on us meeting up with the Poles or my own lot?' he mused.

'Odds are always a matter of luck,' said Caterina. 'One can hope for good luck, but never rely on it.'

'Well, if it arrives, we'll both shake hands with it,' said Nick.

Away to their left, in the east, the heights of the Apennines merged with the sky. Ahead, the aspect was of level countryside, although the ground was a mixture of dips and tufty hillocks. He could not see the road, but it was there in the distance, Caterina assured him. They had to reach it and stay close to it, for it was the road by which the retreating German column had reached Asconi, and Nick assumed, reasonably, that some Allied forward units were also using it in their advance and pursuit.

On they went, and the rough grassy ground gave way to the more difficult terrain that forced them to repeatedly veer and to skirt the tufty hillocks from which sprang thistle and thorn. They ran, they walked, they ran, they walked. A faint buzzing noise began to disturb them. They looked back. About four hundred yards behind them, a small tracked vehicle was eating up the rough ground.

'There, that is bad luck,' breathed Caterina.

'Catie, bad luck is something you have to fight,' said Nick, and they broke from a walk into another run. Nick wondered what good the road would be to them now, since it would put the chasing German vehicle hard on their tails. Germany's treatment of prisoners of war was not always what it should have been, and as for a woman who had sheltered an RAF pilot, only God knew what might happen to her.

Nick ran and Caterina ran, her skirt whipping, his leg now feeling sore and his hand letting go of the bottle of wine. The tracked vehicle dipped and lifted in its chase, its engine a loud buzz. What happened next was an assault on the senses and an attempt to kill or maim them. It was the noisy, repetitive spat of machine-gun fire. Bullets whistled above them and kicked at the rugged, tufty ground behind them.

'*Mama mia*!' gasped Caterina.

'Run, Catie,' hissed Nick, 'it's only an attempt to make us stop. Run.'

It was reasonable, in any case, to assume the machine-gunner couldn't line up his target while the vehicle was rising and dipping. That assumption held good when the next burst of fire went wildly awry. Nick glimpsed the road then, a thin dusty grey line intersecting the green ground.

'There!' panted Caterina.

'Right, go for it.' Nick saw the thin grey line broaden as they ran. Legs were tiring, and the unevenness of their going, the skirting avoidance of hillocks, became a serious handicap. Behind them, the tracked vehicle charged forward with obvious menace, then stopped. The machine-gunner lined up the target, a running man and woman.

Propitiously, Caterina stumbled and fell at the moment the gun fired. Nick threw himself flat beside her. Flights of bullets passed close above them. The vehicle began to charge forward again, its officer suspecting the prey had been hit.

Nick raised his head, saw the oncoming grey gun-carrier, came up on his knees and pulled at Caterina.

'Yes, yes,' she gasped, and then they were both on their feet and running again. From around a bend in the road appeared another tracked vehicle, dark grey and huge, the long barrel of its gun pointing the way, a soldier's head and shoulders visible, field

226

glasses looped around his neck. He was riding a Sherman tank, one of many now being used by the British Eighth Army.

Nick forgot his sore leg and rushed over the ground, waving his flying helmet and gesturing towards the German vehicle. Up went the field glasses to the eyes of the tank commander. He shouted something. The tank came to a halt, its gun turret swivelled and the long snout was laid on the target.

The German vehicle was turning in hasty retreat, tracks gouging the ground. The Sherman's gun fired. The shell struck the rear of the German carrier. The explosion that followed caused it to lift off, to split apart and to burst into flame. Bodies tumbled.

'Oh, my God,' breathed Caterina, white and staring.

'This time, Catie, good luck came our way,' said Nick, hardened to that kind of picture. He put an arm around her shoulders, gave her a squeeze, then ran to speak to the tank commander, a captain, who was leading a detachment of advance armour of 13 Corps, of the British Eighth Army. Nick, having quickly stated who he was and how he came to be here, imparted the news that there were Tiger tanks and some German infantry in Asconi.

'Thanks. We'll chase them out. Get yourself aboard a rear vehicle and we'll drop you in Frosinone in a couple of hours. Who's the lady?'

Nick thought of Bobby and what he had said about Helene.

'The lady's my saviour.'

'Straight from heaven?' asked the unshaven lieutenant.

'No, straight off a bicycle in Asconi,' said Nick.

'Get the lady aboard our medical transport, and we'll drop her back home. What about those buggers over there?'

'I think those buggers over there are all stone dead,' said Nick.

'Can't stop for a look. I'm pushing on. Hope your squadron leader can find you a new plane. Better for your record than mucking about in the wilds of Italy with a beautiful saviour and her bicycle.' The tank commander grinned, issued an order, and as the Sherman began to grind forward again, he gave Nick and Caterina the V for Victory sign.

'Ah, thank you, yes!' called Caterina. '*Viva Winston Churchill!*'

It was back in Asconi a little later that she said goodbye to Nick, while a waiting truck driver gave him five minutes to make his farewell.

'After the war, come to England, Catie, and stay with me and my family for a while,' he said.

'After the war, who knows?' she said. She meant who could tell what might happen to either of them before the war was over?

'You'll get an invitation,' said Nick.

'To meet your wife, Nicki?'

'To meet her and my family,' said Nick.

'Hurry it up, Admiral, I ain't got all bleedin' day!' hollered the truck driver, a veteran Desert Rat who wanted to get to the morning brew-up, which wasn't as easy in Italy as in the Sahara. There, where you and your mates could have umpteen square miles of the desert all to yourselves, you spilled sand into a pan, soaked it with petrol, lit it and brewed up on it.

'Goodbye, Nicki,' said Caterina.

'I don't like goodbyes at the best of times,' said Nick, 'and this one's a swine. What can I say except thanks for everything, and for the privilege of knowing you?'

'That is so English,' said Caterina with a little shake of her head and a smile. She did what came naturally to an Italian woman. She kissed him, full on the mouth, and with warm Latin affection. 'That is to tell you you are a fine man, Nicki, and that my Pietro would have liked you very much.'

'And you are a fine woman, *and* a great runner,' said Nick. '*Ciao*, Catie.'

'*Ciao*, Nicki,' said Caterina, and watched him walk to the truck and climb aboard next to the driver, a British Army corporal.

The truck moved off. Nick waved to her. She blew him another kiss.

She watched until the truck disappeared.

The Germans had gone, retreating in disciplined fashion and without panic at the approach of the British armoured units, and the people around the square were laughing and shouting. Their village had been liberated.

Enrico Bonetti was not there himself. He was dead, along with a German officer and machine-gunner out there in the fields.

Caterina Angeli sighed and went home.

Chapter Twenty

Late May

'A week from today?' said the man known as Roget, leader of Marne's main Resistance group.

'A week,' affirmed a woman known as Lise, a leading light of the Epernay cell. They were drinking wine at an outside table of a café in the main square of Epernay, the classic capital of the champagne industry. The afternoon was warm and caressing. 'The train will leave precisely at ten in the morning. The information comes from our most trustworthy source in Paris.'

'Good,' said Roget, 'although I've known trustworthy sources that have proved regrettably unreliable.'

'Ah, what a miserable France we have,' said Lise, 'pigeons are eating pigeons, dogs are eating dogs. No-one agrees with anyone else about how to redeem our country.'

'Redemption will only begin when de Gaulle has thrown out Hitler's tyrants and French puppets,' said Roget.

'De Gaulle is a long time coming,' said Lise. 'The Communists are already here, waiting, skulking, murdering. They are assassinating our friends as well as our enemies. Where are our new friends?'

'Maurice and Lynette?' said Roget. 'With the truck.'

'And where is the truck?'

'Hidden,' said Roget, watching people. One watched instinctively. The Gestapo planted their agents in every town and city. 'Tonight I'll be driving it to the appointed place.'

'Trucks cost a fortune,' said Lise.

'Yes, old trucks as well as new,' said Roget.

'Has anyone seen a new truck lately?' asked Lise.

'Not lately,' said Roget, 'but Maurice and Lynette have enough funds to buy either old or new.'

Two uniformed SS men strolled by, thumbs in their belts.

Roget, regarding their backs, issued a little dart of spit. It struck the pavement beside his chair.

'That is disgusting,' said Lise.

'Not on this occasion,' said Roget.

'Spitting is always disgusting,' said Lise, while believing nothing was more so than Himmler's Gestapo.

A few miles east of Epernay, a man and a woman climbed down from a capacious old truck that was standing in a clearing deep in a long stretch of woodlands adjacent to a dirt road. The truck had been purchased through the medium of shady and shadowy black marketeers, the equivalent of London spivs. It was still in good working order, with reliability guaranteed. Guaranteed, it must be said, by exhaustive tests over two days, since assurances from any spivs were about as valuable as a bucket of sand in the middle of the Sahara.

The doors locked, the man and woman sat down with their backs against the broad trunk of a tree. The woman unwrapped food. She broke a stick of French bread in half, handed one half to the man, and followed that with a wedge of cheese. They began to eat hungrily. They were alone in a cavern bounded by trees and roofed by the sky.

'Buying this truck and testing it have almost shredded my nerves,' said Helene. 'You are a good negotiator, but a terrible driver.'

'The tests had to be gruelling,' said Bobby, 'I had to throw the truck about before being satisfied it could carry a full load of people up into the hills without breaking down.'

'I feel fortunate to still be alive,' said Helene. 'But I forgive you. I will always be forgiving to you, Bobby.' When they were alone, affectionate intimacy induced them to set aside their code names. 'But I hope Roget will be kinder on my nerves when he drives us out of here tonight. Ah, how I wish this vicious war was over and we could make a home for ourselves.'

'Well, we should aim for that, of course, as a married couple,' said Bobby.

'It will make me very happy,' said Helene. She would not mind living in England, she said, since she was used now to the fact that most of the English were either stuffy or crazy. Bobby said that was a very helpful and civilized attitude, which would encourage him to do his best to knock the stuffiness out of their future neighbours, even if nothing could be done about their peculiarities. 'No, no,' said Helene, 'we must not do anything that will mean a quarrel with people living next to us.'

'Let them stay stuffy, you mean?' said Bobby.

'I am to take you seriously when you speak of knocking them about?' said Helene.

'It was just a thought,' said Bobby.

'A joke, you mean,' said Helene. 'Bobby, perhaps we can buy a farm.'

'That's another thought, an interesting one,' said Bobby, and they talked on about their future, and their wishes and inclinations. That kind of dialogue did much to ease the strains that were the constant affliction of their work for the French Resistance.

Later, when the sun went down and dusk arrived, Roget arrived with it. Within ten minutes, they were on their way, Roget driving the truck, since he knew the area so well and how to stay off the main roads. They headed for their next rendezvous, where they were to meet Roget's group and would have a week to prepare for one more enterprise of risk and danger.

Chinese Lady came out of the kitchen just as the phone rang in the hall.

'Oh, that contraption,' she murmured. However, after years of suspecting the new-fangled thing could electrify a body – she meant electrocute – she had at last accepted it had no dark designs on her, and put herself on friendlier terms with it.

She lifted the receiver.

'Hello?'

'Hi. Who's this?'

Chinese Lady took the receiver away from her ear and looked blankly at it before responding to the peculiar question.

'I'm sure I don't know who you are,' she said, 'and I don't do guessing games. Myself, I'm Mrs Finch.'

'Hi, Granny. Patsy here.'

'Patsy?'

'Patsy Kirk. Is Daniel there?'

'Oh, it's you, Miss Kirk.' What a funny girl, thought Chinese Lady, asking who's this instead of who's that. 'Yes, Daniel's just come in from his work. I'll get him.'

Daniel came on the line after a short while.

'Hello, Patsy girl, how's your good old Pa?'

'Get you, smarty,' said Patsy. 'My good old Pa's in town, broadcasting to the folks back home, as usual. How about taking me to the movies this evening? There's a great fillum on. *Double Indemnity*, with Fred MacMurray and Barbara Stanwyck. Yeah, and Edward G. Robinson as well. Sky-high ratings. You've heard about it, I guess.'

'Actually, no,' said Daniel, 'my life just lately has been revolving round the demanding responsibilities of my job by day, and my new potatoes, spring onions and lettuces by evening. Then there's the news on our wireless, which sort of glues my ears to the set.'

'Daniel, stop being a freak,' said Patsy.

'Beg pardon?' said Daniel.

'Any guy in love with spring onions is a freak,' said Patsy. 'Call for me at twenty after seven. The programme starts at seven forty-five. I'll ride you there on my bike. It's that cinema by Camberwell Green.'

'OK,' said Daniel, 'but I'll do the riding. You sit on the carrier.'

'Listen, handsome,' said Patsy, 'don't push your luck.'

'Listen, saucy,' said Daniel, 'in this country fellers are still on top. Got it?'

'No,' said Patsy, 'it's Stone Age stuff, you dope.'

'Now look here, Topsy—'

'Patsy.'

'Well, Patsy, stop answering me back and take note of our customs. Fellers are on top and, accordingly, treat girls kindly. Got it?'

At the other end, Patsy shrieked with laughter.

'Oh, I like you, Daniel,' she said, her voice a gurgle.

'What's that?' asked Daniel, failing to interpret the gurgle.

'You're cute,' said Patsy.

'That's for kittens, not fellers,' said Daniel. 'Right, call for you later and we'll go by bus. You can't leave your bike outside the cinema. It'll get nicked by some bloke with a sister who wants one for Christmas.'

'But it's not Christmas,' said Patsy.

'In this country,' said Daniel, 'Christmas is always coming.'

'You've got some screwy customs,' said Patsy. 'Still, OK, Daniel, we'll bus there and you can sit next to me.'

'Can't wait,' said Daniel.

'Glad you're thrilled,' said Patsy.

The film was a classic, packed with incidents and suspense. It built up to a terrific climax, and Patsy and Daniel enjoyed it immensely.

Summertime meant twilight was only just beginning to give way to dusk when they left the cinema and walked to the bus stop, but because of the blackout dusk would lead to dense darkness. They talked about the film and how good it was. The night was cool, and there was moisture in the air. Along the South Coast rain was coming down, and the forecast for the immediate future was worrying Churchill and General Eisenhower. Weather for the transport of thousands of troops and tons of armour across the Channel needed to be kind, and it had been finally agreed by the Allies that the last day in May ought to offer the kindest conditions. May was being perverse, however.

A bus pulled up almost as soon as Patsy and Daniel arrived at the stop. They boarded with several other people. Patsy buoyantly climbed the stairs to the upper deck, Daniel following. She put herself in the rear seat. Daniel put himself next to her, and warm hips and shoulders made cosy contact.

The bus, its headlights masked, moved off. Daniel looked at Patsy. Patsy looked at him. The upper deck was semi-dark, for no lights were on, and the few other passengers had their backs to them.

All the same, Patsy made her apparent reservations known by whispering, 'No, you can't, not here.'

'Can't what?' said Daniel.

'Kiss me,' she whispered.

'Is that correct? I mean, I could. What you mean is I mustn't, don't you?'

'Did I say you mustn't?' she asked.

'I said I could,' murmured Daniel.

'Well, go on, then.' Her lips pursed.

'Patsy, you said not here.'

'D'you know you've got a silly smirk on your face?'

'You've got a cute nose on yours.'

'Leave my nose out of it,' said Patsy.

'Well, it's not in the way,' said Daniel, and kissed her. Very nice it was too, her lips fresh and girlish and co-operative.

'My stars,' breathed Patsy, 'you did it.'

'Well, I said I could and you didn't say I mustn't.'

'It didn't mean you had to,' said Patsy.

'But you told me to go on, then.'

'If you don't mind,' said Patsy, 'that was a dare, not an invitation. You're not going to do it again, are you?'

'Do I look as if I am?' whispered Daniel.

'No, you still look kind of smirky,' said Patsy.

'Is it the kind of look you like?'

'How could anyone like a smirky look?'

Up came the conductor, a clippie, a lively lady of

forty or so doing her best with the aid of hydrogen peroxide to hang on to the allure of her blonde hair. GIs fell over themselves to get close to English blondes, whether they were twenty-odd or forty-odd, as long as they hadn't lost control of their figures.

'Fares, if yer please, me lords and ladies,' said the clippie, cap worn at a rakish angle. She turned to Daniel and Patsy.

Something happened to Patsy's skirt. It resulted in a small purse coming to light. She dug into it. Daniel, however, stuck to the custom that as fellers were on top, it was his privilege to stand treat, as he had with the cost of the cinema seats. He pulled coppers from his pocket, and bought two tickets to Danecroft Road. The clippie punched them under the light of a little torch fixed to her dispenser, looked at Patsy, gave Daniel a wink and moved on.

'Wasn't it my turn to pay?' asked Patsy.

'My grandma's against that,' said Daniel. 'Listen, where did that little purse of yours come from?'

'Leg of my panties,' whispered Patsy.

'D'you mean you keep it in your knickers?'

'Yuk. You English guys talk funny about a girl's panties.'

'Where's the purse now?'

'Where it came from.'

'Well,' said Daniel, as the clippie returned to the lower deck, 'I've got to admire how you manage it. Never saw a thing.'

Patsy put her lips to his ear.

'You're not asking to see, are you?'

'See what?'

'Don't play dumb.'

'Look, I'll take your word for it that they're pretty.'

At that point, the air raid sirens blasted off, warning of the approach of German night raiders.

Chapter Twenty-One

The sudden impact of the sirens on unready ears made passengers jump. Patsy, startled, sat bolt upright. Daniel, tensing, wished he'd got her home first. The bus driver, adhering to air raid regulations, brought his vehicle to a stop.

'Air raid, air raid!' yelled the clippie from down below. 'All orf, all orf!'

'Bloody hell,' said one well-dressed top deck passenger, 'I thought the buggers had given up, but they're back.'

Daniel thought the same, since London hadn't suffered any bombing raids for some time.

In fact, Germany had been transferring more squadrons to their hard-pressed Eastern front, where huge Russian armies, backed by countless bombers of their own, were causing certain German generals to curse the day Hitler had launched the invasion of the Soviet Union.

'My stars,' breathed Patsy, 'is it really going to happen?' She and Daniel, with the other top deck passengers, descended and alighted. Lower deck passengers were already scurrying off into the night, towards the nearest public shelter as the staccato wail of the sirens continued. The bus, now carrying only the driver and clippie, moved off to make for its depot at top speed.

'Let's get across the road,' said Daniel. 'We're a bit far from home, and I know where there's a private shelter.'

'Daniel, I don't mind waiting to see where the bombs are going to drop,' said Patsy. 'Well, it's kind of tingling spooky.'

'It'll be kind of tingling blotto if one drops on your head,' said Daniel, standing on the kerb with her. The warning sirens stopped. 'And what would your good old Pa say if all that was left of you were your shoes? Or even only one? Come on.' Darkness had descended, but there was no traffic, and Daniel knew exactly where he was. He took Patsy straight across the road, and edged his way around the remains of a flattened house. They heard the bombers arriving, the heavy drone of Heinkels unmistakable. It was a reminder to Churchill from the *Luftwaffe* chief, Hermann Goering, that he still had an iron fist, even if it was covered with plump flesh.

'Where are we?' asked Patsy, holding Daniel's hand as he skirted the ruins.

'This is my family's old house,' said Daniel. 'That is, it was. A German bomb blew it to pieces over two years ago. That's why we're living with our grandparents. Dad'll have a rebuilding job done after the war.'

'Daniel, it really happened, your house got bombed?' said Patsy, trying to make out exactly what was left of it.

'Fact,' said Daniel, peering ahead in his quest for the now overgrown garden. 'Fortunately, Mum, Dad and Paula were in the shelter. That saved them, and that's where we're going now. By the way, Dad's on standby ARP duty tonight and so is my Uncle Tommy. They'll have put their helmets on and be out by now, I should think.'

The bombers were swarming, the sky vibrating, the noise merging with muffled booms as the first cascades of high explosives struck. The raid was taking in the inner suburbs, the London boroughs and the City. Ack-ack blazed away, the sky too dark for effective action by RAF night fighters. Daniel brought Patsy carefully down some stone steps into the old Anderson shelter at the front of the garden. The shelter was pitch dark, and there was small-sized rubble underfoot. Patsy was awestruck. The shelter and its dark, damp embrace, the riven night sky, the droning bombers and the knowledge that bombs were actually falling, all contributed to a feeling that Satan was lurking and fiendishly grinning. But Daniel's hand was warm and firm around her own.

'Oh, good grief,' she whispered.

'They're getting a lot of this in Germany,' said Daniel. 'Day and night.' Talking, he thought, was better than staying silent. Staying silent was like listening for the bomb that was going to drop on you through the shelter roof. 'I wonder if it's making them think building sandcastles is better than building an empire, after all? That was Hitler's idea, y'know, to build a great German empire. Patsy, are you old enough to remember what the Germans said to that?'

'Wasn't it something like, "*Sieg Heil*, Oh Mighty *Fuehrer*,"?' offered Patsy.

'Sort of "Lead us to it"?' said Daniel. 'Grandpa said to me once that people blind enough to worship the devil end up in hell, the devil's kingdom.' He grimaced in the darkness. 'I suppose they're halfway there now. Should we feel sorry for them, Patsy?'

'Sorry for them?' Patsy sounded slightly over-wrought. 'Daniel, at a time like this, we've got to feel sorry for people who stood and watched Hitler's gorillas beating up Jews and smashing their shops? Listen to all that.' The noise of the bombers was so thunderous and menacing that the shelter seemed absurdly inadequate. 'I think I'm a coward,' she said.

'I know I am,' said Daniel, and talked about life in the West Country as an evacuee in company with sister Bess and brother Jimmy. They were still there. Patsy said she'd been in the West Country herself, at the boarding-school, but braving a raid here was a lot more real than braving the principal there. It made one realize what this sick war was all about.

They talked on, Patsy giving Daniel something to laugh at now and again, and Daniel giving her cause to giggle. It was a courageous dialogue beneath the deadly threat of the laden sky.

'Pa and I were caught in an air raid when we were in London Town one evening,' said Patsy. 'It was during our first week over here. We went down into a deep shelter and never heard a thing, but the raid made Pa send me to that boarding-school well away from London. I hope tonight's bombs won't make him send me back, especially now you're set on taking me to the cinema once a week.'

'Am I?' said Daniel. 'Yes, so I am, and I'll make a note of it.'

'I appreciate the offer, Daniel, I really do,' said Patsy, sharing with him the feeling that talking was good for the beleaguered. The constant droning was oppressive. 'I like it that we're friends.'

'Would you say, in American lingo, that we're buddies?' asked Daniel.

'Sure I would,' said Patsy, then gave it some thought. 'Buddies, you said? Like in an army?'

'No, like you're a girl and I'm a feller,' said Daniel.

'Well, I'm glad you're not a mail box,' said Patsy with a little laugh. There might be rolling thunder above them, but there were no bombs dropping in the immediate area. 'It's crazy dark in here. Daniel, you're my first English guy, d'you know that?'

'I hope your second and third don't get in a hurry to elbow me out,' said Daniel.

'What? Oh, you flathead. Listen, are you going to make a habit of kissing me on buses?'

'Probably,' said Daniel. 'What's your American custom about that?'

'I tell my Pa, and my Pa goes round and kills the guy,' said Patsy.

'That's given me second thoughts about your good old Pa,' said Daniel. He flinched then. Bombs were dropping, after all, in the Herne Hill area, not far from them. The harsh crumping noise of each explosion was unmistakable. Moments later, one bomb crashed down at the foot of Denmark Hill. That brought the roar of an explosion savagely to their ears. Darkened houses shivered, and residents crouched deeper inside their shelters. To Patsy and Daniel, the ground seemed to shudder and the shelter to quiver. Patsy clutched at Daniel.

'Oh, my knees, I'm losing them,' she gasped, at which point the heavy droning mercifully began to lessen.

Noting the receding thunder, Daniel breathed, 'Patsy, let's take a look. If that bomb has smashed some houses, there might be people needing help. Come on, better than staying here and doing nothing.'

'I'll be glad to do anything,' said Patsy, and gritted her teeth as she followed Daniel out of the shelter. He guided her around the remnants of his family's old house, and as soon as they reached the pavement they saw flames flaring high, way down the hill. That and the receding bombers put determined life into them, and they ran. Daniel, who knew every inch of the hill, its road and its pavements, travelled fast through the darkness, hand in hand with Patsy, whose flying legs put their trust in the sureness of his long limbs. The flames gave them light in a short while, enabling them to increase their pace. Down the hill they went. Houses on each side of the road fell away and they reached the empty stretch close to Ruskin Park. There the road was clear of properties, and there on the left, close to the shattered pavement, were the great yellow flames leaping and hissing.

'Bleedin' blind Amy,' gasped Daniel, at one then with his cockney roots. His dad and his Uncle Tommy could still sound off in that way. 'It's gas, Patsy. The bomb smashed a gas main.'

They came to a halt before the searing heat scorched them.

'Daniel, oh, my stars, look!' Patsy was aghast. 'Daniel, look!'

On the other side of the road and a little farther down from the flames, was a car. It was on its side, its bonnet smashed, its windscreen totally absent, its roof crumpled.

'Oh, gawd blimey,' breathed Daniel. 'Stay here, Patsy.'

He ran to the far side of the road, to the pavement, getting himself as far from the hissing, twisting tongues of flame as he could. He felt the heat. It plucked at him. Patsy, watching him running towards the car, gritted her teeth again. If he could get to it, so could she. She went after him.

Daniel reached the car, leaned over it and looked in through the glassless frame of the windscreen. He sucked in breath and expelled it. The light of the flames revealed a man and a woman, both slumped, both unconscious. Their hats were off, their foreheads bleeding. Patsy arrived.

'Daniel—'

'Two people, Patsy. We've got to get them out.'

'Daniel, the auto! It could blow up in this heat.'

Daniel was wrenching at the door handle. It wouldn't even turn. The door was buckled.

'Can you smell petrol?' he panted.

'No – no – Daniel, shouldn't your police and ARP people be here?'

'They'll arrive any moment, Patsy.' Daniel was leaning over the wrecked bonnet now, peering into the car again. 'Let's see what we can do now we're here. Grab my legs.'

He pitched himself over the upturned bonnet, and Patsy, demented with shock but gritty, wrapped her hands around his ankles and held on to him with fingers like limpets. Daniel thrust his head and shoulders through the windscreen frame, and reached in. With the driver's seat uppermost, the driver, the man, was a collapsed bulk, hip and shoulder resting on the unconscious woman, trapped between him and the passenger door.

The sky above Camberwell and Walworth was quiet. The nerve-racking droning had ceased. The last of the bombers had followed other flights north over London to the East End and the docks.

'Daniel, be quick,' begged Patsy, the radiating heat of the burning gas at her back, 'I'm afraid for you.'

Daniel had his hands gripping the lapels of the driver's jacket. He pulled and yanked, but the man was such a dead weight that he had a sick feeling the poor bloke was lifeless. He pulled again, Patsy's tight grip on his ankles giving him leverage. He managed to bring the collapsed victim free of the woman. He simply could not get at her until he had dragged the man out through the windscreen frame. One thing was in his favour. The glass had been completely sucked out, and there were no jagged edges. The loud hissing noise of the flaming gas turned into a roar, and Patsy shuddered as heat seemed to billow around her and Daniel and the car. Daniel was pulling, tugging and wrenching, and the unconscious driver's head appeared at the window frame. Patsy glimpsed a face ghastly white and a bloodstained forehead. Daniel heard a faint moan from the woman. His hands now were under the man's armpits. He pulled with desperate strength. It moved the man only an inch or so.

Down the hill a car came racing. It pulled up with a high-pitched protest from tyres and brakes, and helmeted ARP wardens seemed to expel themselves in a burst of movement. There were five of them, a woman and four men, including Tommy and Sammy. Tommy and Sammy stared in momentary shock at the illuminated figures of a young man and a girl, both recognizable to Sammy. Tommy hadn't yet met Patsy. The young couple looked as if they were trapped around the bonnet of the overturned car. All five wardens rushed at the overturned vehicle as a police car began to approach from the direction of Camberwell Green. At the same time, the clanging bell of a fire-engine was heard.

'Daniel! Patsy!' Sammy shouted as he ran up. 'Leave it, leave it to us!'

'I'd better not let go now, Dad,' gasped Daniel. 'The bloke's a dead weight. All I need is another pair of hands.'

The woman warden, bulky but agile, reached, gripped Daniel's legs just below the knees and used her weight to push Patsy aside. It wasn't a time for begging her pardon first.

'I'll hold him, ducky, you get yourself clear and take a rest.'

'Everything's getting hotter,' gasped Patsy. 'Something's going to blow any moment.'

'Go and wait in Sammy Adams's car, there's a love,' said the ARP lady, applying a beefier grip to Daniel's straining legs to ensure that he didn't tumble in through the windscreen frame. However, she was unable to persuade Patsy to make herself scarce. The American girl stayed where she was. Somehow, in these heart-stopping minutes, she and Daniel had become comrades of the war-torn night.

Sammy ran back to his car, opened the boot and brought out a sledgehammer, something he had kept permanently there since the Blitz on London. He ran back with it. Tommy and Daniel together were heaving at the still unconscious driver, but the dead weight factor and the awkwardness of their position was hardly working in anyone's favour. Sammy swung the sledgehammer and smashed handle and lock of the driving door. The buckled door issued a metallic screech and burst open. Sammy dropped the hammer, put his head and shoulders into the car, and slid his hands around the driver's ribs. He established a firm and strong hold. He hesitated fractionally, then decided however badly damaged the man was, he had to risk worsening his condition in case the heat of the burning gas caused the car to combust.

'Right, got him, Daniel. Got him, Tommy. Let go and let me pull him out.'

Daniel was grateful to let go. His arm and shoulder muscles were at their limit of exertion. Tommy let go and placed his trust in Sammy. Out came the limp body of the driver and another warden lifted the unconscious man clear. Right in over the driving seat went Sammy to take hold of the moaning woman. She was a dead weight too, but only half that of the man. The front of her scalp was seeping blood, staining her forehead. Hit the windscreen, he thought, just before it blew. He dragged her out.

The police had arrived. The fire-engine followed. The gas from the burst main kept feeding the flames, and the heat kept the wardens necessarily distant. The police and the firemen, taking control, pushed everyone even farther back, the injured couple having been gently laid down on a policeman's cape well out of danger. An ambulance was summoned from nearby King's College Hospital to pick up the casualties.

With no further help being required from the wardens, Sammy spoke to Daniel and Patsy.

'Let's get you two home,' he said, 'you're both—' A gusting roar shook the night, and blinding light sprang. 'Holy cows!' he hissed.

The crashed car had blown up and turned into a flaming torch. The safety first precautions insisted on by the police paid off, for no-one was within dangerous distance of the act of explosive combustion, and that included several people who had appeared seemingly out of nowhere to gape at the towering tongues of burning gas. A police inspector was contacting the gas company about shutting off supply, and the firemen turned their hoses on the flaming car. Patsy, standing between Daniel and Sammy, regarded everything with wide-open eyes, little breaths escaping. Sammy said it was time to get her home, and while Tommy and the other wardens remained at the scene of the incident, helping to divert desultory traffic, he drove Daniel and Patsy to Danecroft Road.

'Couldn't get to that incident earlier,' he said. 'We were all at Herne Hill, twenty of us. Jerry chucked several bombs around Half Moon Lane, and made a hell of a mess. A message, relayed through our ARP post, took some of us off. Glad it did, otherwise the people in the car might not have been pulled out in time. You two could have gone up with it. Still, good on you both for having a go, and I'll give you a mention if I ever meet King and Queenie. You could end up being promoted to Lady Patsy Kirk and the hon'rable Duke Daniel of Adams, and receive a fiver each into the bargain.'

'Keep talking, Dad,' said Daniel, seated in the back of the car with Patsy. Not many members of the Adams families ever lost their tongues, never mind the circumstances, and that included himself, he supposed. Well, at the age of twelve and during his last term at school before the war started, his science teacher had said, 'Who's that talking in class? Oh, gasbag Adams, I see.' He grinned at the memory, then thought well, come to that, Patsy hadn't left herself out of the species. She'd contributed any amount of chat in the clammy darkness of that old shelter. Some girls – and some fellers too – would have been struck with nervous silence.

'Mind, I'm not sure either of you ought to have got yourselves that close to the incident,' said Sammy. 'Daniel, me lad, I nearly had kittens when I saw you and Patsy both shaking hands with that car.'

'Oh, we thought we ought to say hello,' said Patsy, now quite exhilarated by the fact that effort had triumphed over disaster. Both occupants of the car had been injured, but an experienced police sergeant had said quite confidently, 'They'll live, miss, they'll live.'

The All-Clear sounded as Sammy turned into Danecroft Road. He stopped outside the large house in which Patsy's father had a rented flat. Patsy and Daniel alighted, and Patsy said goodnight to his dad.

'So long now, Patsy, take care and sleep tight,' said Sammy, giving her a smile.

'Thanks, Mr Adams, you're great,' said Patsy.

'If your dad's doing his wireless talks on Sunday afternoon, come to tea with us,' said Sammy.

'Mr Adams, I'd like that, I really would,' said Patsy.

I'll get some fat shrimps, thought Sammy. Have to touch black market suppliers. Won't tell Susie, she sort of starts walking backwards whenever I mention black market. She's got these Christian principles. So have I, only mine stretch a bit now and again. This time it'll be with the help of John the Baptist, who happens to be a fishy Billingsgate acquaintance of mine.

He waited while Daniel saw Patsy to the front door of the house. In the darkness, Daniel caught the whisk of her skirt. Miraculously, her little purse appeared, and out of it a key. Daniel smiled. She opened the door.

'OK now, Patsy?' he said.

'I'm fine, Daniel,' she said. 'Well, I am now. Call me tomorrow?'

'I'll get you on the blower when I'm home from work,' said Daniel. 'Patsy, I liked having you with me this evening. Proud of you, in fact. Listen, what time will your Pa be home tonight? D'you know?'

'About three in the morning,' said Patsy. 'Over here, we're five or six hours ahead of New England, but I'll be OK, you bet. There are tenants above and below me, and I know them all. 'Night, Daniel, it's been an experience I don't think I'll ever forget.'

He gave her a kiss. She gave him one. They parted, and he went home in the car with his dad. The family had just come back into the house from the shelter.

What happened next, of course, was that Chinese Lady made a large pot of steaming hot tea.

That night, Daniel slept well after lying awake for a while. It was Sammy who couldn't get off. He kept thinking of Daniel and Patsy at that car, lit up by huge flames of burning gas from the other side of the road. If the car had been leaking petrol, it could have blown up and torched them. His repetitive reflections, running about in his head, eventually made him think of the war and how long it had been going on. Nearly five years. Ruddy carbolic, five years. People in their twenties when it started were growing old while it was still going on. They'll have wrinkles by the time it's over. I'll get rheumatism and an old man's trouble with me waterworks. And on wartime rations, Susie and Lizzy'll get so skinny they'll fall through their corsets. The day Susie does that'll be the day I'll take to me bed for good. Well, that's if me business can do without me. Business. I seriously ask myself, are Tommy and me going to spend ten more years turning out uniforms and Army knickers, female issue, while Hitler and Japan keep slogging it out with the Allies? I won't say such business is unprofitable. There's handsome bonuses coming regularly to Gertie and her girls at the factory, and mouthwatering fees for the directors, including Boots, which'll help him keep Polly living in the kind of style that suits her, she being upper class, but where's the challenge like there used to be in promoting each year's fancy female fashions? And if Hitler's starting another Blitz on old London, Susie and me'll have to think about sending Paula and Phoebe to live in the country with Bess and Jimmy. If those two little treasures left, I'd get chronic depression, which means gloomy headaches, which I can do without.

He turned in the bed. Beside him, Susie breathed evenly in sound sleep. He thought about their flattened house, and the fact that Susie favoured building a new one on the site. She liked the position, and she liked the idea of eventually having the now overgrown garden put to rights. Susie liked the familiar, she still liked talking about her times in the old house in Walworth, which her family had taken over from his family in 1921, twenty-three years ago. Twenty-three? Stone the crows, that many? And every one of them related to what they had shared, before and after she became his wife. That had been the best move of his life, getting her to the altar of St John's Church, and getting her to say, 'I do.'

Love, honour and obey, that's what she'd promised. It hadn't worked, not the obedience bit. More like the other way round. By rights, the marriage trousers belonged to him, but when he'd mentioned to Boots that he couldn't get them off Susie, Boots said well, let's face it, Sammy, they fit Susie better. Typical. He mused. He dropped off. He slept. It was gone three in the morning.

* * *

In his headquarters buried deep in a forest in East Prussia, from which he was directing the war against Russia, Hitler was still up. He was keeping his clique of yes-men up with him. He was a compulsive night owl, and rarely rose before midday. At the moment he was ranting about the incompetence of German generals who had failed to smash Russian offensives and obliterate the subhuman hordes of Stalin. Hitler, regarding himself and his directives as infallible, was now given to literally foaming at the mouth when indulging in fits of hysterical rage. Spittle ejected as he cursed the idiots who misunderstood his orders, and the traitors who chose not to obey them. No-one among the yes-men pointed out that it was strict obedience to his orders that caused most of the setbacks.

A signal arrived from Goering to inform the *Fuehrer* that the *Luftwaffe* was bombing London.

Hitler ranted about London, Churchill and the incompetence of Goering, who had promised as long ago as 1940 to bring Britain and its war-mongering Prime Minister crawling to Berlin.

'Ah, promises, *mein Fuehrer*,' said a yes-man, 'and the raid itself is quite unnecessary under the circumstances.'

'Himmler, take that man's name!' raved the Fuehrer.

'But, *mein Fuehrer*—'

'Wait, yes.' Hitler calmed down. His blue eyes, thought magnetic by some people and cold by others, showed a glint. 'My scientists. Am I able to put my trust in them, or will they prove as incompetent as some of my generals?'

A rambling monologue developed, and his clique of yes-men listened like men who were collective in their faith, with not a sign that most hated each other.

Chapter Twenty-Two

Over breakfast in the house on Red Post Hill, the talk was about last night's unexpected air raid. Mr Finch was present, convalescing at home while under orders from the Department to take a month off. Sammy, Susie, Paula, Phoebe and Daniel were all at the table, with Chinese Lady presiding as usual over the large family teapot. Eloise, Boots's French-born daughter, always felt no photograph of her English grandmother was complete unless there was a teapot in the foreground. Eloise was sometimes able to get away from her duties in London to spend a weekend at home, where Chinese Lady's teapot was always in evidence.

At the moment, the family matriarch was against talk about the air raid.

'If no-one minds,' she said, 'I'd like to mention we talked about it before we went to bed last night, and this morning it's been on that wireless, which I had to turn off to save hearing it all through breakfast.' Breakfast was porridge and toast, the toast spread with an imitation butter, made by Chinese Lady from a mixture of margarine, milk, Brown and

Poulson's cornflour, and a dash of salt. It passed with a push and made more of the margarine ration. The butter ration itself was kept for Sunday teas and anything a bit special. 'I don't know any wireless that goes on more than ours does about what we only need to hear once.'

'That's a good point, Maisie,' said Mr Finch. 'Perhaps we're the victims of broadcasters who, when there's nothing new to tell us, are compelled by the nature of their medium to endlessly repeat themselves, since under no circumstances must they fall silent.'

'They could play a bit of nice music,' said Chinese Lady, 'but I don't want you to worry about it or go writing to them, Edwin, not when you're supposed to be resting.'

'I wasn't thinking of writing to the BBC, Maisie,' said Mr Finch.

'That's good,' said Chinese Lady, and gave him a little pat. 'Wait till you're a lot better.'

'Was there any good news, Mum?' asked Susie.

'Well, there was talk about the meat ration being cut again,' said Chinese Lady, 'which I don't suppose anyone could say was good news. I can't think why the Government doesn't grow more.'

'More what, Grandma?' asked Daniel.

'More meat, like lamb and beef,' said Chinese Lady.

'Grow it?' said Daniel.

'Now you know what I mean,' said Chinese Lady. 'There's lots of empty fields in this country that could be used. I've seen a lot myself in my time,

258

especially when I used to go on the train to Southend as a girl, and later when me and Edwin used to go all the way to Salcombe with Boots and Lizzy and their children. I never saw so many empty fields in all my life.'

'You sure they weren't sprouting carrots or cabbages?' said Sammy.

'There weren't any cows or sheep on them, I can tell you that,' said Chinese Lady.

'Granny, p'raps they're all full up now,' said Paula.

'Well, there's still places like Hyde Park and Peckham Rye,' said Chinese Lady. 'The Government could put cows and sheep on them, instead of letting people laze about on the grass.' Noting Sammy was yawning, she said, 'Might I ask if everyone had a good night's sleep after the air raid?'

Phoebe's soft brown eyes regarded Sammy.

'Daddy, I fink you're a bit tired,' she said.

'Don't you worry, pet, I've got all me health and strength under lock and key, which I'll open up when I get to the office,' said Sammy.

'Oh, that's good,' said Phoebe, 'Paula and me wouldn't like you not being able to go to work, Daddy.'

'That's right, Phoebe,' said Daniel, 'we all need your wages, Pa.'

'What's that?' said Chinese Lady. 'Daniel, did I hear you call your dad Pa?'

'We all did, Mum,' said Susie, 'and out loud.'

'It's what Patsy calls her dad,' said Daniel. 'I think it's catching,' he murmured.

'An Americanized diminutive,' said Mr Finch.

'Crumbs, what's that, Paula?' whispered Phoebe.

'Oh, something foreign, I think,' whispered Paula. 'Granddad knows foreign languages.'

'Well, whatever that is, Edwin, it sounds as common to me as Ma,' said Chinese Lady and looked accusingly at Sammy.

Sammy, receiving the look without taking offence, said, 'That reminds me, I've invited Patsy to tea on Sunday.'

'That's nice,' said Susie, in favour of the bright American girl, even if she had once forgotten to wear a slip.

'If I could get some fat shrimps?' offered Sammy.

'Americans have a happy relationship with shrimps,' said Mr Finch, a little wan but still finding enjoyment in the family table talk. All his wife's children and grandchildren had an aptitude for communicating with each other and with their immediate world.

'I'll see what I can do,' said Sammy, 'I've got a few friends.'

'Sammy,' said Susie, 'are we speaking of shady characters?'

'Pardon, Susie?' said Sammy. 'Would you mean gents a bit dubious?'

'Oh, lor',' murmured Paula, who knew her mum was against anything like that.

'Sammy,' said Susie, 'you know exactly what I mean.'

'I think Daddy's for it now,' whispered Paula to Phoebe.

'Oh, crikey,' breathed Phoebe.

Daniel was grinning all over. Nothing was more entertaining than listening to his priceless mum letting his versatile dad know that some of his friends left a lot to be desired. But, of course, whereas she saw them as dubious, his dad saw them as useful.

'Well, Susie love,' said Sammy, 'I admit in my time I've bumped, accidental like, into one or two geezers who've been educated at Borstal, but—'

'Edwin,' said Chinese Lady, shocked, 'did I hear right, did Sammy say that in front of the children?'

'Maisie, to rub shoulders with all kinds and to remain the upright son of one's mother, as Sammy has, can be considered a triumph for the way he's been brought up,' said Mr Finch without a flicker of his eyelashes.

'And as I was going to point out,' said Sammy, 'it's always been a principle of mine as a reputable businessman and the son of me revered Ma, not to consort as a friend with same geezers.' He regarded his daughters confidingly. 'If I see 'em coming, me pets, I cross the road, on account of knowing that's what your highly respectable mum likes me to do.'

'Little girls,' said Susie to Paula and Phoebe, 'd'you know what codswallop is?'

'Mummy, I don't fink it's what we're learning at school,' said Phoebe.

'You don't need to,' said Susie, 'it's what comes out of Daddy's mouth nearly every day.'

Paula giggled.

Phoebe looked impressed.

'Oh, could I learn some from Daddy?' she asked eagerly. 'I fink I'd like to.'

Outside the house, a car horn sounded.

'That's Uncle Tommy for me,' said Daniel, still wearing a grin. Tommy picked him up and drove him to the Belsize Park factory every day. He also brought him home. 'Let's hear some more about Dad tonight, Mum,' he said, pushing his chair back and getting up. 'I'd like to learn about codswallop myself. I've got an idea it's useful.'

'Just push off, my lad,' said Susie, 'or you'll learn something different that'll put a flea in your ear.'

Daniel departed smiling, and when he and his Uncle Tommy reached the foot of Denmark Hill, they found a gang of workmen already busy around the damaged road and pavement. Two men were deep in the crater. There's no end to what this war's doing in the way of ruination here and all over Europe, thought Tommy. Like countless other people, he hoped the Germans were finding out from Allied bombing raids that ruination wasn't exactly what Hitler had promised, and if they weren't sorry about making him their Great-I-Am, then they were off their rockers.

'How did Aunt Vi and cousin Alice take it last night?' asked Daniel.

'Well, your Aunt Vi's 'ad a large share of it for years,' said Tommy, driving past King's College Hospital and towards the morning traffic at Camberwell Green. 'She's used to it. For Alice, it was her first experience of a heavy raid since being back from Devon, and it made her jumpy. Come to that, it still makes me jumpy.'

'Same here,' said Daniel.

'That American girl,' said Tommy, turning into Camberwell New Road to head for Vauxhall Bridge, 'she's got some pluck, I must say. Where'd you find her?'

Daniel related details of how he met Patsy.

'Friendly girl,' he said, 'and I like her.'

'Give the young lady me regards,' said Tommy, 'I like her pluck meself. How's young Phoebe? What a little charmer, and who'd have believed how sad she was when your mum and dad first took her in, eh, my lad? Ruddy rotten time she had before that.'

'She's a little darling,' said Daniel, 'and if she's not following Paula about, she's having a giggly time with Dad. Has Alice got a heart-throb yet?' His cousin Alice, Tommy's eldest, was nineteen.

'I think it's Bristol University,' said Tommy, passing cyclists on their way to work. 'She'll be going there in September. Well, she's in love with education, which I never was, nor Vi. Nor your dad. Your Uncle Boots was the only one who had any real education, which is why he talks educated. I don't suppose he'd have got to be a colonel otherwise, or married to your Aunt Polly. Your grandma still can't believe she's got a colonel and an upper class daughter-in-law in the fam'ly. Come to that, I suppose, your cousin Eloise is an ATS officer. Talk about the fam'ly moving in high places. There, look at that, Daniel. Nasty.'

A building, intact yesterday, lay a shattered and ugly mountain of bricks and girders.

'It's a sign, Uncle Tommy, that we've got to

invade France and get at Hitler's back, or we'll never end this rotten war,' said Daniel.

'Drop a line to Churchill,' said Tommy.

'I've an idea he already knows,' said Daniel.

They chatted all the way to the Belsize Park factory, where Gertie Roper, the faithful charge-hand, greeted them with the news that the East End had caught it last night. Bleedin' noisy it was, she said, excusing her French, and two of the seam-stresses hadn't turned up. Tommy said he hoped that didn't mean they'd caught it too. The factory could make do with two hands absent. What it couldn't stand was hearing that the missing workers were casualties.

'Mister Tommy, you're a caring soul,' said Gertie, who'd been an angular and starved-looking woman when Tommy and Sammy had first known her. Good wages and bonuses, not only for her, but for her husband Bert, factory under-manager, had helped to turn her into a full-bodied woman, with two well-fed sons in the Services. 'I'll find out about them gals tonight,' she said. ''Ere, Daniel, there's a couple of machines want seeing to, like. Bert's put two reserve machines in place. And, Mister Tommy, there's a fault in one of them bales of rayon yarn for ATS reach-me-downs. It wants sendin' back with a complaint form, and a request for a quick replace-ment. Could yer look after that today, Mister Tommy?'

'Noted, Gertie,' said Tommy. 'I'll phone the manufacturers first. We don't want to get into a position that puts the ATS short of bloomers. It'll make things awkward for them on windy days.'

'Oh, the poor dears,' said Gertie. 'It's windy today and all.' It was. Further, it was also chilly. May was in a bit of a temper, much as if it had quarrelled with April and taken a dislike to General Eisenhower, Commander of Overlord, who was in desperate need of good weather. 'Still, can't 'elp laughing at the thought, can we, Daniel?'

'My imagination's going up in smoke,' grinned Daniel, and he and his uncle began work.

Bang went the front door knocker. Cassie answered the summons. Large and unwieldy Mrs Hobday, a smile on her face, was on her step. In view of the smile, Cassie supposed the loud knock hadn't been unfriendly, just the consequence of her beefy-armed neighbour being naturally heavy-handed.

'Oh, 'ello, dearie,' said the fat lady, 'I brought yer some fruit for yer kids, seeing they ain't been jumping up and down on me doormat lately. Here we are.' And she handed Cassie a calico bag with a drawstring. The bag was laden, and Cassie, opening it up, saw the golden gleam of oranges.

'Oranges?' said Cassie. 'Oranges? Mrs Hobday, I haven't seen as many as this since before the war.'

'Jaffas, that's them,' beamed Mrs Hobday. 'Me old man says they're shipping some from the Middle East nowadays.'

'Oh, thanks ever so much,' said Cassie. 'All these?'

'Well, me old man works down at the Nine Elms shunt yards,' said Mrs Hobday, 'and now and again, like, a bit of this and that falls orf a goods waggon. He brought a lot of them oranges 'ome yesterday, and I thought some of 'em might be good for yer kids.'

'I don't know how to thank you,' said Cassie.

'Pleasure, ducky,' said Mrs Hobday. 'Mind, don't tell the coppers. Here, did that noisy air raid frighten yer kids last night?'

'It scared them, and I felt awful about having brought them home,' said Cassie. 'It was the first time they'd known an air raid. I thought raids were supposed to have stopped.'

'Bleedin' cheek of Hitler, that's what I thought meself,' said Mrs Hobday. 'Me old man said it was the last kick of a dying donkey. Did you get yer kids into yer back-yard shelter all right?'

'Yes, and we all cuddled up, and it didn't last long, which was a blessed relief,' said Cassie. 'Thanks again for the oranges.'

'Oh, you're welcome, dearie,' said Mrs Hobday, 'and I'll remember you and yer kiddies if me old man is somewhere around when a bit more of this and that falls orf a goods waggon. Well, he ain't paid for puttin' them back, if you see what I mean. I told 'im when he left for 'is shift this morning, I wouldn't mind a few bananas, I said, and he asked me if I'd like straight or bent ones. Don't be bleedin' daft, I said. Mind, I don't want you to think I ain't fond of him. Well, nice to 'ave had a chat with you. I 'eard there's a few more holes round the Elephant and Castle from last night's bombs, but keep smiling, eh?'

'My children will do a lot of smiling when they see these oranges,' said Cassie.

'Bless 'em, they're little angels, ducky,' said Mrs Hobday.

'Thanks,' smiled Cassie, 'come and have a cup of tea with me this afternoon.'

'Well, that's nice of yer,' said Mrs Hobday, 'I'll do me hair up and put me best blouse on.'

Chapter Twenty-Three

Miss Alice Adams, spending much of her time studying at home in preparation for her entry into Bristol University at the end of summer, had planned a full day of uninterrupted swotting. Keen to obtain an English Literature degree, she had borrowed a set of novels by John Galsworthy from the library. They embraced *The Forsyte Saga.*

Alice, nineteen, was fair-haired like her mum, Mrs Vi Adams, with a slender frame and looks that some people might have said were in need of relaxation. That is, she rarely looked other than earnest, serious or studious. She was certainly studious by nature, something she had in common with Leah's sister, Rebecca, and she practised the kind of precise speech befitting a young lady whose ambition was to become a university tutor. While not actually deprecating her cockney roots, very much alive in her parents, Alice preferred to see herself as a reflection of her Uncle Boots, who may have been born of cockney parents, but had always been a natural cosmopolitan. Boots would have been disappointed in her attitude. Alice, in fact, was a bit toffee-nosed, something Vi and Tommy had not yet noticed since her return from Devon.

Vi only knew she didn't want her daughter to turn into what was called a blue-stocking. She asked Tommy a question. Didn't blue-stockings finish up being married to history books and suchlike? Not much comes out of that except little history books and suchlike, said Tommy. Vi said that wasn't a sensible answer, and Tommy said that as he'd never been intimate with blue-stockings, it was the best answer he could think of. What I mean, said Vi, is that they mostly stay spinsters, don't they?

'Steady, Vi,' said Tommy, 'watch your language, or my dear old mum might get to hear. She'd totter about if she thought there was goin' to be a spinster in the fam'ly. She'd tell us God didn't order women to be spinsters, and to take Alice to see a doctor.'

'Tommy, you can't take a girl of nineteen to see a doctor about that sort of thing,' said Vi, still a woman of soft eyes, gentle voice and kind ways. 'And blessed if I'd want to try. We'd just have to put up with it if Alice left marriage alone.'

'I don't know I'd like it meself,' said Tommy, still a handsome piece of male furniture at forty-four. Impressionable machinists at the factory sometimes had saucy dreams about him, and at Christmas gave him equally saucy presents like sexy male briefs run up by themselves. In vivid colours. 'My Alice married to history books? I'd have to fight that.'

'Tommy love, you mustn't,' said Vi. 'It's her own life, not ours. You and me, well, we did what we wanted to, didn't we?'

'Not till we got married,' said Tommy.

'I didn't mean that, you saucy man,' said Vi. 'I mean, we got married at a time when we really couldn't afford to and only me dad was in favour. I remember him saying we had a right to live our own lives, while Mum said I had a right to live it with someone that had better prospects than you. Still, Dad stood up for me, and together we got round Mum.'

'I'm fond of your dad, Vi,' said Tommy.

'So am I,' said Vi, 'and me mum's a lot more mellow than she was once.'

'All the same—'

'No, we've got to let Alice live her own life,' said Vi.

'Well, I'll tell you this much,' said Tommy, 'I'm glad I'm still living mine with you.'

'Bless you, Tommy,' said Vi, 'and we'll see this rotten old war through, won't we?'

'You can say that twice over,' said Tommy.

'Oh, bother it,' said Alice at the sound of the front door knocker being smartly hammered. She was studying in the parlour, books and writing pad, inkwell and blotting paper, covering the table. During the preceding week she had read her way through all volumes of the *Forsyte Saga,* and the author's subtle darts at the morals and attitudes of the hidebound dynasty had not been lost on her. At the same time, she had come to like many of the characters, and to feel empathy with their outlook.

Her mum being out, visiting her ageing parents,

Alice had to answer the door herself. She did so fretfully.

A gangly young man in a boiler suit stood on the doorstep. Bareheaded, with black hair and the visage of a gypsy, he was as dark as any villainous squire of Victorian melodrama. This aspect, however, was offset by the twinkle in his eye. He carried a toolbox in one hand, and held a smoker's pipe in the other. Alice thought him about twenty-five and eligible for the Army.

'Yes?' she said.

'Och, guid morning to ye, young missus,' he said. A Scot?

'I'm a miss,' said Alice.

'You're no' Mrs Adams?'

'Miss Adams,' said Alice. 'What is your business?'

'Weel now, ye've a suspected gas leak in your airing cupboard, which a Mr Adams of this address reported by phone to the board this morning at the time of eight-ten.'

'Oh, yes, that's right,' said Alice. 'My father phoned just before he left for his office.' She could more correctly have said factory.

'Shall I step in, Miss Adams?'

'Yes – no, wait,' said Alice, thinking of petty crooks who were taking advantage of circumstances brought about by the war. Houses temporarily vacated because of nearby unexploded bombs, damaged houses under repair by Government-sponsored gangs, and houses empty because housewives were doing war work, all offered opportunities to shifty-minded men with no scruples whatever. 'I think I should see your credentials,' she said.

'My credentials?' The gangly young Scot laughed.

'What's funny?' asked Alice, stiffening.

'Weel now, Miss Adams, this being a devil of a war for ladies, wi' no give or take, and lassies dancing their cares away at the Lyceum Ballroom, a man's credentials these days dinna strictly amount to what's on a piece of paper.'

'I don't know what you mean,' said Alice, and she didn't. She was intellectual but unworldly. 'Are you trying to confuse me?'

'Miss Adams, I'm Fergus MacAllister—'

'Who?'

'Dinna lay the blame on me, Miss Adams, it's my grandfather's name. I'm here from the South-Eastern Gas Board to try to trace your suspected gas leak, and if ye'll let me in I'll go about the work as quiet as a moose.'

'Moose?'

'Aye.'

Oh, mouse. His Scottish accent wasn't broad, but it was there. She quite liked the Scottish accent, it gave character of a pleasant kind to English, providing it wasn't too broad. She gave him another look. He smiled and his teeth gleamed. Alice had a flashing mental picture of a villainous Rob Roy laying an ambush.

She put that aside as absurd and said, 'Well, I suppose it'll be all right if I let you in.'

'If the gas isn't turned off, I'd no' recommend closing the door on me,' he said.

'My father turned it off before he left,' said

Alice, and stood aside. Fergus MacAllister stepped in and surveyed the handsome hall, half-panelled in oak.

'Mansions and marble halls,' he said reflectively. There was no envy about him, however. 'Will you lead the way, Miss Adams?'

Alice took him upstairs to the first floor landing. She showed him the airing cupboard, which Vi had emptied of laundry in anticipation of the call. He set down his box of tools and examined pipes.

'Don't forget the gas is turned off,' she said.

'I'm no' forgetting,' said Fergus. 'I'll go down and restore the flow.'

Down he went and out of the house to the gas main situated to one side of the drive. When he was back at the airing cupboard, Alice came out of her bedroom.

'I'll leave you to it,' she said.

'Aye.'

But she lingered, watching him for some minutes before she returned to her bedroom, from where she could listen. There were warnings all over about keeping one's house safe from the wartime crooks. Gasman Fergus MacAllister might be genuine, but he might not, and if he was going to be as quiet as a mouse he could be out of the house with his box full of stolen items without her hearing a thing. Unless she stayed as close as possible. She left her bedroom door open. She listened. She heard him whistling, she heard him tapping. Then she heard nothing. Out she went on quick feet. He was there, however, head inside the airing cupboard, a wet finger running over a pipe joint. Hearing her, he lifted his head out and turned. His pipe was in his mouth. He took it out.

'Ye're wanting me aboot something, Miss Adams?' he asked, and Alice thought his half-smile quite evil.

'Are you smoking that pipe close to a gas leak?' she asked.

'Weel now, Miss Adams, leaking gas and a burning pipe don't make guid companions, so I'm just sucking it. And there's a leak, that's certain.'

'Well, please find it,' said Alice, and went back into her bedroom. She was sure she should keep an eye on him. Yes, at his age and his health and strength, why wasn't he in uniform? Was he a deserter, or was a gas maintenance man in a reserved occupation? She heard him whistling again, a murmurous whistle, and she heard him say something.

Then silence.

Alice fidgeted. Her studying could wait, she had the whole of the summer, and she gave vent to her suspicions by appearing on the landing again. Fergus MacAllister was down on his knees, head deep inside the airing cupboard. His tool box was open, and there was very little room in it for stolen items.

'Have you found it?' she asked.

'I've a wee smell up my nose,' he said, his voice emerging muffledly.

'Yes, both my parents were certain there was a leak,' said Alice. 'How long will it take you to fix it?'

'There's a wee hairline fracture in this T-joint.'

'Can't you fit a new one?'

Out came his dark head. It bumped against the

bottom of the padded hot water boiler on the way. He rubbed at his thick black hair, and made an untidy mop of it.

'Aye, I'll have to, but it's an old pipe system, y'ken, and I dinna have the right kind of replacement joint in my toolbox,' he said, looking up at her. Alice, neat in a plain, simple dress that was in tune with her studiousness, returned his look with one of suspicion.

'I consider that inconvenient,' she said.

'I'm mortified, Miss Adams,' he said, but Alice didn't think he was.

'Your people must know how old our system is,' she said, 'and they should have made sure you brought the right kind of spares.'

'It's the war, y'ken,' said Fergus. 'Shortage of staff, shortage of spares for systems going back to before the '14–18 war, and priority call-outs to incidents. But cheer up, Miss Adams—'

'I beg your pardon?' said Alice.

'Aye, there's a silver lining,' said Fergus. 'First, I'll apply a sealing agent to the joint, which will stop the leak for at least thirty days.'

'That's a month,' said Alice.

'Then when I get back to the depot sometime today, I'll ransack the stores for a T-joint that'll fit. I'll call here again tomorrow. You can use the gas in the meantime.'

'I don't think the Gas Board would consider that procedure in our best interests,' said Alice, 'and perhaps not even correct. Gas is dangerous.'

'I'll no' argue wi' that, Miss Adams,' said Fergus, 'it's powerful stuff when it's on the loose, like an escaped convict's pickaxe.' Rummaging through his toolbox, he asked, 'By the way, are you a school-teacher, Miss Adams, or a lay preacher?'

'No, I am not,' said Alice, 'and I don't know why you should ask such a question.'

'It's no' a great matter,' he said, and his head disappeared into the cupboard again. He applied the sealing agent to the affected T-joint. 'Just that ye've a fine delivery, Miss Adams.' His voice travelled hollowly around the cupboard.

'What do you mean?' asked Alice.

'You speak your words fine and clear,' said Fergus. 'There, that's the wee job done for the time being.' His head re-emerged, he wiped his hands on a duster from his toolbox, put it back, closed the box and came to his feet. Whether it was dust from the cupboard or not, his dark features looked darker and his teeth whiter as he smiled. Alice suddenly felt herself dangerously alone in the house. 'Will I leave the gas on, or turn it off, Miss Adams?'

'I wish you'd been able to replace the joint instead of having to come back tomorrow,' said Alice.

'It's nae bother,' said Fergus.

'I would prefer you to turn the gas off at the main.'

'Och, aye, I'll do that, then,' he said. 'Guid day to you, Miss Adams.'

'Good morning,' she said, and followed him downstairs to make sure he left the house. He opened the front door and turned to her.

'Has it been a grieving war for you?' he asked.

'Do you mean it's been joyful for some?' she countered.

'I'm just thinking ye're a serious young lassie,' he said, and left.

Really, what an obnoxious man, thought Alice. She watched as he uncovered the gas main and turned it off, replaced the cover and went on his way down the drive. He walked like a gangling cowboy, she thought.

She phoned the Gas Board, gave her name and address, and asked if one of their maintenance men was a Scot called Fergus MacAllister.

'Pardon?' said the woman clerk.

'Fergus MacAllister, is he one of your maintenance men?' asked Alice.

'Never heard of anyone with a name like that.'

'Well,' said Alice, 'let me tell you—'

'Oh, wait, d'you mean Mac the Bandit?'

'What?'

'MacAllister, yes, of course, so sorry, only no-one, even the Super, calls him anything but Mac, or Mac the Bandit, and I'm a bit new here, anyway. D'you have a query we can help you with, Miss Adams?'

'No, never mind,' said Alice. 'No, wait. Why do you call him Mac the Bandit?'

'Oh, I can't discuss personal matters, madam.'

'No, of course not, goodbye,' said Alice, and put the phone down. She put two and two together, and decided the man had been given the nickname by his workmates because he looked like a Mexican of the bandit kind.

When her mother came home later, she told her of the man's call, what he had said about the leak, what he had done and what he was going to do. Vi said that was all right, then, as long as he brought the new joint tomorrow. Alice kept quiet about the suspicions she had had of him.

The villainous-looking Scotsman reappeared during the afternoon of the following day, a wet and windy one, and Alice considered it bad luck that she was alone again, her mother out shopping. For all that the Gas Board had confirmed him to be genuine, Alice simply did not think him incapable of quietly lifting an object or two.

However, he brought the necessary T-joint, addressed her with cheerful politeness, put his head into the airing cupboard again, and did his work whistling 'Lili Marlene'. Alice watched him. He broke off his whistling to ask her why she was at home.

'I don't think that is any business of yours,' she said.

'Curiosity, y'ken,' he said, still working away.

'It killed the cat,' said Alice. 'Is yours a reserved occupation, by the way?'

'Come again?' he said, and blew on the newly fixed joint.

'Well, you aren't in uniform, are you?' she said.

He turned his head and looked up at her, a strange expression on his face, and Alice knew she had committed an error that now discomfited her.

'Nor you, Miss Adams,' said Fergus, and finished his work.

'I'm sorry, that was unfair of me,' she said.

'Och, dinna mind yoursel',' he said, 'ye're young

yet.' He came to his feet, picked up his toolbox, and put his empty pipe between his teeth. He took it out again to say, 'I'll turn on the main.'

'Thank you,' said Alice, 'and thanks for fixing everything.'

'Nae bother,' he said, and she followed him down the stairs. He eyed her when he reached the front door, his twinkle back. 'The war's a serious business for all of us, I don't doubt, but d'ye go dancing at the Lyceum a time or two?'

'I do not,' said Alice.

'Will you come with me sometime?'

'Certainly not,' she said, 'I don't care for that at all.'

'Ye're a sad lassie,' he said, and left.

Alice closed the door sharply on him.

She spoke to her dad about him that evening. Tommy shook his head at her.

'Alice, you asked him why he wasn't in uniform and turned down his invitation to go dancing?'

'I apologized for the one thing, I considered I'd given him no encouragement with the other,' said Alice.

'Alice, me love,' said Tommy, 'you talk sometimes like a young lady professor, and you're not at university yet, nor seen much of life.'

'Dad, I know you left school at fourteen and began to see life from then on,' said Alice. 'I'll begin to see it in a different way when I start at university.'

'Of course you will, love,' said Vi.

'And good luck,' said Tommy. 'But I know the bloke. Well, I know about him from a bloke who knows him, and talked about him at the pub.'

Denmark Hill boasted its own pub. 'He was in uniform once, he was in the battles that led to Dunkirk. He was with that Highland Division that tried to hold back Rommel's army and got surrounded, most of the survivors ending up as prisoners. He was lucky enough to be stretchered out of the battle before the Jerries cut the division off. He'd been badly wounded. Full of shrapnel. They took a lot out, but 'ad to leave some in. Some of what's still there pops out through his skin every so often. What's still left in, well, it's a problem, I suppose. He had to leave the Army, of course. They invalided him out, so it must be a problem. Mind, I was told he never looks as if he's carrying some lead weights, and the Gas Board didn't argue about giving 'im a job. Pity you didn't act a bit more gracious, Alice.'

'Tommy, Alice didn't know any of that, and come to that, nor did I,' protested Vi.

'Well, that's true,' said Tommy. 'Yup, true enough. Live and learn, I suppose, eh? Eh, Alice?'

'Yes, live and learn, Dad,' said Alice, feeling about five inches tall.

She bit her lip.

Chapter Twenty-Four

Patsy was tickled at the way Daniel and his family set about Sunday tea, everyone seated around the dining-room table laid with a snowy white cloth. She hadn't imagined anything so formal, with Daniel's mother and grandma obviously in their best Sunday outfits, Paula and Phoebe in Sunday frocks, Daniel in a suit, and his father and grandpa likewise. Not that they all sat up stiff and stuffy, no, everyone talked and reached and passed things and ate, while Granny, with a huge teapot in front of her, addressed the guest hospitably from time to time.

'Another slice of bread and butter, Miss Kirk?'

Miss Kirk, would you believe, what a cute old lady.

'More shrimps, Miss Kirk? I must say my son Sammy has managed to get hold of some nice ones.'

I'm fascinated, thought Patsy, I never knew people as old-fashioned as this were still living.

'More tea, Miss Kirk?'

I'll drown in it.

'Is the cake to your liking, Miss Kirk? I must admit it don't have the kind of ingredients I'm used to when baking, but that's what comes of being at war. I knew that man Hitler would lead us into it, I can't remember how many times I said so to my husband and my only oldest son Boots, but of course no-one took any notice, and look what's happened.'

Boots? Was there someone called that in this family?

'Might I ask what you have for Sunday teas in America, Miss Kirk?'

'Oh, I guess we don't celebrate Sundays like this, Granny, and we mostly crisp-fry our shrimps, which come a bit bigger.'

'They're prawns?' said Mr Finch.

'Excuse me?' said Patsy, wearing a sweater and skirt, which looked fetching enough, but casual compared to Sunday frocks.

'We call big shrimps prawns,' said Daniel.

'What's them?' asked Phoebe of Paula.

'Prawns,' said Paula.

'Yes, but what's them?' asked Phoebe.

'What's prawns, Grandpa?' asked Paula.

'Oh, let's say adult shrimps,' said Mr Finch.

'Crikey,' whispered Phoebe, 'what's them?'

'Grown-up shrimps, I expect,' said Paula, 'like Patsy has in America.'

'Have another slice of cake,' said Daniel to Patsy, and pushed the stand towards her.

'Well, gee whiz, thanks, I will,' said Patsy, and took a slice. It was great. 'Excuse me, Granny, could I—'

'Oh, more tea?' offered Chinese Lady.

'No more tea, thanks,' said Patsy, 'I'd just like to have the recipe for the cake.'

'Well, bless me,' said Chinese Lady, 'd'you do baking, then?'

'Sure I do, for my Pa,' said Patsy.

'Then I must say I'm very admiring of you,' said Chinese Lady.

'I shop, cook, bake and do housework for me and Pa,' said Patsy.

'Well, I never,' said Chinese Lady.

'I'm an also-ran,' said Daniel, 'I only plant potatoes.'

'We're happily awaiting results, Daniel,' said Mr Finch.

'I'm impressed, Daniel, believe me,' said Sammy, 'and so I am with Patsy as her dad's daily help.'

Well, thought Chinese Lady, well, I don't know that Daniel hasn't found himself a proper young lady, already useful around a house, and at a time when too many other girls were acting very flighty. It wouldn't do for Daniel to take up with that kind. She warmed to Patsy.

'About the recipe, Miss Kirk, it's only one of our wartime recipes they print in magazines,' she said.

'Oh, sure,' said Patsy, 'but I'd like to have it.'

'I'll write it down for you when we've finished tea, Miss Kirk,' said Chinese Lady.

'That's sweet,' said the proper young lady. 'Excuse me again, Granny, but I'd care for it if you called me Patsy.'

'I'd be pleasured,' said Chinese Lady, and thought about how to encourage Daniel to take up serious with this respectable and domesticated girl. Otherwise, one of them flighty wartime girls might take up with him.

*　*　*

After tea, when the table had been cleared and the washing-up done, everyone repaired to the parlour, where Paula, a promising pupil, played the piano, and all the others sat around. I'm dreaming again, thought Patsy, this is out of Dickens, and it's only the clothes that are different. I've seen illustrations in his books.

But the music and the family tableau didn't last long. Paula did only a brief stint on the piano, then scampered out of the room and returned with a bagatelle board.

'Let's play, can we, Mummy?'

'I'll get unpopular if I say no,' smiled Susie, and Patsy watched as the bagatelle was placed on the carpet. Immediately, it was surrounded by kids and grown-ups on their knees. Paula, Phoebe, Daniel, Susie and Sammy were all there.

'Come on, Patsy, join in,' said Daniel, and down Patsy went. A circle of six heads hovered above the board, and Patsy was given first go. Ping went the little hammer, up shot the metal ball, and down it came, striking pins before it plonked itself in a hole scoring ten. Shrieks, yells, cries and complaints became the order of the evening from then on.

'Mummy, Daddy's got his elbow in my eye nearly.'

'Daddy's got that kind of elbow, Paula.'

'Someone's pushing.'

'Crikey, look, I went and scored a fifty.'

'How many's that altogether?'

'I don't know, I forgot to count.'

'Here, when's my turn?'

'It's mine.'

'No, it's not.'

'Someone's pushing.'

'Yeah, and I know who. Daniel, I'll sock you.'

'Play up, Patsy.'

'Phoebe, stop yelling in my ear.'

'Paula, I can't do yells yet, I fink I have to wait till I'm older.'

'Your go, Susie.'

'Well, get your head out of my way, Sammy.'

It all convinced Patsy that Daniel and his family were old-fashioned but fun.

When Daniel took her home later, she gave him a kiss outside the front door.

'Ta!' said Daniel, and gave her one in return.

'Did I say you could?' she asked.

'No, but you left your mouth there,' said Daniel.

'It goes with my face,' said Patsy.

'You left your face there, then,' said Daniel.

'Oh, well,' said Patsy, 'accidents will happen. Still, you kiss pretty nice, Daniel. I guess you've known a lot of girls.'

'Schoolgirls down in Devon mostly,' said Daniel.

'It's a crime in states like Alabama, kissing under-age schoolgirls,' said Patsy.

'I didn't do it in Alabama,' said Daniel. 'Down in Devon, didn't I say so?'

'Yes, and you need watching. Well, goodnight, Daniel, thanks for a fun evening.'

'Pa?' said Patsy, when her dad came in at ten o'clock.

'You're going to touch me for an increased allowance?' said Meredith Kirk, a newscaster with a voice built for making a radio deliver exciting vibrations into the ears of lady listeners.

'Thanks, just an extra ten per cent'll be OK,' said Patsy. 'Actually, I wanted to tell you I'm getting to like this English guy.'

'It's always good for the soul, a liking for friends.'

'That's profound, I don't think,' said Patsy. 'A friend's no friend if there's no liking.'

'I'd say you've got something there, Patsy.'

'The point is, Pa, I'd like you to meet him,' said Patsy.

'Is that so?'

'Well, I've met his Pa,' said Patsy, 'and his Ma.'

'Is something going on?'

'Is that a loaded question?' asked Patsy.

'No, an interested one.'

'It's just a friendship,' said Patsy.

'Bring him here Saturday afternoon, sometime before four,' said her Pa, 'and I'll do what I can to get the friendship moving along.'

Patsy smiled.

'It doesn't need any help, Pa,' she said.

Prior to their involvement in the war against Germany, American servicemen had known about the events in troublesome old Europe only from what they read in their newspapers or heard on their radios. Enlisted and trained once the USA was a belligerent, American airmen had arrived in the UK to find the conflict in the skies dangerously unhealthy, but in their Flying Fortresses they participated with all the vigour and panache of their kind. They took severe losses on the chin with rugged fortitude, even if they thought that daylight bombing raids on Germany were ninety-nine per cent suicidal. Off duty, and along with American infantrymen, they formed friendships with the natives, chatted up the dames, and handed out welcome gifts from their PX stores, including fully-fashioned stockings, canned goods and jars of peanut butter.

Britain was the base not only for Americans, but also for the Free Forces of Norway, Belgium, France and Poland. There were also Czechs, Dutch and other European men and women who had escaped the swarming Germans to continue the fight from the UK. And Canadian soldiers and air-men had been stationed in England and Scotland almost from the beginning of the war.

The Canadians were to join the Americans and British in the attempt to establish the Second Front, and one of de Gaulle's Free French divisions was to follow on.

The unseasonal weather, blustery, chilly and un-friendly, meant that nerves at SHAEF (Supreme Headquarters of the Allied Expeditionary Force) were at a high pitch, starting with General Eisen-hower himself, although Montgomery seemed as perky as a cockerel fresh at dawn. His outlook seemed to be on the lines of, 'Never mind the weather, let's get on with it and knock the blighters for six.' Which meant clout them. The appointed American field commanders still had their own ideas about Monty.

'That guy's a nutcase.'

'Sure, but he'll give the Krauts a tough time trying to crack him.'

'Overlord', the attempt by the Allies to form a Second Front, originally scheduled for sometime in May, had been postponed more than once because of unsuitable weather forecasts, and was now set for the beginning of June. The invasion force, concentrated close to the harbours of the South Coast, was stamping its feet, playing cards, writing to mothers or wives, talking, arguing, sleeping, waking, doing press-ups, conducting open-air ablutions, remembering the excitements engendered by relationships with certain girls, thinking about what they were in for, and wondering when the hell it was going to begin.

Boots was there, and Tim and Colonel Lucas were with the Commandos waiting to be airborne.

Sammy Adams, kingpin of Adams Enterprises Ltd and its associate companies, was at the Elephant and Castle, the junction that launched traffic into London Road, New Kent Road, Kennington Park Road, St George's Road, Newington Causeway and Walworth Road. It was a sad sight these days, having suffered massively from Hermann Goering's bombers.

Sammy remembered the old, bustling junction, a place of surging life and old ladies in granny bonnets, old ladies he could often touch for a penny when he was a kid in patched shorts and darned jersey.

'Carry yer shoppin' bag 'ome for yer for a penny, missus?'

'You look to me like you'd run orf with it.'

'Me, missus? Me? Ain't I a Boy Scout when I got me uniform on?' (He never was.) ''Ere, missus, you must be near on forty.' (Usually, the victim was on the wrong side of sixty.) 'It's too much for yer to carry that 'eavy shoppin' bag 'ome yerself, and I'd be pleasured to carry it for yer. Only tuppence.'

'Up to crafty larks now, are yer? You said a penny first.'

'Well, tuppence or a penny, missus, I ain't pertic'ler, specially for a lady that's your age. What's it like being nearly forty? Here, did you know there's other ladies round 'ere that looks over sixty? D'you mind if I ask if you're under or just over forty? Here, give us yer bag, it ain't right for you to 'ave all that weight to carry 'ome. That's it, and I'll tell yer all about me starving sisters on the way, and how me eldest lost a leg when she was run over by a tram.'

And so on, until they reached her doorstep, when he offered to split the difference between a penny and tuppence.

Sammy, shaken when he'd first seen what the bombs had done to the Elephant and Castle, had long since recovered from going into mourning for what had been. He lived for the present and future. Furthermore, he had Rachel with him, and Rachel had never been noted for being a wet female blanket. They were making a tour of bombed properties, each resembling nothing more than a pile of bricks and smashed stone. Sammy kept consulting a list and quoting transaction details. The turn of the tide against Hitler and Japan had made developers interested in post-war prospects. Much money had circulated during these war years, and developers had coined a large share of it.

'This one, Rachel, bought by Adams Properties for nine hundred quid. Sold November, eighteen months ago, for fifteen hundred to Parkinsons Furniture Stores. Profit, sixty-six per cent.'

'Sixty-six, Sammy? My life, that's mouth-watering.'

'Now, this one. Bought for eleven hundred and fifty good 'uns. Sold, April last year to Ambrose and Partners, Accountants, for rich gravy.'

'How rich, Sammy?'

'Two thou, Rachel. Profit, let's see—'

'Just under seventy-four per cent, Sammy.'

'Flash of first-class arithmetic, that was, Rachel. Congratulations.'

'Don't mention it, Sammy.'

'Next, that one across the road. Purchased two years ago for nine hundred guineas.'

'Guineas, Sammy?'

'Well, previous owner being a gent also owning gee-gees, he'd never heard of pound notes. Currently under offer for twelve hundred.'

'Guineas, Sammy?'

'Quids. Prospective buyer says guineas are ruddy chickens.'

'Guinea-fowls, Sammy?'

'Do they lay eggs, Rachel?'

'All fowls do, Sammy.'

'I like you for being informative, Rachel.'

'I like you too, Sammy.'

'Anyway, twelve hundred quid don't rate high enough, not now smart developers can't see Hitler winning the war. Adams Properties are accordingly standing firm for fifteen hundred. Now, place your remarkable mince pies on that great heap of sad ruination over there. Large enough for a store. Collared for two thousand five hundred a year ago, split between the owners of three properties all bombed as one. Going, I'm confident, for four thou to Hurlocks, the Walworth Road store where me sister Lizzy at fourteen landed her first job. Profit, Rachel?'

'We should calculate before completion, Sammy? Not wise.'

'See your point, Rachel.'

They went on. At the end Sammy was able to announce that with the investment in the firm of twenty-five thousand pounds left to Rosie by her late natural father, plus five thousand pounds from Adams Enterprises, Adams Properties had begun trading with a capital of thirty thousand. Eighteen thousand and eighty pounds had been used to purchase bombed sites, and sales so far had amounted to twenty-eight thousand and ninety. Profit so far? Sixty-three per cent plus, said Rachel. You're a walking percentage marvel, said Sammy. I like the plus bit, he said, it takes into account there's still three sites up for sale or completion, purchase price having been included in the total outlay mentioned previous. So a bit more plus should be coming our way, he said. Did Rachel have any comments?

'Well, you brought me here, Sammy, to take a look at these sites,' said Rachel. 'Are you sure you've done the right thing in buying and selling, and not buying for development?'

'Well, development's long term, as my old friend Eli Greenberg pointed out,' said Sammy. 'There's going to be a shortage of building materials after the war and a kind of staggering economy, according to your dad, so there'd be nothing coming back for years with development, and I decided I don't like waiting about. What I do like is investing the profit in Adams Fashions and expanding meself industrially. Along with the directors, of course.'

'Personal expansion would ruin my figure, Sammy,' smiled Rachel, as they took a walk to his car, parked in Newington Causeway.

'It wouldn't ruin your bank figure, Rachel. I'm looking for you and the family to approve Adams Fashions going in for big business.'

'I should object, Sammy? I think your first love is the rag trade.'

'Well, y'know, Rachel, there's always a challenge about that, and a lot of customers. Every year's new fashions grab female women, which reminds me I've never seen you looking like last year's remnants, even if it's my personal opinion that wartime styles could do with serious improving.'

Rachel, wearing a cream-coloured raincoat as protection against the wet and windy day, said, 'I'll bet on you, Sammy, to go in for serious improving when this war's over.'

'I appreciate your encouragement, Rachel,' said Sammy.

'Don't mention it,' said Rachel lightly, but an inward sigh developed. The differences that Leah and Edward seemed willing to set aside were those that had deprived her of the chance of becoming Sammy's wife.

Chapter Twenty-Five

Wednesday, 31 May

The train from Paris was heading for Germany. Its passengers were all French Jews. Men, women and children. Families. Most of them imagined they were going to be resettled outside the country of their birth. Well, that was what they had been told by the French authorities and the French police who had rounded them up. Unfortunately, said the authorities, the present policy of France in these troubled times is to co-operate with Germany, which country, as you know, is Europe's bulwark against the terror of Communism. Germany wishes to replace the Old Order with the New Order, and that means the establishment of an independent homeland for Europeans of the Jewish faith. Yes, the uprooting is very unhappy for you, but others who have already gone are adapting well, and we are sure you will too. Germany guarantees you will not be threatened by the menace of Communism, and that is an important consideration.

What the authorities did not mention was that

the homeland in question consisted of a series of concentration camps specializing in either working the inmates to death or summarily gassing them on arrival, something that would have been so incompehensible to these Jewish families that, even if they had been told, they would have been unable to believe it. Deliberate liquidation? Of children as well as parents? No, no, who could believe anything so infamous? No, no. After all, they were French citizens, weren't they? They obeyed the law, and some of the older men had fought with distinction for France in the Great War. Further, several of the younger ones had served in the Army during the battles against the Nazi hordes in 1940, even if those battles had been conducted only half-heartedly by the French generals.

Most believed the assurance that they were to be resettled in a civilized and understanding way, and certainly the train journey was very civilized. (They did not know just how civilized it was compared to the inhuman and suffocating conditions endured by the Jews of other countries in cattle waggons.) However, despite what comfort they took in re-assurances and promises, they were bewildered by their expulsion from France, their native land. Some, a few, took no comfort and nor did they believe. They distrusted authorities who obeyed the German order to uproot them, and they suspected expulsion was going to lead to something frightening, for in their minds it related horrifyingly to rumours that German Jews sent for resettlement actually ended up being murdered. Would French Jews fare better? The doubters kept trying to convince the believers that resettlement was a mirage, especially as the train was in the hands of German soldiers and Gestapo officers. Their attempts were not welcomed.

'Don't talk like that, you fool.'

'We have to consider unpleasant possibilities, we must.'

'Go away, or my children will hear you.'

'First tell me where you think all the Jews of France and Germany and, yes, Poland, are being sent for resettlement. A Greek island? The South of France? Palestine, with British permission?'

'What I think is that you have water on your brain.'

'I do ask you very seriously, have any of us ever heard from friends and neighbours who have gone before us for resettlement?'

'You can't expect all the work and process of fitting into a new life to allow time for writing letters.'

'I haven't myself heard of one single letter from anybody, and I don't like it that there are German soldiers armed to the teeth on this train.'

'That is to make sure the train isn't attacked by Communists, and that we reach our destination safely. It's sad, yes, that France no longer wants its Jewish citizens, but it would never be responsible for betraying us.'

'In my opinion, and that of others, it has already betrayed us.'

'You and the others are crazy, and see, everyone in this compartment agrees with me. Go away.'

'What can be done with people who are blinding

themselves to the intentions and actions of France's anti-Semitics and their German overlords?'

'Go away, do you hear, you rabble-rouser!'

The train steamed on towards the Department of Marne, noted for its champagne vineyards and pine forests.

A certain section of the railway line in the east of Marne was cut through a deeply wooded area, and the foremost pine trees on either side of the track stood like towering sentinels. Trains, travelling at reduced speed, entered this wooded stretch from around a long bend.

The pine forest was usually quiet except for the snuffles and rustles of foraging wild life. It was not so quiet this afternoon, for an invasion by humans had caused the wild life to retreat noisily into the heart of their habitat, and the invasion itself had been a scrambling and disturbing affair. However, after the invaders, a number of men and women, had settled down, a comparative silence ensued. Now and again, whispers were heard.

After quite some time, one man addressed another in a murmur.

'Twenty-five minutes, I think, if it left on time, Roget.'

'It always leaves on time,' whispered Roget, leader of Marne's main Resistance group. Dark, bristly of jaw, Roget was a man of courage and fixed loyalties. Under no circumstances would he betray France or his comrades. He was a man Bobby and Helene had come to like and admire. 'That is the way of Germans. They make a fetish of punctuality and paperwork. How are your nerves, eh, Maurice?'

'Critical,' said Bobby. 'I need to see a doctor.'

'We're all in need, we're all crazy,' said Roget, 'but who is sane in a Europe governed by a criminal lunatic?'

'Don't ask me,' said Bobby, 'I'm an innocent abroad.'

'You're no innocent, my friend,' said Roget.

'I was once,' said Bobby.

'So were we all at the age of five,' said Roget.

On the other side of Bobby, Helene dug an elbow into his ribs.

'If you must talk, talk to me,' she breathed.

'Don't worry, Lynette,' murmured Bobby, 'I know you're with me.'

Roget grinned.

'Your tigress is awake, Maurice,' he said.

'And spitting,' said Helene, always in a fierce mood when girding herself for a brush with Hitler's Nazi Boches. She hated them for what they had done to France, reducing it to humiliation and turning it into a nation bitterly divided.

Today, another hold-up had been planned. This time a train was their target, the objective the release of its passengers. Helene was keyed up. Bobby had implied he was too, but she knew him and his ability to control his nerves and concentrate on the need for action at the right time. Ah, that English blood of his, it never rushed hot through his veins, it flowed like the sluggish Thames. Well, perhaps not all the time. There were the occasions when he was as hot-blooded as she could wish for. As for the Thames, she would like to see it again, from a place called Marlow, where Bobby had once taken her on a summer day. There the river was clear and running, the banks green, the gardens of houses sloping down to the waters, where ducks and drakes glided, flapped and dipped. The sun dappled the swirling currents and produced moving fingers of light on the surface. Bobby had taken her rowing in a rented boat, and they had laughed the afternoon away.

He was a crazy man, her Bobby, doing the most reckless things with never a shout or a tremor. The men and women of the Resistance liked him, and one or two of the women would have endeavoured to make love with him if she had not threatened to cut their throats.

'Hands off, you peasants.'

'But we don't ask for each other alone, we're willing to share.'

'Share? Share? How would you like your filthy tongue pulled out?'

'Lynette, we aren't playing a game with the re- pulsive Nazis. We belong, as you do, to those who may be alive today and dead by torture tomorrow. What is the point of acting as if little things are important?'

'Little things?'

'Jealousy. Possessiveness. And even love.'

'Love is a little thing, you moth-eaten donkey?'

'Cheating Hitler and avoidance of death are the only things of real importance at present. Love is for the future, if France has a future.'

'Stupid woman, you know nothing of love.'

Helene ground her teeth at her recollections.

Beside her, Bobby was quite still. He was probably trying to estimate the number of running footsteps it would take him to reach the track. His strength was his single-mindedness. All through the days he had spent on her parents' farm following the Dunkirk evacuation, his unalterable objective had been his homeland. He had made up his mind from the beginning that the only way to get there was by sailing the Channel. That fixed purpose wore her down, and so in the end she set sail with him in her own boat that had miraculously survived the bombing of Dunkirk. Quite crazy, and only the arrival of an MTB boat saved them when her dinghy capsized.

The forest was still. Not a breath of wind disturbed any part of it. Roget had split his group, some lying in wait on this side of the track, the rest opposite. Everyone was down on one knee within the shelter of the foremost pines. It was easier that way to spring into action. And everyone was armed with a British Sten gun, provided by London and brought over by the SOE agents known to the group only by their code names of Lynette and Maurice.

Helene whispered into Bobby's ear.

'Be careful. If you behave like a man running happily into a warm sea, I will knock you to the ground for your own good.'

'And if I break a leg, that'll be good?' murmured Bobby, watching the track through the trees.

'Idiot. Where are your emotions?'

'Tucked away under my shirt.'

Helene, always instantly changeable, wanted to

shriek with laughter. Instead, she whispered, 'Ah, I like what is under your shirt.'

'You French saucebox, stop saying things like that.'

'What is Lynette whispering about now?' asked Roget.

'Don't ask me,' said Bobby, 'she's a woman, and I can't understand any of them. I'll go through life trying to work out how they tick.'

An elbow hit him in his ribs again.

Roget glanced at his wristwatch.

'Tell her, Maurice, that there's to be no more talking or whispering. Only listening and watching.'

'I hear you, Roget,' said Helene.

Roget issued a low whistle, and complete silence descended on the two groups lying in wait, the railway lines between them. Roget had control of a detonating plunger. The cable ran a long way down the track to the clamped explosive laid there by Lynette and Maurice, the experts who had been trained in England, and who, Roget had quickly noticed, were inseparable. God help the other if one fell into the hands of the Gestapo. Both would suffer, one from torture, the other from unbearable thoughts. That was the trouble with such relationships when what was called for permitted of nothing except dedication to the cause of stricken France. Lovers should not work together as agents, but one could not help accepting the partnership of Lynette and Maurice, resolute, quick-thinking and experienced agents, and it was Roget's understanding that their entry into the SOE had been conditional on operating as a team.

He had agreed with them that the reduced speed of the train as it entered the straight stretch from the bend would enable it to pull up well before it reached the buckled lines. It would not do for engine and coaches to be wrecked. Attending to casualties was not the purpose of the exercise at all.

It should not be long now before the train was heard and seen, no more than ten to fifteen minutes. Every ear was straining and listening.

What every ear heard then was not the sound of an approaching train, but of a vibrating hum in the sky, a hum that quickly turned into a loud and recognizable drone.

'Bombers,' murmured Roget.

'Flying Fortresses?' said Bobby. 'Another American daylight raid on Germany?'

The planes were high, invisible, but the drone was heavy and unmistakably that of bombers.

'I hope so,' said Roget, 'but watch, Maurice, watch. In this noise we'll hear nothing of the train.'

The blue sky gave birth to streaks of white as French-based German fighters shot upwards in pursuit of the raiders, the first flight of which was now overhead, but still too high to be seen. The drone continued as other flights followed the first.

Again Roget looked at his watch.

'How long now?' asked Bobby.

'Six minutes,' said Roget.

His partisans watched while the reaches of the sky filled with the drone of giant bombers.

Something caught Helene's eye. She glanced down. A large stag beetle was climbing over the toe of her right boot. In the way of its kind, its movements were erratic. It slipped, it clung, it scrambled and darted. Little crab, thought Helene, why don't you go round my boot instead of climbing it? The beetle went gamely on, reached the curve of a precipice and fell into crushed brown pine needles, where it happily righted itself and went walking. *Au revoir*, my friend, I hope we shall succeed in our endeavours as well as you have in yours.

The droning died, and the sky above returned to quiet. Roget heard the train then, two minutes only behind the estimated time. He lightly touched Bobby's arm. Bobby nodded, and Roget issued another whistle.

Tension took hold of every man and woman comprising the ambuscade. The sound of the train's approach became clear, its speed governed by the demands of the long curving bend. Roget, hand on the plunger, rammed it down hard and fast the moment the engine came into view. Away down the line the explosive, detonated, went up with a crack and a roar. Twisted steel leapt, sleepers were torn from their beds, stone chips spouted, and the whole seemed to turn into a whirligig of disintegrating matter for the space of a few seconds. The train ran on unchecked for a moment or two before a German Army corporal, riding with the driver and fireman, yelled in frantic alarm. Sparks flew and metal shrieked as brakes clamped on wheels, and wheels grated on steel. The train shuddered and lurched, its weight forcing it on. The engine passed the place of ambush, coaches passed, and windows passed, windows that framed pictures of passengers thrown about. It took the train time to come to a noisy, suffering halt, and directly in front of Roget and his group was a flat car coupled at the centre, four coaches ahead of it and four behind it, with the guard's van. On the flat car were six German soldiers and two mounted machine-guns, one on each side. The soldiers were an untidy heap, erupting into shouts as they struggled to right themselves.

From either side of the track, from the fringes of the split forest, Sten guns opened up, all trained on the flat car. The fusillade of fire caused the Germans to stay down and to duck their heads low. Bobby and two other men, under covering fire, broke out of the forest, pulled the pins from grenades and lobbed them. Two struck the rail beneath the car, and the third hit a wheel. All three exploded. The car, despite its enormous weight, shuddered, clanged and danced, rolling the Germans about. The mounted machine-guns keeled over.

Roget's partisans leapt from concealment on both sides of the track, and rushed forward. By the time the stunned Germans righted themselves they were under the threat of Sten guns, their sergeant swearing at the top of his voice. At the guard's van, Bobby, Helene and a Resistance man were outside the open door, which had slid back to reveal two Gestapo officers with Aryan good looks. The unpleasantness of finding themselves confronted by an armed trio turned their good looks ugly. Mouths tightened, eyes reflected fury and disgust.

'So sorry,' said Bobby in French, 'but stay where you are.'

On the flat car, the German sergeant was beside himself with rage. Insurgents lined both sides of the shallow embankment. Yes, insurgents, what else? Every one of them, women included, had a Sten gun and, in his opinion, a repulsive countenance typical of a race of decadent Latins. Curse them, they were a collective ugliness. Swines, all of them, fit only to be hanged.

The standing engine hissed steam as Roget made himself heard in loud accented German.

'Attention, soldiers of Hitler's infamous Reich! Come down! Quickly, or we shall fire!'

'Dirty swine!' shouted the sergeant.

A woman partisan fired. The brief burst of bullets whistled over the heads of the Germans.

'A warning!' shouted Roget. 'Come down!'

Sergeant Erich Hoenloe, blaspheming, clambered down over the side of the car, his men following. From there, with their sidearms confiscated, they were forced to join the Gestapo officers in the guard's van. The sliding door was closed, a jemmy jamming it, and the van's inner door leading to the last coach was attended to by a couple of Resistance men. One thrust the sharp end of a wide iron wedge under the foot of the door, and the other gave it a huge kick. The door, which opened outwards, became firmly jammed. The Resistance men remained there as a precaution. One of the imprisoned Germans made an attempt to open the door. A booted foot clamped hard down against the wedge, rendering the attempt useless.

The guard's van became a place of noisy, raging

Germans. It was unheard of anywhere in German-occupied France, an attack on a train carrying Jewish people.

Down at the engine, the German corporal who had been riding with the driver and fireman to ensure they would bring the train to its destination, was now a prisoner of some of Roget's other men. Arriving at the engine, which had come to a stop only twenty metres from the damaged track, they made short work of keeping the corporal quiet by flooring him, gagging him and tying him up.

There was time now, a limited amount of time, to do other work. The area was uninhabited, and the nearest vineyards were out of sight, but it was all too probable that somewhere along the line, at a station, a railway official would soon begin to wonder why a special non-stop train had not passed.

Chapter Twenty-Six

With the train at a standstill, the passengers, having recovered from a tumbling, were newly bewildered. What had happened to bring the train to an emergency stop? They did not suspect for a moment that it was an attempt to spring them free from the hands of the Gestapo. They did not really think themselves prisoners, although they had been warned it would be unwise of any of them to attempt to leave the train. They pressed faces to windows, for they were unable to get out. All doors were locked, except the sliding doors that enabled them to use the corridors and the toilets. But they could not get through to adjoining coaches.

'What's happening?'

'I heard shots being fired a minute ago.'

'Yes, but what's happening?'

'Are we being attacked by Communists? What are our German guards doing?'

'Yes, I'd like to know. We were told they would prevent any trouble, that our journey would be safe and uninterrupted.'

'I can't understand why anyone should attack us, can you?'

'Communists, I tell you. They're everyone's enemies. A bomb went off on the line, didn't it?'

'I heard something. Was it a bomb? I don't know, I couldn't say.'

'I can hear frightened children crying in the next compartment. Can anyone see what's happening?'

'I can only see trees.'

'Let the window down.'

'We were told not to open windows.'

'I'll open it. Stand aside.'

Similar confusion and apprehension existed in all compartments, which provoked braver souls into pulling down windows and putting their heads out.

Roget and several of his band were outside a compartment of the last coach, Roget speaking to people crowding the open window.

'Do you want to go free? Then come out. We have a large truck waiting for the women and children.'

'We can't come out,' said a man, 'the door's locked.'

'If you'll all stand back, we'll blow the lock, or you can climb out through the window,' said Roget. Other partisans were hurrying alongside the train to speak to other passengers, to tell them escape was possible, and that all who wished to should come out. The Jewish people responded with a babble of words, all indicative of reluctance. Resigned to resettlement, they felt escape would only be temporary, that they would be rounded up again.

'No, we can hide you,' said Helene to a collection of faces at one window, but expressions suggested an extraordinary lack of enthusiasm. Helene was informed that mothers were afraid of what might happen to their children if escape meant a family would be hunted down and punished. 'If I were such a mother,' said Helene, 'I'd be far more afraid of what might happen to all your children at the end of your journey. Come with us, give yourselves and your children the chance to be free.'

'No, we have accepted resettlement, and guarantees of our welfare have been given.'

My God, thought Helene, they're either mad or stupidly deluded.

Bobby, urgently addressing people in another compartment, became appalled by their obvious wish to be left alone and by their belief that resettlement was a genuine thing. Christ Almighty, he thought, are we risking our necks for people who trust the word of authorities acting for Himmler, their worst enemy? Am I to believe they really don't want to leave this train? The large truck, acquired at great risk and expense, would take scores of the women and children, but they had to make their minds up quickly, bloody quickly. There was no time for argument or for prolonged debate with parents convinced that resettlement was better for them and their children than a hiding-place.

'Come out, for God's sake,' he said.

'We can't, the door's locked.'

'The window, man, the window. Climb out. I'll help. Hand me your children.'

'No, there's our luggage, anyway, everyone's luggage, in the guard's van.'

A woman, becoming hysterical, brought about a

greater reluctance to leave the train. But a young man suddenly shouted.

'We're fools. Of course we must get out. I for one will.'

He pushed his way through to the window and levered himself out. Bobby helped him down.

That impulsive act was repeated elsewhere, by those passengers who had voiced doubts and suspicions. Within minutes, two middle-aged men and their wives, three young men, one young woman and a family of five, had also left the train via windows. That, however, amounted to only fourteen people out of what Himmler would have called a consignment of over three hundred subhumans, including fifty-one children.

Roget, who had expected all of them to jump at the chance of escape, had planned for the children and their mothers to be taken aboard the large truck, and for the men and other women to follow on foot, the whole under the escort of his group, the temporary destination a remote mountain monastery, the permanent refuge Switzerland. He had thought the freeing of the trainload of Jews would be a blow struck for the tarnished honour of France, and it shocked him that only a few chose freedom.

Arguments, warnings and appeals could not break down the attitude of the men and women whose trust in promises was so fixed. Helene was dismayed and even angry. She saw acceptance of resettlement as stupidity. Bobby said to her that in a way he hoped the trusting believers were right and he was wrong, that European Jews really were being resettled somewhere. Otherwise, he said, he would always bitterly regret not pulling every man, woman and child forcibly off the train, never mind their beliefs.

'I've a feeling we'll both have to live with that regret,' said Helene, watching partisans escorting the fourteen refugees into the forest to face a trek through to the far side, where the truck was hidden and guarded.

Roget, now impatient to get away, spared a moment to point out to an elderly man that the train wasn't going to be able to move until the track was repaired.

'We will wait,' said the venerable Jew from his compartment window.

'More fool you, all of you,' said Roget in disgust, and whistled up his band. Down from the last coach came the two men who had been keeping watch on the jammed inner door of the guard's van.

Inside the van, Sergeant Hoenloe and his men, directed by the Gestapo officers to a mountain of luggage and boxes, succeeded in uncovering a sealed crate containing submachine-guns and a cache of ammunition. They smashed it open. Sergeant Hoenloe grabbed one gun, peeled off its oily wrapping and loaded it from the cache.

'Arm yourselves,' he hissed, and his men and the Gestapo officers snatched at the weapons. He moved to the communicating door and sprayed it with bullets. The bullets burst through but struck no targets. Still firing, Sergeant Hoenloe applied a savage kick to the splintered door and it crashed open, despite the wedge. He was out in a flash, rushing to the landing step of the coach, from where he saw the running figures of the swinish insurgents. Alerted by the sound of gunfire, Roget and a number of men and women were going head-long for the shelter of the massed pines.

Sergeant Hoenloe fired again, and roared for his men as he gave chase. They followed with their loaded weapons, the Gestapo duo with them. All eight Germans spread out, went down on one knee and searched for targets among the disappearing partisans. They fired.

Helene ran, Bobby ran, they all ran. One man, hit in the leg, went down on the very edge of the forest. Roget stopped, and with the help of a comrade, took hold of the wounded man's arms and dragged him fast over the ground into shelter. The rest of the men and women disappeared amid the pines, although not before the sickening disaster of a bullet through the back of his head killed one man outright, and a second fell dying, his body riddled with bullets.

Sergeant Hoenloe, a man of action furiously set on a need to take prisoners, ran forward, his men on his heels. Reaching the foremost trees, they sprayed fiery lead into the forest. The prey, how-ever, had gone quickly to ground and were flat on their stomachs. Bullets passed above them, smack-ing and thudding into tree trunks, or whining through gaps to smash into undergrowth. Bobby knew the band had to stay for a while to hold off the opposition long enough to give the escaping Jews and their escort time to reach the truck. From the ground, the partisans returned fire for a few moments, then fell silent, Bobby inwardly cursing a ricocheting bullet that had struck his left arm above his elbow.

Sergeant Hoenloe gestured to his men with a flailing hand, signalling the need for a flanking manoeuvre.

'Get round them before they start moving again,' he hissed.

Four soldiers divided into two pairs. One pair darted to the left, the other to the right. Each pair covered thirty metres before entering the forest. But Roget, no fool, had men waiting for just such a move, the obvious one. The Germans encountered continued silence as they crept forward left and right. It was a silence that made them wonder if the partisans had managed to melt away unheard.

From the train the confused passengers watched and listened. They saw two German soldiers and two plainclothes men flat on the ground facing the forest, their weapons sighted. What they did not see for the moment was the small group responsible for immobilizing the driver, fireman and German corporal. These men and women, on the blind side of the train, began to edge quietly round the guard's van, the nearest point to Sergeant Hoenloe and the three Germans with him.

In the forest, the two left-flanking soldiers, easing slowly and carefully forward, froze as a woman's voice, speaking German, came softly to their ears.

'Stop. Drop your guns and turn.'

They stopped, yes, but did not drop their weapons, and their turn was calculated. A man and a woman confronted them, each with a levelled Sten gun, unfriendly fingers curled around triggers. Other men were backing them up from various points.

'Drop, drop,' said Helene, attired in beret, leather jacket, trousers and sturdy boots. Beside her, Bobby, similarly clad, eyed the Germans like a man who'd be happy to blow their heads off. Not only was his left arm hurting like hell, but he was remembering something Colonel Buckmaster of SOE had told him, that a company of Waffen-SS troops had massacred scores of British soldiers taken prisoner during the fighting retreat to Dunkirk.

The two Germans, tight-lipped, flung down their weapons, and at that moment their right-flanking comrades were downed fifty metres away. Three partisans, rising up from cover, simply leapt on their backs and sent them crashing. Roget wanted no killing, if possible. There were bloody reprisals for the killing of German troops by the Resistance.

Sergeant Hoenloe, cooler now, was waiting for the sound of fire that would tell him his flanking men were attacking the swines who had sabotaged the railway line. He and his men would then go in, firing as they went. From the train, the watching Jewish passengers held their breath as they saw several men and women suddenly appear at a run, a run that brought them speedily at the backs of the grounded Germans.

'*Achtung! Kaput!*'

Attention. You're finished. The warning and the

message came from a Resistance man. The two Gestapo officers and the soldier rolled over to stare up the small group of insurgents, all armed. Sergeant Hoenloe did not roll over. He came calmly to his feet, still facing the forest, and he lifted his submachine-gun and let go a burst that emptied the magazines. The bullets whined and smacked into the forest. It was to let his flanking men know he wanted immediate action. He did not get it. There was no response at all, neither from his men nor the skulking partisans. Nor did the swines at his back take any action. Or so he thought until something heavy struck the back of his head. He blacked out.

Not long after, he and his men, together with the bitter-faced Gestapo officers, were back in the guard's van, tied hand and foot. The corporal up with the driver and fireman remained trussed, and the latter men, tied to the controls, were left like that.

The passengers, heads out of windows, saw exactly what happened to the sergeant, his men and the two Gestapo officers. One man, withdrawing his head spoke urgently to the people in his compartment, telling them that if nothing was done to help their German guards, everyone on the train would suffer. That led to a number of men climbing out of windows as soon as the partisans had disappeared. They opened up the guard's van and released the Germans.

Thirty minutes later, Sergeant Hoenloe and one of his men caught up with the trekking Resistance group. He had had to leave four men behind to ensure the Jews remained on the train. The Gestapo officers had insisted. He was a good soldier, a competent sergeant and wholly in favour of Hitler's Reich, and that sent him pounding in pursuit of the Resistance group, along with only one man. The moment he saw a lone figure flitting ahead of him, he and his sole companion opened fire with their submachine-guns. Ahead, the partisans scattered. The two Germans swept the area with bursts of fire. The partisans melted away fast. The Germans rushed and came upon a man lying on his back, a woman and another man down on their knees beside him. Sergeant Hoenloe glimpsed the face of the wounded man. It was deathly white beneath its darkness. That's one dog on his way to hell, he thought. The others are what I need for handing over to the Gestapo.

'Flatten yourselves, you swines, on your dirty faces!' he hissed in guttural French.

Bobby and Helene looked up at him, pain in their eyes.

'Your turn to crow,' said Bobby. 'Perhaps,' he added.

From high in the pines men dropped on the two Germans, who folded like sacks beneath the weight of plunging bodies. They smashed, faces and stomachs, into a thick carpet of needles.

Bobby and Helene could do nothing for the man who had caught the best part of a burst of fire. Roget, leader of the group, died quietly, however, speaking not a word from the moment the burst had felled him. He, Bobby and Helene had formed the protective rear of the retreating partisans, but at a distance from each other. That had saved Bobby and Helene, and they found it bitterly painful to watch Roget, the best of men, die, to hear the long shuddering sigh that came from him seconds before he stopped breathing amid a silent grieving circle of his men and women. Roget was a man of the old France, the France of liberty, fraternity and honour, not the France of the defeatist Pétain and Weygand, or the corrupt France of Laval and other pro-Nazis. There were regrettably many such people, all of whom had come out of the rotting fabric of 1940. The rehabilitation of the country was in the hands of General de Gaulle, his Free French and partisans of the same breed as Roget. Bobby and Helene desperately hoped they would succeed.

The partisans hammered a stake into the ground where Roget had fallen, and carried his body away with them to bury it in the ground adjacent to his family's vineyard. They left Sergeant Hoenloe and the other German soldier tightly lashed together, and the lashed bodies further lashed to a tree. It would take them hours to release themselves.

The group finally caught up with the truck, previously reached by the Jewish refugees and their escort. Everyone went aboard, and space was found on which to place the body of Roget. Before Bobby climbed up with the driver, however, Helene, as adept at First Aid as any FANY officer, took the bullet out of his arm and dressed the wound.

'Thanks,' he said, sweating a bit.

'See, it isn't so bad, no,' she said, 'just a flesh wound. But—' She grimaced.

'It's nothing compared to our losses?' said Bobby. 'You're right, you sweet woman, it's a large empty nothing. Three dead men, including Roget, by Christ.'

'I know, Bobby, I know,' whispered Helene.

'Time to go home again, Helene.'

'How bitter,' said Helene that night.

'God, yes,' said Bobby. They were bivouacking, along with everyone else, under the starry sky. They were, however, very much by themselves. 'How the hell did those two Germans get free quickly enough to tail us as they did?'

'Bobby, could some of the Jews have released them?' asked Helene.

'Oh, Christ,' said Bobby, 'could they have been indirectly responsible for the death of a man whose single purpose had been to engineer their escape?'

'If so, how fortunate for them that they'll never know,' said Helene. 'Ah, those poor people, so passive, so resigned. At first, I was angry with them. Now I am sad. Who could not be sad for people who believe resettlement is Himmler's idea of being kind to them? Himmler is the world's filthiest specimen of a diseased pig on two legs. I say that knowing only what his Gestapo swine are doing to France. What are they doing, I wonder, to other countries?'

'And to the Jews,' said Bobby. 'All these rumours

of concentration camps. I don't think I'm going to get much sleep tonight.'

'Is your arm hurting?' asked Helene.

'No, just a bit stiff and sore,' said Bobby, lying on his back, head pillowed on his folded right arm, new moon a bright crescent high above him. It had been a bad and sad day, the operation only minutely successful, and the Resistance leader gone, shot to pieces in the space of a second. The death of a brave man who'd become a fine friend and comrade was bloody bitter.

'Ourselves, we have been lucky, yes?' said Helene.

Yes, they had, thought Bobby, lucky in all their missions so far. The missions had made them act as one, think as one, and he could not visualize life without his fearless French love. He wondered if he should put aside his belief that a wartime marriage was fraught with too many uncertainties to be fair to a woman. Perhaps he ought to marry Helene. He knew it was what she wanted, and that she would like to tell her parents through the help of the Resistance. Messages had been sent periodically to Jacob and Estelle Aarlberg in that way, to let them know he and Helene were alive and well.

'Helene?'

'Bobby?' She was lying beside him, sad for Roget, sad for the day.

'Shall we get married, chicken?'

She sat up.

'Before the war is over, you mean?'

'As soon as London gets us back to England again. Would you like that?'

'Yes, I would, *chéri*, very much.'

'Well, so would I, Helene, so would I, and so would the family. Let's go for it, shall we, and damn Hitler, Himmler and all the other Nazi hellhounds.'

'I'm for you, Bobby, today, tomorrow and always,' whispered Helene, and dipped her head and kissed him.

Chapter Twenty-Seven

Felicity awoke and sat up. There was a new moon, but she saw nothing of its light. She saw nothing at all. Her world was always in darkness. Very often she lived only with her thoughts and her imagination.

There was a thought now, a thought that had played on her subconscious and woken her up.

She was well overdue. She was, of course she was. She had known it for days.

She sank back.

Soon I must see Dr Gillespie of Bere. See? God, what a hope, you silly woman. Consult him.

Tim, you lovely man, I think, I just think, I might be going to have a baby.

It took her a while to get back to sleep.

She spoke to Rosie during the morning.

'You darling,' said Rosie, 'I'll phone Dr Gillespie and make an appointment for you.'

'It's not too soon?' said Felicity. 'Or too imaginative? I mean, there are women, aren't there, who only imagine the condition?'

'Don't let's join those unfortunate ladies,' said Rosie. 'We're not the kind.'

'We?' said Felicity.

'Felicity, we're together all the way about this,' said Rosie. 'It's our baby.'

'Oh, hell,' said Felicity, 'you're counting my chickens.'

'Chick,' said Rosie, and laughed. 'Unless it's twins,' she said.

Felicity yelled.

Dr Gillespie gave Felicity a consultation during his evening surgery and promised to let her have the result of his tests as soon as possible.

'In five minutes?' said Felicity. 'Shall I wait?'

'Ah, wait?'

'Just a joke from off the top of my dizzy head,' said Felicity.

'I like that kind of joke, Mrs Adams,' said Dr Gillespie, 'and I think I'll let you go home with Mrs Chapman now, and phone you when I have the result.'

'It's a hairy old world at the moment,' said Felicity, 'and wouldn't be worth living in if certain kind of professionals went missing.'

'What certain kind?'

'Doctors,' said Felicity.

'Mrs Adams, allow me to say a certain kind of person makes every doctor's life worthwhile. Your kind.' Dr Gillespie opened his door then and called Rosie in. Giles and Emily were with her in the waiting-room, Emily in her pram. Rosie collected Felicity, and they made their way home with the children. Felicity did not use a stick. She was hand in hand with Giles, who knew what her dark glasses meant, and was accordingly her earnest little guide.

'Mind, there's a kerb now, Aunt F'licity.'

'Yes, darling,' she said.

God, she said to herself, what have I done? As I am now, dependent on a small boy, I'm mad to have persuaded Tim.

But to have a little boy like Giles, or an infant girl like Emily? Tim's child? Hold me up, someone, I'm giddy at the prospect.

Alice came out of the local library, having returned *The Forsyte Saga* and borrowed *Lorna Doone* by R. D. Blackmore. A man in a peaked blue cap and a workman's boiler suit was approaching. He was chewing on a pipe, and carrying a toolbox. He seemed to be checking house numbers. Alice bit her lip, and wondered if she should pass him by or speak. He looked at her as she began to pass, and a little smile touched his face.

'Guid afternoon, Miss Adams.'

Alice stopped.

'Oh, it's you,' she said.

'The same,' he said, removing his empty pipe.

'I remember you, of course,' she said.

'I'll no' forget you,' he said, 'all of sixteen and training to be a preacher.'

'Sixteen? Training to be a preacher? How dare you!' Alice flamed into hot vexation. 'Really, what an impertinent man you are!'

Fergus MacAllister laughed.

'Whisht, lassie, dinna blow up,' he said.

'I ought not to say so,' fumed Alice, 'but I think you quite hateful.'

'Och, aye,' said Fergus, 'I'm a blackhearted fellow, y'ken, wi' fearful designs on young lassies.'

'I believe you,' said Alice.

'Try a smile,' said Fergus.

'I beg your pardon?' said Alice.

'Dinna be so serious, young lady, we'll win the war yet,' said Fergus. 'And guid day to you while I go looking for number twenty-one.'

'I hope you find it,' said Alice, 'for I'm sure everyone there will be tremendously happy to see you.'

Fergus laughed again, and Alice stormed off.

If I never see him again, she thought, I'll be tremendously happy myself. Sixteen? Sixteen? And training to be a preacher? He's off his head. Oh, bother it, I meant to tell him I was sorry for not being more hospitable when he fixed our gas leak. Well, I shan't worry about that now.

Chinese Lady, Mr Finch, Susie and Sammy were listening to the news. Prior to their bedtime, Paula and Phoebe were romping about with Daniel, and the stairs were taking a thumping.

The Allied advance in Italy had brought the American 5th Army into Rome, and Rome was delirious with joy. The GIs, from their trucks and tanks, were throwing candy bars into the uplifted hands of elated Italian females. Fully-fashioned stockings would follow later, when some personal relationships were established. If the BBC news-reader did not mention that, his controlled description of events and scenes gave a clear picture of the fall of Rome to the Americans, and the advance of the Free French Force, the Canadians and the British Eighth Army east of the American drive.

'A splendid campaign,' said Mr Finch, fully recovered, back at work before expected, and giving Intelligence the benefit of his talents and experience.

'Edwin, I don't know what we're doing in Rome,' said Chinese Lady, 'the Pope hasn't been fighting us, has he?'

'No, he's been sitting on his throne not fighting anybody,' said Sammy. 'He's a peacemonger.'

'Sammy, don't you mean peacemaker?' suggested Susie.

'Same thing,' said Sammy.

'Yes, same thing, Sammy,' said Mr Finch, although he knew there were doubts about the Pope's strange refusal to condemn Germany's rabid anti-Semitism. It was being put down to His Holiness's approval of Germany's war against Russian Communism, the enemy of the Church.

'Well, then,' said Chinese Lady, 'what's all our tanks and guns and things doing in Rome?'

'Chasing the Germans out, Mum,' said Susie.

'Susie, you sure our wireless has got it right?' said Chinese Lady. 'I often wonder if it knows what it's talking about. It's given me many a chronic headache, I can tell you. I was down in Walworth yesterday, visiting Mrs Brown while Cassie was there, and she was telling me they can't wait to change their own wireless for a new one when new ones are in the shops. She's had headaches too. Edwin, there ought to be a law against wirelesses giving people headaches. Can't you speak to the Government about it?'

'As soon as the Government can spare a moment, Maisie, I'll deliver a note,' said Mr Finch, one ear on the wireless, the other on the family.

'Yes, I wish you would,' said Chinese Lady, who considered her husband the kind of gentleman any government would be pleased to listen to.

The phone rang. They heard Daniel call.

'I'll go, Dad. I'll go, Mum. I'll go, Grandma. I'll go, Grandpa.'

'That young man, well, I don't know, what's he telling all of us for?' asked Chinese Lady.

'To get a laugh out of Paula and Phoebe,' said Susie. 'Listen to them shrieking.'

'I prefer any loud noises from kids to the air raid sirens,' said Sammy.

'Hello?' said Daniel into the hall phone.

'Hi, handsome,' said Patsy.

'Who's he?' asked Daniel.

'Oh, some smarty-pants,' said Patsy. 'Hi, smarty-pants, can I come round? My Pa's given me a bottle of hooch and a box of candy for your parents and grandparents, and I'll bring them with me.'

'Happy to know you'll bring yourself as well,' said Daniel, 'you can help me put Paula and Phoebe to bed. Dad's been disqualified.'

'Disqualified?' said Patsy.

'From putting the girls to bed,' said Daniel. 'He gets them into a giggly tizzy and it keeps them awake.'

'They don't put themselves to bed?' said Patsy.

'They could, but it's not as much fun,' said Daniel.

'We'll have to make some rules,' said Patsy.

'Rules?' said Daniel.

'Sure,' said Patsy. 'You have to have rules. We'll work some out.'

'Um, I don't think rules are very popular in this family,' said Daniel.

'I can hear those girls,' said Patsy, 'you've got mayhem. We'll make some rules.'

'You make 'em,' said Daniel, 'I'll duck.'

'Don't be a funk, Daniel,' said Patsy, 'I'll be on my way in five minutes.'

She brought a bottle of American 'Southern Comfort' for Sammy and Mr Finch, and a box of chocolates for Susie and Chinese Lady, also an excited exposition of how the GIs had taken Rome. Then up she went with Daniel and the girls to get the latter quietly into bed. Rule one, she said: undress. Rule two: put on nightwear. Rule three: clean teeth. Rule four: say prayers. Rule five: get into bed quietly. Rule six: go to sleep.

'What could be more simple, given sensible adult supervision?' she said.

'Leave it to you,' said Daniel. 'There's a war on, and that's enough for me. I'll sit on the stairs.'

'You'll see,' said Patsy.

The first thing that happened concerned Paula's attitude. Paula mostly gave no trouble at bedtime. It was Phoebe who always looked for games and giggles. But the mention of rules was a challenge to

Paula, and she immediately asked if she could do rule six first, then she wouldn't need to do any of the others. And Phoebe spoke up.

'What's rules, please?'

'Instructions,' said Patsy.

'What's them?'

'Orders to be obeyed,' said Patsy.

'Oh, crikey,' said Phoebe.

'Patsy, you been and forgot rule seven,' said Paula.

'Oh, yeah?' said Patsy. 'So what's rule seven?'

'Mummy comes up and says goodnight to us,' said Paula.

'And kisses us,' said Phoebe.

'That's rule eight,' said Paula. 'Then there's rule nine. Daddy comes and says goodnight.'

'And kisses us,' said Phoebe.

'And that brings on rule ten, when Daddy kisses you?' said Patsy. 'Well, we'll work a quick way through rules one to six first, get it? Start by undressing.'

She was on a hiding to nothing. Daniel, sitting on the foot of the stairs, with a grin on his face, heard giggles, then laughs, then shrieks. Susie came out into the hall.

'What's going on up there?' she asked.

'Oh, just a few rules, Mum,' said Daniel.

'What rules?' asked Susie.

'Patsy's,' said Daniel.

'Well, they're not working,' said Susie. 'Daniel, go up and get those girls into bed.'

'All three of 'em?' said Daniel.

'Listen, my lad,' said Susie, 'in our respected families, there's your dad, there's your Uncle Boots, there's your cousin Rosie and cousin Tim. They're all comics, so we don't want any more, not even one more, you hear?'

'Mum, are you looking at me?'

'Yes, so get those sisters of yours into bed, or I'll send your grandma up to quieten the little monkeys,' said Susie.

'I thought I'd let Patsy give it a go,' said Daniel.

'Well, we all love Patsy,' said Susie, 'but I don't think she's got the hang of it. Go on, Daniel, put your foot down.' And she left him to it. Out of the girls' bedroom came Patsy, flushed and giggling. She sat down on the top stair.

'Who's winning?' asked Daniel from down below.

'I've got a headache,' said Patsy.

There was a yell from Paula. Patsy jumped and disaster struck. She slid all the way down the stairs on her bottom, and although her skirt and slip stayed with her they were very much out of place.

'Blind O'Reilly,' said Daniel, 'is that what the butler saw?'

'Blow the butler,' said Patsy, covering up her pants and stockings, 'and the rules. You go and get them into bed, Daniel.'

To Daniel, it all amounted to an hilarious break from the strained atmosphere of a prolonged war that had had its effect on the whole country. The wish for it to be brought to an end was intense. Mind, the arrival of Patsy into his life was a pretty uplifting event.

He walked her home later and kissed her good-night at her door. Patsy thought his kisses kind of clean and fresh, and that he never groped. Which was kind of nice.

'Look, you can hold me, if you like,' she said.

'Hold you?' said Daniel.

'Put your arms round me,' said Patsy.

'What for?' asked Daniel, who always played this sort of thing for laughs.

'What for? What for? Well, you like me, don't you?'

'Not half,' said Daniel, 'especially after what the butler saw.'

Patsy giggled.

'Listen, funny guy,' she said, 'when you come and meet my Pa tomorrow, keep off what the butler saw or he'll shoot you.'

'How big is your Pa?' asked Daniel, not for the first time.

'Seven feet,' said Patsy.

'I think I'll stay home,' said Daniel.

'Daniel, you'll be here by three,' said Patsy.

'All right, I'll risk it,' said Daniel. 'Any rules?'

Patsy gave a little yell and aimed a blow. Daniel ducked and left.

The weather was discouraging. General Eisenhower was fidgeting. The locked-in invasion force was suffering restlessness and boredom. Prime Minister Churchill was calming his nerves with a Scotch or two. Montgomery was itching for the off. The harassed meteorological boffins came up with a forecast of slightly improved conditions in two days' time, the sixth of June.

'Gentlemen, given that, we'll go,' said Eisenhower.

'We'll still be seasick all the way,' said an American commander.

Montgomery, perky, intimated that seasick men would be off their landing-craft like bats out of hell, and who could ask for more?

If Field Marshal Rommel suspected an imminent invasion attempt, he was confident it could be broken and beaten.

He advised the German High Command accordingly.

'The main defence zone on the coast is strongly fortified and defended. There are large tactical and operational reserves in the rear areas. Thousands of pieces of artillery, anti-tank guns, rocket projectiles and flame throwers await the enemy. Millions of mines under water and on land lie in wait for him. In spite of the enemy's great air superiority, we can face coming events with the greatest confidence.'

It was a fact, however, that this enormous defensive concentration was aimed at smashing Allied landings on the Pas de Calais coast, the German High Command having been convinced by subtle Allied machinations that that was the selected area.

It was another fact that the landings were to take place on the coast of Normandy, in an area well over one hundred and fifty miles south-east of Calais.

To 30 Corps and all other units under his direct command, Montgomery sent a personal message of

special encouragement. He ended with this famous
military quotation:

'He either fears his fate too much,
Or his deserts are small,
Who dare not put to the touch,
To win or lose it all.'

Earlier that day, a letter dropped lightly on the mat
of a house on Denmark Hill. Mrs Vi Adams picked
it up. It was addressed to *Miss Adams*. Vi gave it to
Alice.

'It must be for you, love.'

'There's no address or stamp,' said Alice.

'It must have come by hand,' said Vi.

Alice opened it.

Dear Miss Adams,
I think I'd like to say sorry for pulling your leg when
we ran into each other. Yes, there you are, sorry. I
thought I'd drop you a line to apologize and to
mention that if you'd like to change your mind
about a visit to the Lyceum Ballroom any Saturday
evening, I'd be willing to call for you. Or do you
prefer the cinema?
Yours sincerely,
Fergus MacAllister

'Well, of all the nerve,' said Alice, 'look at that,
Mum.'

She passed the letter to her mother, and Vi read
it.

'Alice, who's Fergus MacAllister?' she asked.

'You know, that man from the Gas Board who fitted a new joint to the airing cupboard pipe,' said Alice. 'The man Dad said he knew about.'

'Oh, that one,' said Vi. 'The one you didn't like.'

'Yes, and I met the gentleman near the library yesterday,' said Alice.

'What, by arrangement?' said Vi, wondering if her daughter liked the man, after all, and had actually found an interest outside her studying.

'Arrangement?' Alice looked offended. 'I should say not. I bumped into him by accident, worse luck, and as for going dancing with him, even if I had time for social activities of a recreational kind, I wouldn't wish to share them with Mr MacAllister. He's short of personal graces.'

Social activities of a recreational kind? Personal graces? Bless the girl, thought Vi, I hope all this studying isn't making her old before her time.

'Still, his letter has got a bit of grace to it,' she said. 'Alice, isn't he the young man your dad said was wounded near Dunkirk and has got some shrapnel left in him?'

'Yes, and I'm sorry about that, but I wasn't given a chance to say so,' complained Alice. 'He said I talked like a sixteen-year-old girl training to be a preacher. Can you believe anyone could be so rude?'

Lord, what an odd thing to say to a girl, thought Vi. Mind, Alice was a bit formal at times, and didn't have much in common with her cousins Annabelle and Emma, who'd both been happy to leave school at seventeen and sort of dance into the excitements of life.

'Alice, I can't believe the young man dislikes you if he wants to take you dancing,' said Vi. 'Still, you can decide for yourself, love, and let him know when you reply.'

'I'm not going to reply,' said Alice, 'I'm simply going to ignore his letter.'

Vi, the most gentle of women and the most affectionate of mothers, for once felt a lack of sympathy with her daughter.

'Now, Alice, if he was rude to you he's been gracious enough to say he's sorry,' she said, 'and I think you should be gracious enough to reply. And if you want to turn his invitation down, you can be gracious about that too. I won't have you going about with your nose in the air.'

Alice stared at her mum. The rebuke, spoken so firmly, astonished her. Neither of her cockney parents had ever dressed her down like that.

'Well, all right,' she said, 'I'll write to him, then.'

'Do it now, love,' said Vi, and stood by while Alice composed a reply.

Dear Mr MacAllister,
Thank you for your kind letter and for your apology, and I have no hard feelings. However, I really don't have time for dancing or the cinema as I'm terribly busy studying the subject of English Literature. But thank you for asking me.
Yours sincerely,
Alice Adams

'Yes, that's gracious,' said Vi, having read it. Fergus MacAllister had given his address in Grove

Lane, Camberwell, not far from Denmark Hill.

Vi posted the letter when she went shopping. Conditions were better for young people who did want to go dancing or to enjoy other forms of entertainment. Apart from the recent air raid, which had been very brief, London was being left alone by the Germans. Cinemas, theatres and dance halls were crowded most evenings, and trains, trams and buses carried people to and from the West End without having to worry about bombs.

Nor was the German High Command thinking in terms of orthodox assaults from the air. From Calais to Cherbourg, sites for the launching of rocket-powered bombs had been built, all pointing in the direction of London. These sites were being periodically attacked by the Allied Air Forces.

The Allied High Command knew something the people didn't. The hope and prayer were that by dint of deadly accurate bombing, the people wouldn't have that knowledge carried to them in a brutally practical way.

Chapter Twenty-Eight

'Hello there, hello,' breezed Mr Meredith Kirk, Patsy's Pa, on Saturday afternoon. 'I'm delighted to meet you, Daniel.'

'Same here, Mr Kirk,' said Daniel. The meeting was taking place in the living-room of the apartment, its double windows letting in the grey light of another cloudy and blustery day. June was playing up as if it had taken on a fit of stormy vexation. 'I've heard a lot about you from Miss Kirk, your daughter.'

'Miss Kirk?' said Pa Kirk.

'Patsy,' said Daniel. 'I just thought I ought to show good manners.'

'That's good manners, calling me Miss Kirk?' said Patsy.

'I'm not against it,' said Pa Kirk.

'It's a hoot,' said Patsy, 'but Daniel's like that sometimes. Kind of eccentric. Well, most times, actually. Don't take too much notice, Pa.'

'Eccentric?' said Pa Kirk, a handsome man of forty-five with a deep baritone. 'In the way of the English?'

'In the way of Daniel Adams,' said Patsy, 'but I don't let it bother me. I'm a good-natured girl guy.'

Pa Kirk smiled.

'Is that how you find Patsy, Daniel?' he asked. 'A good-natured girl guy?'

'Well, to be frank, Mr Kirk,' said Daniel, 'your daughter's got funny ideas about who sits on the carrier when we're riding her bike. I've told her that in this country, fellers sit on the saddle, girls on the carrier, otherwise one of our old native customs goes to pot.'

Patsy shrieked.

'Told you, Pa, didn't I tell you? He's a kook, and an old-fashioned one.'

'Let's discuss it,' said Pa Kirk genially. 'Take a seat, Daniel, and if Patsy would serve us coffee, I guess we could kick a few British and American customs around, and then I'd like to hear what you think about the war generally. I'd be interested in a young man's point of view and include it in my newscast tonight.'

Daniel spent a couple of very entertaining hours with Patsy's gregarious dad and Patsy herself, and he delivered himself of his opinions on the war, which he eventually said would never have come about if his paternal grandma could have had half an hour alone with Hitler as far back as the time of Munich. She was a good old rousing London cockney, and wouldn't have thought twice about knocking Hitler off his mountain balcony once he started to bawl at her. Pa Kirk wanted to know more about this redoubtable cockney lady, and Daniel supplied the works, along with anecdotal asides concerning what she thought about his dad's pre-war rag trade involvement with the manufacture and sale of ladies' underwear. Namely, decidedly improper, which made Patsy fall about.

Pa Kirk had to leave at five-thirty for his evening commitments in town. He said goodbye to Daniel and hoped he'd see more of him. Patsy went down to the front door with him.

'So what d'you think of my fun guy, Pa?' she asked.

'Clean as a whistle, Patsy, a fine young man, and amusing,' said Pa Kirk.

'I think I'm getting a crush,' said Patsy.

'Well, don't fight it, honey,' said Pa Kirk. 'You can take it from me, you could do a hell of a lot worse for your first boyfriend at this time in your life.'

'Thanks, Pa,' said Patsy.

She and Daniel went to the cinema in the evening, while clouds tumbled about in the sky, the Channel waters tossed, and landing craft were brought to loading points.

Patsy sat with her knee touching Daniel's knee, and felt remarkably happy. On the upper deck of the darkened bus going home, she whispered a comment.

'Pa says he doesn't mind you're English.'

'I don't mind, either,' said Daniel. 'Well, I was born that way, and a feller's got to honour his birthright.'

'D'you know how loopy you sound sometimes?'

'I don't mind that, either,' said Daniel. 'My

338

cousin Emma told me once that our Uncle Boots is convinced that everyone's a bit barmy, and she thought that sort of reassuring. Well, at the time she was a bit potty herself.'

'Potty? Potty?'

'Dotty,' said Daniel. 'About a Sussex bloke. She married him later. She said if she didn't, she'd end up being certified.'

Patsy linked arms with him, and whispered again.

'Daniel, I like you, I really do.'

'Well, I like you too, Patsy.'

'Really like me?'

'On my oath,' said Daniel.

'On your oath? That's wacky,' murmured Patsy. 'Oh, well, can't be helped, and next time we ride my bike together, you can sit on the saddle and I'll sit on the carrier.'

'You sure?' said Daniel.

'Sure I'm sure,' said Patsy, 'I've decided I don't mind observing one of your old and quaint English customs. Help,' she added, 'I hope it won't turn me old and quaint myself.'

'Who cares, as long as the war's over by Christmas?' said Daniel.

The bus dropped them off, and he walked her to her front door in the light of a half-sized moon. There he told her he'd enjoyed meeting her good old Pa and taking her to the cinema. Patsy said she'd invite him up, only it was late and she knew her Pa wouldn't like her to be alone with a guy at this time of night. Daniel asked what kind of a guy.

'What kind?' said Patsy. 'Your kind. I bet I'd have to yell for help.'

339

Daniel laughed.

'Goodnight, Patsy,' he said, 'see you again.'

'Hey, wait a moment, don't I get a kiss?' demanded Patsy.

'Oh, nearly forgot,' said Daniel, and kissed her. Somehow, it was a new kind of kiss, and Patsy experienced exciting little vibrations unknown before.

'Daniel – oh, I never liked anything as much as that,' she said.

'Same here, me too,' said Daniel, 'we'll do it again next time I see you home. You're sweet. So long, Patsy.'

'No, wait,' said Patsy. 'Daniel, d'you mean this is the beginning of a long and faithful friendship?'

'That's it,' said Daniel, 'be faithful and keep other fellers off your doorstep.'

'I will, I really will,' said Patsy. 'Goodnight, Daniel.'

'Goodnight, Patsy.'

Daniel walked home through the moonlight. The surging clouds had gone, although the night was still blustery. At SHAEF in London, the word 'Go' was still the operative one for when midnight had passed and the sixth of June had begun.

Of all things, earnest Miss Alice Adams, whose mind constantly dwelt on the fulfilling years of university life to come, dreamt that she was nowhere near any seat of learning. She was running in panic through endless woods, her limbs leaden, her running reduced to slow motion. Behind her loomed a dark figure, and each time she turned her head, the villainous face of a pirate grinned at her, white teeth huge. Thorns reached to rip and shred her dress, and an evil chuckling voice reached for her ears.

'Hold there, me young beauty, hold there and come aboard, won't ye?'

'Never! Never!'

Her legs could hardly carry her, his hot breath fanned the back of her neck, and her shredded dress fell off. In front of her loomed a black pit. She tumbled into it and found herself sitting at a table writing a letter. She looked up and there he was, in a kilt this time. She screamed and woke up. She was hot all over, but she breathed in deep relief.

Oh, you wait, Fergus MacAllister, next time I see you I'll push your rotten face in.

That was drastic for Alice.

Fergus, asleep in his lodgings in Grove Road, Camberwell, woke up himself, a dull ache in his ribcage.

Aye, that's the bloody shrapnel getting a wee bit restless again, he thought. Then he wondered why he had an oddly compulsive interest in a young lady so serious that she never smiled. A challenge? Perhaps.

There had been two brief letters for him during the day. One was from his father in Aberdeen.

Come home, Fergus. You belong up here, not down there. What are you doing, for God's sake, working as a maintenance mechanic for a gas company? There's a position for you in our sheet metal company as manager, you know that. Come home.

Aye, I will one day, but not yet, thought Fergus. London is where it's happening, the pulse of the war, and a battalion of the Highland laddies is here down South, I know that from a letter sent by Ian McGregor a few weeks ago. Something big is in the wind, I feel it and so does this bloody shrapnel. Further, I've got customers I like, and then there's that Adams lassie.

The other letter had been from her. It was very polite, but it simmered between the lines, and she turned down his invitation.

Well, he'd thought she would. She was living in a small corner of the world all on her own, with only English Literature to keep her company. English Literature had a lot to answer for.

Did the lassie need saving from herself?

Sunday morning

Susie, in her Sunday best, was ready to take Paula and Phoebe to church, and to make sure Sammy went with them.

'Paula, where's Daddy?' she asked.

'Hiding, I expect,' said Paula.

'He's in the garden, Mummy,' said Phoebe, both girls delectable in their frocks and round hats. Church Sundays were always hat Sundays, even for little girls. 'Well, I fink he is. I'll get him.'

'We'd both better go,' said Paula, wiser in the ways of her dad than Phoebe.

'Tell him I'll give him just two minutes,' said Susie.

Out into the garden went the girls. Sammy wasn't

hiding, however, he was standing in the middle of the lawn, looking up at the sky, where clouds were racing.

'Daddy, you've got to come to church,' called Phoebe.

'You've got just two minutes before Mummy comes after you herself,' said Paula.

'I'm ready,' said Sammy, turning. 'See that sky, me pets? It's our sky, looked after by the lads in RAF blue, and I daresay if they could keep the rain off, Queen Liz might be having some friends to tea in her garden this afternoon.'

'Yes, Daddy, but you've still got to come to church,' said Paula.

'I know, I've had notice of that,' said Sammy, and joined the girls. 'Would you two like to have tea with Queenie?'

'Oh, I don't mind,' said Phoebe, 'but I like it best with you and Mummy.' Sammy took her hand. Her fingers curled around his. He took Paula's hand. She clung too.

'Daddy, you look ever so respectable,' she said. Sammy was in a well-cut grey suit with a dark grey tie.

'Well, I promised the vicar,' he said. He looked down at his young daughters, pictures of innocence, and thought about the sky, full of clouds but clear of the enemy, an enemy who'd had a last-gasp go the other night, but was now reduced by Bolshevik Joe to hanging on to his shirt buttons. I'm betting that the young and the very young are safe now. The old country had taken a hell of a bashing, but Paula, Phoebe, Daniel and all the other grandchildren of Chinese Lady, and the grandchildren of grannies everywhere in the land, could surely from here on look forward to no more bombs and to eventual peace.

'Come on, Daddy,' urged Phoebe, looking up at him. Sammy smiled down at her.

'Lead on, Phoebe,' he said, 'lead on, Paula.' That's it, he thought, in twenty years' time when I'm looking at bathchairs, it'll be Phoebe, Paula and his other kids who'll be running the business and shaping the country.

They joined Susie in the hall.

'Oh, you're conscious, Sammy?' said Susie.

'Alive and kicking,' said Sammy, and thought so is Boots, I hope, and Tim, Bobby and Nick.

'Daniel!' called Susie.

Daniel responded from upstairs.

'I'm following with Grandma and Grandpa, Mum.'

'Hooray, Daniel's alive and kicking too,' said Susie.

'Mummy, you are funny,' said Paula.

'Something I caught from your dad and Uncle Boots,' said Susie. 'I was normal once.'

It was a moving service that morning, the church full. Patsy was there too, by arrangement, sitting next to Daniel, and Vi and Tommy were close by, with Alice. The hymns were sung full-throatedly, the responses to prayers fervent with 'Amens', and the vicar in his sermon dealt with the sacrifices that had been made and were still to be made in the elimination of the unhappy anti-Christ of Berlin. It was a regrettable sign of the times that this Christian nation needed to subdue the godless by force of arms.

He concluded with a compassionate reference to the enemy and the availability of forgiveness.

'Let us not forget the unhappy German people themselves on whom our bombs are falling. Let us remember to pray for them in their forgetfulness of God and their misguided worship of a man born of Satan himself and sadly in need of forgiveness.'

'There,' whispered Chinese Lady to Mr Finch, 'haven't I always said likewise more than once?'

'Indeed you have, Maisie,' murmured Mr Finch.

'Those who have lived by the sword must and will perish by its bright steel,' intoned the vicar, 'but with the knowledge that in the moment when life is ebbing and death is waiting, God is forgiving of all.'

'He's goin' to forgive Hitler? Well, I dunno about that,' whispered an old bloke to his old Dutch.

'God's forgiveness encompasses all transgressors,' smiled the vicar, attuned to catching asides. He welcomed asides. They were a tribute to the pungent points of his sermons. 'Providing that at the last there is repentance.'

'I'd like to listen to Hitler repenting,' whispered Daniel to Patsy.

'Shush,' whispered Patsy.

'All things are possible when we stand before the gates of God's heaven,' said the vicar.

'Ruddy hell,' muttered the old bloke, 'if Hitler gets through them gates, I ain't sure I want to follow.'

'Percy,' breathed his old Dutch, 'you just wait till I get you home. We're in church.'

'Better off down the pub, Gertie.'

'I'm willing to allow intercessions,' smiled the vicar.

'Oh, we didn't bring nothing like them with us, Your Reverence,' said the flustered old Dutch.

'I'm not believing this,' whispered Patsy.

'All of you are welcome, though you might come unclothed and empty-handed,' said the vicar benignly.

'That's the cue for the last hymn and the collection,' said Tommy to Vi.

'What's he mean, unclothed, Edwin?' whispered a slightly shocked Chinese Lady.

'Without worldly goods,' murmured Mr Finch, and the vicar bestowed his blessing and announced the last hymn, *Onward Christian Soldiers.*

The congregation liked that. It was very topical, and they sang it lustily, as if it meant one in the eye for Hitler. After all, they could leave it to God to forgive him. They didn't have to themselves, and were all for Eisenhower or Montgomery beating his brains out.

The service over, the congregation filed out, the vicar at the door shaking hands with all.

'Oh, I did enjoy your sermon, vicar,' said Chinese Lady, 'except I wouldn't ever come unclothed to church.'

'Dear Mrs Finch,' smiled the vicar, 'that merely referred to the unfortunate poor.'

'Yes, my husband explained,' said Chinese Lady, 'but even if I had nothing else, I'd always bring me handbag with me.'

'I've been unfortunately poor in me earlier days,

vicar,' said Sammy, 'but always managed to find a penny for the collection.'

'Yes, out of our mum's purse,' said Tommy.

'Tommy, not here,' said Vi.

'Come again,' smiled the vicar. 'Come again, come again,' he said to Alice, Daniel, Patsy and others.

'Are your church services always like that?' asked Patsy of Daniel when they were on the forecourt.

'Yes, always,' said Daniel, 'hymns, prayers, amens, reverence and a collection.'

'Reverence?' Patsy, in dress, light coat and cute hat, giggled. 'You could have fooled me. All the same—' She paused.

'All the same what?' asked Daniel.

'I liked it,' said Patsy, 'and I like your family.'

'Well, they all like you,' said Daniel, 'and so do I.'

'Daniel, we could have a really special friendship, couldn't we?'

'I thought we'd already got there,' said Daniel. 'Well, I have.'

Patsy smiled. Happily.

Tommy and Vi stood around talking to their relatives. Alice said she'd go on home.

'Yes, all right, love,' said Vi, and Alice left. A young man, emerging from a group of people, crossed her path.

'Hello, and a guid morning to you, Miss Adams,' said Fergus MacAllister. 'Was the sermon to your liking?'

'Pardon?' Alice quivered, the Scot as much of a blackhaired pirate in a suit of charcoal grey as in her dream. 'The sermon?'

'I'm fond of the brimstone-and-treacle kind mysel',' said Fergus. 'May they be cast into the black pit, darkness descend on their eyes and worms devour their bodies. That kind of stuff, y'ken. I'm no' believing it, of course, but it stirs the blood and keeps a man awake.'

'But it's very much Old Testament brimstone,' said Alice, 'and I prefer the generally more compassionate aspect of the New Testament.'

'I canna say I'm a great authority on the Bible,' said Fergus, 'and doubt if I'll ever read it from cover to cover. Rabbie Burns now, and Robert Louis Stevenson, aye, and Walter Scott, I've read my share of them.'

'Oh, have you read *Ivanhoe*?' asked Alice.

'At school,' said Fergus, 'and again when things were at a bit of a standstill.'

'Such detailed descriptions, such period authenticity, don't you think so?' said Alice.

'I didna think of it like that,' said Fergus, 'only that I enjoyed it, even if I found it long in the wind at times. By the way, thanks for your letter, Miss Adams. All understood, y'ken.'

'Oh, that's all right,' said Alice. 'I—'

'Fergus? Fergie?'

A full-bodied woman in her thirties was calling to him from the open gate of the forecourt.

'That's my bonny landlady,' said Fergus. 'I promised to walk her hame in case the Huns dropped on her by parachute. Guid morning to you, Miss Adams, and fine luck to your English Literature whatever.'

'Oh, goodbye, Mr MacAllister,' said Alice.

It was a relief in a way to see him go, a young man who at his age ought not to look like – like who?

Long John Silver from *Treasure Island*? Or Blackbeard the demon pirate?

Alice shook herself and went on the short walk home.

What had he meant about reading *Ivanhoe* again when things were at a bit of a standstill?

Fergus had meant when the Chamberlain Government and the French Government had been in charge of the 'phony war', and the BEF had dug the kind of trenches familiar to the troops in the 1914–18 conflict. There had been no attempt whatever to cross swords with the German Army, when the bulk of their Panzers had been engaged in scorching Poland.

Sunday evening

Pa Kirk arrived from town to spend an hour or two with Patsy before returning to transmissions.

'Patsy, we may be shaking the dust,' he said.

'What d'you mean?' asked Patsy, making coffee and peanut butter sandwiches. All kinds of goodies were brought to the apartment by her Pa. Americans had unlimited sources of fodder available for representatives of their Press and radio.

'I've been offered an assignment in Rome,' smiled Pa Kirk. 'It looks like we'll be upping sticks next Thursday.'

'Rome?' said Patsy.

'Recently liberated by our boys,' said Pa Kirk. 'I've been invited to cover the continuing war in

Italy, since so many American divisions are there.'

'You go, Pa, I'll stay here,' said Patsy.

'Hold your horses, honey,' said Pa Kirk. 'I go, you go, we both go.'

'Pa, no.'

'Have you got a good argument?' asked Pa Kirk.

'Yes.'

'Spill it, Patsy.'

'I don't want to go.'

'That's an argument?'

'Pa, I'm not going.'

'Well, I guess I've got a problem,' said Pa Kirk.

'Pa, we're settled here, we've got friends, and anyway, it's not what we ought to do, fly off to the fleshpots of Rome and Italian ice cream.'

'It's an assignment I don't want to turn down, honey.'

'But if you accept, it'll – it'll be like an act of desertion,' said Patsy, patently upset.

'Desertion?'

'Yes, and I couldn't do it, Pa. I'll go on strike, I'll burn all my clothes, everything, and go to bed unclothed and empty-handed, and stay there.'

'You'll do what?' said Pa Kirk.

'All that, and I will too,' said Patsy.

'Unclothed and empty-handed?'

'Sure.'

'Patsy, where'd you get that from?'

'The preacher at this morning's service,' said Patsy. '"Oh, my good people," he said, "come unto me thus—"'

'Thus?'

'Yes, without any belongings. "Come unto me

350

thus," he said "and you shall be welcome." That's what Jesus said to the multitude. "Come unto me all ye who are heavy-laden and I will give ye comfort." Heavy-laden meant laden with dire poverty, and not even a spare pair of pants. Pa, if you try to make me go to Rome, I'll ask the preacher for sanctuary.'

'You'll run to his church unclothed and empty-handed?' said Pa Kirk.

'In a flour sack,' said Patsy.

'Well, Patsy,' said Pa Kirk, 'we've both got problems. You sleep on yours and I'll sleep on mine, and we'll hit the high road of compromise or agreement over breakfast.'

'I'm sorry, Pa, but there's not going to be any breakfast.'

'That's a fact, Patsy?'

'I'm going on strike at midnight pronto,' said Patsy.

'Well, before that happens, Patsy, is there any chance of a coffee now?'

'Yes, you can have that, Pa. It's ready. But don't think I'm weakening. Pa, have you got a cold?'

'No, Patsy, I'm just coughing fit to bust.'

Chapter Twenty-Nine

The invasion armada was on the waters. The first landing-craft, laden with British and American troops, had been launched late on the night of the fifth of June to reach the beaches next morning.

Prior to that, bridges over the Seine and the Loir had been bombed and destroyed by thunderous waves of Allied planes. Attacks on railway bridges, lines and roads had been effected to cripple the movements of any German units intent on re-inforcing the defence forces in the Normandy landing area.

Paratroops and airborne Commandos were on their way before one in the morning.

East of a town called Montebourg, the commander of a German infantry battalion, disturbed by the continuous drone of aircraft, left his bunker to investigate. He could not, for a moment, believe his eyes. Several giant aircraft, clearly visible in the moonlight, were heading directly for his head-quarters. From them spilled what at first seemed to be little white clouds.

'*Mein Gott!*'

He knew then what he was seeing, an airborne landing.

'*Achtung! Achtung!*'

Down, down to earth dropped hundreds of American paratroops.

Fifty miles away, a German sentry patrolling a bridge over the Caen canal stood rigid as a strangely soundless aircraft glided downwards only a short distance from him. He stared, he blinked. It disappeared, it crashed, but with only a splintering noise. A stricken bomber that had lost engine power, he thought. Bombers had been roaring in from the coast for longer than he cared to estimate. He shouted, and his comrades came up from their dugout to be told an Allied bomber had crashed close by, and then came the spectacle of land and earth being invaded by giant birds from the sky. Gliders. The moon disappeared behind clouds, and by instinct and at random the German soldiers fired in all directions. Out of the darkness came phosphorous grenades that burst into searing white flame, blinding vision.

Commandos landed. Colonel Lucas landed, Tim landed, and their detachment landed. They put the men in the nearby German pillbox out of action by tossing explosive grenades into its aperture.

The combat teams of the British 6th Airborne Division all landed. In very short time, at the expense of a few casualties, the bridge was in their hands.

The Commandos formed an arc of defence to

retain their hold. Colonel Lucas peered at Tim.

'For Christ's sake, Tim, is that blood all over your face?'

'No, Colonel Lucas, it's a faceful of sweat,' said Tim, taking a breather. God, what a night this was going to be. Were the landing-craft and the naval escorts at sea yet? How long before the Jerries bring up a unit to try to shift us from here? 'Luke, I'm going home. When's the next ferry?'

'Christmas.'

'Might get there by Boxing Day, then.'

'Save your jokes, Charlie Chaplin.'

'You think that's a joke? I tell you, I wish I'd never joined. How far's Berlin?'

The fight for a foothold in Normandy had begun, the advance airborne troops detailed to capture and hold strategic objectives, and so create conditions that would help the main invasion force to establish important footholds.

These objectives were numerous. American and British airborne units took them in rushing sorties, and held them against German troops who, recovering from confusion, became certain the offensive by the Allied paratroops presaged an invasion. Local German commanders, telephoning higher authorities, were told they must be mistaken. German Intelligence had long possessed information to the effect that when the invasion did come, it would be in the Pas de Calais area.

'You are dealing with a feint.'

'It's a damned widespread feint that's costing us bridgeheads and casualties.'

'Don't panic. Retake the bridgeheads.'

*   *   *

The landing-craft, the supply ships and the escorting warships were on the broad surface of the heaving Channel, the moon alternately coming and going, the wind chilly, the vast armada of a thousand vessels heading on a hugely broad front for the coast of Normandy. Conditions were appalling for the men packed into landing-craft, which rolled, pitched and staggered through the high swell. Seasickness hit thousands of stomachs, causing the troops to vomit. If they had had qualms about what awaited them on the designated beaches of Normandy, those qualms disappeared beneath a Godalmighty urge to feel land, any kind of land, under their feet, never mind if they ran into a hell of fire. Any kind of hell was preferable to that of constant vomiting. Husky Americans, all built like John Wayne, were green, groaning and vilely sick. Lean, toughened British soldiers cared not if their landing-craft sank.

Nevertheless, the armada sailed on, early morning beginning its approach to dawn, the skies roaring to the thunderous waves of Allied bomber formations that never stopped coming.

The officers of 30 Corps Headquarters, Boots among them, were making the crossing aboard an escort ship. That did not prevent some of them being sick. Boots escaped that by positioning himself amidships, the least affected area of the heaving vessel. He thought of his wife Polly, his twins Gemma and James, and his son Tim. Polly and the twins were in the haven of Dorset, but where were Tim and Colonel Lucas and their Commando team? Already there, already in France. Boots was sure of that. Wars asked a lot of some men, those whose fighting qualities were of a kind that influenced commanders to detail them for participation in one hair-raising action after another. It asked even more of a man whose blinded wife needed him just as much as his country did.

Telephones were dancing a ringing jig in the Paris headquarters of Germany's Naval Group West. Report after report from Normandy radar stations concerned huge numbers of blips on screens.

'It's some kind of technical interference, it must be.'

It was not possible that these blips represented ships. Never. There were hundreds.

The Chief of Staff suggested that what was not possible in such inclement weather might very well be happening. He made up his mind that it was, and signalled the *Fuehrer*.

'Allied invasion force on its way to Normandy coast.'

Hitler, sceptical, said that if this was true, the armada was to be blown up and sunk. No-one cared to mention that the concentration of guns was sited in the wrong area, the Pas de Calais. After all, as the *Fuehrer* himself suspected, the signal might be based on mistaken conclusions, and it was known that the weather over the English Channel was entirely unsuitable for a seaborne invasion.

At grey dawn the sea off the coast of Normandy presented an unbelievable picture to German lookouts. It was covered with ships of every description. Formidable battleships, sleek destroyers, flak ships, supply ships, minesweepers and countless landing craft. And the landing-craft were coming in to disgorge men whose immediate needs were to find terra firma and then to engage with the Hun, very much in that order. Tanks were swimming ashore. Swimming!

The great guns of the battleships were booming, the extensive bombardment pinning Germans down. Fighters and bombers were at their own kind of work.

On their respective beaches, the seasick Americans and British began to land, some to throw up for the last time before engaging with the enemy.

The invasion from the sea, an effort of colossal magnitude, had begun, and there was a day's furious fighting ahead to establish an invincible foothold.

London and Washington were awaiting the morning's outcome. Neither Churchill nor Roosevelt realized that the German High Command and their defensive units covering the North-West coast of France were in a stage of hopeless confusion. This state, engineered by the brilliant work of Allied Intelligence, was such that there was no move by the Germans to despatch reinforcements from the Pas de Calais to Normandy, since Hitler and his generals still believed the Normandy landings were a deceptive ploy.

This confusion helped the British units to sweep aside opposition and to begin a first day advance that was beyond Churchill's happiest dreams. The Americans were having a tougher time, suffering heavy casualties, but they were sticking it out and gradually pushing forward. General Eisenhower was receiving reports minute by minute, and so far no deeply worried frowns had creased his handsome brow. Montgomery was ebullient, chirpy and confident.

Churchill's cigar kept going out. Not that he was short of puff. In his exultation, he was simply unable to determine which was his cigar and which was his glass of Scotch.

The old boy wasn't counting his chickens. There had been too many setbacks, too many disappointments and too many failures. But the years of endeavour, the protracted and difficult planning of Overlord, the need for secrecy and colossal bluff, all had at last culminated in a successful landing, and with the unstoppable air might of the Allied Air Forces pounding the Germans, Field Marshal Rommel was faced with the task of a lifetime to push the Americans and British back into the sea.

In a mood of fresh exultation, the Prime Minister treated himself to a new cigar, from which the smoke rose with positive buoyancy.

Chapter Thirty

The apartment phone rang. It woke Patsy. Sleepily, she checked the time. Seven. Seven? Who was calling at this time? She slipped from her bed, padded into the living-room and picked up the phone.

'Who's this?'

'Patsy?' said Pa Kirk. He was often not back from town until the early hours. This time, he'd been out all night. 'It's me, honey.'

'Oh, is that a fact?' said Patsy. 'Well, this is a lousy time to get me out of bed. What's kept you in town all night, and why—'

'Patsy, listen.' There were vibrations drumming through Pa Kirk's baritone. 'They're over, they've made it.'

'Who's over where, and who's made what?'

'The Allies. Press and radio have been standing by all night here on the promise of a sensational news flash. Patsy, we've landed an army in Normandy. A whole armada made it, and put the GIs and the Brits on the beaches. There's been a total clampdown on any news until this morning.

Switch the radio on now, if you want, and you'll find there's nothing but continuous communiqués being broadcast. Patsy, we're over there, we're in Hitler's back yard. There's a million Allied warships standing off and shelling the German positions. Patsy, the Krauts are throwing in everything, but they can't shift the boys. We're there, honey, and we're staying. Patsy? You there?'

'Pa, I'm here and I've lost my breath. We're really over there, we're in France? It's the Second Front?'

'It's the end of the loudmouth Nazis, Patsy, the end of German totalitarianism. It's only a matter of time. Naturally, I shan't be going to Rome, I'd be crazy if I left London now, particularly as there'll be a chance of moving across to France with the Press and radio corps when Ike's armies are well on their way to Germany. Paris, Patsy, how does that grab you? Not tomorrow, of course, but sometime, if I can slip you through as an interpreter or secretary.'

'Pa, I'm dizzy, I'm standing on my head,' said Patsy, 'I never heard anything more exciting. A landing in France, isn't that great?'

'The planning, the operation, Patsy. Titanic. Stand on your head all day, if it suits you.'

'I'm so pleased for our friends, for all the Brits, Pa, and I'll be pleased for you too, if you make Paris eventually. Sure, you go and cover the war from there. I'll follow when it's all over. Listen, if you meet up with a nice, well-preserved Paris lady who'll take your shirts to a French laundry for you, I'll honestly root for you.'

'You're giving me a free hand, is that it, Patsy?'

'Ma's been gone three years now, Pa, and you've paid your respects. Any time you feel like getting married again, you go ahead.'

'Hold your horses, Patsy, I think we've still got problems. No way am I going to leave you here alone.'

'Pa, I'm an adult.'

'On several counts, you're not. It's either under my wing for you, or a return to Boston to stay with your Aunt Martha in Northboro.'

'Aunt Martha?' said Patsy in disgust. 'She's still living the Revolution. She still sits on her porch with a loaded blunderbuss on her lap, and any guy wearing something red is in danger of having his head blown off.'

'I think I'm listening to slight exaggerations,' said Pa Kirk.

'Well, don't push me,' said Patsy, 'or I'll—'

'Hightail it for sanctuary in a flour sack?' Pa Kirk sounded amused. 'I'll pass on that one. I'll have to hang up in a moment. Patsy, we'll talk about it, and in any case, a Paris assignment isn't going to come off for quite a while. There'll be some tremendous battles to fight as soon as Rommel can fill Normandy with extra divisions. I'll see you some-time later today. Hang in there, honey.'

'I'll do that, Pa, and we'll talk about who does what and who goes where when I next see you?'

'Sure,' said Pa Kirk, and hung up.

Patsy stood for a moment, then rushed to switch on the radio, and within seconds it was all coming forth, news upon news of the Normandy landings. Patsy danced barefooted and in her nightie, then ran back to the phone.

It rang in the house on Red Post Hill, the time just gone seven.

Sammy woke up.

'Wassat?' he mumbled.

Chinese Lady woke up.

'Oh, that blessed contraption,' she said.

Daniel woke up, looked at the time, wondered who was phoning and who was going to answer the call.

Paula woke up and went down to the phone.

'Hello?'

'Hello?' said Patsy.

'We're not up yet,' said Paula. 'Is that the lady milkman?'

'No, it's Patsy here, and could you be Paula?'

'Crikey,' said Paula, 'have you fallen out of bed or something? D'you want a doctor?'

Patsy laughed.

'You're a sweetie,' she said. 'Can I talk to Daniel?'

'He's still in bed, he doesn't get up till half-past seven, nor me, nor Phoebe, nor Mummy.'

'He'll get up when he knows what's happening,' said Patsy. 'Could you go up and tell him our armies are in Normandy? Could you do that, Paula?'

'Oh, crikey, oh, lor',' breathed Paula, who knew enough about the war to understand what Patsy meant. She dropped the receiver and let it dangle by its cord. She went scrambling up the stairs, intent on running from bedroom to bedroom.

So it was from nine-year-old Paula that, in turn,

Daniel, Susie, Sammy, Granny Finch and Grandpa Finch came to hear that which brought them all out of bed to listen to the wireless. The day of the invasion had already been named.

D-Day.

Daniel dashed from the kitchen to find that Patsy was still hanging on.

'You took a long time to crawl out of bed on a day like this,' she said.

'Patsy, you beauty,' said Daniel.

'You sure you mean that?' she said. 'After all, I'm not eighteen yet—'

'And not quite seventeen, either,' said Daniel.

'And genuine beauty doesn't clothe a woman until she's at least twenty-one, according to artists,' said Patsy.

'Don't they paint them in no clothes?' said Daniel. 'Anyway, don't talk yourself out of it, count yourself an exception. You're worth framing for phoning the news. Patsy, the invasion, they've done it, the Second Front's been opened up.'

'Daniel, it's exciting, really exciting, isn't it?' said Patsy. 'And I'm proud, aren't you, your guys and my guys hitting Hitler's pitchers out of the stadium?'

'You've lost me there,' said Daniel. 'Now if you'd said knocked 'em for six down the Old Kent Road, I'd be with you.'

'We're losing each other,' said Patsy.

'Come and join the family tonight,' said Daniel.

'Could I do that, Daniel, could I come round and listen to your radio with you?'

'You bet,' said Daniel, 'and bring your legs with you.'

'Daniel, I guess they'll just come with me kind of naturally.'

'Good-oh,' said Daniel, 'I like 'em.'

'You're kinky,' said Patsy, but she was laughing as she hung up. No way was she going to let her Pa divorce her from Daniel and his old-fashioned English family.

It was D-Day 2, and follow-up landing-craft were swarming over the waters of the still heaving Channel, where the wind was beginning to lessen a little. The Americans and British were consolidating their footholds, reinforcements pouring onto the beaches, and the sounds of war crashed on the ears. The Germans, desperate to break the footholds, were up against men trained for months for just this kind of battle, and they were, moreover, relentlessly attacked by air forces that never stopped coming at them.

The British 30 Corps, Montgomery's crack troops, forged ahead, smashing into the opposition with tanks and guns, and from the established headquarters Boots and the rest of the staff could barely keep up with the reports detailing progress.

The Commando teams, behind the German forward lines, were engaged with enemy reserve formations. Colonel Lucas was in his element, and Tim was a hundred per cent supportive. They had known the humiliation that had driven the BEF, beaten and disorganized, to the beaches of Dunkirk. Now they were back in France, something Colonel Lucas had promised himself the moment he stepped off a fishing-boat at Ramsgate and picked out Eloise Adams of the ATS as the young lady most likely to give him the help he was set on at the time.

At this moment, Eloise, on liaison duty at the London headquarters of the Free French, was beside herself with exultation. He was over there, husband Luke, he was at the commencement of the bruising journey to Berlin with the invasion army. On reaching Berlin, he would, she was sure, be the one to drag Hitler the monster from his lair and hang him for all the misery and torment he had inflicted on the people of Europe.

Eloise had enjoyed many imaginative moments in picturing her barnstorming husband as the people's avenger. Her imagination was preposterous, her French temperament volatile, her little conceits absurd, which all in all made Luke regard her as irresistible, such was the weakness of strong men hopelessly in love.

Eloise was sure her half-brother Tim was with the invading Commandos, and sure too that her father was over there, her English father, the man her French mother had known for only a few weeks, but who had loved him very much.

A French officer, Captain Debret, entered the room she used as a makeshift office. He was forty, handsome, moustached and amorous. He had a bottle of wine in his hand, and was slightly flushed. Eloise was seated on a small settee, reading a Free French circular relating to the Normandy landings. It had just been issued.

'Ah, my beautiful Eloise—'

'*Mon Capitaine*, I am not your beautiful Eloise.'

'But why not? It could be achieved easily. We only need to make love.'

'You're drunk,' said Eloise.

'Of course.' Captain Debret eyed her khaki-clad legs. Pointedly, Eloise gave her skirt a tug. 'France will be ours again. I am—' An involuntary hiccup emerged. 'I am celebrating.'

'One can celebrate, but it's disgusting to be drunk at ten in the morning,' said Eloise.

'Not on a morning like this. Drink wine with me, angel of France.'

'I don't deny I'm angelic, but now is not the time to get drunk,' said Eloise. Captain Debret seated himself, a little gratefully on account of a generous amount of tipple, and a little happily on account of placing himself close to her. 'You must know there's a public relations meeting with representatives of the Free French newspaper and a BBC interviewer in half an hour,' said Eloise, 'when you will be one of the officers expected to give the Free French view of the Normandy landings.'

'Ah, half an hour,' murmured the enamoured captain. 'In that time, we could accomplish much.' He put a hand on her knee. 'First, some wine.'

'If you insist,' said Eloise. She took the bottle from him and poured some over his head. 'It is an offence to touch the person of a lady officer, but I shan't report you. Not on a morning like this. Yes, how wonderful to know France will belong again to those who truly love her. *Mon Capitaine*, I think you need a towel. Here is one. It's only a hand towel, but it will do, I think.'

*   *   *

'Rosie!' An excited Polly was on the line. 'You've heard, of course.'

'Over and over,' said Rosie, 'we're simply letting our radio run on and on. Felicity's given in to compulsive listening, she's got Emily on her lap and Giles sitting on the floor at her feet. She's hoping Giles is understanding just a little of what D-Day represents. It's all passing over his head, of course, but Felicity says that one day he might tell his grandchildren he was indirectly present at the battle for Normandy.'

'I can't settle,' said Polly. 'I listen, I walk about, I listen, I go and look at my vegetables, I listen again, and the twins think I've got my knickers in a twist.'

'Do they think that?' asked Rosie.

'My dear, Gemma asked if I was wearing something that didn't fit. Can you believe an infant of two and a half capable of coming to that kind of conclusion?'

'I can believe anything of yours and mine,' said Rosie, 'they're infant marvels. Of course, yours are my brother and sister.'

'Yes, I still realize they're all related, Rosie old sport,' said Polly. 'Put any complaints in writing.'

'Complaints?' Rosie laughed. 'One day I'm going to send you a certificate of merit for producing them.'

'Rosie, I can't settle here today,' said Polly, 'I'm driving over with the twins to spend the day with you and yours and Felicity. Any objections?'

'None!' said Rosie. 'All of us and our talking wireless would love to have you, and you are, as well, Felicity's favourite mother-in-law.'

'Rosie, you stinker,' said Polly, 'I don't want to be known as anyone's mother-in-law. It's not my style.'

'Come over,' said Rosie.

Neither of them had mentioned Boots, Tim or Colonel Lucas. It was as if they were keeping their fingers crossed, and that any mention would break the spell. Nor had Rosie mentioned that Felicity thought she might be pregnant. Felicity, naturally, didn't want anything said about it until the doctor had confirmed it. The test might prove negative. She would know tomorrow.

30 Corps, pressing on, were worrying the Germans, and the Americans, badly mauled during their D-Day landing, had recovered, won their beach-heads, and were massing for a forward charge. Back-up units were wallowing across the Channel in fully-laden landing-craft, and supply ships were riding in. The beaches were swarming with men, stores, tanks, guns, ambulances and everything else necessary to sustain the impetus of yesterday's landings and 30 Corps's battering advance. Again, the skies were patterned with Allied warplanes swooping in to target German defence positions. Naval guns pounded away, and shells from German guns caused the sea to erupt around the ships. Men worked feverishly amid the hell of the back-up of D-Day 2. It reflected a courage and effort that could never have been put down on the most detailed of plans. True, plans asked for such endeavours, but only when the time came could commanders expect answers.

*　　*　　*

Cassie, her children at the re-opened church school, was shopping in Walworth Road when she met Mrs Hobday. Cassie walked in the lively way of her kind. Bulky Mrs Hobday had a kind of cheerful waddle.

'Hello, ducks, nice to see yer,' said the neighbourly fat lady, 'ain't it good news we're gettin'? Me old man brought me 'ome a bottle of Guinness last night when he come rolling in from the pub, like he knew about the landings when nobody else did. Well, he's always saying he's prophetic.'

'I feel all excited,' said Cassie. 'I mean, it really does look as if the Army's done the Germans in the eye.'

'Yes, and ain't they givin' it to them Japs in Burma as well?' said Mrs Hobday. 'I dunno where Burma is meself – here, love, didn't you tell me your hubby's there?'

'Yes, he's there,' said Cassie, and wondered if there was any country farther away than Burma, if any husbands were farther away from their wives than those in Burma. She hadn't heard from Freddy for ages, but refused to consider the possibility that the Japanese might have got him at last.

In the steamy heat, the British 14th Army was coming to the end of the greatest land battle of the war against Japan, the prolonged and savage battle for Kohima, the gateway to Burma, Mandalay and Rangoon. Freddy and his Chindit comrades had been in the thick of things for months, Freddy twice wounded, patched up and returned to combat duties.

The Japanese were at last in retreat after what they themselves described as one of the greatest battles in history.

As far as Freddy was concerned it had been something he'd be glad to forget.

He longed for home, for Cassie and his kids.

'Leah, my dear,' said Mr Isaac Moses, father of Rachel, 'I've been giving much thought to your attachment to Edward Somers. Much thought.'

'Yes, Granddad, I expect you have,' said Leah.

'I've left it until now to speak to you,' said Isaac, 'but am no more certain in my mind about how to advise you than when your mother first showed me Edward's letter.'

'I understand, Granddad,' said Leah.

'And do you understand that I wish this attachment had not been formed?' said Isaac gently. He was not an authoritarian, any more than he was strictly orthodox, but he was faithful to his religion and the people of Israel.

'Yes, I understand that too,' said Leah, quite sure that she did not want to hurt her grandfather, or her mother, by adopting a rebellious or precocious stance.

'There's to be a year, I believe, before you and Edward make up your minds about whether or not you wish to marry,' said Isaac.

'We both think that would be right, Granddad,' said Leah.

'In the event that you did marry, would you convert?' asked Isaac.

'No, Granddad, I wouldn't change my religion,' said Leah.

'And if you had children?' said Isaac.

'Edward and I would have to discuss that,' said Leah.

'I think, Leah my dear, I will sit back and wait to see what effect the passing of a year has on the situation,' said Isaac.

'Yes, a year might change things,' said Leah, but she didn't think it would. 'Granddad, thanks for being so kind.'

Isaac smiled.

'No good ever came out of loud voices, Leah,' he said. 'Not even the smallest good ever came out of Hitler's loud voice, except for people like Goering, who has been given the privilege of stealing the treasures of nations.'

'Is that what has happened, Grandad?' said Leah.

'I know it has, my child, and one day the whole world will know it, along with other perfidies,' said Isaac.

Chapter Thirty-One

Hitler's reaction to the Allied invasion was not one of anger or alarm. He actually expressed a kind of satisfaction. He said, in effect, that now the hitherto skulking armies of the warmongers had at last shown themselves, it would avail them nothing, for they had given the Germans the opportunity to confront them face to face and smash them. It was an opportunity he himself had long wanted.

'My *Fuehrer*,' said Goebbels, Hitler's number one yes-man, 'as you inspire those of us who serve you, so you will inspire our invincible German soldiers.'

Well, he said something like that, being what he was, an acolyte of self-delusion. He was also intellectually superior to the rest of the Nazi hierarchy, and a brilliant propagandist. That, combined with his self-delusion, enabled him in his speeches concerning the war against Russia to make defeats sound like victories.

Stiffening German resistance in Normandy was not affecting the build-up of Allied resources, but it was causing casualties, most of which were speedily dealt with by the well-organized medical machinery. They were carried across the Channel in hospital ships to be treated in the United Kingdom.

D-Day 10. Montgomery's British and Canadian troops had taken Bayeux, and been given a joyful welcome by its people. The seizure of important bridges was effected, and this opened the way for an attack on Caen, heavily defended by German Panzers and infantry. Montgomery's plan was to draw the bulk of Germany's divisions to Caen and give the American forces the opportunity for a wholesale breakout elsewhere.

At home, phones were ringing everywhere, such was the need for communication of all kinds at this particular time in the war. Rosie answered hers.

'Hello, Rosie Chapman here.'

'What-ho, Rosie Chapman, how's your famous self and your bundles of chubby joy?'

'Tim!'

'Yup, me myself,' said Tim.

'Oh, you lovely man for phoning,' said Rosie, who had always enjoyed a very happy relationship with the son of her adoptive father. 'It tells me you're somewhere over here and not over there. Are you?'

'Guildford,' said Tim. 'Hospitalized with a smashed left arm. Happened four days ago. Bloody marvellous journey home, nurses kissing me all the way. What a sacrifice! I was five days unshaven, six days sweating, filthy togs and all over lice and BO. I tell you, getting kisses from those nurses must have cost them something. Mind, I think they shut their eyes and held their noses, but it was still a sacrifice.'

'Tim, is your arm badly smashed?'

'Well, it's a mess and it hurts a bit, and I won't deny it,' said Tim. 'I've given up being a brave bloke, I go in for hollering when there's pain about. Luke – Colonel Lucas – was close by when I caught my packet. He asked me what the hell I was bawling about. I asked him if he'd seen my arm. He said I was still wearing it, wasn't I? He took a look and said he didn't know what I was fussing about, that there wasn't all that much blood. I said see that, it's a piece of my armbone. All right, shove off and get it seen to, he said. He's an uplifting brother-in-law.'

'Tim, I think you're telling me you've got an arm that's in crisis,' said Rosie.

'Oh, they're trying to put the pieces back in place,' said Tim. 'I've had my operation, and my bedside nurse, Captain Daisy Bell—'

'Daisy Bell?' said Rosie.

'Well, she's a Daisy, so I've hung a bell on her,' said Tim. 'She's given me a bedside phone today, and I'm sufficiently compos mentis to be able to use it. Rosie, is Felicity around?'

'Tim love, yes, she is,' said Rosie, and wondered just how bad his arm was. He'd been severely wounded during the war in the desert, and she hoped to God that if he was returned to duty, lightning wouldn't strike a third time. 'I'll get her.' She could have told Tim something, but no, that had to be Felicity's own special moment.

Tim heard her call.

'Giles? Giles, bring Aunt Felicity to the phone, will you, darling?'

Felicity answered.

'Rosie, if I can't get myself to the phone, I'll spit.'

'Not in front of the children, old thing,' said Rosie.

'Who's calling, anyway?' Felicity was on the move.

'Guess.'

'My mother, bless her?'

'No, your husband, bless you.'

A little yell sprang from Felicity.

She was at the phone moments later.

'Tim? Tim?'

'Hello, Puss, how are you, you darling woman?'

'Where are you, where are you?'

'Guildford.'

'*Guildford?*' Felicity did half a jump. '*Guildford!*' It was almost a shout.

'Rosie will tell you all about it—'

'No, you tell me.'

'All right, Puss,' said Tim and repeated much of what he had told Rosie. And, of course, Felicity asked the same question as Rosie, just how bad was his arm. 'I can't see,' said Tim, 'there's all these bandages, but better some holes in an arm than holes in the head. Holes in the head are fatal, and I've seen some. Meanwhile, for the time being, I can't get out of here to see you, but I'll give you a daily phone call.'

'Tim, if Rosie will look after all the kids and I can get Polly to drive me, can I come and see you?' asked Felicity.

'Can you do that?' asked Tim.

'See you?' said Felicity. 'Well, curses that I still can't even see my hand in front of my nose, but I can sit with you, can't I?'

'It shouldn't be a problem,' said Tim, 'I smell better now that I've been scraped and bathed.'

'Then I'll ask Polly to drive me to Guildford,' said Felicity, 'I'm sure she'll say yes.'

'Tell her she can't say no, she's my mother,' said Tim.

'Stepmother,' said Felicity, 'but don't call her that, she's got a thing about the frightful curse of being anyone's stepmother or mother-in-law.'

'She's still a flapper,' said Tim, 'and I'll always regret I never saw her doing the Charleston in half a dress, which is what the flappers wore, didn't they?'

'I was an infant at the time,' said Felicity. 'Tim, I'm dreadfully sorry about your arm, but grateful you're being looked after not too far away from me, and you'll beat all the gremlins, won't you?'

'There's an armistice at the moment,' said Tim, 'but I'll be hollering as soon as they start firing their burning arrows again.'

'Little devils,' said Felicity.

'Nothing compared to those you had to suffer,' said Tim. 'And still do, don't you?'

'Now and again in my waking moments,' said Felicity. 'But Tim, I've something to tell you. I'm pregnant.'

'Felicity?'

'Yes, it's a fact.'

'You're going to have a baby?'

'Yes. You and me.'

'Who said so?'

'The doctor.'

'What doctor?'

'Our village doctor, a few days ago.'

'How does he know?'

'He's a doctor. Tim, what's up with you?'

'I'm punch-drunk,' said Tim.

'In a celebratory way?'

'Look, Puss, am I really going to be a dad?'

'Yes, about January.'

'And you're going to be a mum?'

'Yes, about the same time.'

'Well, we did talk about it.'

'We did more than that,' said Felicity.

'And you're sure you can cope?'

'We talked about that too.'

'What a woman,' said Tim.

'Your kind, Tim?'

'My kind, Puss.'

My dear Polly,

I expect the radio is keeping you up-to-date with events, and you won't need any forbidden details from me about present operations. I can tell you French wine by the case has become available to Corps headquarters, but that Scotch seems to be in short supply. Enjoyed the sea trip only up to a point, and I'll stick to the Thames in future, or just the bath. When you've seen one wave as high as a house, there's a dread feeling you're going to see a lot more. Everyone damned glad to get ashore. Had a rousing welcome from the Jerries, but nothing like their bombardments of our other war. Had a suspicion the RAF *were giving their batteries a hard time.*

Corps Commander jovial about progress, yours truly not so jovial. Someone's made off with head-quarters' last bottle of Scotch, an unspeakable crime. On the unexpected side, had a report from our forward units that when several German prisoners were being escorted out of a certain village, two young French ladies threw stones at our men. It seemed that liberation didn't count as much with these ma-demoiselles as the fact that they were engaged to two of our prisoners.

Thinking of you and the twins, thinking of joining you in our post-war garden and growing marrows. They're big but friendly. We're all overdue for a friendlier world, and I've a feeling the people who'll need it most, eventually, will be Bertha and Fritz.

Have you heard from Tim? Let me know if you have. Kiss Gemma and James for me, and tell them I hope to be home for Christmas. All my love, Polly.

Ever yours
Boots

Christmas, thought Polly, Christmas? Not until then? Doesn't he realize I'm getting older week by week? He'll arrive on Christmas Eve, look at me, look at the twins and say, 'Who's the old lady, Santa Claus's grandmother?'

An RAF truck pulled up outside a cottage in a small Wiltshire village. A pilot-officer, sitting beside the driver, jumped down and pulled two laden valises from the back of the truck.

'*Ciao*,' he said to the driver.

'You'll get arrested, sir, using that kind of language,' said the driver. The truck moved off. The door of the cottage opened, and Annabelle, expecting the caller, showed herself.

'Hooray,' she said, and a smile lit up her face.

'You look good to come home to,' said Nick.

'Give me the bad news first,' said Annabelle.

'No bad news, Annabelle, I'm promoted to training duties at Cranwell,' said Nick.

'That's my best present ever,' said Annabelle, 'so drop those valises and let's have a cuddle. Come on, don't just stand there.'

The valises were still on the doorstep twenty minutes later. Annabelle and Nick were making up for lost time while their children were still at school. It was that kind of a cuddle.

Sammy, home from the office, was having a word with Susie.

'Considering things are looking better, Susie, and considering there's benefits to be had from a change of scenery—'

'You're after something I'm not going to agree with,' said Susie.

'Susie, have I ever—'

'Yes, frequently,' said Susie, 'like cornering markets, consorting with spivs and giving me a Christmas present last year of a black nightie you could see through.'

'Well, Susie, you're still—'

'Yes, I know,' said Susie, 'but see-through nighties aren't for respectable wives and mothers, and your mum would faint if she saw me wearing it, and I'll have you know I only ever wear it under protest.'

'All the same, Susie, it shows you've still got a lot of Hollywood oomph,' said Sammy.

'My oomph is nothing to do with Hollywood,' said Susie, 'it was born and brought up in Walworth, which I'm proud of. Anyway, I'm nearly forty and you shouldn't talk about me having – Sammy, have I really still got a lot?'

'Yes, both of 'em,' said Sammy.

'Where's my egg saucepan?' said Susie.

'No, listen, Susie, I've been thinking about you being a deserving woman, and seeing the war's beginning to make Hitler cry his eyes out, I'm suggesting a holiday down in Cornwall as soon as Paula and Phoebe break up.'

'Sammy, oh, yes,' said Susie, delighted.

'I happened to be conversing with me contractual friend, old Blenkinsop of the Air Ministry,' said Sammy. 'He's got a large cottage by the coast of North Cornwall, and says he'd be pleasured to offer us use of it for two weeks. You, me, Paula, Phoebe, Daniel, and Jimmy and Bess, plus Chinese Lady and our stepdad. Plenty of room for nine of us, Blenkinsop said. We pick up Jimmy and Bess from Devon on our way, and at the end of the holiday, we bring 'em back here, which I think would be safe to do now, especially seeing Bess had been pointing out lately in her letters that Paula and Phoebe are permanent here. She wants to come home. The holiday would be a nice change, wouldn't it, and I'd buy you a new bucket and spade.'

'Oh, you don't have to ask me twice,' said Susie, glowing. 'But we can't all drive there in the car.'

'I'll ask Daniel to go on the train with his grand-parents and keep 'em company,' said Sammy.

'I'm sure he will,' said Susie, 'he's a kind boy.'

Sammy coughed.

'I know you're his loving mum, Susie,' he said, 'but haven't you noticed he's been wearing long trousers for a few years, that he's a working bloke and what you'd call a young man?'

'Oh, dear,' sighed Susie, 'don't one's children grow up quick, Sammy?'

'Patsy?' Daniel was on the phone that evening.

'This is you, Daniel?' said Patsy.

'I think so,' said Daniel. 'In fact, I'm sure it is. How's your good old Pa?'

'Having a ball about Normandy,' said Patsy, 'and I'm fine myself, thanks. That's in case you were going to ask.'

'Granted,' said Daniel.

'What d'you mean, granted?' asked Patsy.

'Yes, I was going to ask,' said Daniel.

'I like you over the phone,' said Patsy, 'it does things to your baritone.'

'Hope you like me off the phone,' said Daniel. 'Listen, we're off to Cornwall for the last week in July and the first week in August. Dad's got the use of a large cottage by the coast. Would your Pa let you come with us, and if he would, would you like to come?'

'Gee whizz, I'm really invited?' said Patsy.

'I pointed out to Mum and Dad I'd be sorrowful if we left you behind,' said Daniel. 'It'll be beaches and sand, buckets and spades, and swimsuits. Got a swimsuit?'

'Daniel, no, I don't go swimming here.'

'Never mind, make do with your bra and knickers,' said Daniel.

'You'd like that, would you?' said Patsy.

'Well, I would,' said Daniel, 'but Grandma wouldn't. She'd give you a talking-to.'

'I'll get fixed up,' said Patsy, 'I'm not going to miss out on Cornwall.' Her Pa had agreed to let problems rest, and to wait on the outcome of the Normandy campaign. 'Daniel, it sounds great, and you'd really like me there with you?'

'I'd miss you if you weren't,' said Daniel.

'Daniel, do you like me a lot?'

'A lot and some more,' said Daniel. 'Don't you know that by now?'

'Oh, I guess I just need telling,' said Patsy, 'and now that you have, do you know where I could buy a really sexy swimsuit, if clothes rationing hasn't sunk them?'

'I'll ask my dad,' said Daniel, 'he's tops in the rag trade, and knows where to find stuff that's still floating.'

'Would you do that for me, Daniel?'

'Ask Dad about a sexy swimsuit? Yes, when my mum's not listening,' said Daniel. 'Oh, and when can I come round and measure you?'

Patsy shrieked.

Her English fun guy was a hoot.

Mid-June

At various sites along the coast of Northern France, sites that had escaped Allied destruction, German scientists were just about ready to launch a deadly new weapon at London.

The flying bomb.

THE END